Shattered

Dreams

DEDICATION

Those we love memories will never go away. They walk beside us every second of each day while we live without them. They are unseen, unheard, and untouched, but they are always near.

Still loved and still missed.

This book is dedicated to those who have lost a loved one.

-LM-

CONTENTS

Acknowledgment

ACKNOWLEDGMENTS

Let me start off by saying, I am forever thankful for your support. Through the first and second editions of Wikked and my creative twist and turns, I wanted to show my audience there is more to me than Wikked. I have an amazing support team with my family and friends, and I can't thank you enough. I have started this project many moons ago, and I'm thankful for the listening ear, the back and forth, the ideas, the suggestions and everything it takes to be friends with an 'Author.' I pray that you will appreciate this story. In closing, I want to say, I always look to the Heavens and give Him praise for every single thing that has happened to me. Thank you Lord for blessing me.

If I could just...

"You see what you made me do!"

Alana tried to scream, but the knot in her throat and the fear in her heart wouldn't allow her to make a sound. She heard a noise drawing near her, but she couldn't turn her head to see what or who was around her. She could only move her eyes. In desperation, she tried to move her hands to feel what was beside her, but her hands wouldn't move either. She weakly tried to scan her bedroom as she lay motionless on the bed. Before she knew it, she was staring into her attacker's familiar eyes. Terrified, she closed her eyes when the intruder's breath stained her neck as her breathing became rapid. She never would've believed in a million years that the person standing over her would be the cause of her death. She heard the front door open, but was too exhausted and defeated to scream out.

"Alana?" Skyler called out as she walked through the front door. *"That's odd...., why is the door unlocked?"* she mused.

Skyler called her name again as she closed the door to her once shared living quarters with Alana. She noticed a single wine glass and a bottle of wine sitting on Alana's grandmother's antique coffee table in the living room. The place was dimly lit as if she was having a rendezvous or some sort, so turning on the light wasn't an option. Startled by a gust of wind, Skyler walked toward the terrace as the curtains swayed slightly until she noticed a silhouette. She slowly walked in the kitchen, eased a knife from the set she'd given Alana as a house warming gift and held on to it for dear life. She tiptoed toward the terrace, took a deep breath, and slid the curtains to the side with the knife cautiously. She shook her head and wondered if she was overreacting to the silence, but Alana's unlocked door still puzzled her. She reached for her phone to dial Alana's number again, but it went to voicemail.

"I should've kept my damn mouth shut," she mumbled as she closed her phone and placed the knife on the bar. "I know I was out of line."

She walked towards the restroom when a faint chirping noise caught her attention. She turned her head toward Alana's room and quietly walked toward it, until broken glass underneath her feet stopped her stroll.

"What in the ....?" she said to herself.

She then noticed Alana's bedroom door was ajar and it was dreadfully dark. A feeling of terror rushed over her as she anticipated what stood behind the door. She slightly pushed the door open until she was staring into Alana's infamous mirrored wall. It reflected her once beautiful body now drenched in blood, stretched out on her bed. Shocked at what she'd seen, she quickly covered her mouth as her shaky voice crept through her hands.

"Oh my go...."

She ran toward Alana's lifeless body as her mind drew blank and her heart weighed heavy with guilt. She quickly searched for a pulse, but there wasn't one. Tears streamed down her face as she cradled Alana's lifeless body while her fixated eyes stared at the ceiling. Skyler clutched her best friend's body to her when the bedroom door squeaked and she saw Alana's murderer's shadow.

Three Months prior...

Flash. Flash. Rafael Jai, a local renowned photographer smiled to himself when he zoomed his camera lens and admired Alana's beautifully sculptured 5'10 olive brown complexion.

"Just five more frames, beautiful," he said as he climbed on a ladder to take a couple of frames above her.

While Alana posed for Rafael, her assistant, Micah, was busy prioritizing Alana's schedule on her iPhone. She kept one eye on Alana and the other one on her flirty boyfriend as he drooled over the Brazilian beauty. Micah chuckled to herself when she walked toward Alana with a white terry-cloth hooded robe in hand after Rafael announced he was finished.

Rafael stood 5'11 with droopy dark hood eyes and a tailored goatee that matched his smooth coco dark-brown complexion. Nothing was out of line with him from his style of dress to the way he spoke British English. He attracted all type of femme's with his line of business, but he made sure Micah knew she was his woman.

"Thank you, Micah, you're the best," Alana said.

Micah Richardson was born and raised in Miami, Florida.

3

Her skin was sun kissed by Miami's rays, with her golden covered skin with streaks of blonde in her naturally coiled hair. Standing 5'4, she studied law at the University of Miami, but after graduation she took a job offer at a local modeling agency. Realizing she was too short, she became an agent, a manager, and a publicist before acquiring her license and formed her own agency, SunKiss Lady, which Rafael also financially acquired. The payout was remarkable, and so was their budding relationship. A few months later, Micah ran into a twenty-three-year-old Afro-Brazilian girl named Alana Inacio who had beauty gleaming from her pores standing at the post office.

Born and raised in a small village in Brazil, Alana was the last child born to the Inacio's. Her mother, Aelah, disappointed that she would not be able to carry another child, prayed and hoped for a daughter when she became pregnant unexpectedly. When the midwife delivered and covered the baby's shivering body, Aelah immediately stared at her beautiful brown eyed joy and named her Alana. When she uncovered the blanket to discover that she was born a male, Aelah's world changed.

Upset that she didn't get what she wanted, she told the midwife to never speak that Alana was born a male or tell her husband, Luis, they had a girl with complications. Luis was so excited, he never bothered to question her with details.

Aelah stared at Alana for months to see if she resembled a boy, but everyone complimented on how beautiful her daughter was. She had beautiful features, long eyelashes, and soft feminine features. She created what she wanted, a daughter. By the time Alana reached the age of eleven, mother and daughter was back and forth to several doctors. Luis demanded to know the outcome of her frequent doctor visits. When he learned that his child was born a male, he was heartbroken, livid, and embarrassed and wanted absolutely nothing to do with the pair.

Distancing himself from his once beloved wife and daughter, so at least he thought, he entrapped himself with anything outside of his house until a photographer showed interest in Alana's pictures. Luis grew leery of the offer, but the photographer insisted on the financial opportunities he could invest in. Luis still devastated by the revelation; knew he had an attractive child, but his broken-heart wouldn't allow him to look at ...her. But his love of money made him look at things differently. He put her in modeling competition and she would win. Now, at the age of 17, she stood 5'7, and was offered an opportunity in the United States as an international model six weeks' shy of her 18th birthday.

Alana and her mother moved to Miami, Florida with high hopes of her modeling career skyrocketing, but knew she had to take care of some personal business first. Aelah scheduled Alana's sex reassignment surgery and stayed with her during and after her recovery. Now that Aelah physically had a daughter, they celebrated their womanhood. Alana always felt like a girl and never wanted the genital assigned to her at birth. She expressed to her mother that she wanted to cut off her extremity, never referencing it as a penis, but Aelah promised her the surgery on her 18th birthday. Alana knew her father's disinterest, but her mother's love filled both shoes for her parents.

Once Aelah confirmed the successful surgery to Luis, he provided all the money they needed if Alana never returned to Brazil. In return, he bought her a condo, a brand-new car of her choice and deposited continual funds in her account. Aelah asked her older brother to keep an eye on Alana until she moved back to Miami in a year. She was finally leaving Luis.

Alana noticed an anxious Rafael walking toward them.

"I know you need to get going, so I won't waste any more of your time. Micah has a keen eye for beauty and I must admit you are absolutely beautiful. It was a pleasure to have met and worked with you Alana."

"Thank you. It was a pleasure to work with you too."

"You know, Micah showed me some of your earlier work, but I must admit you're more beautiful now. It's just so hard to believe that you're not a professional model."

"I've had some false promotions and most of the contracts haven't been to my liking so that caused me to turn down a lot of work. Right now, I'm looking for whatever is in my best interest."

"And that's how it should be. There are too many young women eager to make money but all money isn't good money. They tend to jump at any and every opportunity that comes their way without thinking of the repercussions," Rafael added.

Alana nodded and agreed.

"You know, I would like to use one of your pictures for the cover of the magazine my work is featured in."

"Really?" she said, looking at Micah then back at Rafael with large eyes.

"Yes, I-I mean if it's alright with you. Of course, we need to discuss the legalities of it," he said as he smiled at Micah.

"Sure," she said, looking at Micah then back at him.

"This exposure just might be the push that you need and I know you will become an overnight success. I give you my word," Rafael replied.

"It's due. She's put in a lot of hard work," Micah voiced proudly.

Alana smiled at them because she felt like her dream was finally coming true, or at least it seemed like it.

"Micah, I would like for you and Alana to come with my team when we start our tour in Las Vegas. She's the perfect model. She's eye candy and with her face and *that* body, she should spill her beauty in every major city. What do you think?"

"I don't think it'll be a problem, unless Alana disagrees," Micah said, looking at Alana with a smile.

"I don't disagree," Alana replied anxiously. "Do I have anything on my schedule Micah?"

"Even if you did, we would clear it. This is a very good opportunity for exposure for you. Let's sit down and go over our contractual obligation and go from there?"

Six weeks later, SunKiss was gaining notoriety and journalists were trying to get quick interviews. They were putting Alana everywhere in Dade county and the surrounding cities. Micah took a deep breath when the journalist walked up to her and pleaded for a five-minute interview with Alana, but she knew they were pressed for time. She politely declined the interview until the journalist begged for a reduced two-minute interview. Micah was skeptical at first, but quickly agreed to the it. She caught up with Alana as she walked toward her dressing room trailer.

"Do I have anything else set up for today, Micah?" Alana asked Micah.

"Let me check," she said as she looked through her phone, avoiding mentioning the two-minute interview, "You have a couple things to attend first thing Monday morning and...."

Alana continued to listen to Micah read her schedule aloud while her cloudy mind suffocated Micah's voice. Alana's phone hummed from a text when they walked in the trailer. She quickly glanced at it then walked toward the bathroom. She pushed the shower curtain to the side then turned on the shower and let the water steam the bathroom.

"Don't forget that you have a luncheon at Night's Owl at noon today," Micah yelled before Alana closed the door.

Alana leaned against the bathroom door for a second to catch her breath. She looked at her trembling hands just as the steam from the shower misted the mid-length mirror. She stared at her reflection and watched her streaming tears caress her beautiful face. She could only think of Anthony, her boyfriend of three years, who just gave her an ultimatum five minutes prior to her most important photo shoot.

Anthony Carnes was a business man from nine to five, but one minute after five, he was a bonafide crook. He was a ladies' man by far, standing 6'6 with broad shoulders, an impressionable smile and perfect teeth that sat behind beautiful caramel skin and hazel brown eyes. Being recognized as a retired NBA player enticed his female fans. He spotted Alana at his friend's beachfront upscale bar and restaurant called Night's Owl three years ago at his retirement party. Immediately love sparked for the pair.

"I can't do this anymore. It's either me or your career," his voice replayed.

She peeled the robe from her body, stepped into the shower while the water soothed her trembling body. She sat in the tub, bringing her knees to her chest and cried silently into the spraying waters.

The deception and manipulation pained her, but she knew the only way she could come out of this was to focus solely on herself. She'd fallen in love without fears with a man who led her to believe that he supported her dream, but he was scorned at her success and his failures. She never would've imagined that he would want her to compromise her career for him, surely that was asking too much of her. As much as she wanted him, needed him, she couldn't sacrifice what meant the most to her. Modeling.

She couldn't pretend she wasn't affected, but she refused to release her pain to anyone including the camera lens. It was too embarrassing, so instead she had to find the will to mask her hurt and deal with it alone. She stood on her feet, gaining more control of her emotions before washing her body and trying to think of something other than Anthony. But it was no use. He had a hold on her. She stepped out of the shower, hoping it had flushed the heavy burden down the drain, but it didn't. The pain continuously pulsated. She finally grabbed a towel, wiped the tears from her eyes as she walked into her dressing room and glanced at the roses he'd given to her minutes before his ultimatum.

She closed her eyes, took a deep breath then oiled her body. She slipped on a nice lacey bra and thong set before dressing into a wrap-around dress. She quickly brushed her wet hair into a ponytail and applied her lip gloss just as Micah knocked on her door.

"Are you decent?"

"Yes."

"There's a journalist outside who wants an inter...," she stopped abruptly. "What's wrong? Are you okay?" she said, noticing Alana's red eyes.

"Yes," she said then quickly looked away.

"You sure? You don't look like you're okay," Micah quizzed.

"I'm okay."

"You're telling me you're okay, but I'm seeing you with puffy eyes which is not okay, so out with it. What's wrong?"

Alana paused.

"Micah, it seems like when I get closer to my dreams, something else goes wrong."

"What do you mean Alana? Everything is great. This was the most important photo shoot for you."

"Yea, I know, but...."

"But what? So, what's the problem? It's Anthony, isn't it?"

"I need to focus on modeling only."

"Whoa, wait a minute. What happened with you and Anthony? Are you guys ok? You guys were perfect, so what..."

"Yea, snap shot perfect? I guess things were great when everything went his way and I never complained, but I caught a whiff of his dirty laundry and now things are very complicated."

"How so?" Micah quizzed.

"He gave me an ultimatum. Can you believe that? I mean after

8

all I went through with him and he pulls this? He had an affair when I went back home to visit my family and she had his child. Who was there? Me, if anyone was issuing out ultimatums it should've been me," Alana said angrily, tossing her towel on the bed.

Micah listened intensely while Alana spoke. She didn't know what shocked her the most. Alana finally opening up to her or Anthony giving her an ultimatum.

"Well, I know you know this already, but you're better off without him anyway."

"Yea, I guess."

"You guess? Alana, he had a child with another woman and you guess? He gave you an ultimatum and you guess? He's selfish, obnoxious and inconsiderate and you're standing here telling me you *guess?*"

Alana looked away.

"Sometimes we get caught up and only see what we want to see. You deserve more, but sometimes more means being without. Welcome to dating," Micah said with compassion.

Micah tried to lighten her mood, but Alana was empty.

"Alana?"

"Yes Micah?"

"There will be another man out there who will respect you and your dreams. Don't give up just yet. Just let him walk into your life, its effortless when he does."

"It's not about giving up. It's about doing what I love the most and that's modeling."

"And that should be your focus because no man is worth giving up your dream," Micah stated.

Alana opened the door and stared into the awaiting young journalist eyes.

Alana quickly looked at Micah, rolled her eyes before looking back at the journalist. She really didn't feel like being bothered and an interview was the last thing on her mind. She smiled and hurriedly asked Micah to give the young journalist the dozens of roses that were on her table while she answered a few questions. The bystanders watched, smiled, and took pictures. She liked the attention, but it came from the wrong person.

She placed her sunglasses on after she concluded her interview and walked toward her 2018 special edition Silver

Audi, which was parked in the garage. She opened the door, threw her purse in the passenger's seat and started the engine. As soon as she closed the door, she dropped the top, pulled out her cell phone and redialed the missed number.

"Hello?" Skyler answered quickly.

"Hi. Sorry about the delay," Alana said when she pulled off. "I was in a photo shoot."

"Oh, I forgot, you're a celebrity now."

"Whatever. I am not a celebrity."

"Mmm hmm, where are you? I can't wait to see you."

"I'm on my way to the airport."

"Girl, you were taking too long, I caught an Uber."

"Tell him to take you to Night's Owl."

"Uber, take me to Night's Owl," Skyler said aloud.

He quickly made a u turn in the middle of the street and sped toward the opposite direction where Skyler anticipated seeing her childhood friend.

Alana drove toward Night's Owl and thought back to how they met. Skyler Sutton sat in the back of her small eighth grade classroom on the first day of school as an exchange student in a relatively small city in Brazil called Belem. She would often have scuffles which led her to principal's office. Since Alana's mother was the vice principal, she would hear the elders say that being an exchange student wasn't the easiest experience, but they were grateful that their school was chosen to only get a hand full of Americans. They expressed how different the two cultures were and how this could be fundamentally challenging for both sets of children.

"Ms. Sutton, I'm afraid I'm going to have to call your parents."

"What? I said I was sorry! I didn't mean to do it," her young voice pleaded.

"Ms. Sutton, you have brought us nothing but havoc and unless someone can come here and prove that you weren't involved then we don't have any other choice. We do not tolerate that type of behavior from our students and we will certainly not accept it from our guests."

"I-I...," she stammered.

"Anything you would like to add?" the principal said.

"I... I..."

"I did it!" Alana blurted when she walked through the door.

"Ms. Inacio?" the principal questioned.

"Yes?"

"Wha-what are you doing.... you're accepting responsibility for this?" he yelled furiously.

"Yes sir," she said when she tried to pass his office.

"Where do you think you're going young lady?"

"I was going to see my...."

"Sit down and don't you move."

The principal snatched the receiver to his ear as the pair chatted quietly. His native tongued spilled over the phone to his vice principal they sat in front of him.

"You didn't have to do that," Skyler whispered.

"Yea, I know, but I never get into trouble..., consider it a favor," Alana replied shyly.

"Favors aren't fair."

"Huh? What does that mean?"

"People aren't fair. You don't even know me."

"You're right. My name is Alana Inacio."

"I'm Skyler Sutton."

"It's nice to meet you," she smiled at her first American friend.

"You too."

"So, what happened?"

"It's kind of a long story."

"We're not going anywhere anytime soon, so...," Alana said as she slouched into her seat folding her arms across her chest.

They burst into a quiet laughter as they watched the tomato red faced principal rant and rave in the receiver as he paced back and forth in his closed office. He shoved the receiver into the cradle and stormed into the vice principal's office as if he was about to spit fire. They watched him pace and point toward them before the vice principal called for them while he was storming out.

"What is the problem Lana?"

"Mamã I know I shouldn't have butted in, but...."

"Mamã?" Skyler voiced before quickly looking at Alana.

"Yes, she's my mom," she whispered.

"Alana, your father is going to be more upset with you." Alana dropped her head in disappointment as her mother spat. "I know you are not responsible for this nonsense Lana. I don't believe you were in the restroom throwing a trash can at one of the mirrors in the girls' restroom and cracked it. So, who did it?"

They looked at each other without uttering a word.

"Okay, so neither one of you are going to say anything?" she looked at them staring at their shoes, "*Não minta a mim Lana,*" she stated in Portuguese.

"I'm not lying," Alana whined.

"Okay then I'm sending both of you to detention, do you hear me?"

"Yes ma'am," they both said in unison.

They walked toward the door until she called out their names.

"Skyler. Alana, come here."

"Yes?"

"I don't want to hear a word about this leniency, am I understood?" she whispered.

"Yes ma'am."

"And Lana?"

She turned around reluctantly and stared at her mother. Skyler listened to them speak rapidly in their native tongue, but couldn't figure out a word they were saying.

"Let's go," Alana whispered.

Skyler quickly asked what she had said as they left.

"She's really mad at me," she said dryly.

They walked inside of the principal office as strangers facing two different battles, but left out as friends facing the same problem. What Alana didn't know was that her lasting friendship with Skyler would be a host of many dark secrets.

Alana arrived in front of Night's Owl and parked in her usual spot when a car pulled up alongside, honking its horn.

"Lana?" a familiar voice yelled out.

She could recognize that voice from anywhere. Alana looked toward the car as Skyler stepped from the backseat, ran toward her, and hugged her tightly.

"Oh my goodness, look at you," Skyler admired.

"No, look at you. You look great," Alana said. "wait, where's your luggage?"

"In the trunk," Skyler said as they walked toward the car.

The driver got out and ask, can I please take one picture with you? My friends will never believe that I saw you."

She glanced at Skyler and flashed her million-dollar smile. "Sure, no problem."

He pulled out a local magazine with her on its cover and handed it to her.

"Is it too much to ask for your autograph, too?"

"Not at all," she said politely.

"I heard you're about to put out a calendar, is that true?" he said lustfully while pulling out his camera.

"Well, I'm working on some material, so just check out my websites for releases," she replied, still flashing her smile.

Alana asked Skyler to take the picture while he took off his hat and leaned close enough to her to smell the Pantene residue in her hair. Snap. Snap. Snap. He smiled at her and thanked her for taking the pictures with him. He asked Skyler would she take a picture with him too, but she declined, stating she was camera shy. He ran to his trunk, pulled out her luggage and placed her luggage in Alana's trunk. He thanked her again before rushing off back to his car. Skyler watched him dash off and sped off.

"Camera shy?" Alana repeated, with a raised eyebrow.

"This is about you, not me," Skyler shot back. "What was that all about?"

"But camera shy? Are you hungry?" Alana asked.

"I sure am. What's on the menu?"

"Depends on what you have a taste for. Night's Owl food is fresh and delicious."

Skyler looked at the restaurant's marquee and smiled to herself. They walked toward the entrance of Night's Owl while Skyler continued to compliment Alana's appearance.

"Thank you, I'm on a low carb diet these days."

"I should be asking you are you hungry then," Skyler chuckled.

Thanks to Anthony, I really don't have an appetite, Alana thought.

They walked in as the host greeted Alana while Skyler looked around the new atmosphere.

"This is *nice*," Skyler said as the music played in the background.

Alana walked toward her usual table, secluded from the rest of the customers, facing the door, but hidden from the onlookers. She pulled out a chair while Skyler looked around in awe.

"This is nice," Skyler said.

"It's a Beachfront bar and restaurant. There's a patio near the back with a dynamic view of the beach. Clifton wanted to create a place where people could mingle and whatnot."

"Who is Clifton?"

"He's the owner."

The Owner? Skyler mused.

Alana looked around Clifton's establishment as if it were her first time there. Although she'd seen it before, she never really admired the exquisite art work until now. She looked at it with Skyler and thought back to a time when she and Anthony sipped away their problems. She stared off as her ears enjoyed the song that played in the background which was her song, 'Naked,' by an artist named Ella Mai. She listened intensely until she saw Clifton walking toward her.

"Clifton is walking toward us now," she whispered.

Skyler smiled, slightly curious about the owner of such a nice establishment. He walked toward Alana and kissed her softly on her check. She noticed his baby blue linen outfit with sandals and his masculine manicured nails. With a raised eyebrow, Skyler watched the pair interact intimately without saying a word.

"Hello beautiful," he said in his raspy voice.

"Hello Clif."

"It's about time you showed up. Alana, I was looking for you, hours ago."

"I had a photo shoot today."

"I heard. Well, I'm glad your beauty has graced Night's Owl," he said flirtatiously.

Skyler cleared her throat as she watched him drool over Alana. He quickly darted his eyes toward her guest, slightly raising an eyebrow at the chestnut brown- haired woman with eyes to match.

"Alana, who is this gorgeous woman sitting with you?" he said flirtingly.

"My best friend Skyler, I was telling you about. Skyler, this is Clifton."

"Skyler?" he asked playfully.

"Skyler Sutton and yes, that would be me," she said impassively.

"She's more beautiful than you lead me to believe Alana," he said in awe.

He extended his hand to her as she wrapped her beautiful sculptured manicured hands around his, delicately.

"Hello, I'm Clifton, but please call me Clif."

"It's a pleasure to meet you. I'm Skyler," she said in a whisper tone, "but please call me Sky."

"I will," he shot back matching her whisper.

He was mesmerized by her beauty, quick wit and seemingly fast paced humor. Immediately, his mind danced with thoughts while he eyed her long legs as she crossed them beside the table when Alana's phone buzzed. Skyler glanced at Alana, but licked her lips seductively toward Clifton catching his full attention.

"Lana told me this is yours?" she said as she looked around.

"It is," he said as he grabbed a seat.

"A man with some business about himself," she said with a raised eyebrow. "Nice."

He leaned closer toward her while Alana chatted on her phone.

"Well, I can't take all the credit, some of this wasn't my idea. It belonged to my uncle who was like a father to me. He was in an accident about several years ago."

"I'm sure he would be proud."

"I would like to think so," he said as he looked around. "So, are you only in town for the weekend?"

"Yes. Unless I have a reason or an invitation to stay longer."

Clifton liked her slick passive aggression.

"Excuse me, but I need to take this call. I'll be right back," Alana whispered as she covered the phone.

"Everything okay?" Skyler mouthed.

"Yes. I need a little privacy that's all. You ok?" Alana asked as she eyed Clifton.

"I'm fine. Handle your business," she whispered.

"Would you like for me to order your usual, Alana?" Clifton asked.

"Please," she mouthed before walking away.

"What about you gorgeous?"

"I'll have what she's having."

"You sure?"

"Of course," she mused when he walked off.

Skyler watched Alana walk toward the patio. Just as she leaned back to get a better glance at her, Clifton returned with their drinks.

"Two bottles of water."

"Water? This is her usual?" she quizzed.

Clifton chuckled to himself at Skyler's assumption.

"She's not much of a drinker, but I can get you whatever you like. Matter of fact, I have *just* the drink for you."

He waved at Mesa, his server, to come to their table. He placed an order, while keeping his eyes on Skyler the entire time while she sparingly sipped from her water bottle.

"So, what brings you here?" he asked, as he continued to caress her legs with his eyes.

"What? Let's just say, I wanted to get away from Vegas for a little while. I'm thinking about possibly relocating?"

"Vegas? It's beautiful out there, why leave?"

"I need a change."

"Change is good. Welcome to South Beach," he chimed, "maybe if you're not so busy, I can show you around."

"Sounds like a plan."

Mesa returned with a beautifully decorative glass topped off with a couple of umbrellas and several cherries. Clifton handed Skyler the drink and watched her wrap her lips around the straw as she took her first sip.

"Mmmm. This is delicious. I absolutely love Mangos, but I never thought to make a Mango Martini when I bartended."

"You bartend?"

"I have my license. I got a couple of tricks under my sleeves."

"I bet," he said with raised eyebrows.

"Is this on your menu?"

"Nope, this is Mesa's concoction."

"Why not? This is *so* good. You need to consider it," Skyler said as she tipped Mesa.

"You think so?"

"Of course. This is very good. You need to have a happy martini hour and let her make different Martini's to see how well they do," she smiled then looked away when their eyes met. "That's how you incorporate 'Happy Hour drinks' and that my friend will generate quick sales."

"Look at you, and you're quite the business woman."

"I dabble here and there."

"I see. Alana should you keep you around, beauty and brains."

"I'm sure you say that to all the beautiful women you meet."

"I have no problem complimenting a woman's beauty."

"Me either," she smiled.

He liked the idea that she was the opposite of Alana; she was flirty and quick witted. She had a glaze of confidence that was alarmingly attractive.

"You know, she told me you modeled before too. Have you two ever considered taking some pictures together?"

"It never came up."

"Well, I can see it now, the two of you in a bikini, soaking wet seductively leaning on each other..."

"You can see that? She's not as racy as me so she might blow it off," she chuckled.

He laughed and slyly looked back to make sure Alana was still near the patio before leaning forward.

"So, where's your man?" he quizzed.

"Who says I have one?" she asked.

"Why are you answering my question with a question?"

Instead of answering his question, she sipped from her straw.

"I'm just curious, that's all," he added when she didn't respond.

"Curious?" she smiled at him.

"I'm saying, you're too fine to not have a man."

"I don't have a man."

"Tsk. I find that hard to believe."

Alana walked up behind Clifton entertaining Skyler. She could only imagine what lies Clifton was telling her. She smiled to herself before shaking her head at the pair.

"What?" he said as he threw his hand up playfully.

"You know what."

"Don't be so hard on me Alana. You know a woman is my favorite delicacy."

"I know," she said, rolling her eyes.

Clifton looked around his establishment and saw his attractive female companion walking from the host stand. He politely and quickly excused himself from their table when he noticed her walking toward Mesa. He swiftly walked toward Mesa near the bar.

"Mesa, I need you to do me a favor," Clifton said hurriedly and anxiously. "Make sure Alana and her guest are taken care of while I entertain my lady friend, alright? Let them order whatever they want, it's on me."

His Cubaña friend walked up to him, leaned toward him, and tried to plant a kiss on his lips. He quickly peeled away from her and looked at her for a few seconds. No woman had ever disrespected him and she was no different.

"Aye papi."

"Hey beautiful, don't do that right now. Why don't you have a seat until I get my guests situated, okay?" he said politely, as he pulled out a bar stool.

He raised his eyebrows toward Mesa then walked toward Alana and Skyler. He flashed his perfectly white teeth which revealed two deeply set dimples in his cheeks.

"Hey ladies, Mesa is your server and she's going to take good care of you. So, order whatever you want on the menu, it's on me."

"Thank you, Clifton."

"No problem Alana," he winked. "I hope you two enjoy your meal and it was nice meeting you Skyler," he said with an extended hand.

She shook his hand while he glanced at the bar. A bona-fide flirt was the only way to describe Clifton Parks who was a thirty-six-year-old fair skinned Dominican who stood 6'1. He moved to Miami from Chicago when his father was sentenced to life in prison without parole. He stayed with his legal guardian, his dad's best friend whom he called Uncle, when he was only seven. When his uncle passed, he left his entire estate to Clifton, but Clifton's overnight success didn't come easy for him. He had his share of run-ins with the law for gambling, prostitution, and drug trafficking, but Night's Owl was his only safe haven. He tied up most of his loose ends with his, but his biggest downfall was women. He was an out of control womanizer.

"Damn, he's gorgeous," Skyler complemented.

"Tsk. He is," Alana said with hesitation.

Alana's demeanor alarmed Skyler.

"So, what's been going on?" Skyler said, hoping to change the mood.

"Same ol' stuff...," Alana replied.

"Tsk. You know what I'm talking about," she laughed under her breath.

"Oh. Oh. Oh....," Alana fanned at her. "I'm doing great."

"Does it work?"

Alana laughed, "yes it works."

"I am so glad your mom was here with you during the procedure. You know I would've came."

"I know you would've, but it happened so fast like I said over the phone. We moved here and then literally I was walking into my appointment."

"So, do you feel different?"

"No. The only thing that is 'different' is that I finally have a vagina."

"Girl bye! I mean, even to this day, I don't believe it. You have always been a girl to me. You never even hit puberty."

"I was on hormone pills."

"I swear to you, you fooled everyone."

"Like I said and will always say, I never fooled anyone. I was fooled. My mother told me I was born with an extremity, I didn't even know what that meant. I mean, everyone, doctors, teachers, friends, and I can remember as early as dressing up like a ballerina. And because my mom never referenced me as a boy, she just said I was born with a defect so my life was normal for me. To be honest, I have never even used the bathroom standing up."

"Never?"

"Never."

"You never wanted to use it, explore your sexual thoughts?"

"My psychiatrist used to ask me that all the time to confirm if this was my mother's choice or mine. My sexual thoughts were normal except I had this birth defect, which mamá would call it. Does that make sense?"

"It does. You look amazing."

"Like I said, my body was so full of estrogen, I didn't grow facial or body hair like my brothers."

Skyler smiled.

"And what about you? What's been brewing in your life," Alana quizzed.

"So much drama that's why I'm here. I need to get away and think about my life."

"Well your timing couldn't have been better."

"So, what's up with Clifton?" Skyler chuckled.

"He's too flirty," Alana said with pause. "He doesn't know how to commit to one woman."

Skyler glanced at him and his Cubaña. She smiled at Alana politely, but she couldn't lie to herself, she wanted to know more about him.

"Whatever you have in mind, let it go Sky. Don't get all loose and wild down here on me. You're only here for the weekend plus HIV/AIDS is real serious down here."

"HIV/AIDS is serious everywhere. You just have to protect yourself," she laughed. "But I will keep that in mind."

"Skyler, this is not a joke."

"Yea, yea, yea... so, enough with the lecture, where's Anthony?"

"I don't know, we're not an item anymore," she shrugged her shoulders.

"Wha-....? Since when? Oh my goodness, so ya'll done?" she asked in a hushed voice. "Did he find out?"

"Yes, we are done, and there is nothing to find out. But, he did give me an ultimatum."

"An ultimatum?" she fumed. "Who the hell does he think he is? Just because he's an ex-ball player doesn't give him the right to spit out ultimatums to nobody. Hell, that's what's wrong with these men who got money. I guess they think they can just talk to us any kind of damn way."

"Well, I'm not choosing him over my career."

"And you better damn not," she added.

"So enough about me, what about you? How have you been? It's been years since I've physically seen you, and FaceTime doesn't count. How's life back home? Are you still with...um...what's his name? Ric?"

"'Lana, please don't even say his name."

"Well, dang I thought my situation was bad."

"Girl, put it like this. I'm so over Ric and his selfish ass ways, it's not worth discussing."

"Oh, I truly understand."

"So anyway, what is there to do down here?"

"It depends on what you're into. We can hang out and I can show you around, but it'll have to be after my photo shoot."

"Okay."

"Do you want to take some pictures Sky?"

"No, I'll pass."

"You'll pass? You used to jump in front of the lens."

"Well, things have changed," she said, stirring her drink.

"You're not modeling anymore?" she quizzed, hoping she said yes.

"No."

"What happened?"

"I dance now."

"You dance? Hip hop or Ballet?"

"Neither, exotic dancing."

"Exotic dancing? You got to be kidding me, you're a stripper?"

"Call it whatever you want to call it, but it pays nicely. I wanted to make some quick money and things kind of spiraled out of control so yea, I kept dancing. You know, it's a very lucrative business."

"Lucrative business?" Alana questioned, then looked away.

"Anyway, I thought about looking into some clubs out here. Who knows what I might come up with?"

"So how long are you going to stay?"

"It depends."

"I'll take care of the expenses if you stay for a while unless you have a reason to go back to Vegas or Ric?"

"Damn Ric," Skyler hissed.

"Damn Anthony."

"Let's drink to that," Skyler said with a grin.

Alana looked around for Clifton so he could celebrate with them, but it was no use. She spotted him in a dark corner lip locking with his Cubaña friend with his hands fondling and stroking her curvaceous body. Skyler stared at the pair.

"Skyler?" Alana repeated. "Skyler?"

"Yyyessss?" Skyler grimaced.

"I've been sitting here calling your name. You want a frozen Mint Daiquiri?" Alana asked.

Skyler laughed it off when she noticed the pair staring at her suspiciously. She chuckled to herself and agreed to the drink. Mesa walked toward the bar to prepare their drinks.

"Did you find what you were looking for?" Alana said

jokingly.

"Huh?"

"Over there with Clifton because you were all in his mouth," Alana said.

"Who? Me? Please," she brushed off.

Alana took note of Skyler's interest. They chatted about everything except Anthony and Ric while Skyler took quick glances toward Clifton.

"Let's make a toast," Alana suggested.

They tapped their glasses and sipped their daiquiri. After the ladies sipped their drinks, they stood to their feet.

"Whoa, wait a minute. Are you two leaving right now? I wanted to announce to everyone that we have chosen you as the face of Night's Owl."

"Why didn't you tell me?" Alana asked surprisingly.

"It's called a surprise," he said.

"Aye, that calls for a celebration. Why don't we celebrate at Lana's?" Sky suggested.

"That'll work, I'll bring the bar to you," he said with a wink.

"No, that's not going to work," Alana replied.

"Why not? This is your moment," Skyler said.

"We can't have it here?" Alana asked.

"Because this is a special occasion and it won't be overly crowded. It can be an intimate setting, just a small number of guests."

"I guess," she said doubtfully.

"Okay, see you two later," he said before they walked outside into the bleak visage of summer.

I should've followed my instinct

The sweltering heat suffocated Alana and Skyler as they stepped outside of Night's Owl while the remnant of their frozen Mint Daiquiri rested on their tongues. The breeze from the Atlantic Ocean combed through their hair as the aroma from the sea shells permeated their nostrils as they drove away.

"*I can't imagine life without you,*" Anthony's voice replayed in Alana's mind.

Immediately her thoughts came to an abrupt halt when she heard Sky arguing on her phone. She wondered what made her want to be an exotic dancer because she was flawlessly beautiful. Something stirred inside of her, but she couldn't put her finger on the eerie feeling that Skyler wasn't being totally honest with her. There were so many things she wanted to ask, but knew how she reacted when forced into a corner with too many questions. Instead, she listened to her curse into the phone while she drove through the city.

"...What the hell do you mean? You can't just throw my shit out... I told you already.... I'm trying to stack my money, so I can give it...... What?...As soon as possible. .... Ric? ...Hello? Hello? Ric? Ric?"

She redialed the number as she cursed into the phone.

"Ric, I don't appreciate you hanging up in my damn face! You bastard!" Skyler yelled before leaning into Alana's passenger seat.

"Is everything alright?" Alana asked Skyler when her phone buzzed again.

"I don't.... hold on, Ric, why the hell did you hang up in my face? ...I'm not gonna....Whatchu mean?.... So we can't even talk about this?.... No? Whatchu mean no?...... Didn't I tell you I was ...Yea and I told you I'm gon' ...I'm not in Vegas... Yes...... I already told you.... You're not listening to me, you're cutting me off and shit, how 'bout....no, how 'bout I send you your money when I make it...You're a liar!...Me. Hell no! ....That's not how I gave it to you....Man whatever ...," Skyler said just as she ended the call then tossed the phone out of the window.

"I swear I hate him!" she voiced.

"Did you just throw your phone out of the window?"

"Hell yea. I was trying to be cordial, but he *wants* me to be a bitch."

"Who Ric?"

"Yes, he's fucking unbelievable," Skyler mumbled.

Alana listened as Skyler continued to curse under her breath. Something else was going on with Skyler and a part of her didn't want to know anymore.

"You know Lana, I wish I could turn back the hands of time."

"You and me both," Alana sighed.

Skyler folded her arms across her chest, held her head back on the seat then closed her eyes.

"Can I ask you something?" Alana asked cautiously.

"Sure Lana," she replied with closed eyes while taking a deep breath."

"Is he on drugs or something?"

"Drugs?" Skyler chuckled.

"Yea, drugs? Is he hitting you?"

Skyler didn't answer which made Alana more aware to her silence.

"Hello?" Alana glanced over, trying her best to look at the road and Skyler as she drove.

"N-nah. He's just going through some really hard times right now."

"That doesn't give him a reason to put his hands on you."

"Alana, every relationship has its problems."

"I agree, but hitting draws the line. You need to leave him alone."

"And go where?"

"What do you mean go where? You said you had your own place, a nice job and a car."

"Well, technically, I do but we're sharing a place together."

"Is it in *his* name?" Alana asked sarcastically.

"Y-yes, but that's only because my credit isn't that good."

"I tell you the truth Skyler, you ought to....," Alana replied, shaking her head.

Skyler quickly ignored her and stared out of the window with only one thing on her mind. Vegas. She thought back to how it all started. When she returned to Vegas from Brazil, she tried to continue pursuing modeling but her growing belly wasn't appealing to the agency. The day her agency declined her being a young mother, she vowed she wouldn't get behind a lens ever again.

After the defeat of rejection, she then met a man by the name of Mark, the manager of Scores. Impressed by her young and tender beauty, he invited her to lunch and treated her like a queen. He bought her whatever his money could buy and she loved every second of it. He catered to her, but she found herself wanting something more. Something exciting. She had to admit, being eighteen and having a sponsor was good until he leaned over to kiss her. His distinctive features, salt, and peppered hair, was a sensitive topic for her when she noticed the frequent stares, but she refused to admit it. Instead, she continued to play her role until his estranged wife resurfaced and seized all their accounts, leaving him with nothing in his accounts except for his private savings.

In order to keep her around, he offered her a job bartending and paid for her bartending license at Scores, one of the hottest gentlemen's clubs in Las Vegas, Nevada. For almost two and a half years, she'd made a name for herself as the best and sexiest bartender at Scores. She noticed his frequent lady friends paying him a visit or two every night at different times. When she questioned it, he would brush her off by saying they were paying their debt. She eventually ignored it and started to entertain the men who sat at the bar with her. One man in particular, Ricardo Simmons was mesmerized by her beauty and paid for her company as he occupied a seat at the bar. He then offered her to dance at his club where she could make a week's pay in one night, but she declined. After working countless nights at Scores, she began calculating how much she could really make if she danced. Finally, she asked Mark if she could dance at Scores, but he quickly dismissed it when he noticed Ric, a no good slickster, hanging out at the bar a little too much with too much interest in Skyler. Ric would only frequent different clubs in

Vegas to recruit young naïve women for his personal gain, and his charm always sealed the deal.

Skyler became more interested in dancing than bartending every time Ric was around; Mark noticed. As soon as Ric noticed her growing interest, he invited her to dance at amateur night at a local club across town he was sponsoring. He mentioned the first-place winnings of seven hundred dollars and immediately she was drawn in. She danced at the amateur night and won first place and soon began dancing two nights a week. When she returned to Scores, she found herself watching the ladies dance and interact with their customers and perfected her dance routines at the other club.

Finally, Ric tried to offer Mark another bartender to replace Skyler, but Mark showed no interest. Ric then placed five one hundred dollar bills on the counter, assuring him that he would take care of him. Mark needed the money, but declined because he didn't want her getting too involved with his dirty and grimy schemes. He tried to keep a close eye on her by giving her a promotion and giving her more hours, but that only fueled her persistence to want to dance even more. He tried to ignore it until one of his headliners was in a serious accident and he needed an immediate replacement.

Skyler used it to her advantage as she poured her customers drinks and danced behind the bar for them. Disgusted at what he saw, Mark instantly took note of it and noticed how his customers were more focused on his sexy bartender instead of the girls on the stage.

"What the hell do you think you're doing?" he asked acidly.

"Nothing just dancing," she smiled.

"I can't have you distracting my customers," he said. "No one is paying attention to the dancers."

"Man, let her dance," a male customer spat.

Mark cut his eyes at him, then at her.

"Come on Mark, give her a break. At least she dances better than the girls on the stage," a second man yelled. "Yea, I rather give the bartender my money," he fussed.

Mark looked around the room and noticed how disinterested the men were with his dancers. He took a deep breath and leaned toward her.

"You're leaving me with no choice." He sighed. "Go into the

dressing room and talk to Claudette. She'll get you into something tasteful so you can work your.... magic," he mumbled.

"Don't lie to me," she answered excitedly.

"Do I look like I'm playing right now? I have a club full of unhappy men who have deep pockets and as much as I don't want to do this, you're leaving me with no choice."

"I will not disappoint you."

"It's not about you disappointing me. I just don't want to see you get enticed by quick money."

"Mark, we all want quick money."

"But quick money isn't always good money."

He looked toward his unhappy patrons as the discouraged dancer continued to dance.

"I really don't want you to do this, but I really need you to do me this one favor, just this one time and then you'll be back at the bar tomorrow night, okay?"

"All I need is just one chance," she said excitedly.

"Well, I don't need you on my stage I need you behind my bar."

"I don't want to bartend anymore."

She reached under the bar, grabbed her purse just as Mark leaned down and grabbed her hand.

"I ain't trying to get all in your business, but Ric isn't the man you think he is," he whispered.

"And neither are you," she said in disbelief.

"I've seen what he does to young girls like you."

"What? Treat 'em good and make 'em feel like they matter until wifey comes back. Oh, you've already prepped me for that Mark, thanks," she hissed.

"You know what, you already got your mind made up so who am I? Just know, when he's done with you he'll leave you broke and flat on your face."

"I hear you."

"Trust me, after he's done with you, he'll drain you dry and leave you owing him thousands."

"Yeah...."

He stared at her for a second. She sounded like all the other girls that came before her, but there was no use trying to explain to her what kind of man he was. She would know soon enough.

"Don't let me stop you," he said as he stepped back.

She smiled and walked passed him with only one thing on her mind. Money.

"Hey ladies, where's Claudette?" she said as she entered the dressing room.

"In the back listening to Sade. You know how she gets when she's in her mood. So we just let Sade sing away her problems."

"Yea, I know." She chuckled to herself and walked toward Claudette who was pulling on a cigarette and rocking her head to the melodic sounds of Sade. "Ms. Claudette, you alright?"

"Yea, I guess I'm alright, how ya doing baby girl?"

"I'm well. Looks like something got you down, you sure you're okay?"

"I'm alright I guess. No need to talk about a no good son of a bitch who won't even bring his ass home. What brings you back here? Somebody ordered a drink?"

"No, Mark sent me back here."

"For what? All week he's been bitchin' bout his liquor and I'm getting real sick and tired of hearing his shit," she fussed as she sat straight up in her chair.

Skyler chuckled.

"Anyway, just 'tween you and me, I won't be here too much longer. I got me another gig down the road," she said as she stretched.

"Oh yea? When you leaving Ms. C.?"

"I don't know yet, but mark my word, one of these days, you gon' come back here and Ms. Claudette's shit will be long gone. I'ma make sure I leave his damn locker wide open and empty. Mark is too damn selfish and all he wants is my damn money. I already played the fool when I was young and dumb. It seems like every time I turn around he has another damn reason to get my money."

"Well, you and I both know how Mark is. I'm making some plays of my own."

"You better," she said, counting her money with her cigarette hanging from her lip. Claudette shook her head and mumbled under her breath. "So, what's up Sky? You said he sent you back here but you never said for what."

"He told me I to come back here and dance."

"He told you what! That's the shit I be talking 'bout. Just wait 'til I see his ass, I'ma give him a good tongue lashing. The only thing he can think of is getting some ass out there on that damn stage so he can beat himself off."

Skyler raised an eyebrow disgustingly. Claudette removed her cigarette from her mouth and placed it in the ashtray while she eyed Skyler.

"I can't believe he asked the bartender to dance, he must be mighty desperate," she laughed boisterously. "You don't know shit 'bout dancing. This here is for grown folks. Shit, you still got Similac on your tongue," she said sarcastically.

"I dance across town on my off days."

"Since when?"

"For about six months."

"Damn girl, if you've been dancing you should've came and talked to me sooner. I could've put you on to some things and you could've made you some real money."

"Oh, I'm good. My guy friend is putting me on."

"Who?"

"A guy named Ric Simmons."

"Ricardo?"

"Yea, you know him?"

"Do I know him? Who doesn't? He's too money hungry for me chile. Believe you me, that money you 'bout to make will never hit the bottom of your purse."

"He's never took my money."

"Oh, he will. He will have you eating out the palm of his hands before he's through with you. Trust me when I say, he's not the man you think he is. He's not worthy of your time. I'm only telling you what I know and what others failed to tell me when I was your age. I stood in your shoes many moons ago when he first got into the game. Now he's better, stronger, manipulative and vindictive."

"Ric?"

"I'm telling you what I know and I ain't got no reason to lie to you. If I were you, I'd drop him like a bad habit quick, fast and in a hurry."

"Ric?"

"All he does is get silly ass young dumb girls, then trick 'em out. If you stick around him long enough, you'll be next."

"Oh no, he won't do that to me. I have too much respect for myself."

"Do you?" She chuckled. "So, you telling me that shaking your ass for a dollar or getting a twenty-dollar lap dance is respecting yourself?" she laughed. "Listen to me, baby he's bad news. Don't get too caught up with him. He's a charmer. I give him that, and only that, but his bite is full of venom."

"That's weird, everywhere we go people show him nothing but love."

"Show him love?" she scoffed. "Well, take note, no one shows him love, its fear. Don't get side swiped, once he gets his hooks in you, you'll be worthless and useless. Anyway baby, let's get you into something quick 'cause I don't want Mark marching back here bitchin' bout what's taking you so long."

Skyler followed a marching Claudette while her thoughts lingered back to Ric. She stood behind Claudette as she fumbled through her locker of outfits before handing them to Skyler. Skyler fingered through her selection and tried them on until she found one that fit like a glove. She walked toward a singing Claudette who was baffled when Skyler stood in front of her.

"Lawd ham mercy girl. You sho'll gon' make us some money tonight," she sang, waving her hand in the air like she was a faithful member of the local church. "I didn't know you had all that under them clothes. Um...Um...Umm. Girl, I think we might've hit jackpot," she said as she scurried around. "We got to make sure we put some glitter on you." She stepped back. "Oh, don't forget what you have on had a price tag hanging from it so pay me when you take your first break."

"No problem."

"Okay, now let me lay down some house rules before you go on the floor. One, don't fuck up my money 'cause then I'll have to fuck you up. I'm serious about my shit. Two, never get too enticed with my money before you start fucking up yours, turning tricks and shit, and three I don't give a damn how tired you are, if you on the floor, money is to be made."

Skyler paused for a second until Claudette raised an eyebrow. "Yes ma'am?"

"And oh, before I forget, I don't care what Mark tells you, don't get your ass on that stage unless you are called. If they want to see you dance, you only give them lap dances, you hear me?"

"Yes."

"all right now, I'll send someone out there to check on you to see how you're doing."

"Ok."

"Now, go 'head and get our money," Claudette said as she shooed her away.

Skyler walked away feeling like she was lectured by her mother, but as soon as she stepped to the bar and ordered a drink, Claudette and her lecture had dissipated. She noticed she had a few admiring eyes so she did what she knew best. She asked Mark for two shots of Patron, dashed the salt on the back of her hand, chased it with a lime and tossed them in her mouth then slowly licked the salt from her hand as they lustfully watched. She slid the shot glasses to Mark then winked at her admirers, leaving them at the bar as they watched her white and sky blue stringy outfit compliment her curvaceous ass. She never thought she would ever dance at Scores, but since Ric had someone to run ole' girl off the road, someone had to make the money whether Mark agreed to it or not. Her audience was captivated when she stepped across the floor in cadence with the melody as her fragrance tantalized them. The sexy bartender danced seductively, grabbing everyone's attention including Mark and Claudette as they watched her make an easy six hundred dollars in the first hour.

"....so, what you think?" Alana voice interrupted her thoughts.

"I think that's fine," she replied without knowing what she agreed to.

Skyler was so engulfed with her own thoughts she hadn't heard a single word from Alana, but asking her to repeat whatever she said was out of the question. Instead, she leaned into the passenger seat and tried to figure out how something so great backfired in the worst way. She knew she'd lost control when cocaine became part of her wardrobe, a serious habit she couldn't kick thanks to Ric.

Alana looked at her and noticed a blank expression on her face and mentally noted to self to talk with her after she settled in when she drove into the parking deck.

"Damn girl, this is nice...," Skyler complimented.

"Thank you, but it's just the parking deck."

"I bet the inside is sweet, isn't it?" she said with raised eyebrows.

"Girl, help me with this doggone luggage. What's inside of this? A dead man?"

Sky looked at her with a wikked smile and a raised brow.

"Hold on for a second, let me call security."

Alana reached inside of her purse and pulled out her phone. She noticed three missed calls from Anthony and quickly dialed security's number. They waited for security with the luggage cart loaded the cart.

"Hello Ms. Inacio, how are we this evening?"

"I'm good thank you, how are you?"

"Ah, you know me. I'm alright."

He stared at her guest before Alana introduced him to her.

"Oh, I'm sorry. Brian this is Skyler. Skyler this is Brian, one of the building's security guys."

"Hello Brian," she muffled.

Skyler carried her small bag while Alana pulled her luggage carrier from her photo shoot toward the parking deck elevator. Skyler reached into her purse and pulled out her phone.

"Hey, I thought you tossed your phone out of the window?" Alana asked.

"I did, but I always keep a backup."

"You haven't changed a bit," Alana chuckled when the elevator door opened.

Skyler pressed her lips together as she admired the glass building.

"Now, this is real living," Skyler complemented as they walked inside of the lobby.

"Okay Skyler, so what's really going on with you?" she whispered as Brian trailed behind them.

"What do you mean, what's really going on?" she scoffed.

"I know something is wrong, I heard it in your voice when you were on the phone with Ric."

Skyler struggled to find the right words as Alana carefully watched her facial expression just as the elevator signaled and the occupied guests walked passed them, smelling like a mobile liquor store. Alana and Skyler looked at each other after the guests walked passed and burst into laughter as they exited the lobby. Skyler walked into the elevator then leaned against the elevator wall. Alana pressed the number six of her floor highlighted in red. Skyler looked around the elevator and noticed a small television inserted in the wall of the elevator.

"Girl, even the elevator is nice."

"Ms. Inacio, I will catch the next one. I need to stop by the desk for a second, okay?"

"Sure, no problem."

Brian walked toward the front desk with the luggage cart while the ladies stood inside of the elevator.

"Yea, I thought the same thing when I first saw it, but I'm still waiting for my answer," she said as the doors closed.

"Okay see, Ric and I....," she said as a hand propped the doors from closing.

The doors bounced opened and a guy in a maintenance uniform stepped inside holding onto his crates as he smiled at them. They both returned the smiled at him, while their eyes covered his muscular physique. Alana noticed his muscular arms, chocolate skin and piercing almond shaped dark -brown eyes which complimented his dark features. On the other hand, Skyler noticed his well-toned arms and raised an eyebrow. She looked at him again and noticed a familiarity about him as if she'd seen him before. But between dancing at different clubs, traveling from Vegas to South Beach, nothing came to mind.

They say we all have a twin somewhere in the world, she mused.

They both raised an eyebrow at each other when he pressed the number five button. Alana noticed while Skyler cleared her throat.

"Well, hey number five, we're number six," she said flirtingly.

"Well hello," he said, turning to look at her with a raspy voice.

"I'm Skyler and this is my girl, Alana."

"Skyler and Alana? I'm Monte," he said smiling at Alana.

"Hi," Alana replied before looking away.

"We're having a small celebration tonight. If you're not too busy, why don't you stop by 'round nine o'clock if you want to hang out?" Skyler invited as the doors opened.

"Oh yea, where about?" he said, glancing at Alana.

"L," Skyler blurted when the elevator signaled.

"L? I may swing by for a second if I step out," he told her.

"Ok, well we look forward to seeing you later then," Skyler said as the doors closed. Alana cut her eyes at Skyler, but Skyler stared at Alana with a wide grin.

"Now, that's what I call sexy, did you hear how raspy his voice was?" Skyler cooed.

"I did, but that's the last thing on my mind right now," Alana said as she rubbed her temples. "I can't believe you just did that," Alana said with disdain.

"What are you talking about?"

"What am I talking about? You just invited that man to my apartment like you know him."

"Lana, I was just....."

"If I wanted him to come over, don't you think I would've invited him myself?" she said as the elevator doors opened.

Alana stormed out of the elevator leaving Skyler behind. Skyler swiftly grabbed her luggage as she tried to catch up with Alana and explain her reasons, but it fell on deaf ears. Instead Alana just opened her door leaving it slightly opened for Skyler.

"Look, I'm sorry Lana. I didn't look at it that way. I was just trying to invite your neighbor over, ya know, being neighborly.

Alana looked at her then shook her head. "You just can't invite people over. You never know a person's intentions and I'm not trying to find out anyone else's no time soon."

"I'm sorry. He just doesn't look like the type of guy who would hurt a fly."

"Regardless if he looks like it or not, I'm still cautious about who I let into my space. To be very honest with you, I really don't want a lot of people up here anyway. Maybe Clifton will only invite a couple of his friends," she said as she shut the door behind her.

Alana's calm and welcoming Brazilian culture set the ambience of her condo.

"Here's the guest room," Alana showed her.

Skyler walked in the guest bedroom and adored the earth tone colors accented with sea shells in the corner of the room near her balcony.

"Just beautiful," she said when she stretched across the bed.

Nine o' clock arrived quickly and Alana's spacious condo was now overly crowded. Had she known Clifton was bringing his entire entourage, she would've had the celebration at Night's Owl, at least her personal space wouldn't have been invaded. She tried to mask the intrusion by smiling and interacting with her guests, but deep inside it sickened her that her condo was full of lurking guests. Alana looked around the room and noticed Skyler clinging to Clifton like he was static on her dress. She watched them chat and laugh like they were the only two people in the room. Disgusted at what she'd seen, she walked toward the bar until her phone rang. She answered the phone without looking at the screen then disappeared amongst the crowd while Skyler clawed Clifton with her conversation.

"So Clif, when are you going to take me out and show me a good time?" she asked while sipping on her drink.

"It's on you baby. Just let me know when you're ready."

"Oh, I'm ready. I know tonight is about Lana, so what about tomorrow night?"

"Tomorrow is good for me. Where do you wanna go?"

"I wanna check out a couple of strip clubs and...."

"Strip clubs?" he repeated with a piercing stare.

"Yea...I want to see what's out here."

"Is that, right?" he said with a raised eyebrow. "You wanna see some ladies?"

"I want to see my competition," she said as he shoved him a little.

She laughed to herself while shaking her head.

"Wanna step on the balcony with me?"

"Sure, but I don't want Alana to see us. I don't want her asking any more questions I'm sure she already has some for me when all of this is over with."

"She's pretty occupied, she's on the phone," he noted.

They stepped on the crowded balcony and found an empty corner spot. Clifton pulled out a small blue teardrop saran wrap while Skyler leaned against the balcony rail and admired the Oceanside view. Clifton noticed her admiration then leaned against the rail beside her.

"It's beautiful, isn't it?" she said with awe.

"It sure is."

He dipped his pinkie fingernail inside of the package and sniffed it into his nostrils then passed the bag to her. She smiled to herself, took a dip and ran her finger across her front teeth.

"This is good," she said, tracing her tongue across her teeth.

"I get this from the best."

"Yea?" she said with a raised eyebrow. "You get it from here?"

"Oh no," he said, dipping again.

"So, where do you get it from?"

"Don't worry 'bout all that lil' lady. I have my sources."

"Okay then, so you know people. Do you know anyone that owns strip clubs?" she said as she turned her back toward the ocean.

"I do. I have a homeboy that owns several clubs out here. Sniff. I'll holla at him."

"So, what time are you picking me up?"

Sniff.

"Depends. Is Alana coming?"

"No. When I told her that I was dancing, man she freaked out."

"Well you know how Alana is." Sniff. "She probably just freaked out because of all the negative things people say about it."

"I guess."

"Anyway, you know how she is. Just explain to her the business side of it. She'll understand if you break it down to her like that." Sniff. "Explain it from a different perspective."

"I'll keep that in mind, but knowing Lana, that's not gonna fly with her."

"So, how about I show you the strip tomorrow night?"

"Sure."

Clifton couldn't believe how drawn he was becoming to her. She was dangerous. It hadn't been a full twenty-four hours since they'd met and yet he found himself comparing some of her qualifying qualities that most women lacked. She was just his kind of girl, but he didn't want Alana to know. It was something about their friendship that he valued. No matter how much he kept quiet about it, he had feelings for her but knew he could never act on them. He tucked the bag in his pocket when he saw her hang up her phone.

"We need to go back inside."

They hurriedly walked back inside and stood next to the fireplace as if they had never left. Clifton glanced around the room to see if everyone was socializing and realized he needed to interact with his guests. He grabbed a napkin near the fireplace, scribbled his number on it and handed it to Skyler.

"Call me," he said.

She folded the napkin and slid it inside of her bra before

walking away. He watched her sway away while his rising impression in his pants slight jumped just when his phone vibrated in his pocket.

"Yea, hello?......Umm, maybe an hour or so, what's up? ...Yea? Is that right? ....Right now?.... Damn, well don't stop your party, let me wrap this up so I can come on over there, alright?...... Oh, and don't you move a muscle. ....Alright ....Talk to you soon."

He quickly hung up the phone and headed to the bar for another drink. He didn't want to seem like he was in a rush, but the sooner this party ended the sooner he could leave and blow off some steam with his little Cubaña play toy.

"Are you having a good time?" Skyler whispered to Alana.

Alana turned around quickly and grabbed her chest.

"Oh my goodness, you startled me."

"Loosen up girl, you're so uptight. It's just me. I had to get away from Clifton, he's so flirty."

"I thought you liked that?"

"I do, but on my terms," she said, avoiding her eyes.

"Hmph," Alana mumbled to herself when her doorbell chimed.

"This place can't fit another person," Skyler scoffed.

"Tell me about it."

Alana walked toward the door then stared out of the peephole. She smiled to herself and snatched the door opened when she saw Micah standing outside of her door.

"Micah, you made it," she smiled.

"Yes I did, but I'm sorry I'm late."

"Better late than never. I love that yellow dress."

"Thank you. I wouldn't have missed this for nothing in the world. I brought Rafael?"

"Hello Rafael, please come on in."

Skyler quickly made eye connection with Micah's male acquaintance while she leaned on the bar. Alana welcomed them inside and accepted the bouquet of flowers from Rafael. Skyler walked toward them while Alana introduced Micah and Rafael to her friend and vice versa. Micah and Alana stepped aside leaving Skyler alone with Rafael as they chatted and watched Skyler flirt with Rafael. Micah laughed under her breath before shaking her head at them.

"She doesn't waste any time, does she?"

"I see."

"And she's your best friend? But you guys are like night and day."

"I know."

"Why haven't you ever mentioned her?"

"It's a long story," she said dryly.

"We'll talk about it later. Honey, it's packed like sardines in here," Micah said, noticing Alana's dryness.

"Tell me about it. You know I don't like too many people in my space," Alana frowned.

"Yea, I know. How did you manage to have your celebration here? That's not like you."

"Oh, this was definitely Clifton and Skyler's idea. I was against it, but he made it sound like he was only going to invite a handful of people and she suggested my place."

"You call this a handful of people?"

"Ha," Alana laughed sarcastically.

Micah looked at Alana's overcrowded condo until the door bell rung again. Alana took a deep breath when she walked toward the door because now she was slightly aggravated with the entire celebration. She wanted it to end as soon as possible but to her surprise the man who stood behind the door would enlighten her mood.

"Well, hello beautiful."

"Hi Mo-Monte, how are you?" she grinned.

"I'm wonderful now. I wanted to come by earlier, but I didn't want to seem like a stalker."

"You're fine, come in," she giggled.

He walked in and admired her Brazilian styled eccentric look which was complimented by her Ultra-Premium Orange Fruit wall color. She offered him a drink and vittles, but he politely declined.

"So, where's your date?" Monte asked as he looked around.

"I don't have one."

"What? Now please tell me, why is the most beautiful woman in this room dateless?" he said playfully.

"Well, I-I..," she stammered until Skyler interrupted.

"Well, look who decided to show up," Skyler voiced coyly, "Mr. Monte."

"Hello."

He smiled uncomfortably at her rudeness before looking away.

"Do you want something to drink?" she offered.

"No thank you, Alana already offered me something to drink. I'm good."

"Oh, okay then. You need anything Alana?"

"No, I'm fine Skyler."

"I just wanted to make sure you were good."

"Thank you, I am."

She smiled at them before walking toward Clifton.

"Who is she to you?" he asked suspiciously.

"My friend from Vegas," she said dryly.

"Your friend? She's visiting or is she your new roommate?" he inquired.

"I invited her to stay a little while longer, so I guess she is my new roommate for a couple of weeks. Why are you asking about Skyler?"

"I don't want to sound like that guy, but she's pretty presumptuous," Monte said.

"Yea..., I see. She's only been here one day, but we have a lot to catch up on. It's been a long time since we've seen each other."

"Well, I'm sure that's going to be quite interesting. I went through that myself just a few weeks ago, me and one of my homeboys linked up after we graduated from college. It was cool at first then I realized how much I had outgrown him. In high school, we just kicked it and didn't worry about nothing except getting girls."

She chuckled at him before staring at Skyler.

Maybe she's just excited to be in Miami, she mused.

Alana wanted to know the real reason why Skyler wanted to visit her out of the blue. She'd offered her a plane ticket for the past four years, but Skyler always declined and blamed it on bad timing. Monte glanced at Alana and noticed her wrinkled forehead.

"Hey, you alright? You look like something is weighing heavy on your mind."

"Yea, just a little, but I will be alright. So anyway, Mr. Monte, where are you from?" she said, quickly changing the subject.

"Virginia," he said without pressing the issue.

"Virginia?"

"Yep, born and somewhat raised. What about you?"

"Brazil. I moved down here about five years ago."

"Okay then. So, if you don't mind me asking, what are we celebrating?" he asked.

"I'm the face of Night's Owl, Clifton's club. He's the guy walking toward us now."

Clifton swiftly walked toward them with his eye only on Monte. He stood in front of him and extended his hand to him.

"I haven't seen you around here, my name is Clifton Parks."

"Monte. J. Monte," he replied as he shook his hand firmly.

Clifton studied him until Alana eyed Clifton's stares. He tried to look away, but found himself staring at the dark-skinned guy who was standing beside Alana. She knew that look Clifton gave Monte and reintroduced him as her neighbor from downstairs. He relaxed a little when he learned that he was the maintenance man for the building and wanted no parts of anyone's drama. Monte also told him he had just moved to Miami and wasn't familiar with the area, but Clifton still wasn't convinced he could be trusted. Clifton looked at his watch and told her he was about to make his announcement. Quickly, he turned around and asked everyone to please join them for a moment.

"Can I have your attention for a second or two?" he said while everyone formed a circle. "I just wanted to thank all of the participants for running for the face of Night's Owl, but at this time we have made our selection. It is with great pleasure that I introduce her to you. *Alana Inacio*," he said as he stepped back.

Everyone clapped as she stood in the middle of the circle before a loud knock sounded on her door. Skyler swiftly walked toward the door so they could continue, but when she slowly opened it the door pushed her back.

"Hey what the hell?" she said aloud when the door hit her.

"Get out of my damn way!" Anthony responded tartly.

"What are you doing here? You didn't get an invite," Micah said matter of factly.

"Where's Lana?" he slurred. "Lana!" he called out.

"You're not welcomed here," Skyler said.

"The hell I'm not! I know she's here, now where the hell is she? Lana!" he called out again.

Immediately, Anthony's raised voice caught everyone's attention, especially Clifton and Alana's. Clifton handed his glass flute to Micah before rushing toward the commotion near the door.

"Hey, hey, hey! Anthony, what the hell are you doing?"

"What the hell are you doing here? You at my girl house throwing her a damn party? What are you trying to do? Throw her in my face? Take what's mine?" he spoke dizzily.

"Man, you got this all wrong. We're celebra....."

"I got it all wrong? Man, get the hell out of my face! Lana!" Anthony said interrupting Clifton.

"You've had too much to drink and this is not that kind of party. You need to go home Anthony."

Monte stepped in front of Alana as Rafael and a couple of other guys rushed toward the door.

"Ant, what the hell is your problem?" Clifton said.

"You're my damn problem! I know you want Alana for yourself. You think I don't know it, but I see how you look at her. I see it man," he yelled as he rushed into him.

"Whoa wait a minute," the guys at the door voiced.

Immediately, Monte rushed toward the door as Anthony yelled out Alana's name in a rage when things seemed to get out of hand and the havoc was causing a distraction outside of Alana's door.

"Who the hell are you?" he asked Monte.

"Man, you need to take this somewhere else," Monte said with a stern voice.

Clifton looked on with the other men while Monte tried to calm the drunken visitor at the door. He was angry, loud and intoxicated and seeing a new face trumpeted his anger. Monte noticed the man wasn't backing down so he did the only thing he knew how to do. He walked past the guys who tried to restrain Anthony, picked him up by his shirt collar then tossed him on the opposite side of the wall. He stood eye to eye with him without blinking an eye.

"Now, this can go one or two ways. I'm not in the mood for this shit," Monte growled as he pushed him away from him.

Anthony stumbled sideways before hitting the floor while staring at him bizarrely before spitting on Monte's shoe. Monte looked at his shoe disgustingly then kicked Anthony in the stomach. Anthony tried to stand to his feet, but fell backwards when he felt Monte strike him again. Monte pulled him up from the ground then pushed him back into the wall.

"Get your fucking hands off of me!" Anthony yelled.

"Get the hell out of here before I...," Monte said as he drew back his fist before Alana rushed out and grabbed his arm.

"Don't hit him Monte. Just let him go."

Monte glanced at her before looking back at Anthony. She stared at Anthony as her heart raced in her chest.

"You need to leave before I call the police."

Anthony picked up his jacket from the floor then looked at Alana apologetically. He tried to walk toward Alana, but Monte pushed him back into the wall.

"Did you hear what she said," Monte replied.

"You son of a bitch! I'll be back," Anthony voiced before storming away. "I'll be back," he said as he wiped the blood from his lip.

"I'll be right here if you want another ass whoopin'."

Monte, Clifton, and Rafael stood in the hallway until Anthony disappeared. Monte stood behind Alana as she stood in a trance. Monte asked her if she was okay, but she simply nodded without looking at him until Skyler stood beside her.

"What the hell was that all about?" she asked.

"Same old mess. He called earlier, we had another disagreement and he went ballistic when he heard the chatter in the background. You already know how jealous he is."

"He got some serious issues," Skyler said.

"Tell me about it."

"Well, I tell you what. If anyone else wants to throw you something, they need to have it somewhere else," Monte suggested.

"Who are you telling," Alana shot back.

Alana turned around and walked back inside of her place as everyone followed her. Clifton noticed how uncomfortable she looked when she saw her guests stirring around in her condo. Clifton immediately walked toward the bar and told the servers to shut it down and pack it up. He quickly announced to everyone that the party was over. Micah leaned toward her and told her to call her first thing in the morning so they could discuss shooting fifteen frames for Night's Owl ad for the local magazine. She agreed and apologized again for Anthony's outbursts when she walked them to the door. Everyone congratulated her again as they left. He stayed back and thanked every last person for joining Alana's celebration until her condo was cleared out with the exception for Monte. When Clifton noticed Alana talking to Monte, he sat near the coffee table while Skyler tried to occupy his time. He wasn't paying any attention to Skyler's small talk. He kept his eyes on Alana while she conversed and laughed with Monte across from them. He dashed to his feet when Monte leaned closer to her and abruptly pulled Alana to the side. Clifton insisted on staying if she'd like, but she assured him that everything was under control. Still, he wasn't convinced that her neighbor was the nice man he portrayed to be.

"It's something about him that makes me uncomfortable," Clifton whispered to Alana.

"Clifton he's fine," she whispered without taking her eyes from Monte, "after all, did you see the way he stepped up and handled Anthony?"

"Yea, maybe he was trying to impress you," he whispered.

"Clifton? Come on, he's my neighbor. Besides, Sky invited him. He doesn't look like he's a bad guy."

"Looks are deceiving."

"You're right, but I'm okay."

Clifton glanced at Monte before looking at Alana. She quickly noticed and reassured him that she was fine just as Monte walked toward them.

"Well, it's getting late, so I'm gonna head home," Monte said politely to Alana.

"Okay."

"Nice meeting you," he said to a skeptical Clifton.

"Yea, likewise," Clifton replied.

Alana stepped away from Clifton and walked Monte to the door.

"Ya know, I get the feeling that ole' boy don't really care for me," he said with caution.

"Clifton is usually like that like when someone new comes around. My dad asked him to be his extra set of eyes, but sometimes it's a little too much," she said just as they reached the door.

"I'm sure."

"No, you have no idea.

"Ya know, I'm not trying to get all in your business, but can I ask you something?"

"Sure."

"Who was that guy that came by earlier in a rage?"

"That was my ex- fiancé?"

"Hmm, is he always like that?"

"Yes, he's very jealous."

"You may need to look into getting a restraining order on him, just to make sure he won't hurt you."

"He'll never hurt me."

"You don't know what a jealous person will do. You should at least give it some thought."

"I will," she said nonchalantly.

"Okay, well get some rest and don't be a stranger," he said.

A smiled formed in the corner of her mouth just as she opened her door and he stepped outside of it.

"Good night Monte."

"Good night to you too," he said politely before walking off.

She closed the door then turned around just as Clifton walked toward her.

"I am so glad it's finally over. There were just too many people in here Clifton."

"Yea, I apologize for the stampede in here. I only invite a couple of people and word must've spread quickly. Actually, I have over forty text messages from people wanting to know your address, but I know how you are about your space. Next time, we'll have it at Night's Owl."

"I think that's the best news I received all night," she said playfully.

"Well, since your neighbor is gone I guess I'm about to head out myself. If you need anything let me know."

"Okay. Thank you for tonight it was nice until....."

"Don't fret. I will talk with Ant about his jealous rampage."

"Good because I was so embarrassed."

"I know, like I said I'll take care of it," he said reassuringly. "Ladies, have a good night."

"Okay you too. Good night," they said in unison.

Alana closed and locked the door then blew out a long sigh before Skyler walked toward her.

"Girl this place was packed like sardines, wasn't it? Do you know if you would've charged cover that would've taken care of your rent?" Skyler joked.

"I'm glad you're amused because this is your fault."

"My fault?"

"Yea, you were the one who suggested my place for the celebration," Alana said as she walked toward her bedroom leaving Skyler in the living room.

Alana woke up the next morning with a migraine headache. She peeled her eye mask from her eyes to glance at her digital clock displayed on her ceiling.

"What in the ....? It's five forty freaking five," she huffed, as the banging noise echoed in her room.

She stuffed her ear plugs in her ears, covered her eyes with her sleep mask then pulled the covers over her head, but the noise continued. No sooner as she leaned deeper into her pillow, her bedroom door flung open.

"What is that? And who is making all that noise this early in the morning?" Skyler questioned.

Alana pressed her head into her pillow, irritated and frustrated with her new noisy neighbor and agitated by Skyler hastily entering her room. She pulled her mask above her eyes, leaned back onto her elbows and shook her head in dismay when she looked at the time. Skyler stood at Alana's door with one of her hands on her hips and the other one covering her temples.

"I'm assuming that would be Mr. Monte," Alana yawned.

"Monte, the maintenance man?"

"Yes."

"If he has to do all that, he needs to find another job."

Skyler looked around Alana's room and walked toward her infamous mirrored wall.

"Dayum, where did you get this big ass mirror from?" Skyler said.

Alana laughed at her then shook her head.

"Whatever."

"I mean like for real, what the hell do you need to see in this mirror?"

Alana chuckled without giving her an answer.

"Ok, okay well who put this mirror on your wall?"

"Anthony and a couple of his friends."

"Anthony? Oh, that's why you got it, for panoramic porno poses?"

Alana chuckled to herself just as Monte started the banging noises again.

"Tsk. Do you hear that? I mean, it makes no damn sense for him to be making all that noise this early. I tell you what, I'ma go downstairs and tell his ass to...," Skyler said just as she spun around.

"No, I'll take care of it," Alana said, quickly jumping to her feet.

"You sure because I have no problem telling his ass it's too early for all that damn noise."

"No, I got it. I'll tell him that we have a long day ahead of us and we need as much rest as we can get," Alana said.

"You sure you don't want me to go down there with you?" Skyler said with her hands on her hips.

"I'm sure."

Alana slipped on a pair of leggings, grabbed her keys and headed toward the staircase which was closer than the elevator. As she walked down the flight of stairs, a part of her wished she'd gotten his number last night since he was the maintenance man. There was no way she was going to ask for it, she didn't want to seem too anxious to get his number especially at this time of the morning.

A phone call would've been much easier, she thought while shaking her head.

When she reached his floor, she quickly tapped on his door, but there was no answer. She patiently tapped again then looked down the hall.

"Who is it?" he called out.

She quickly stuffed her hands in her pockets and toyed with her keys when she yelled out her name.

"Alana."

The disturbance slightly irritated her, but she remained calm despite the situation. Just as she held her hand up to tap on the door, he snatched the door open, as if someone had disturbed him. Immediately, he formed a wide smile when he saw her standing at his door.

"Good Morning beautiful, what brings you by this early?" he asked, wiping his hands and checking out his watch.

She was taken aback when she noticed his dirty jeans and torn black t-shirt which complimented his toned biceps. She eyed his personalized tool belt wrapped around his waist as he wiped his hands on a small towel.

"Alana, is everything okay?" he asked again.

"Y-yea. I-I mean no. No, I'm not okay," she stammered.

"What's wrong?"

"Umm, it's almost six o'clock in the morning and I've got a migraine headache from your banging. What in the world are you doing?"

"I'm so sorry. Is it that loud?" he said as he covered his mouth.

"Yes."

"This damn pipe burst in the bathroom and I'm trying my best to stop this leak, but it's not working."

"Early this morning? Is there someone else that can help you out?"

"No. I replaced the last one so it's just me. The store doesn't open until eight o'clock and if I don't put a bandage on this, water will be everywhere and I don't want to hear the other tenants complaining about it. I need my job."

She rubbed her temples as the cool breeze past her, chilling her. She folded her arms, realizing she didn't have on a bra and didn't want him to get the impression that she was happy to see him.

"Yea, I'm sure they will complain."

"Well pretty lady, let me wrap this up. I'm sorry that I've disturbed you, but can I make it up to you? How 'bout we grab something to eat later today?"

She had to admit, he was quite the charmer and she liked it. She looked away, slightly impressed by his mannerism before answering. He noticed her hesitation and quickly took another approach.

"Maybe we can walk on the beach. I mean, we can grab a bite to eat in a public place, nothing intimate or private," he suggested.

"I-I didn't say...."

"I just wanted to clear the air. I'm not trying to make any sudden moves, just trying to get out and see the area. Plus, I heard the view it is nice. Figured it would be a little lonely walking on the beach by myself."

"Yea, the beach can stir up a lot of emotions if you're by yourself."

"Oh, my manners, would you like to come in?" he invited.

"Oh no, I need to get back upstairs. I have a photo shoot today and I need to get in a few more hours of sleep before Micah calls me."

"Micah?"

"My personal assistant, the young lady who had on a yellow dress last night."

"Oh yea, must be nice to have a personal assistant," he teased.

"She takes care of my personal errands and arranges all my appointments."

He leaned on his door and folded his arms across his chest while admiring how gorgeous she was without a drop of makeup and only wearing sleep wear.

"Well, I need to go back upstairs so I can get a few more hours of sleep."

"Oh, wait a minute," he quickly stepped away and scribbled something on a piece of paper, "here's my number, call me later if you want to join me at the beach. I'll be here. I have a few work orders that the last guy didn't fill."

"Okay."

She looked at it then slipped it in her pocket as she walked off. She knew Micah was planning a hectic day for her so jumping in bed was the only thing on her mind when she reached up the stairs. She hurried up the stairs, rushed inside and laid across her bed until she heard her phone buzzing on her nightstand.

Catching a break...

Three hours later, Micah and Rafael were setting up the photo shoot for Alana and Skyler. Micah playfully grabbed his camera and snapped a couple of pictures of him before the ladies arrived. He grabbed the camera with his left hand, her with his right and pulled her close to him.

"You are the best thing that ever happened to me Micah," he said as he planted a small kiss on her nose.

"Aw, you're just trying to get some," she said while playfully pushing him away.

He laughed at her as he adjusted his camera while Alana and Skyler walked in together. Micah turned around and smiled at them as they walked toward her.

"Hey ladies."

"Hey Micah," they said in unison.

"Alana, Rafael is waiting on you."

"Okay, sorry we're running a little late," Alana said. "We had some technical difficulties," she said jokingly.

"You're fine."

Alana walked toward the dressing room while Skyler stayed behind with Micah.

"So are you ready to take your frames?" Micah asked Skyler.

"Not really, but if I don't take these pictures Alana won't let me hear the end of it."

"Well, let me just reassure you that Alana just thinks you are too beautiful not to be in front of a camera."

"She told you that?" Skyler asked with a smile.

"Of course."

Skyler paused for a second.

"So, Alana tells me you're going to be here for a little while longer?" Micah said with a question.

"Yea."

"So, while you're here, is there anything you want to do?"

"Um..., I guess I'll look at some job opportunities while I'm down here."

"Anything in modeling? We're hiring."

"Nah, I stopped modeling to pursue other avenues."

"Well maybe after you take your pictures, you might change your mind. He's really good."

"You sound like his spokesperson," Skyler joked.

Micah chuckled under breath when Skyler flashed a smile at her.

"Well, I tell you what, if you ever change your mind and you want a couple of gigs to make some money, feel free to call me," Micah said as she handed her a card.

"I'll keep that in mind," Skyler replied.

Skyler looked at the card then smiled to herself without looking back at Micah, all awhile shaking her head to herself. She was tired of people trying to convince her to get back into modeling. She tried to convince herself a couple of times that she could easily slip back into it if she wanted to, but the money she received from dancing reminded her why she stopped in the first place.

"Skyler?" Rafael called out.

"Yes?" she blurted out.

"Want to shoot some frames with Alana?"

"Nah, go 'head."

Alana looked at Skyler pleadingly when she seemed disinterested in Rafael's offer. Micah noticed and insisted that she should take a couple of frames and in return she would tell Alana to stop pressuring her to go back to modeling. Skyler made a deal with Micah and walked toward Alana. The two of them shot several frames and Skyler thought about Clifton's proposal. She wanted to ask Alana what she thought about it, but thought against it when Alana stepped aside and let Rafael work on her.

Micah watched Rafael adjust his lens while Skyler position herself for him on one of his hottest displays. Micah took note of Skyler's beauty and wondered the real reason why Skyler wasn't modeling. Alana slipped on her robe and watched Skyler pose for Rafael with her own private thoughts. Skyler was beautiful, but Alana knew it wouldn't matter how much she reminded or complimented her beauty, she didn't think Skyler knew her worth. She stared at Skyler's 5'7 inch frame and wondered to herself how many men actually paid to see her dance in her nakedness. She shook her head at the thought and quickly looked away when Micah walked beside her.

"She's actually doing pretty well. She follows direction well and she isn't camera shy," Micah chuckled.

"I know," Alana said with a smile. "You know, I never realized how natural she was with the camera."

"Well, she is a beautiful woman. I just can't believe she stopped modeling to pursue other avenues."

Alana wished Skyler would've told her that so she didn't have a visual image of what she traded modeling for. She listened to Micah read her daily schedule for her upcoming week and informed her that Rafael had drawn up the contracts for her to sign what they discussed.

"So, did you enjoy the party last night?" Micah asked.

"You know, I have to be honest with you, I did not. I know that was supposed to be one of the best times for me and I'm very grateful for it, but all I could focus on was everyone in my space. Did you see how crowded my living room was?"

"I could tell by the look on your face that you were displeased."

"Displeased? Oh, that's an understatement."

"And Anthony showing up acting like a clown?"

"Please don't talk about him. I can't believe he had the nerve to show up uninvited and drunk," Alana said, shaking her head.

"That boy is out of his mind. Okay, but I tell you one thing though," she paused, "Monte was checking you out."

Monte. The sound of his name made Alana smile.

"Is that a smile?" Micah asked playfully.

"No," Alana tried to look serious.

"Sure looks like a smile to me."

"That wasn't a smile," Alana replied.

"Well it wasn't a frown," Micah mumbled.

"Anyway," Alana quickly changed the subject, "I need to change my clothes."

Alana and Micah walked toward the dressing room which

was near the stage Skyler was on.

"Have you heard from Clifton?" Alana asked.

"No, that's odd. He usually calls around the same time every day."

"Come to think of it, you're right Micah."

"He might've had a late night."

"Oh, I'm sure he did," Alana said with raised eye brows.

"Can I ask you something?" Micah asked in a hushed voice.

"Sure," Alana said as she changed into a sundress and a pair of sandals.

"How well do you know him?"

"I know what he tells me. When it comes to Clifton, you don't know what you're going to get. But then again, I guess he's just like most people. They tend to show you only what they want you to see, sometimes people can't handle the truth. Why do you ask?"

"Well.....it's nothing," Micah stammered.

"Micah?" Alana asked as she combed her hair.

"Okay Alana," Micah said in a whisper, "did you see how friendly he was with Skyler last night?"

"I did."

"Did you see that powder residue near his nose?"

"Who's? Clifton?" she said, turning her head toward her with a bulging stare.

"That's right Alana."

"Power residue?"

"I don't know what he's into, but make sure you keep your eyes open. Do you know if Skyler is into drugs?" Micah asked.

"I honestly don't know. We have a lot of history together, but there are a lot of things I still don't know about, so....."

"Honestly, she's seems sneaky. What about Clifton? You think there is more to him?" Micah asked.

"There is always another side of everyone."

"Okay...," Micah interjected when she noticed Skyler approaching them. "So, are you excited that you're the face of Night's Owl?"

"I'm not quite sure yet," she said dryly.

"Hey ladies, what's going on?" Skyler greeted as she walked into the dressing room.

Micah picked up on Alana's dry response and made a mental

note to inquire about it when they were alone.

"So Skyler, what do you think? You looked great," Micah mentioned.

"It was fun, thank you," Skyler smiled and looked at Alana.

"Wanna go to Night's Owl and grab a drink first?" Micah offered.

"Heck yea, I'm down with that," Skyler added.

I'm sure you are, Alana thought.

"What about you Alana?" Micah asked.

"That's fine."

Micah noticed Alana's hesitation toward Skyler and tried her best to keep Skyler entertained until Rafael called out her name.

"Micah?"

"Give me second, let me talk with Rafael. I'll be right back," Micah said before leaving them alone.

"We'll be right here," Skyler said as she watched Micah walk away before looking at Alana. "What's wrong?"

"Nothing," Alana said without looking at her.

"So, after we leave Night's Owl, what do you want to do?"

"I was thinking about going back home. I'm not in the mood to do anything."

"I spoke to Clifton earlier, he said he wants to take me to the club."

"Clifton? You don't even know *him*," she scoffed.

"He's your friend, isn't he?"

"He is," she paused, "but I still don't *know* him. You don't even know what kind of place Miami is and you're already looking for trouble."

"Trouble? He asked me out, how is that looking for trouble?"

"You might as well say that's trouble. You don't know what kind of company he keeps and of all places, you're going to a club with him Sky?"

"What's wrong with a club?"

Alana shook her head before looking the opposite way.

"Hello? What's wrong with the club Lana?" she asked while walking toward her. "Did you want to go?"

"No."

"Listen, the only reason why Clifton asked me is ...."

"I really don't want to know why he asked," she replied

disappointedly.

Skyler looked at Alana with a puzzling stare before responding.

"Did I do something to you?"

Alana looked away when Skyler walked closer to her.

"Alana!"

"What Skyler?"

"Have I done something to you?"

"No," Alana said while shaking her head. "Not at all, you're grown and you're going to do whatever you want to do anyways, right?"

"Lana, come on. Why are you acting like this?"

Alana looked at her then took a deep breath before walking away from her. Skyler picked up her bag and hurriedly walked beside her.

"Look, I'm not here to get you all rattled up. I came to South Beach to hang out with you and to see what kind of clubs they have down here."

"Okay then, don't let me stop you," Alana said, swiftly walking away from Skyler.

Skyler noticed how dry Alana was toward her, but she continued to speak as Alana walked away.

"Look," Skyler said as she stepped in front of Alana, in mid step, "I know you don't agree with my choices, but at least I thought you would understand that modeling wasn't working out for me like it is for you. You have something really special here."

"But I thought..."

"You thought what Alana? I don't want to live in someone else's shadow. You're doing your thing and its working for you. Now for me, that's another story."

"But you told me......"

"I know what I told you, but that's not paying my bills right now Lana. People change. Things change. My dad didn't get me a condo and he damn sure didn't pay for my ride of choice."

"What does that have to do with you?" Alana said with tears in her eyes.

"All I'm saying is...... having a supportive family helps," Skyler said before looking away, "one way or another."

"Supportive? You have no idea of what I'm going through. But hey, you've made it obvious why you're here, so don't let me stop you."

Skyler watched Alana walk away then mumbled something under her breath. She felt a breeze crawl up behind her then spun around and stared in Micah's bulging eyes. Micah was abashed by Skyler's comment, but her phone interrupted her thoughts when it buzzed in her hand. It was a message from Alana indicating that she was ready to go. Micah relayed the message to Skyler before walking toward Rafael so she could ride with him.

Alana didn't want to argue with Skyler and tried her best to shake away her feelings toward Skyler's actions. Skyler was right, people do change. She only wished for Skyler to be her own woman and thought modeling could restore that for her. Skyler walked up to Lana.

"I'm sorry Lana."

"Me too. I have never and will never judge you. I just want the best for you..."

"Likewise."

"I do feel like you're not being honest with me Sky. Ever since you've been here, it's like you're someone else. It's almost like I don't recognize you."

"Someone else?" she chuckled. "I'm just going through a rough time, that's all. All I want to do is take care of it and move on."

"And how do you plan on doing that, by stripping?"

"Yes Lana. It's really not that bad. Girl, I can make a few bands in one weekend. Shoot, all I need now is a sponsor."

"A sponsor?" Alana asked shockingly.

"Yea, someone who will take care of me financially."

"Oh, you mean a pimp? And in return what do you have to do for him?"

"Or her. It just depends," Skyler joked.

"Or her? Oh my goodness," Alana said while shaking her head, "you don't have any boundaries, do you?"

"Does a dollar bill have a gender?"

"So, you're resulting in gender bills?"

"I result to currency, not who spends it," Skyler corrected.

Alana pressed her lips together then shook her head. She cringed with what she was hearing. Alana secretly debated whether or not if she was now regretting that she'd offered her to stay longer.

"All I'm saying is I need a sponsor," Skyler stated.

"How much money do you need?"

"I-It's too much."

"Just tell me," Alana sighed.

"About thirty thousand dollars," she mumbled.

"Thirty thousand freaking dollars! Are you out of your mind?" she yelled.

"I know it's a lot that's why I didn't say anything. I'll get it in about...."

"Wait a minute. So wait, you're here to get all of the money?"

"Sort of, but I had to get away from him."

"This is dangerous Skyler, why not get the police involved?"

"Lana, I don' t want them involved. I just want to get this money then I'm out. Besides, I'm not giving him shit."

"Wait, that's him money? Thirty thousand dollars?"

"No! I worked my ass off for that damn money. I was the one who worked two damn jobs, stacking up cash. He told me he needed some money and I gave it to him, but when I asked for it back, he started tripping."

"What does he do anyway?" Alana asked.

Skyler folded her arms and leaned into Alana's passenger seat. She stared out of the window before answering.

"When he told me he had his own business, I never questioned him. As long as I had my own money and he had his, why question it?"

"Um, you never wanted to know what kind of business he was in," Alana said with a curious tone.

"Not really. He had connections and that was my only concern. Things started getting a little messy when I was bringing more money home than him."

Alana knew Skyler was dancing around her questions. A part of her wanted to know, but something was telling her to let it go. Her curiosity was getting the best of her when Skyler fell mute.

"Okay, so let me get this straight. He's your boyfriend?"

"Something like that."

"Where is your car?"

"It's at the Vegas airport."

"Does he know?"

"No, and that's the last place he's going to check."

"Ok," Alana shifted in her seat, "how long will it take you to get the money up?"

"Depends on the crowd and how much they spending in the club."

"If you need some help, I can help you."

"Thank you Lana, but this is really my problem. I just need to get my shit together so I can get this money up."

Alana was slightly cautious about Skyler's apprehension. Skyler's lifestyle was becoming too problematic for her own good. She was definitely mixed up with the wrong type of crowd. Whatever her problem was, Alana really didn't mind Skyler keeping it to herself. She didn't want any parts of it and asked no further questions.

"Why don't you speak to him. At least see if you guys can work out something."

"He doesn't want to work out anything. He's an all or nothing type of guy. So, I refuse to give him anything and my mind is made up."

"I can respect that. Just tell me what you need."

"If I did accept your offer, I promise I will pay you back."

"You don't have a choice," Alana snidely replied.

Skyler smiled to herself and quickly thanked her for her support. She apologized for keeping this from her and linked her recent behavior to it, but she wasn't that dumb. She only told Alana what she wanted her to know, the other stuff she would sort out herself. Alana glanced at her, but still knew that wasn't the end of that story. The closer they reached to Night's Owl, the more Alana thought of going to the beach with Monte didn't seem like a bad idea after all.

While they were headed to Night's Owl, Clifton was thinking about the conversation he and Skyler had the night before about her dancing. He had an associate he dealt with by the name of Russ, who owned several strip clubs in Miami. He picked up his phone and dialed his number, but it went to his voicemail. He left a quick message then hung up right before he saw him walk in. He slipped the phone in his pocket and greeted him.

"What's up stranger? Long time, no see," Clifton voiced as he extended his hand.

"I agree. What's good?"

"Man, you won't believe this," Clifton said with wide eyes. "What are you drinking?"

"The usual, Cuervo Black."

Clifton snapped his fingers, catching Mesa's attention. She walked toward him and took his order.

"So, what got you all excited these days?" Russ asked when the server walked away.

"Man, I met this doll who is new to the city and she say she wanna dance."

"Oh yea?" he said before Mesa placed his drink in front of him. "Thank you sexy."

She smiled and walked toward another awaiting customer.

"Yea and she's a piece of work. She makes Stallion looks like a pony."

"You know Clifton you got some fine ass ladies working for you in here. Your Mesa is very sexy, she can come to the club any time."

"You already know Mesa isn't feeling the strip clubs like that."

"I'm just saying you never know. Money talks homeboy."

"So anyway, man let me put it to you like this, this girl is dripping in sex."

"Ooh, where did you meet her?"

"She's Alana's friend."

"Alana...," he paused, "I keep telling her that she needs to stop playing around and get a real cat like myself. A business man who's gonna support her every move," he said as he sipped from his drink. "Man, your boy Ant didn't know what to do with a woman like that."

Clifton laughed under his breath while his own personal thoughts of Alana danced around in his own mind.

Wait on it, Clifton mused. "Anyway, Alana's friend is here from Vegas and man let me tell you, she's ...."

"Vegas?" he said abruptly.

Russ hadn't heard of his hometown since he left over twenty years ago and the sound of it gave him chills. For a few long seconds he didn't respond, instead he stirred the ice in his Cuervo Black while his mind raced back to the very beginning.

He was very charismatic and with his manipulative, conniving ways, he got cars, rims, shoes, clothes, jewelry, sex and money in exchange. When his peers noticed, they wanted him to teach them his tricks but he laughed it off. Truth was, he didn't want anyone to knock his hustle and he believed every man stood for himself. He finally told one person, his younger brother, but he didn't have the natural charm like Russ. He tried to teach him how to be charismatic with the ladies, but he was too selfish and stubborn to think of anyone besides himself. Once Russ mastered the game, he gave his brother one final golden rule to live by, never get emotionally connected.

As the years passed the brothers ran the streets of Vegas until Russ met a girl named Passion. Russ soon began to fall in love with her and the pair planned to leave Vegas after he settled his reckless affairs. When Russ ended all of his flings, he confided to his brother about marrying Passion. His brother, Ric, congratulated him and offered to throw him a bachelor's party without revealing his interest in her as well, but Russ noticed Passion's growing distance.

One night after a long argument she and Russ had, he went back to his office to clear his mind. He stopped his stride. He heard moaning coming from the next room. His curiosity grew as he walked toward the moans and noticed the door slightly opened. He thought about the countless conversations he had with his male customers having sex in the back of his club with his girls. He walked toward the door and pushed it open, but his heart dropped in the pit of his stomach. He quickly felt a sharp dagger pain in his heart when he saw Passion's legs wrapped around his brother's waist on the wall in the back of their club next to his office.

Immediately, with his heart pulsating like a raging bull and his palms slick, dripping with sweat, he lunged toward them in despair landing several punches on his brother's face causing her to fall onto the floor. Passion crawled away from the mayhem toward her purse as their money and jewelry fell from their pockets. Passion quickly scanned the room as the brothers swung at each other, landing a few punches into the dry wall and kicking over boxes before Passion ran past them.

Without even noticing her fleeing the room, the brothers took out their blades and swung at each other. Russ listened to

Ric boasted about stealing his girl. In a rage, Russ blurted out that Passion was a junkie stealing his money and drugs. Ric looked around for Passion, but once he knew she was gone he slashed the right side of his brother's face. Instinctively, Ric ran out the back door leaving Russ in the office dripping in blood seconds before the police and the paramedics arrived.

The ambulance rushed Russ to the hospital while Ric fled home and gathered his entourage. He instructed everyone to comb the Midwest until they found Passion. As soon as he caught up with her, she was too stoned to talk. All he wanted to do was take her from his brother just to prove a point. After realizing she was a lost call, he walked away from her and let his boys' torture her before slicing her throat and leaving her dead on the dusty road in the middle of nowhere.

Once Russ heard the news, he quickly signed himself from the hospital then hopped on the first flight to Florida. He didn't want to be anywhere near his delusional brother and at that point broke all ties with him. To him, his brother was dead.

"Russ?" Clifton called out.

"Yea?" he said calmly.

"You alright, looked like you went down memory lane," Clifton added.

"Yea, I did for a minute," Russ said as he tossed half of his drink in the back of his throat. "So, what's her name?"

"Skyler. When can we stop through?"

"Come through after you get off, but let her know that she can't dance tonight. You already know the rule, she gotta dance for me first so I can see what she's working with."

"Ten o'clock good?"

"That'll work," Russ said after he placed the empty glass in front of Clifton.

Russ left with only one thing on his mind. Ric. He pulled out his cell phone and called an old friend by the name of Mark, just to touch basis with him. He needed to know if he heard of a Skyler and if she had any connections with Ric. He smiled to himself when his old friend started to disclose layers of information about her just as he closed the door to Night's Owl behind him leaving Clifton puzzled by his abruptness.

Thirty minutes had passed, Alana, Micah and Skyler sat at Alana's usual spot at Night's Owl. Clifton saw them and made an announcement that the face of Night's Owl was in the house. Everyone stood to their feet and applauded in Alana's direction. She was slightly embarrassed, but sat at her table and smiled. Micah shared the news with Clifton about Alana touring with Rafael in thirty states for his promotion tour.

He smiled widely, excited for her tour because all of her long hours at different photo shoots, outside in the sweltering heat, runways and plenty of faulty promotions were about to pay off.

Skyler and Micah celebrated with her, but Skyler secretly envied her. Skyler knew she was just as beautiful as Alana and more of a woman than she could ever be.

"Well ladies, this calls for a celebration."

Skyler excused herself to the restroom when Clifton didn't look at her. She felt like he disrespected her when he kept his eyes only on Alana. He swiftly grabbed a server to distract them when he noticed Skyler walking away. He calmly followed a marching Skyler three minutes after she left the table.

"Hey what's up? Slow down," he said, trailing behind her.

"Oh, now you want to talk to me?" she shot back without looking at him as she marched toward the back.

"What's your problem?" he said, swiftly catching up to her and grabbing her arm.

"My problem? Last night you were all on me, but now your acting brand new," she said while spinning around.

"Brand new? Listen, I'm feeling you, but I ain't that type of cat to run behind no chick. Me and Alana have history, but I don't want her all up in my business like that, feel me?"

She looked away, not believing a word he was saying.

"'Sides," he said as he rubbed his hands together, "we're just getting to know each other and I'm not looking for any obligations. I mean, I'm just trying to make everyone comfortable, ya dig? I have a business to run first and foremost and you should respect that. Now when it comes to playing ....that gets pushed to the side 'til business is squared away."

"I hear you," she replied nonchalantly.

"Don't act like that beautiful. Besides, I want to get to know you. I got some powder. Want some?" he offered.

She folded her arms stubbornly until he pulled out a small tear drop plastic bag.

"See, I was looking out for you," he said as he shook it

slightly.

He walked toward his office then looked back at her while she stood in a trance. "You coming or what?"

She followed him until they walked inside of his modern style office. His office was a mini size loft apartment complimented with burgundy and black furniture with walls to match. He closed the door and ripped the tear drop bag before dipping his pinky nail inside of it.

"This is nice," she complimented. "I'm impressed."

"Thank you, I damn near spend more time here than at my crib so I made it feel like home."

"I'm sure you didn't decorate this yourself," she replied, looking around.

"Nah, I know a decorator," he laughed to himself. "Oh before I forget, I talked to my homeboy." Sniff. "He wants us to swing by his club tonight."

"Yea? He's going to let me make some money tonight?" she asked as she walked toward him.

"Whoa, slow down mama. He said he wanna check you out," he said as he handed her the bag.

"I need to make some money." Sniff. "I need to make some money."

"You can dance for me, how 'bout that?"

"You paying?" she asked.

She dipped her nail inside of the plastic bag and ran it across her teeth while she waited for his answer.

"Money is never a problem, I guess it depends on how much money you trying to make tonight. I can invite some of my boys over, ya know if you wanna make some money tonight, but it's on you."

"How much you trying to spend?" she asked.

"Depends."

"On?" Sniff. "Either you're spending or not. I'm a business woman first and foremost." Sniff. "Now when it comes to playing, that gets pushed to the side 'til business is squared away...," she repeated his statement.

He smiled.

"Well, since you don't know if you're spending or not, how 'bout you get with me later."

They sniffed the powder and mentally escaped to another

place until someone knocked on the door. They quickly looked at each other then glanced at the door. Clifton whispered to her not to move or say anything as he walked towards it.

"Who is it?" he called out.

He wiped his nose and took a deep breath when one of his bartenders called out his name.

"Ay yo Clifton, it's me Raymond."

Clifton felt relieved that is was Raymond because he knew Raymond always stood clear out of his way. He took a deep breath then opened the door.

"What's going on Raymond?"

"Clifton, we're running out of Vodka at the patio bar."

"Get it from the cellar," Clifton said as he handed him the keys. "And whatever you do hold on to them, I'll be out shortly."

"Okay."

Clifton closed the door after Raymond walked away. He looked toward Skyler and noticed her wiping her nose.

"I need to get back to the ladies. I'm pretty sure they are looking for me," she said softly.

"Can I have a kiss?" he said as he grabbed her arm softly.

"A what?"

"A kiss?" he said, pulling her to him.

She looked at him for a quick second then leaned toward him and slowly traced her tongue on the rim of his lips before taking his bottom lip into her mouth. He pulled her closer to him so she could feel him against her. Instead of letting the mood captivate her, she quickly pushed him away and winked at him before stepping out of his office.

"Thank goodness," she said when she saw the restroom near her.

She opened the door and headed for the sink. She looked in the mirror and noticed the white residue in her nose. She quickly grabbed a paper towel and wiped it away just as Alana opened the restroom door.

"Are you alright? You been gone for about fifteen minutes."

"Y-yea," she said nervously trying to regain her composure.

Skyler's heart sped through her chest while she tried to think of a believable story, but she couldn't think of one because her body and mind wasn't on the same page. Alana looked around to see if there were any other patrons in the restrooms, but before she could open her mouth to ask any more questions. Alana didn't want to make a fuss, so she settled to ask one question.

"You don't look okay," she whispered.

"I'm okay. I'm just a ....little disappointed in myself."

"Why? For what?"

"Here I am selfishly thinking about making money and this is your moment. I just feel like ......" she said until Alana interrupted her.

"Sky, don't be in here stressing out about it. I understand that you have a lot on your plate. Maybe you should go out and have fun with Clifton, I'm sure he'll keep you occupied."

"You sure? I fully respect what you said earlier about me not really knowing him and I don't want to impose or ....."

"You're not imposing. He's never disrespected me, so you should be fine."

"Cause we can always go back to your place and..."

"No, you should go out and have fun. I'll be fine."

"And you don't mind?"

"Not at all."

"What are you going to do then?"

"I don't know yet, probably nothing."

Skyler walked up to Alana and embraced her as the ladies in the restroom stopped and looked at them. She didn't know if she was more thankful that Alana insisted on her going out with Clifton or that she didn't choke on her words. They soon returned to their table and carried out the rest of the afternoon.

A few hours passed and Alana found herself looking at her watch wondering what her new neighbor was doing. She paced back and forth in her bedroom nervously with his number in her hand while rehearsing what she was going to say to him after she dialed his number.

"Hey Monte, I was just calling to see if...," she said aloud. "Hey, Monte, I wanted to know if you were still going to the beach and ....," she huffed. *"I'll just call him and ask him if wants to...,"* she said to herself, when she heard a knock on her door. "Who is it?" she called out.

"Monte."

"Monte, oh my goodness, my hair isn't done. I'm not even dressed," she mused.

"Coming," she called out as she quickly slipped on a sundress.

She took a deep breath, ran her hands through her hair, threw it in a ponytail then opened the door with a smile. He stood outside the door with a short sleeved blue and white striped Ralph Lauren Polo shirt that accented the blue shorts to match. His charming, sneaky, and infectious smile lingered her stare longer than she'd expected.

"Hey, I hope I didn't bother you. I was headed to the beach and wanted to know if you wanted to take a walk with me."

"I was just about to call you...," she said as she showed him her phone in her hand. "Let me grab my keys and lock up. I'll be out in a few seconds."

She turned around, exhaled softly then grabbed her keys from the counter and closed the door behind her. He looked at her and shook his head then chuckled to himself.

"What's so funny?" she asked.

"Nothing," he said with a smile.

"Then why the smile? I want to smile too."

He looked at her smile, her essence was innocent.

"Just didn't want to come off too pushy by coming up here uninvited," he said as they stepped on the elevator together.

They both smiled as they walked outside the building and down a couple of blocks. He was in awe with the scenery as he looked around.

"Beautiful, isn't it?" she asked.

"It is. Don't get me wrong, I've seen pictures of South Beach, but being here with the most beautiful woman is priceless," he said flirtingly.

She held her head down and smiled to herself, hoping that he didn't see her blush, but he did. She purposely avoided his eyes while he trailed behind her as they walked toward the sand, closest to the water. He stood in one spot, pushed his hands in his pockets then looked out into the ocean as the orange-like sky painted the scenic view behind the horizon.

"This is absolutely breathtaking," he said, as he took a deep breath, "can I take a picture of you?"

"Sure," she said while the glowing sun kissed her.

She admired the view herself. Not even Anthony wanted to take a picture of her. It had only been just a few weeks ago that she stood in the very spot they were standing and cried over

Anthony while the sunset caressed her. She stood beside Monte, inhaling the scent of the ocean's air without taking her eyes away from the water.

"So, how long are you here for?" she asked, without looking at him.

"Um...I don't know yet," he said with a blank stare as he looked at the ocean. "It depends."

"Depends on?" she turned her eyes to him. "May I ask?"

"Well," he said as he kicked the sand, "it depends on how things go for me here."

She wondered what would come out of their friendship if he chose to stay. Although it was too soon to weigh out, she found him very intriguing and attractive. She quickly took off her shoes before walking into the water as the ocean sprays slightly covered her feet. He watched her at first then removed his shoes and joined her.

"So, are you seeing someone?" she asked.

"Nah."

She raised her eyebrows then said before looking away..., "tell me anything."

He chuckled lightly.

"You okay?"

"Yea, I'm good. Just thinking about my life and where I wanna go and what I wanna do."

"Well what do you want to do?"

"I don't know. I want to live. Be happy. Meet someone with substance."

"I wish I could give you some advice in that department, but I do believe you will get what you put in the universe. If you want to be happy, be happy within. Everything else will fall in place. I believe, we have to get some things wrong in order to get them right."

"That's deep, but you're right," he said as he looked towards the ocean.

"I can only speak from experience, just enjoy the moment."

"Speaking of moments...," he said as the ocean spray washed on his legs.

"Whew, that's cold," he interrupted loudly.

She burst out into laughter when he looked slightly uncomfortable.

"I didn't realize how cold the water is."

"Yea, it gets pretty cold."

They shared a laugh. It was innocently spoken in sound.

"What do you like to do Alana?"

"Honestly, you're going to laugh."

"Me? Why you say that?"

"Because I like walking on the beach and enjoying the scenery. I love the smell of the fresh ocean breeze. This is also where I spend most of my solitary time."

"I can see why you come out here, the water is very soothing."

"It is," she replied while looking at the water.

He looked at her when she moved away from him, allowing the water to reach her calves.

"Whoa, I don't know how to swim..."

She kicked the water in his direction.

"You don't know how to swim?"

"Nah. I almost drowned when I was a kid and ever since then, I stay far away from pools and um....beaches."

"I swim like a fish so you won't drown."

He slightly raised his right eyebrow before flashing a half smile, evoked by her comment. They walked alongside the shore without saying a word, they watched the seagulls fly over the ocean as couples, young and old, walked toward them holding hands. The sight of seeing the couples brought back memories of her and Anthony when they used to walk the shore for hours at a time.

"You still love him, don't you?" he asked, interrupting her thoughts.

She hesitated for a second.

"I'm not here to play match maker or anything, but I can tell your feelings are still there for him."

"Is it that obvious?"

"Guess it depends on who's looking. I don't know what he did to you, but I'm sure he's regretting it. As men, sometimes we say stuff we really don't mean. Ya know, we just get caught up in the moment and end up learning the hard lessons."

"Hard lessons," she repeated.

"I'm not saying that you should go back to him. All I'm saying is if you feel like he's worth it, maybe you need to let him explain himself."

"He's not worth it," she said as she kicked the water.

"Maybe his is," he said with compassion. "You know if you continue to allow him to have that type of hold you on, you will block your love blessings."

She listened with no response.

"Love will knock on your door again, it's up to you whether or not you open that door."

"Right now, I just need to focus on me and if it's meant for me to love again, I will surely make sure it's with someone who respects me and what I'm trying to do."

"I feel you. You deserve to have someone who wants you to better yourself."

She glanced at him and made another mental note of his charming responses.

"Thank you Monte."

"You're welcome. I wish you enough..."

"Enough what?" she looked at him with a puzzled stare.

"Enough happiness, enough patience. Enough time to heal your broken heart, ya know enough," he said while looking at her. "Whatever it is that you need, I just wish you enough of it. I really mean that Alana."

She looked at him. His seriousness soothed her. She eyed his stature but his confidence snagged her attention. She didn't see him as a man who tried to impress her, be the life of a party or portray to be something he wasn't. He was a different type of man, one she'd never met before. She now understood the saying that people from different walks of life come into other people's lives for a reason, but for her, his reason was unclear. So instead of trying to figure it out, she basked in the moment as the sun set, leaving the once orange sun kissed sky behind while he held her in his arms as they sat on the ocean's bank.

Three weeks passed, and things were finally looking good for Alana. She signed Rafael's contract, but since she was an overnight success, he extended it. Before she left to go on tour, Alana skeptically asked Skyler to house sit. Alana had reservations about Skyler house-sitting for her because she felt like she wasn't being completely honest about her past, due to her erratic behavior. Alana knew she had to set some house rules expressing how unfavorable she was about hosting parties after she left, but wanted to be fair. She agreed to let Skyler invite her guests, but not a crowd. Alana also told her that she would be gone for only thirty days, but for Skyler that was more than enough time to make some money moves.

Alana concluded her conversation with Skyler and darted downstairs to talk with Monte as well. Since their walk on the beach, Alana welcomed his charming intrusion. His conversation stimulated her mind and his physical attributes lingered in her thoughts. He was the first person, outside of Micah and Rafael, she told about her tour and asked could he periodically keep an eye out on things and update her while she was gone. He wanted to say more, felt like he should say more, but when Micah called her phone to tell her that they were outside, he fell mute. He didn't want to say anything prematurely about his feelings, but instead grabbed her luggage and walked her to Rafael's car.

While Alana was on tour, she and Monte stayed on the phone. She found herself picking up whatnots for him when her and Micah toured different cities. Micah noticed her blossoming friendship with him and started asking questions.

"So, what's going on with you and Monte?" she asked when she sat beside her on the end of the bed.

"Nothing," she paused before responding, "we're just friends."

"Friends?" Micah repeated.

"I can only offer him a friendship, nothing more," Alana said without looking at her.

Micah chuckled under her breath.

"So, then why are you so giddy these days?"

"I'm not giddy. I'm just ...I don't know....happy," she said with a smile until she noticed Micah's seriousness. "Umm, did I miss something?"

"Alana, I just don't want you to get hurt, again," Micah said as she stood up and folded Alana things neatly inside of her suitcase.

"Hurt? Oh, you have nothing to worry about. We're only friends."

"Does he know that? Or is he another guy trying to fancy his way with you?"

Alana gave Micah a pausing stare before she sat straight up.

"Fancy his way? It's not like that Micah," she said with a furtive glance.

Alana listened, but her mind lingered to Micah's previous

statement.

Fancy? she mused.

"Look Alana, I'm not trying to discourage you from being friends with him or anyone else for that matter. I just want you to be more aware of the people you surround yourself with," Micah said cautiously.

Alana listened.

"I usually don't say anything about your personal life because that's your business. I've gotten used to you keeping your business to yourself, but when you shared with me what Anthony said to you I felt like I should've said something sooner when I saw the signs. Instead, I just saw your hurt and waited for you to come to me."

"I know. I just didn't want to burden you with my problems."

"It's no burden. Anytime you need to talk, I'm always here for you and you don't have to ever feel like you're burdening me. Believe it or not, I see a whole lot of stuff."

"Like what?"

"Your friends. Skyler, Clifton, and Monte. Three different people with three different intentions."

"Intentions?"

"I'm serious Lana. I respect what you're doing and what you're trying to do, but I don't think the people around you do."

"How can you say that? I'm the face of Night's Owl and I've..."

"And what does that really mean? He's just exploiting you. Have you been compensated by 'being the face of Night's Owl?' What's in it for you? I mean, do you at least get a free meal? Geesh. How much is he paying you for displaying your pictures and advertising your name like he discovered you?"

"I mean....," Alana said until Micah kept talking.

"And your friend Skyler is just freeloading off you."

"Micah, she's just having a hard time."

"Is she? Did she tell you that?" Micah asked.

"Micah, she's my childhood friend."

"Again, is she or was she?"

Alana leaned back on the bed and pressed her head into the pillow without taking her eyes from the ceiling.

"Micah, I do appreciate your honesty..., but... "

"I apologize if I'm out of line, but it's not what I see. It's what you need to see. I'm just not sure you want to see it."

"What am I supposed to be seeing?"

"Alana, anytime you make changes in your life sometimes you have to change your selection of friends. It just seems like the people around you are enjoying your success a little more than you. Just take a look at things before you were here and compare the two."

"What about you?" Alana asked.

"What about me?"

"Aren't you enjoying my success too?"

"I'm working. You pay me to do a job and I do it with no excuses. No regrets. I enjoy seeing you do something you've worked hard for. I don't take advantage of you and I have my own money. I have never once taken you for granted and I like to think that we are friends and will remain friends when you don't even need my services anymore."

"Don't talk like that. You're not going anywhere," she chuckled "do you want a raise?"

"No," Micah smiled.

"Do you want a vacation?"

"I would like one if it doesn't interfere with your schedule."

"When we go home, take off for the week and we'll meet back up when we leave Friday morning?"

"You sure?"

"Yes, why not? You deserve to be on a vacation. I apologize for being inconsiderate."

"Don't apologize. I'm not your enemy and I don't ever want you to forget that. Now, get some rest," she said when she walked toward the door.

"Micah?"

"Yes?"

"What about Monte? Do you think he's really trying to fancy me?"

"I'm not sure. The only thing I can tell you is to be careful. If he is really a friend, allow him to be that friend. Don't force it," were her final words before she left Alana's room.

Alana looked at her flashing light on her phone indicating that she'd missed a call from Monte. She opened her phone and searched for Skyler's last call, but shuddered when she noticed she hadn't called since her arrival in Los Angeles. Suddenly, she thought about what Micah said. Was there some truth in what she said or was she in denial about their friendship? So many different thoughts ran through her mind when she realized Skyler hadn't called. She also found it disturbing that Monte told her that Clifton was over there quite regularly. She sat on the bed trying to sort out some things when her phone rang.

"Hello?"

"Hey beautiful, how's the weather treating you?"

"It's nice," she said nonchalantly.

"What's wrong?" he said when he noticed her distance.

"Nothing."

"Your voice is telling me something different."

"I just have a lot on my mind."

"Want to talk about it?"

"Not really."

"Well, you know I'm here if you want to talk."

"Thank you," she paused, "can I ask you something?"

"Sure."

"What do you want from me?"

"Nothing. I told you that from the get go, what's this all about Alana?"

"Nothing, I really don't want to talk about it."

"Whoa wait a minute. You can't just say something heavy like that then turn around and say you don't want to talk about it. Did I say anything offensive?"

"No. It's just...."

"Just what? Alana, I'm fond of you and I thought we were building a friendship."

"We are."

"So, what's the problem?"

"Do you have any expectations or intentions?"

"No, do you?"

"No," she paused, undecided if she should say what was on her mind, "do you think Skyler has intentions or expectations?"

"I don't think my opinion is..."

"Just tell me."

"....yes."

"Why would you say that?"

"I'm sure everyone except you see how she acts like the world owes her something."

"It's not that, she's having some really hard times right now."

"And that's what she told you?"

"Yea, she was telling me how...."

"Alana she's lying to you. She's not being honest with you, she's playing games."

"Games?"

"Yes. She's telling you one thing and doing another. Since you've been gone, she's been having the time of her life."

"No one else knows what she is going through right now and that's the reason why she's in South Beach."

"What do you mean, that's the reason why she's in South Beach?

"She was in an abusive relationship with some guy name Ric in Vegas, but she left him. I don't know much about him or their situation."

"I don't buy it."

"I was sitting next to her when they were having an argument before she threw the phone out of the window when she refused to tell him where she was."

"And you believed that?"

"Yes," she said.

"Alana, she sold you a sob story and you bought it."

She paused for a second when his words left his lips. She didn't know how to respond to his comment nor did she know where all of this was coming from.

"Alana, you don't need anyone to validate your dreams or your intuition."

"I know."

"Look around you, how many people can you honestly trust?"

"At this point, to be honest with you, I'm not sure who to trust."

"Trust your instincts. They'll never let you down. I trust people as far as I see them."

She listened to him then concluded the call. She called Micah.

"Hello?"

"Are you busy?"

"No. Everything alright Alana?"

"Yes, I just wanted to say thank you for telling me what you told me. I don't want to seem ungrateful."

"You're fine. I've been trying to find a way to tell you without overstepping my boundaries."

"Micah, you're hardly overstepping your boundaries. I really do appreciate your honesty."

"I'm glad. You're family to me and I know sometimes the hardest thing we have to do is tell people we care about what they don't want to hear."

"You're right."

"Get some rest, we're leaving in a couple of hours and Rafael is sending someone up here in an hour to get our luggage."

"Alright."

Alana disconnected the call and attempted to dial Skyler's number, but realized she needed to have a face to face conversation.

I was warned...

She caught the red eye plane with only one thing on her mind, Monte. She was drawn to his energy and enjoyed their late night flirty conversations filled with laughter. As soon as she stepped onto the elevator, she pulled out her cell phone and dialed his number, but it went to his voicemail. She leaned against the wall of the elevator and closed her eyes just as the elevator stopped one floor before hers. When the doors opened, she slowly opened her eyes and stared at the man who occupied her mind.

"You're back?" Monte smiled.

"I did. I just called your phone to let you know I was back, but it went straight to voicemail."

"Ah man, I don't even have my phone on me," he said as he patted his pockets. "Had I known you were coming back this early I would've personally picked you up from the airport."

"It's okay, Micah and Rafael brought me home," she said with a smile.

She was very attracted to him, but felt it was too soon to voice or act it out. She would one day tell him how she felt, but now was not the time. He grabbed her luggage as he walked alongside her as they chatted, as if they were high school sweethearts.

"So, you're leaving again on Friday, right?"

"Yes."

"You want to go to dinner when you get settled later on today?"

"Sure, I would like that," she said with a gaze.

He stood behind her when she unlocked her door until she stepped aside so he could enter first with her luggage. He walked in, cut on her lights then sat her luggage on the floor before she walked in and looked at her living room in disbelief. She looked at him then at the beer bottles and garbage strewn across her grandmother's antique coffee table. She closed the door behind her and noticed the curtains from the balcony swaying.

"Didn't you fix that door?" she said without looking at him.

"I did," he said with a puzzled look.

He walked toward the balcony and closed the French-styled doors. She stared at her trashed condo as if she was standing on a merry go round.

"What in the hell?" she said as she walked toward the kitchen.

She noticed the sink filled with dirty dishes and trash. The garbage hadn't been removed in several days and a foul odor arose. She looked at Monte and marched a few steps toward Skyler's room before he quickly pulled her to him. Monte gently grabbed her hand and walked her to her room then shut her door behind them. She cursed under her breath before walking on her balcony. He walked behind her paralleling his hands on the rail so she could fit in his personal space so he could inhale the Pantene shampoo residue in her hair. He whispered in her ear and told her to calm down. He listened to her while she ranted until he told her to take a deep breath and relax. She folded her arms across her chest then took a deep breath while listening to the sea gulls cry. At that moment, he wanted to plant small kisses behind her ears as she stared at the darkness, what would be the ocean.

He remembered telling her while she was on tour that he wanted to tell her something very important face to face. He didn't want to seem selfish to her needs, so he made a note to discuss it later. She turned around and leaned against the rail while his hands were still paralleled to the rail beside her.

His calmness soothed her, but his body turned her on. She took a deep breath as she stood under him and stared at him without saying a word. He looked into her eyes and licked his lips slowly before he leaned closer to her lips as the moon shined above them. He brushed his lips against hers slowly and softly until she stopped him. Before anything escalated, she had to give him her truth so he could make the rightful decision.

She smiled at him just as her eyes lingered toward his lips before leaving him on the balcony by himself. He refused to look at her when she walked behind him. Instead he just leaned on the rail and held his head down. Her lips tasted good against his but he knew he didn't want to rush anything with her. She was more than that, he respected her. He respected her bruised heart and wanted to make sure she was ready to explore new adventures. Until then, he tried to serve his purpose for her, and if that was to heal to her heart, he was willing to do that. When he finally turned around, he found her asleep, lying on top of her covers. She looked peaceful and as much as he wanted to tell her his truth, he just grabbed a blanket near the foot of her bed and covered her up. He turned off the light and laid beside her before drifting off to sleep.

Later that morning, he straightened her living room and placed all the trash by the door. He tried to clean up as quietly as possible without waking anyone up, but Skyler startled him.

"What the hell are you doing here?" Skyler said.

"Alana and I came last night."

"Alana? Last night?" she said while spinning around in circles, looking around. "Oh my...she's here? Why didn't she call me? What did she say when she walked in and saw this mess?" she said in a hush voice, with wide eyes.

"You should ask her. She's standing right behind you."

She turned around and stared at a very serious faced Alana.

"Hey girl, h-how was the trip?" she chuckled softly.

"You would've known if you'd call. Oh, but I see why you haven't called...too busy throwing parties?" she said without a smile.

"You said you were going to be busy, so I......."

"Asked you not to throw a party. I see you didn't bother cleaning up either!"

"I-I was going to....."

"I'm sure. I thought you were responsible enough to ...."

"I know. I know, I can explain .....I partied too hard last night and I was drunk, but I had every intention to clean up this mess first thing this morning."

"Skyler, do you see this mess? You let your company come in here and trash my place!"

"Alana, I am so sorry. I was sick to my stomach so I laid

down. Monte doesn't have to clean up my mess, I can clean it up."

Monte continued to put all the empty beer bottles and trash in a plastic garbage bag without saying a word. At this point, there was no need for him to comment because he warned Skyler about throwing a party at Alana's when he stopped by a few days ago.

"Alana, I'm really sorry," she said apologetically.

Alana stared at her then shook her head as Micah and Monte's words replayed in her mind.

"No need to apologize. I think its best that you look for a place to stay by Friday."

"By Friday? How is that possible? I don't know anyone here like that Lana."

"I can't tell, you're throwing parties. I'm leaving to go back out of town on Friday and I don't want anyone here while I'm gone."

"What about me? Where am I going to go?"

"You probably should've thought about that while you were having a party."

"Alana, I'm really sorry, but where am I going to go?"

"Ask Clifton. I heard he's been keeping you company while I've been gone."

"Alana!" Skyler voiced.

Skyler tried to apologize, but it went unanswered. Once Skyler realized that Alana was ignoring her, she walked to her room and dialed Clifton's number.

"Hello?" Clifton said hurriedly.

"Hey, you busy?"

"Kind of, what's up?"

"Alana came home early this morning after everybody left their shit everywhere," she whispered.

"Damn," he paused, "what did she say?"

"She's so pissed, she wants me out."

"Damn."

"And you know what's fucked up?"

"What's that?"

"I didn't even know they were here until I woke up. I was going to..."

"Hold up, what do you mean they? Who is they?"

78

"Monte and Lana."

"What the hell is he doing there?"

"Hell if I know. He was the one cleaning up this shit ya'll left behind."

He politely ignored her comment, only concentrating on Alana and her escort.

"Hold on for a second, didn't he stop by the party?" Clifton quizzed.

"He only came by to make sure everything was cool."

"Hmph. He's starting to get on my damn nerves, who the hell does he thinks he is?"

"Her snitch," she sighed.

"Well, I tell you what, if you ever decide to housesit for anyone else, you need to be one step ahead of them."

She sighed as he continued to speak into the phone.

"I already know how Alana is and she probably didn't want you to have a party in her place in the first place. You already know how the last party went."

"She said I could invite a few people over."

"Yea, a few people, not an entourage. So now what, are you going back to Vegas?"

"Hell no. I was wondering if I can stay with you for a minute."

"Me? Oh I don't know about that."

"You didn't say that when you were banging my back out the other night."

"You already know how I feel about chicks staying with me. No disrespect. You should ask Stallion, I'm sure she wouldn't mind," he chuckled.

"Stallion...?"

"Skyler, we are cool but we aren't really like that. I mean we've messed around, but living with me? You don't think that's ...," he said until she interrupted his excuse.

"Alright then."

She quickly disconnected the call, but he called right back.

"Why did you hang up?"

"I can't believe you. You're an assho....."

"Look, you already knew what it was from the jump. No need to act like this is new. If you don't have anywhere else to go, you can chill over here."

"Nah, don't worry about it," she said before she disconnected.

She paced back and forth in her room until she cooled down from his blatant comment. She walked toward her balcony and thought about Stallion.

She drifted back to the night Stallion walked inside of Russel's office. Stallion was known as the best dancer in Miami and was asked to familiarized Skyler with the club. Skyler tried not to stare at her but she had to admit, she was bad. Stallion, government name is Z'Dania, but they called her Dana for short. She was Dominican and Black with complimentary bone structures. The pair introduced themselves to each other and immediately sparked a friendship. As the hours passed and the drinks became frequent, Stallion revealed to Skyler that she'd been dancing since the tender age of sixteen, thanks to Russ, but was planning on hanging up her strings and heels in the very near future. Skyler listened as she watched Stallion throw back three shots of Patron in less than five minutes.

Skyler matched her shots of Patrons while sharing her reason for dancing as well. It seemed like the pair had more in common besides clubs and men, and before the night ended the ladies had exchanged numbers. Skyler was drawn to Dana's hot headed attitude and Dana was drawn to Skyler's hustler tactics. Instantly, they became the club's favorite pair and in a matter of weeks, they started dancing together to double the pleasure for their guests. They came up with a plan to make more money without Russ, since he was double dipping in their pockets.

Dana was Russ's main girl, but she had other intentions and a new interest. Skyler Sutton. She and Skyler secretly tip toed with each other without anyone suspecting it. Outside the club, Dana danced at several private parties to make side money, but when she saw the opportunity to make more money by adding another girl, she quickly added Skyler. If it had anything to do with money, Skyler was all in.

She looked at her phone then called Dana.

"Hey, I was just dialing your number," Dana said.

"Really, I need a favor," Skyler asked.

"Anything for you, what's up?"

"Can I stay with you until I figure out some things."

"Sure, you're ok? What happened?"

"Alana's mad at me because I threw that party last night."

"Are you fucking serious? There was only like five or six

80

people over there, right?"

"Actually, there was like fifteen to twenty people over here," Skyler corrected.

"Well dayum... I'm surprised you didn't call Clifton."

"I'm over it. You sure its ok, I don't want to impose."

"You're not imposing. I'm sure you need some time to figure some things out, so it's an open invite for you," Dana offered compassionately.

"Thank you so much."

"Girl, last night was crazy, wasn't it?"

"It was all about the schmoney..."

"Sky, if Russ knew we were making this kind of money without him, he would shit bricks."

"Hell, not only would he shit bricks, he could finally get some legit business about himself."

"Right, lame ass," Dana chuckled.

Skyler laughed until she heard Alana's voice from the next room.

"Let me call you right back."

"Okay, what time you need me to swing your way?"

"Now, call me when you're outside."

"Will do."

Skyler ended the call while her ears struggled to hear Alana's soft voice.

"I don't know. I just want to....," she heard Alana say as she walked Monte toward the door.

Alana closed the door behind Monte then turned to face Skyler.

"Alana, I just wanted to tell you again that I'm sorry. I really didn't mean to disrespect you or your place in any way."

"Skyler," Alana said as she walked past Skyler, "I have a lot on my plate, but I need you to work with me and not against me. Maybe when I come back, we can revisit this conversation. Right now, I have a lot of stuff I need to take care of," she said as she walked off.

"Okay. Well before I forget, Clifton wanted me to tell you that he is throwing you a party Thursday night at Night's Owl," Skyler said as she followed her.

"Tell him I'm all partied out, maybe later."

"Why don't you just show your face? Everyone is so proud of

you."

Alana paused for a second. She remembered Monte planned a dinner date that night and didn't want any interferences.

"Monte and I have plans and it'll ...."

"Just stop through, show your face and then still leave in time for your plans. Leave the rest to me," Sky said convincingly.

"What time does it start?"

"He hasn't set a time, but tell me what time is your dinner, and I will make sure he can work around it. That's the least I can do."

Skyler reached into her purse and tried to hand her some money.

"Sky, you don't have to do that."

"No really, I do. I don't want my carelessness to be the demise of our friendship. You mean that much to me."

"I don't want your money Sky, but I really appreciate the offer," Alana said with a smile. "I really do."

"I'm sorry Alana," Skyler said as she placed her overnight bag near the door.

"No worries, we will talk about everything when I come back."

Skyler apologized again before hurrying out of the front door. Alana sat and leaned back on her couch then closed her eyes. Her phone rang and she quickly answered it without looking at it.

"Hello?"

"Well, hello stranger. Did Skyler tell you about the party Thursday?"

"Clifton, I don't want to entertain a lot of people right now."

"Come on Alana, just this one time for me. I'm just excited that you're the face of my spot."

"Speaking of, you and I need to talk about all of this when I get back."

"Sure, so how was the tour?"

"It was nice. It was good to get out of Miami. I've seen some very beautiful places."

"Is that right?"

"Yes."

She laughed and listened to his flirtatious comments until Monte walked through the door and called out her name. Clifton heard his voice in the background. He grew silent.

"I'm in my room," she said aloud, covering the phone. "I'm sorry, what were you saying Clif?"

"You have company?"

"Yes, so what were you saying?"

"I can call you back or better yet call me when your guest leave."

"You sure? I'm not busy or anything, I'm just sitting here relaxing. It's just Monte."

"Monte?" he asked sharply.

"Yes."

Clifton paused for a second when he heard him speak in her background.

"What's up with you and him? I've been hearing his name a lot lately."

"We're friends," she said.

"Alana, you and I are just friends."

"And I hang around you, don't I?"

"Not as much as I'd like. Have you talked to Anthony?' he blurted.

"No, but on that note, I'm about to go. I'll call you later," she said.

The evening was filled with laughter between Monte and Alana. Monte decided to enjoy the evening without having a heavy discussion. He would save that for a later date.

The day finally came for Monte to take Alana on their date and Night's Owl ceremony in her honor. Alana and Micah were putting the final touches on their makeup until the doorbell chimed. Alana extended the invitation to Micah and Rafael to join them at the Night's Owl so they could also enjoy themselves before they left the next day. Micah agreed to go along with them, but assured Alana whenever she was ready to leave she wouldn't argue with her.

Alana placed on her diamond earrings her mother sent her just days ago so she can look picture perfect for Monte. Micah looked out of the peep hole and quickly opened the door for a handsome Monte, standing with a bouquet of silk white roses and wearing a chocolate linen suit that complimented Alana's dress.

"Alana, Monte is here," Micah called out.

"How are you doing tonight beautiful?" he said.

"I'm great, and you? Thank you, oh please come in," she said as she stepped to the side.

"Thank you, I'm good."

Micah skeptically kept her eyes on him because she knew the conversation she and Alana had days ago was nothing more to Alana than a faded picture. She didn't want to seem apprehensive, but she still couldn't shake the suspicious feeling she had about him. She watched him walk until Rafael walked up behind her and cleared his throat.

"Ahem, I'm looking for this incredible beautiful woman by the name of Micah, could you tell me where I can find her?" he said in a low raspy sultry tone.

"Oh, may I ask who's looking for her?" she shot back as they role played in Alana's doorway.

"Um, sure tell her my name is.....," he paused, "Casanova."

As Rafael entered inside Alana's condo, Monte stood near the balcony until Alana walked from her room like an angel looking radiant and more beautiful than he ever witnessed before. His pulse raced. His forehead perspired and his heart shuddered when she walked toward him. His tongue was paralyzed and wouldn't allow him to say anything, but his eyes said it all. She smiled at him while her butterflies swam around inside of her stomach.

"You look very handsome tonight Monte."

"You do too. I-I meant to say that you're absolutely gorgeous tonight," he said nervously, hoping he didn't sound corny.

"Thank you," she giggled, with a smile.

Monte immediately handed her the silk bouquet of roses. She quickly placed then in empty vase that was sitting on the counter behind her before they headed toward Night's Owl. Truthfully, Alana dreaded going and the only thing she wanted to do was spend a romantic evening with Monte. It felt like love was in the air for the pair, but she didn't want to get ahead of herself. A conversation was mandated. They arrived at six forty-five, just as Clifton walked outside looking for them. Clifton watched the limousine driver jump out of the front seat and opened the door. Micah was the first to step out and he quickly took her hand. She was more beautiful tonight than ever before. Their eyes locked as he complimented her until Rafael stepped out of the limo seconds later behind her. He quickly released her hand and shook Rafael's hand as he welcomed him to Night's Owl.

Alana stepped out of the limo next, but Clifton nearly knocked over the limousine driver out of the way just to grab her hand. She was breathtakingly beautiful and at that moment, his heart raced. He knew if she would only give him half a chance, he would gladly trade in his player card for her, but she never took the time to see him for the man he could be. She leaned toward him then kissed him on the cheek. She pulled away then quickly turned around and reached inside the limo. Clifton was so engulfed by her beauty that he didn't pay any attention that she reached for Monte's hand until he stood to his feet. Startled, Clifton took a step back as his heart race with rage.

"Hello Clifton," Monte said as he extended his hand.

Clifton looked at Monte's hand disapprovingly. He stared at Monte for a bulging five seconds then quickly turned around and led the couples inside of his restaurant until he sat them at their table, almost in the middle of his establishment. Alana looked around and noticed her pictures displayed on the walls. Everyone smiled and nodded in approval. Monte quickly looked at his watch so he could make sure they didn't go pass their time. He arranged for a driver to pick them up at exactly eight o'clock. Clifton stood at the podium to make an announcement before the food was served and the music played.

"Excuse me, before we start this celebration, I want to let everyone know that Alana Inacio is touring from city to city and she's leaving tomorrow. I just want to say congratulations for your dreams finally coming true. I know it's been a journey for you and as a friend I just want to say 'Congrats.'"

Balloons filled the room rising to the ceiling after he finished speaking. Alana didn't want to make a public statement, but she waved and bowed her head graciously. Skyler walked over to her table with a dozen of tulips.

"Here's to you. Congratulations. You did it and I'm really proud of you."

"Thank you," Alana said with a smile.

She placed the tulips on the table when the music came on. Everyone clapped and celebrated as Monte pulled her on the dance floor and moved from side to side. She laughed at him while they danced for the first time. She watched him snap his fingers while the melody surrounded them. When the song was over, Monte escorted her to her chair while Micah and Rafael laughed while their plates were being served.

"Girl, you two look pretty good out there," Micah whispered to her.

She laughed until she noticed Anthony walking into the club looking around. She dropped her smile immediately as she stiffened. Monte noticed and asked her what was wrong, but she didn't say anything. Micah saw Anthony and told Rafael as they watched him walk toward Clifton then handed him a small package.

Anthony swiftly walked away from Clifton and headed toward Alana's table, leaving him standing near the exit door. He saw the guy that roughed him up at her party and chuckled to himself. At first, he wanted to grab him by his neck and wipe that smile he was wearing off his face, but thought against it since they were in a public place. Instead he politely walked up to the table and took another approach.

"Hello everyone, how are you?"

Everyone looked at him then scoffed without replying. Once he noticed no one was happy to see him, he turned and faced Alana.

"Alana, can I please speak to you privately?"

"For what?" she replied.

"I need to talk to you about something."

"No thank you."

"Alana, I promise you this will not take long."

"What do you want Anthony?" she said in a low growl.

"Can I talk to you alone? I don't want to do this in front of your guests."

She paused then looked around for a place for them to talk. She spotted two chairs near the bar and quickly stood to her feet.

"I'll be right back," she said to Monte.

"You sure you're going to be alright?" Monte asked as he grabbed her hand.

"Yes, I'm just going to the bar for a second, this will not take long."

"Okay," he said with concern.

Micah stood up beside her before Alana walked away.

"I don't think that's a good idea. He's too unstable and he can hurt you. This is your night. You really don't have to entertain him."

"It's all right Micah, like I said this will be very short."

"You sure? I'm getting really bad vibes."

"You worry too much Micah."

"And you trust too much Alana."

Alana patted Micah's hand then walked away. Micah looked at Monte and shook her head before taking her seat. She couldn't shake the vibes that something wasn't right.

There was something about Anthony that Monte did not trust. He couldn't put his finger on it, but Anthony was becoming a thorn. It didn't matter how much Monte tried to protect her from him, Anthony always managed to show up uninvited.

"You wanna sit down?" Anthony asked her.

"Not really, what do you want Anthony?"

"I want to apologize for giving you an ultimatum a few months ago. I was really upset that day, but baby you know I would never want you to choose me over your career. You have worked too hard for too long. I'm so proud of you," he said as he reached for her hand.

She swiftly moved her hand away. There was a time when she hoped he would tell her how proud he was of her, but that day never came and now it didn't matter. He looked at her while she stared in a trance.

"What's on your mind?"

"Anthony, please leave me alone. You expressed how you felt so now what? You think you can just turn your words around just like that?"

"What? Alana, it's not like that."

"Goodbye Anthony," she said as she walked off.

He stepped in front of her, cutting off her stride. "Will you give me another chance?"

"That chapter has now closed."

"Oh, so you don't want to give me a chance because of your new interest," he said as he tilted his head toward her table.

"I don't have to explain anything to you."

She tried to walk away, but he quickly grabbed her arm.

"Let me go."

"Oh, so is your little boyfriend gonna come to your rescue?"

"Anthony, let me go!" she said, as Monte approached her.

"If I can't have you, I'll be damn if I sit back and watch him have you," he said before storming off.

"Are you okay Alana?" Monte asked.

"I'm ok."

"Damn, what was that about?" Skyler asked before they encircled her.

"Nothing."

"Seemed like an intense conversation to me," Skyler said annoyingly.

"Mind your own business Sky," Alana replied.

"Well geesh, what's wrong with you?" Skyler asked sarcastically.

"Let's go Micah," Alana voiced.

Alana and Micah walked away with Skyler trailing behind. Alana whispered something in Monte's ear. He quickly reached in his pocket, pulled out a twenty-dollar bill and informed Micah and Rafael that they were leaving. Micah looked at Alana with a concerned look, but Alana looked away disgusted. Micah was right, something was wrong. The best thing Alana could do was leave.

"You're leaving? You can't leave, Clifton hasn't even...," Skyler said as she sipped on her drink.

Clifton walked toward Alana's table with a tray of drinks. He stopped in mid step when he saw Alana reach for her purse. He placed the drinks down on their table and walked toward Alana. He placed his hand on the small of her back and leaned toward her ear.

"Hey, can I talk to you for a second?"

"No, we're leaving," she said as she stepped away from the table.

"So soon, we're just getting started," he whispered.

"I'm sorry, this was nice, but I need to leave."

"Aw, come on Alana. The party just started. Don't let him or anyone mess up this night for you, please stay awhile longer."

"Let her go if she wants to go," Skyler hissed.

Clifton spun around and stared at Skyler.

"Clifton, it's best that we go. Just call me later," Alana said while staring at Skyler.

Micah noticed Alana's growing frustration. She didn't like how this was going and things were now getting intensely uncomfortable. Clifton stood in disbelief as he watched Alana's table collect their things, thanks to Skyler. Her sporadic behavior was unattractive and it all belonged to her sniffing habit.

"Oh, so now you're better than us? Skyler said as she walked behind Alana.

"Cut it out Skyler," Clifton said when he walked beside her.

"No, I don't," Alana said in disbelief.

"Tsk. Yes you do and you know it," Skyler said with a scoff. "Ever since I've been here, it's all about you. Alana this, Alana that."

"Cool it Skyler," Clifton said politely.

"Hell, it could be about you too, but you chose another path," Alana shot back.

"Another path?" Skyler quizzed. "Oh you think I'm throwing my life away?"

"Never said that Sky."

"Bitch, I'm not throwing my life away. I'm making money," Skyler spat, while walking closer toward her.

"You have the nerve to call Alana a *bitch*?" Micah voiced angrily, cutting off her stride.

"I'm not bowing down to Alana like everybody else. Hell, that bitch wish she bleeds like I bleed."

"Let's go. I refuse to do this," Alana said.

"I'm sure, oh but I forgot you're always hiding behind masks," Skyler said.

"Whatever Skyler, just like the residue lingering under your nose right? But who's hiding?" Alana shot back.

"Ladies. Ladies, come on now. This is not the time or the place," Monte interrupted.

Alana looked Skyler up and down before turning her head. Clifton looked at with disgust while Skyler looked away without saying a word. She didn't know what embarrassed her more, Alana noticing her residue or verbalizing it. She paused for a second, unsure if she should reveal what Alana really was, but thought against it. Instead she just wiped the residue away from her nose while her anger festered. Alana looked at Clifton then turned to walk away.

"Oh so, you're leaving with the maintenance man? He can't do shit for you but take out your damn trash," she laughed cynically. "I mean, be real Lana. What can he do for you? You can never have a baby because you were born a ..."

Before the words left Skyler's lips, Alana slapped her across her face. Immediately, Micah pulled Alana back while Clifton pushed Skyler back.

"What the hell is your problem? You are so fucking unbelievable," he yelled at Skyler.

The curious onlookers stopped and stared at the dramatic scenery without saying anything. Their lingering eyes felt Alana's embarrassment as they gathered their items from their tables as well, leaving Night Owl abruptly. Alana stormed out of the restaurant with Monte and Micah by her side. Skyler held her face then laughed under her breath while Clifton stared at her. Rafael stayed behind for a few seconds and pulled Clifton to the side.

"Hey look, I hate to bail on you, but we can talk about the pictures whenever you get a moment. From the looks of things, you have a mess on your hands to clean up, so just call me when you can."

"Sure. Oh, before I forget Raf," he said as he handed him a very small package, "I got what you asked for."

"Good," Rafael said as he stuffed it in his pocket without looking at it before walking away.

Clifton marched towards Skyler.

"You know what, you're a bigger asshole than I imagined. Do you see what you have done? You've ruined a perfectly good ass party!"

"Yea I'm not the only asshole in the building sir. I mean damn Clifton, you damn near begged her to stay. For what? You don't have to kiss her ass."

"You have no fucking boundaries, do you? I mean, you had me fooled, but trust me when I say, you're gonna get what's coming to you. I promise," he said as he left her standing in the middle of the floor.

Alana stood outside Night's Owl feeling violated and embarrassed. She covered her face while the customers walked passed her. She was appalled how Skyler tried to blurt out something she shared with her so openly to complete strangers.

Monte noticed her distance and wrapped his arm around her to console her without saying a word. Micah walked up beside her and wrapped her arm around Alana.

Monte signaled the driver as the rotating circling lights lit the sky above them as the two couples waited patiently outside of Night's Owl. As soon as Rafael walked up behind them, the limousine driver pulled up beside them, but Rafael insisted that the couple ride alone while he grabbed a cab for him and Micah. Monte offered again, but Rafael politely refused, shook his hand and smiled at him. Monte knew the timing wasn't still right so he requested the driver to take them back to the South Beach Estates.

As the cab driver drove them to their destination, Alana stepped out of the limo and opened the lobby door leaving Monte behind. He thanked the driver for his patience and tipped him nicely. The driver insisted that he should take the chilled bottle of wine and the two golden wrapped flutes. He walked toward the lobby and noticed tears falling from her eyes as she waited for the elevator. He pulled her close to his chest until the elevator took them to her floor. After she opened her door, she quickly tossed the keys on the coffee table and stormed around in the kitchen.

I can't believe her, she said to herself as tears fell from her eyes.

Monte walked toward her then reached for her hand gently toward the couch as he sat down beside her. Monte looked at her as he wiped her tears away.

"Alright now, just calm down. You two shouldn't even be in this space. I know you are frustrated with her, but don't let that compromise your friendship. It's not worth it."

"I refuse to air out her dirty laundry, but she is clearly not the person I thought she was. I opened my home to her, I tried to help her."

"You can't help everyone."

"I can't believe her. The nerve of her to air my..."

"Listen, you don't have to explain yourself to me or anyone. Everyone has secrets. She was wrong for trying to expose them publicly. I'm sure the way she acted tonight confirmed what we talked about."

"Yea," she said dryly. "I wanted to be the one to tell you about my discrepancies. Family is important to me."

"Animals are family too."

She smiled.

"I knew that would put a smile on that beautiful face of yours," he said as he rubbed her back.

"Can I ask you something?" she asked.

"Sure."

"Do you want kids?"

"I would love to have kids, do you?"

"Yes, but I can't have kids."

"Well there are alternatives. You can always be a mother, as long as you're willing to be open," he said with sincerity.

She smiled to herself then looked away.

"Let's change the subject on something more positive. Are you excited about tomorrow? I mean, you finally have what you've always dreamt, you've been signed to a major modeling contract. Your modeling career is about to take flight and tomorrow is officially your first day on the job."

"I am. Micah and Rafael really made my dreams come true, I'm very thankful."

"You deserve it. Now on another note, I need to discuss something with you."

"Like what?"

"Before I get into that, let's have a toast for your accomplishment."

She wasn't quite interested in a toast, but figured a glass of wine would help collect her thoughts and help her relax. He picked up the glass flutes then poured the wine perfectly.

"Alana ...," he said as he handed her a flute.

"Yes."

"I just want to say you that in my time of knowing you, you are the most perfect woman any man could ever ask for. I toast this to you for a job well done and to new beginnings."

...I am not a perfect woman," she thought. "New beginnings."

They tapped glasses and Alana drank the wine in one gulp. She placed her flute on the table then poured herself another glass.

"Whoa, don't drink too much, remember we didn't eat."

"I'll be fine," she said as she poured her another glass of wine.

She sipped on the second glass of wine before complimenting the taste.

"Now, what did you want to tell me?"

As soon as the words slipped through her mouth, his pounding heart began to race in his chest. This was the day he dreaded, but he needed to be the only one to tell her this.

"Um, I haven't been completely honest with you," he said as he placed his glass of wine on the table in front of him.

...I need to tell him my truth too.

"What do you mean, you haven't been completely honest with me?" she said with a blank stare.

"Do you remember when we walked on the beach a couple of months ago?" he asked.

"Yes?"

"Well truth is ...."

"Oh my goodness," she said, placing her glass beside his, "don't tell me that you're married and have a couple of kids?"

"No. I'm not married and I don't have any kids, will you let me finish?"

"Do you have a fiancé back home or someone waiting on you?" she asked anxiously.

"No, I was honest with you when I told you that I was single."

"Okay then, so what is it?"

"I-I'm really not the maintenance man."

She looked at him for a few seconds before bursting out into laughter and throwing her head back on the couch, relieved that she wasn't catching feelings for *the maintenance man*, like Skyler had mention earlier. For a minute, she smiled at the ceiling until her mind brewed before she sat up and stared at him.

"So, if you're not the maintenance man, then who are you?" she asked cautiously before moving away from him.

"I'm not supposed to tell anyone this, but I...," he said in a whispery like tone, "I'm working undercover."

"Undercover?" she said with a returned whisper.

"I'm an undercover cop. My boss wants me to report back to the office first thing in the morning, but my heart won't let me leave without telling you this. I told him I was still working on a lead, but he is demanding that I return or he's taking my badge away from me permanently."

"So, all this time you've been playing a role?"

"Yes. My father was a maintenance man and that was the easiest way to mask as a decoy, then I met you. It wasn't in my plan to come to Florida to meet anyone or get attached, but I was immediately drawn to you. Your conversations made me think about how I speak. Your softness reminded me of the very reason why I need to be more delicate and attentive to a woman's needs, but it was your calmness that taught me that I'm ready to be open and honest about myself."

"My calmness?" she said, as she glanced at him.

"Yes, your calmness. It's been a while since I felt like I could trust someone with the truth without being judged. If you think about it, who wants to hang out with the undercover cop? So when you left to go on your tour, I didn't think it was appropriate to tell you over the phone that I was catching feelings. I wanted to tell you when you came home the other day, but when we came inside and found your place trashed, you were too pissed. I didn't see any sense in pouring out my feelings at that moment. Instead, I just wanted to be there for you. When we were on the balcony I just wanted to enjoy the moment. So as far as my feelings for you, they're real and that's not a role."

She took a deep breath and looked at him, not sure if she should believe his words. "Why didn't you tell me how you felt?"

"I didn't want to tell you that until I told you the truth. What's the use of telling you how I feel, if I'm not being honest with you?"

"I can respect that. So, are you really from Virginia?"

"I'm from Virginia."

"Where do you work?"

"In Vegas."

"Vegas? What brings you all the way here? It's not like Vegas is three hours away, you know."

"I followed Skyler here."

"You did what?" she paused. "You got to be kidding me, so you're interested in Skyler?"

"Not at all. Skyler is really not the person you think she is. She has serious charges pending against her back home and I was just steps away from arresting her until she fled this way. She is facing money laundering and racketeering charges."

"What! She didn't tell me that, she said her boyfriend was threatening her with her own money."

"Not exactly," he shook his head, with raised eyebrows. "It's a very complicated case when it comes to linking their personal roles."

"Oh my goodness," she said in disbelief.

"Well that's why I told you she sold you a sob story because she knew you would buy it."

"You mean to tell me you've known and you didn't say anything?"

"How could I tell you? I didn't want to chance it and put you at risk."

"Put me at risk? What does this have to do with me?"

"Everything. I'm guessing you're her outlet away from Vegas or why else did she come all the way down here?"

"She said she needed to get away."

"Yea well, she's in hiding. Before she left, the Vegas Police Department found out she caught a plane to Miami. I had no idea who she knew down here neither did my team and they put me on the first plane smoking so I could trail her. We even tapped her phone. She called someone by the name of Ty before you two linked up."

"Ty?"

"Yes and she told her that she was going to be staying with you. She gave her the address so I immediately called the management staff at your condo, explained my position and they set everything up. They gave me the assigned task, thanks to my boss, and I filled out the paperwork and took over as the full-time maintenance man's position so it could look legit. They allowed him to work late nights while I allegedly worked in the day time. The agreement was that he and I would work as one, but I was the face only my floor and your floor would see."

"Oh my goodness, so does she know you?"

"No."

"Have she seen you before?"

"Yes, but she doesn't remember where, she was too messed up to remember anything that night."

"So, she doesn't even know that you're watching her?"

"Not at all."

"So, now what?"

"My orders are to report back to Vegas in the morning and turn in my paperwork on Ms. Sutton. Since no one can trace that

I've been here it will be like I've never existed and I didn't want to do that to you."

"So you're leaving for good?"

"Just for now, but who knows? My life in Vegas is over. I'm open for a transfer, but I don't want to invade your space without knowing where I stand in your life. I would love for us to stay in touch and I'll fly down here to spend some time with you whenever your schedule allows it. I really do adore and care about you. I know you're still getting over Anthony, but you have to believe me when I tell you that I don't want to leave you, but I promise you I'm coming back."

"You're not obligated to come back."

"You're right but I want to. I really do care about you."

"So let me get this straight, you're not really the maintenance man, you're a cop for Vegas?"

"Yes."

"And is Monte your real name?"

"Sort of, but its Jared Montgomery."

"Jared? You look like a Monte to me."

"Well, my birth name is Jared, but my pops was the only one who called me Monte."

"So, can I still call you Monte?"

"Sure, you can call me whatever you want."

She put her head down then smiled. She was glad they talked, but sad that he was leaving. He pulled out his wallet, and showed her his license to verify what he was saying was true.

"You don't have to do all that."

"I know, but I don't want any more secrets between us. There is another lead I'm working on in Vegas and that's Ricardo Simmons, he's a drug lord. I just need to have Skyler in my custody to seal the deal first."

"This is serious."

"This is very serious and I don't want you anywhere near it. The only reason why I'm telling you this is because I need you to know everything. Skyler is very shiesty and whatever you do, don't get caught up in her web of deceit."

"Yea, well I kind of feel like it's a little too late for that now. I see now that everything was a lie."

"I told you to trust your instincts. It's a hard pill to swallow since you're the innocent one in this."

"Yes you did, and I'm thankful," she said. "So, I need to tell you something too."

"Yes?"

She paused. She never wanted to take anyone's ability to decide what's best for them by lying about her true identity. She wanted to give them the chance to choose without fears. She took a deep breath.

"Monte..., I was born with a deformity, well that's what I was told all my life until I became aware."

"I don't care what it is."

"I need to be the one to tell you."

"And I respect that, but I don't want to know."

"It's important for me to reveal my truth like I have with everyone I was involved with."

"Whatever you tell me, it wouldn't matter."

"...I was born a male.

He stiffened without looking at Alana.

"My mother wanted a girl and made me one."

"What do you m-mean, she made you one?"

Alana rubbed her hands together nervously.

"When I was born, my mother told me I was the most beautiful child she'd ever seen. She never thought twice about it. She saw my face, named me Alana and then found out that I wasn't her beautiful daughter. She kept my true identity to herself, not revealing my sex to my brothers or my father. I had surgery so now I have all female organs and never associated myself as a male. I've always been a girl and my name is on my birth certificate, listed as a female."

He paused. His words were stripped from his voice and he was slow to speak. Unsure what to say..., he sat still with his heart racing.

"I know it's a lot but I can't live my life with a lie and pretend that I was born a woman. I wish I could. I wish I can have a natural child," she said softly.

He paused. She looked away and stood up. Anthony had the same reaction, but she vowed that she would always reveal her truth. She knew she was altered. It was only right that she faced it like adult.

He paused.

She poured more wine and took a couple of gulps.

"Are you okay?" she said softly.

"Yes. I don't know what to say. I-I don't know how to say it because I don't want to say anything hurtful..."

"Just say it..."

"I would've never thought you were born a ...."

"I don't associate with that."

"Ok...umm., I've never.....well damn, not to my knowledge ever been with a woman of your... type."

"You never know honestly. I mean, transgender women are slow to speak their truth because we don't want to be labeled as..."

"Men."

"No, we don't want to be labeled as creeps. We are all born into a body some don't feel they can associate with and now medicine can allow us to be who we feel we are."

He stood up, took a deep breath and covered his mouth.

"I'm ..."

"You're what?"

"I'm attracted to you."

"I'm attracted to you too," she laughed.

"Your ex knew?"

"Yes. I am very honest about my identity and I will not trick someone for my selfishness."

"I can respect that."

"Look, I know it's a lot to process so process it. The way I feel about you isn't going anywhere. I just wanted to tell you my truth."

"I-I do have a question."

"Yes."

"You've always associated yourself as a female so you never really were a boy? Like... is there a picture of you floating around of you as a boy?"

"No. From birth, I've always been a girl. I never wore pants, always had long hair. No one knew of my deformity until I was thirteen and only my mother, father, Skyler, and Anthony knows. My brothers don't even know."

"Get the hell out of here."

"I'm serious. At 18, I got the reassignment surgery so I have all female parts."

"I see," he said before he poured another glass of wine. "Just gonna take me a second to wrap my mind around this. This is all new to me."

"I know several transgender women, but they are not honest with their partners. I just wanted to be honest with you. Too much dishonesty in the world and it should be your choice if you want to deal with me or not. I hope you look at me the same but if not, I can respect it."

"That's fair," he replied.

"So, now what? You're a cop and I'm a model. My flight leaves out at 6 am."

"Speaking of that, I need to run downstairs and pack my things. While I'm down there, I'm going to call my boss so I can let him know that I'll be on the first flight tomorrow morning too, okay?"

"Well, do you want to spend the night so we can leave out together in the morning?"

"Sure, I would like that. I'll be back in few."

"Okay," she said with a smile.

She leaned toward him as hugged him. His arms wrapped around her which made her feel safe. She inhaled his essence, hoping her news didn't scare him off. They locked eyes ..., but he pulled back. He pulled away then smiled at her with his eyes. She wanted him but knew the shock factor would bring hesitation. She knew their time apart could make or break their friendship. So, she hoped for the best, the second time around. He brought her close to him and kissed her forehead.

"Um, let me go so I can handle my business real quick," he said as he took a deep breath.

"I'm going to leave the door unlocked for you," she said as she watched him leave.

She closed the door, poured herself a glass of wine, turned off all the lights except the nightlight in the kitchen and quickly darted in her bedroom. She removed her dress, slipped on a pair of shorts and a t-shirt. She closed her balcony door in her bedroom when the breeze crept through, but quickly smiled to herself when she heard the front door open. She was hopeful that they could continue to talk. She grabbed her glass and walked towards the door.

She found herself smiling like a school girl as she walked toward the living room, but stopped in mid step when she didn't see Monte. She called out his name, but he didn't respond. She thought she heard the front door open and began to second guess herself when she didn't see him. She quickly opened the front door and peeped outside, but there were no signs of him. She closed the door, but before she turned around, she felt a prick in her neck.

She quickly grabbed her neck then turned around and was immediately startled when she saw her intruder. She noticed her intruder stood in front of her with a serious face, not revealing the smile she once seen. She quickly turned away and tried to turn toward the door, but her intruder grabbed her and snatched her. She gasped as her legs felt heavy while her intruder picked her up and slung her over his shoulder. The only thing she could do was look at his shoes while her numb limbs disabled her fight. Immediately, she dropped her wineglass before he slowly walked her into her room and tossed her on her bed. Her eyes were soon fixated on the ceiling, but now her room was dark and cold from the breeze of the opened balcony door.

"You see what you made me do!"

Alana tried to scream, but the knot in her throat and the fear in her heart wouldn't allow her to make a sound. She heard a noise drawing near her, but she couldn't turn her head to see what or who was around her. She could only move her eyes. In desperation, she tried to move her hands to feel what was beside her, but her hands wouldn't move either. She weakly tried to scan her bedroom as she lay motionless on the bed. Before she knew it, she was staring into her attacker's familiar eyes. Terrified, she closed her eyes when the intruder's breath stained her neck as her breathing became rapid. She never would've believed in a million years that the person standing over her would be the cause of her death. She heard the front door open, but was too exhausted and defeated to scream out.

"Alana?" Skyler called out as she walked through the front door. "*That's odd...., why is the door unlocked?*" she mused.

Skyler called her name again as she closed the door to her once shared living quarters with Alana. She noticed a single wine glass and a bottle of wine sitting on Alana's grandmother's antique coffee table in the living room. The place was dimly lit as if she was having a rendezvous or some sort, so turning on the light wasn't an option. Startled by a gust of wind, Skyler walked toward the terrace as the curtains swayed slightly until she noticed a silhouette. She slowly walked in the kitchen, eased a knife from the set she'd given Alana as a house warming gift and held on to it for dear life. She tiptoed toward the terrace, took a deep breath, and slid the curtains to the side with the knife cautiously. She shook her head and wondered if she was overreacting to the silence, but Alana's unlocked door still puzzled her. She reached for her phone to dial Alana's number again, but it went to voicemail.

"I should've kept my damn mouth shut," she mumbled as she closed her phone and placed the knife on the bar. "I know I was out of line."

She walked towards the restroom when a faint chirping noise caught her attention. She turned her head toward Alana's room and quietly walked toward it, until broken glass underneath her feet stopped her stroll.

"What in the ....?" she said to herself.

She then noticed Alana's bedroom door was ajar and it was dreadfully dark. A feeling of terror rushed over her as she anticipated what stood behind the door. She slightly pushed the door open until she was staring into Alana's infamous mirrored wall. It reflected her once beautiful body now drenched in blood, stretched out on her bed. Shocked at what she'd seen, she quickly covered her mouth as her shaky voice crept through her hands.

"Oh my go...."

She ran toward Alana's lifeless body as her mind drew blank and her heart weighed heavy with guilt. She quickly searched for a pulse, but there wasn't one. Tears streamed down her face as she cradled Alana's lifeless body while her fixated eyes stared at the ceiling. Skyler clutched her best friend's body to her when the bedroom door squeaked and she saw Alana's murderer's shadow.

She swiftly moved Alana's body away from her then darted out the front door rushing down the stairs without looking back. Immediately, the murderer calmly walked away as well, but took the elevator. About twenty minutes later, Monte opened her front door and called out her name.

"Lana, I'm sorry I took so long. I couldn't find my badge and my supervisor called, he was a little long winded. He was pissed that I wasn't on the plane tonight but I told him all the information I'd gathered and guess what he said......," he stopped when she didn't respond. "Alana....?"

He walked toward her room and called out her name again, but noticed her bedroom lights were off. He walked toward her room and stepped on the glass in front of her door then dropped his bag on the floor. He pulled out his weapon, took a deep breath, hoping what he feared wasn't behind her door and pushed it opened only to see her body on her bed from the reflection from her mirror. He ran up to her and pulled out his cell phone and dialed 911. He grabbed her body and searched for a pulse. He screamed into the receiver and told the dispatcher everything she needed to know. He pushed her hair back and looked at her beautiful face as he rocked her back and forth near his chest. No more smiles. No more pictures. No more conversations. No more laughter. Finally, he'd met someone who took the time to understand him and now she lay in his arms lifeless close to his chest.

"I shouldn't have left you Lana. I'm sorry."

He cradled her as the police and paramedics came rushing in. The police officers asked him to step in the living room. He stood to his feet, carefully placing her back on the bed and walked towards the living room. He saw Micah's business card on the counter, grabbed it then dialed her number.

"Micah, this is Monte ..It's Alana....Umm,,,, you need to get over her right now, it's not good...I rather you come here ASAP...It's not good."

The dreadful call...

Thirty minutes prior, Lieutenant Dezio Garcia and his female companion were sitting at one of South Beach's finest seafood restaurants looking over a menu when his phone rang. He weakly smiled at his companion before pulling out his work cell phone. He quickly apologized for the phone interrupting their highly anticipated date and promised to make it very quick.

"Duty calls," he mumbled with a raised brow. "Lieutenant Dezio Garcia," he said in the phone.

Report to South Beach Estates. Officers on the scene," the dispatcher voiced loudly, "there's been a homicide."

"What do we have?" he said as he signaled the server to come to his table.

"Single female victim."

The server arrived at their table with a pleasant smile. He whispered to his companion to order whatever she wanted, before he stepped away from the table.

"Have you dispatched Phelps?"

"Captain's order was to dispatch you first, sir."

"Damn it," he cursed under his breath. "Make sure you dispatch Phelps immediately," he said authoritatively.

"Acknowledged. Dispatch out."

Lt. Garcia slipped his phone back into his jacket pocket then blew out a long sigh before walking back to the table. He'd promised Catalina, his sexy Cubaña lady friend, a romantic dinner without any disturbances from the office. He shook his head to himself, dreading to tell her the disappointing news once again, interrupting another date. He glanced at his watch before locking eyes with hers. She smiled patiently and grabbed her purse when he walked toward her.

"Let me guess, you need to go again, right?" she said as she stood to her feet.

"Yea," he sighed. "I'm so sorry Catalina. I know I promised you a night with no interruptions, but it's ...."

"No need to apologize. I do understand Lieutenant. I tell you what, how about you call me when you've wrapped things up and I'll meet you at your place with nothing on, but a laced teddy," she said flirtingly as she pulled his tie toward her.

"Now, I can do that," he said with a smile.

She planted a soft kiss on his lips before they parted ways. He watched her walk away while he pictured himself doing all the little naughty things he could think of in a couple of hours. He reached inside of his pants pockets while his eyes followed Catalina exiting the door. He hurriedly paid the waitress for their drinks, apologized for the sudden abruptness and tipped her nicely. He tried to follow Catalina's footsteps, but she was long gone by the time he reached the door. He walked toward his 2018 Chevrolet Camero and headed toward the Estates, which was no more than five minutes away. He pulled out his cell and dialed Phelps number.

"Phelps," his partner voiced.

"What's your ten-twenty?"

"Pulling up at the Estates. Dispatch hit me about five minutes ago, but I was already in the area."

"Where the hell is Williamson? Clark or Brown? And all those other boys who are always volunteering for cases like these?" Garcia said, slightly irritated.

"Apparently, Captain specifically wanted you on the case."

"Yea, I gather that. I'll see you in a few," Garcia said before disconnecting the call.

Lt. Dezio Garcia was less than thirty days from retiring, but wondered why his Captain assigned him to a homicide case. He made a mental note to meet with him first thing in the morning to request for someone else to work on this case instead of him. He didn't want to work on any serious cases just weeks from his retirement. He pulled up beside the other police vehicles and walked toward a couple of uniformed officers while placing a piece of chewing gum in his mouth.

"Why isn't this area taped off?" he said while pointing at the perimeter. "You know the protocol. Tape this area and no one, and I mean absolutely no one, is allowed inside of this building unless they get clearance from me. Anyone that steps on this soil who is not wearing a badge is carded, am I understood?"

"Yes sir."

Garcia watched them scatter off until they disappeared from his sight. He shook his head and mumbled 'rookies' under his breath before walking toward the building. He admired the beautiful building when a uniformed officer advised him that the victim was on the sixth floor when they reached the elevator. When he pressed the number six button and pulled out his pad, thoughts ran back to Catalina. They'd been seeing each other for more than three years and now that his retirement was approaching, he wanted to surprise her with the yacht he was soon purchasing and was hoping to invite her to sail with him. He glanced at his watch, hoping that this was an open and closed type of case because the thought of her in a lace teddy was his growing focus. He dealt with several cases similar to this one in the past and they usually ended up the same way; young girl meets a man, brings him to her place, things get out of hand and so on. When he reached her floor, he didn't expect to see the chaos and distressed officers pacing back and forth shaking their heads outside of her door.

When Garcia arrived at her door, the officer standing inside of her doorway filled him in about the victim. When he stepped inside, he spotted a uniformed officer talking to a young man covered in blood on the other side of the room near the balcony looking distraught. Garcia quickly looked at the officer standing in front of him with a baffled look as the officer read the report.

"What did you just say?" he asked, tilting his head.

"We found her driver's license and it indicated that she is Alana Inacio, a twenty-three-year-old woman. It appears that she's been here for ......," the officer said, before Garcia tuned him out.

Garcia's heart fell to the pit of his stomach and he immediately stepped back as the officer told him her body was still in her bedroom covered up. He thanked the officer then slowly walked toward the back room noticing the broken glass on the floor. He peeped into the first bedroom, but nothing piqued his concern. He took a long, deep breath before walking into the victim's room.

"So talk to me Phelps...," Garcia said as he covered his mouth.

"Looks like a number of things. Sexual assault, rape, strangulation and stabbing," Phelps voiced, unmoved.

"Oh man, sexual assault?" Garcia winced to himself.

Phelps noticed a blank faced Garcia standing across the bed with a puzzled look on his face as he stared at the body.

"Are you okay Lieutenant?"

"Y-yea, I'm okay. Cases like these are never easy," Garcia said with a blank stare.

"You're right, but you know how many young girls we find in this type of predicament."

"Yea," Garcia replied dryly as he scanned the bedroom. "Um, who is the guy covered with blood in the living room?"

"It hasn't been confirmed if that's her boyfriend or not."

"Confirmed? Let's get on that and why is he covered in blood? Tell someone to get a medic up here and check him out right now."

"The victim's body was tampered with by him."

"What? Are you fucking kidding me?" he said in a harsh tone.

"He was the one who called it in. The officer near the door said they found her wrapped in his arms."

Garcia covered his mouth then shook his head as Phelps elaborated.

"Let's make sure Kris collects a kit as soon as she gets in," he said agitatedly.

"Already on top of it. Also, no sign of forced entry."

"Strange," Garcia noted, as he looked around.

"It must be someone she knows."

"Like a boyfriend," he replied sarcastically when he looked back at the guy in the living room.

"No sign of a murder weapon either," Phelps added.

"Looks like our murderer brought his weapon then took it with him."

"Doesn't look like a kitchen knife," Phelps stated.

"This is no ordinary knife wound Phelps."

"Seems like the murderer wanted to make a statement."

"Or make her suffer and from the looks of things, he made her watch," Garcia said as he leaned over and shined his pencil flashlight in her eyes.

"This man is sick. Who could do her like this?"

"Typically in cases like these Phelps, she's the murderers' prey. What I don't understand is the type of statement was he trying to make? He pleased himself first then killed her."

"Or did he kill her then please himself?" Phelps asked.

Garcia studied the position of her body and her dilated eyes as she stared at the ceiling. He scanned the room and noticed her jewelry wasn't touched, indicating that it wasn't a robbery or a random act.

"Hello guys," Dr. Kris Dawson greeted as she studied the bedroom when she walked in.

"Hey Kris, we've been waiting for you to come up."

"There's a stampede out there with all the media trying to get inside," she said as she placed her briefcase down near the bed. "This girl was a model."

"Phelps, make sure you let Captain know what's going on downstairs. He needs to get a hold of that before it gets out of hand. I'm not sure if the family has been notified, but we don't need anyone lurking around for a story just yet. Hopefully, he can make a quick statement to the press."

"I sure will," Phelps said as he left the bedroom.

"So, Kris what do we have?" Garcia said with folded arms.

"I don't know Garcia. From what I've seen, some of her wounds are abraded, but these wounds are just brutal," Kris pointed out.

"So, tell me about the wounds," Garcia said as he walked around her room looking at her pictures of her family.

"I see visual evidence of physical and sexual assault, but there's no matter under her nails. From the looks of things, she must've known who it was because there is no sign that she tried to fight him off, but once I take her down and do a full exam I can give you more feedback," she said as she eyed the victim.

"Alright," Garcia said as he lifted her fingers with his pen.

"And it looks like a blow to the head and a stab wound in her thigh with a double-edged blade."

"Was that the fatal wound?"

"I'm not sure until I perform an autopsy then I'll be able to give you a more thorough evaluation of the victim. She lost a lot of blood from this wound," pointing at her thigh, "but I'm not convinced this is what killed her," she said as she snapped her camera.

"Hello Dr. Dawson and Lt. Garcia," the forensic team greeted when they walked in.

"Hey guys," they said in unison.

"Kris, I'm going to speak to the boyfriend make sure you see me before you leave."

"Will do Garcia."

"And Hunter, make sure you dust the entire bedroom and the broken glass near her bedroom door for prints. I'll be in the living room if you see anything that looks suspicious," Garcia said before he walked toward the living room.

Garcia pulled out his notepad so he could jot down a few notes he could refer to later. He walked toward the pacing gentleman covered in blood apprehensively.

"Excuse me sir, my name is Lt. Garcia. Do you mind if I ask you a couple of questions?"

"No, not at all."

"Were you the one who called 911?"

"Yes I am," Monte said as he faced him.

"What is your full name?"

"Jared Montgomery, but call me Monte."

"And who are you to the victim?"

"A friend."

"A friend or a boyfriend?" Garcia quizzed when he looked up from his notepad.

"We were just starting to get to know one another."

"So, is it safe to say that you two were dating?"

"Like I said, we were just starting to get to know one another," Monte repeated sternly.

Garcia scribbled on his pad without looking at him. "How long have you known Ms. Inacio, Monte?"

"'Bout three months."

"...and you two were here all night?" he asked, looking around.

"No, actually we went out to Night's Owl for a little while, but things kind of got excited there so we left and came here."

"Night's Owl? What do you mean things kind of 'got excited'?"

"Just a small altercation between her ex-fiancé and her best friend. We left because she was really upset."

"What are the ex-fiancé and best friend names?"

"I just know his name is Anthony and her best friend's name is Skyler Sutton."

"Okay," he said as he jotted it down. "Do you remember what time it was when the two of you left?"

"Um, I believe it was probably around seven thirty."

"Seven thirty? So after you left Night's Owl, you two came here?"

"Yes. We sipped on a couple of glasses of wine and talked for a little while."

"You two sat here, sipped on a couple of glasses of wine and talked?" Garcia repeated suspiciously.

"Yes. We were just talking before we both left to go out of town."

"Are you vacationing?"

"No. I work for Las Vegas Drug Enforcement Agency and I'm working on a case against a young lady by the name of Skyler Sutton."

"Aren't you outside your jurisdiction?" Garcia questioned.

"Yes I am, but when I was about to arrest her, she fled this way. Turns out she was Alana's best friend."

"Is that right?" he jotted down. "So, what happened next?"

"Anyway, I told her that I needed to run downstairs to call my supervisor and I would be right back."

"Why did you have to run downstairs?"

"I was staged downstairs, directly below hers."

"And you didn't hear anything?" he quizzed.

"No. I was on the phone explaining to my supervisor why I was still in Florida. I asked him for another extension, but he denied it."

"Can your superior confirm that you were on a call with him at that time?"

"Yes he can."

Monte pulled out his wallet and searched for his supervisor's business card. Once he found it, he handed it to him then stuffed his hands back in his pockets.

"You know the routine, don't leave town. I may need to ask you some questions later at the precinct," Garcia said as he looked at the card before Phelps walked towards him.

"Yea I know."

Garcia quickly wrapped up his conversation with Monte when Phelps walked toward him and nodded his head toward the door. They walked outside in the hallway while Phelps informed Garcia that he checked out the perimeter and noticed that it was equipped with Security Cameras. Garcia made a note to request a copy of the tape from the last two hours from the building.

While the detectives were searching for clues at South Beach Estates, Skyler tried her best to blend back into Night's Owl crowd. She rushed into the ladies restroom without anyone noticing her. Her heart raced in her chest when she closed the door behind her, trying to catch her breath. She tried to calm down, but was still frightened and confused at what she'd witnessed. Had Alana's murderer seen her? She stared at her reflection in the mirror as puddles of tears fell from her eyes. She looked in the mirror then splashed water on her face until she noticed Alana's blood stain on her dress. She hurriedly blotted the blood from her dress with someone's soda water they left behind until she heard voices outside of the restroom. She took a deep breath before she left the restroom then walked toward Dana near the bar.

"Where in the hell have you been?" Dana asked Skyler with a puzzled look.

"In the restroom," she said nervously, hoping Dana didn't notice the wet spot on her dress.

"All this time?" she quizzed.

"No. I told you I needed to make a few calls, plus I got us some powder," she said as she scanned the restaurant.

"From who? Clifton?"

"Hell no," she said, trying to remain calm. "From another friend of mine, don't worry too much about it."

"He'll have a damn fit if he knew we had other connections."

"That's why this is between us," Skyler laughed nervously. "Besides, we need to get going so we can head to the club because I swear I don't want to hear Russ's mouth tonight."

Dana looked at the time on her cell phone and realized they were running late. She cursed under her breath, grabbed her purse as they scurried out of Night's Owl toward the car. Skyler's hands trembled as she pulled the keys out of her purse.

"The car wasn't parked here earlier, was it?" Dana asked,

spinning around looking at the other parked cars.

"Yes it was," Skyler replied nervously.

"You sure? I could've sworn we parked near the fire hydrant," Dana replied, looking around.

"Girl, you're tripping. That powder got you delusional," Skyler chuckled nervously.

"Maybe I am. Can you get more of it?" she quizzed.

"Damn, what's up with all of the questions Dana?" she snapped.

"Why the hell are you snapping at me? I didn't do shit to you," she spat.

"I'm sorry, I didn't mean to snap. I just...got a migraine and I'm really not in the mood to hear Russ's mouth again. Shit, he's going to act a fool cause it's Celebrity night," Skyler retracted as they got in the car.

Skyler glanced past Dana just to make sure she didn't have another pair of eyes watching her. Once she sat in the car and the coast was clear, she quickly sped off and looked in the rearview mirror to make sure no one followed them. She still envisioned Alana's body drenched across her bed in her own blood as she sped through the traffic lights.

As she drove in silence, she wondered if she was making a huge mistake by not calling the police or telling someone. If it were not for the pending charges she had in Vegas, she would've called the police herself and reported it. She felt shallow, less than a friend because if it were not for the argument at the bar, Alana wouldn't have left and went home. She could still be alive. She had to think quickly for an alibi and the only person who could vouch for her presence was Dana, she didn't know it just yet.

Dana mumbled under her breath, but Skyler's mind was elsewhere.

"What did you say?"

"I'm not in the mood to hear Russ's fucking mouth."

"I know, he reminds me of someone I know," Skyler mumbled.

"Well, you better push the petal to the metal then, Sky."

Skyler rushed in and out of traffic until they reached the club's parking lot. They grabbed their bags and tried to rush inside the club, but the bouncer stepped in front of the entrance with his arms crossed, blocking their entrance.

"Ladies?"

"Skip?"

"Just wanted to give you heads up about Russ, he's pissed off at everyone. This is not a good night and he told me to make sure when you two showed up, to send you straight to his office, immediately."

"Ah damn, what now?" Skyler hissed.

"All I can say is you know how he is with his money," he whispered.

"Damn. I already know he's about to milk every bitch shaking their asses in here tonight. I'm not surprised he called every bitch in his damn phone to come through," Skyler said while shaking her head.

"Oh he did and he's making everyone pay up when they hit the door from the rip. Late or not."

"The fuck? This is the shit I be talking 'bout! Every time someone fucks up his money, he starts fucking with mine," Dana spat.

The ladies walked toward Russ office trying to rehearse their conversations before they faced him. They knocked on his closed door until someone snatched it opened. Russ yelled vehemently for them to get in his office.

"Close my mother fuckin' door!" he shouted to the bouncer. "Where the fuck you two been? I've been calling ya'll asses for two straight hours!" he yelled then pounded on his desk.

"We were at Night's Ow......," Skyler replied.

"I don't give a fuck where you been! You two know where the hell you're supposed to be!"

Skyler looked at him and fixed her mouth to speak, but before she could respond, Dana scoffed under her breath which made Russ furious.

"Look at me when I speak to you damn it!" he shouted.

She reluctantly looked at him.

"You got a problem with me Stallion? Huh?" he said, rushing toward her while towering over her.

"Hell yea, you're my damn problem! You all in my face like I'm a bitch on the street and you asking me do I have a problem with you? What the hell do you think?" Dana spat without biting her tongue.

"Oh, I see you just don't give a fuck, do you Dana?"

"No, why should I?"

"You know what, just for talking shit you can go 'head and give me my cut now then get the fuck out of my face!" he yelled.

"Man, this shit doesn't make any sense," Dana said loudly.

They reached into their purses, but Dana kept her eyes on Russ as she counted her money slowly and carefully.

"If I didn't know any better, I feel like I'm 'bout to pay your damn rent!" Dana fussed.

"Keep on and you will! All that shit you talking just landed you and your girl a personal visit from me as soon as ya'll asses come from the mother fuckin' stage. I'll get the rest of my fucking money later on tonight," he snarled as he snatched the money from their hands. "Now get the fuck out of my face and get out of my damn office."

Skyler looked at him disgustedly then at Dana before turning around without saying a word to either one of them. Dana followed Skyler out of the door just as Russ called out Dana's name. She turned to look at him, but as soon as he stormed toward her she slammed the door in his face. He quickly snatched the door opened then grabbed her arm.

"What the fuck is your problem?"

"I already told you that you're my damn problem, you didn't hear me the first time?" she shouted and snatched her arm away from him.

Skyler looked at them while thinking about Ric and his demanding ways. Just the mere thought of Ric made her skin crawl and the more she thought about it, every inch of Russ reminded her of Ric. Dana stormed past her speaking in Spanish just as Skyler caught her by her purse and pulled her toward her.

"You need to calm the fuck down Dana," Skyler snapped.

"Calm down? Did you see how he disrespected me?"

"Me and everyone else in that room did, but do you think he's losing sleep over that shit?"

"Fuck no."

"Then why the hell did you tit for tat with him?"

"'Cause he thinks he owns me and I...."

"Shit, he thinks he owns every one of us! Trust me, the best thing you can do is let him throw his temper tantrum without fueling his fire. I'm tired of hearing his damn mouth anyway."

"I fucking hate him Sky!" she bellowed. "I can't do this shit no more!"

"Me either, that's why I'm leaving Miami after my last damn customer. I'll be damned if he thinks he going to take my money after I shake my ass all night, thanks to your damn mouth."

"My mouth?"

"Hell yea! Every time he starts yelling, you have to yell too. Sometimes you should just shut the fuck up Dana. You make shit worse than what it is and then he drags my ass along with yours. I'm tired of that shit!"

Dana stepped back instead of saying anything else when Skyler stared her down without blinking. Dana didn't want to piss Skyler off any more than she already had, so she quickly changed the subject.

"Well damn my bad. I ain't trying to get you all riled up. Are you serious about leaving, where are you going?"

"The hell away from here," Skyler said. "I'm tired of Russ's bitchassness. I refuse to do this shit again. Hell, I played the fool for my ex but I refuse to do it again for someone else I'm not fucking," she spat.

"He ain't always this bad," Dana said.

"Well then you stay and play by his fucking rules!"

"Ain't nobody playing by his rules, I'm just....."

"Playing by his fucking rules Dana!" Skyler said sarcastically. "I'm tired of having this conversation, I'm 'bout to get dressed," Skyler said before walking away.

Skyler left Dana standing in the hallway and headed toward the dressing room without saying a word. She immediately snatched her towel from her bag before heading toward the shower stalls in a rage. She was pissed off at Russ and now Dana, but too many things occupied her mind. First it was Ric then Alana, Micah, Clifton, Russ and now Dana. She heard the door close behind, indicating that Dana was just a few steps behind her. Without saying a word, she quickly stepped out of her dress and balled it up inside of her bag before walking toward the shower stalls. The only thing she could think of was getting rid of her dress and rinsing off Alana's blood off of her body. When she stepped under the nozzle, she closed her eyes and cried softly to herself.

I shouldn't have said it. I should've just let it go, but now I can never say

I'm sorry to her.

Engulfed with a guilty conscience, she stood in the shower with her eyes closed while her haunting thoughts danced around in her mind. When she heard Dana's voice approaching, she quickly poured her shower gel on her pouf then lathered her body while convincing herself that she didn't see anything and come up with a believable plan.

"Can you believe Russ?" Dana said as she stepped in the stall beside Skyler.

That was the furthest thing on Skyler's mind, but she had to play it cool. She didn't need to bring any more attention to herself. She only said a few words before stepping out of the shower, leaving Dana behind while she sprayed on her body mist and oiled her body before slipping into her outfit. She reached inside of her purse, looked at her cell phone and noticed Clifton's missed calls. She powered the phone off then placed it back inside of her purse beside the powder she'd purchased earlier. She pulled it out and dipped inside of it just as Dana walked out of the shower. Skyler offered her some powder just as she ran some of the substance across her teeth before sniffing a thin line into her nose. She knew no matter what differences she and Dana had, she was going to make sure that she kept everything on the up and up. She thought about the way she snapped on her earlier and felt the need to apologize to her.

"Hey Dana, I'm sorry I went off on you earlier."

"You alright. I should've just kept my mouth shut like you said without getting all upset," she said while getting dressed.

"I mean don't get me wrong, I pop off at the mouth too so who am I to tell you what you should and shouldn't say? All I'm saying is when it comes to Russ just fall back. Let him fuss with his damn self, he'll eventually shut the fuck up."

Dana looked away when a flood of girls rushed in the dressing room.

"Russ wants every bitch in here to get their asses on the floor?" a girl voiced.

"What the hell is his problem?" Dana whispered to Skyler.

Skyler and Dana stood to their feet and looked at the mirror in front of them. Skyler's thoughts flashed of Alana's body stretched on her bloodied bed. Skyler quickly closed her eyes then walked away without saying a word. They walked on the floor and noticed a full house. Just as they walked toward the bar, Skyler whispered to Dana to make as much money tonight so they could leave South Beach before they ordered their drinks. Skyler turned around so she could see who was on the stage while glancing at the floor. She looked through the crowd and saw her clients smiling at her as they waited for her. She swallowed her drink just as the DJ announced that she was next on the stage. She took a deep breath then placed her glass on the bar.

She walked to the stage slowly as she swayed her hips while the music caressed her ears. She stepped on the stairs seductively as the crowd stared and smiled at her long legs lustfully. She turned around and looked in the mirror as she swayed her hips side to side while cleaning the pole with her hand towel that matched her sky blue outfit. Her body was curvaceous and her thirty D's were firm and tender. She moved her right leg to the side so her audience could look at her ass when she bent over and placed the towel neatly on the floor. She rolled her hips in a circular motion to the music as if she created the art of dancing. She gripped the pole when the beat dropped and moved a single ass cheek to the beat as she warmed the crowd.

The audience quickly encircled her and pulled out their money before she turned around and flashed her infamous smile. She leaned toward the pole and jumped as high as she could so she could wipe away the last dancers' perspiration. She slid down seductively while the music played. She quickly tossed her towel to the side before reaching towards the pole and wrapping her legs around it once more for their entertainment. She slid upside down with her legs crossed with only moving her torso before slowing opening her legs wide enough for the tippers welcomed intrusion.

Money was thrown on the stage as she performed. She continued to entertain her submerged audience. She rolled her tongue across her teeth as the powder residue still stained them while she escaped her reality. Dana came on stage and placed her hands around Skyler's hips as they danced close, rolling their hips melodically, tantalizing the audience as the ladies seduced each other.

Finally, they all waited for the clubs favorite and they never disappointed. The patrons spoke of Stallion's dance partner and it was a pleasurable treat. Russ was pleased with the outcome even though he rejected the idea at first. He watched the crowd stand to their feet and praise the women as they rushed toward the stage. He did have two of the finest women in the area, but he was still pissed. Dana slowly walked up behind Skyler and as the pair danced methodically together, Dana gently grabbed her neck, tracing her free hand on her, leaving nothing untouched. Skyler was in a zone but the look on her faces displayed pure arousal and the crowd loved it. The crowd exploded with tippers and the stage was on their only focus. Dana whispered to Skyler that a guy near the back wanted a lap dance when she got off the stage. She finished dancing with her until their song ended. Skyler walked off the stage and headed toward the dressing room while Dana stayed on the stage finishing up her act.

Skyler freshened herself in the dressing room while a couple of ladies were discussing the guy who was tossing around stacks of bills easily. She wondered was that the same guy who wanted her to dance for him, but she didn't say anything. She returned to the floor and saw Clifton walking in the front door. Their eyes met, but she quickly turned around without acknowledging him and smiled at an anxious customer waiting on a dance.

She gave her customer a welcoming smile, but underneath it all her skin crawled when she saw Clifton. So many different emotions batted her and she needed something to take the edge off quickly. She felt an eerier feeling and knew something wasn't quite right. She looked at her customer, but the only thing he wanted was to see her naked and sway her hips in front of his lap while he salivated over her.

In the meantime, she tried to get Dana's attention, but Dana was fixated on the money that her customers were throwing at her. Skyler knew it was no use trying to get Dana's attention until she noticed the guy sitting in the back throwing stacks of bills was Ric. She stared at him in a frozen stare just to make sure she'd seen correctly. He nodded his head toward her then pulled his jacket back slightly so she could see his gun holster on his side.

"What the fuck is your problem?" Russ said in her ear as he snatched her away from her customer.

She looked at him nervously then shook her head.

"No-nothing."

"I can't tell. You act like you saw a damn ghost."

"I-I...."

"Keep shaking your ass on my damn floor and make my damn money. Keep fucking up, you'll leave outta here with nothing, but the shit you came in with just like your girl."

He looked at her customer and apologized to him, when she walked back to him. He took a glance at the men in the back and noticed someone sitting in the reserved VIP section which was roped off. He called two of his six bouncers, Skip and Dale, to handle the situation that stared at them when they walked toward the VIP section.

"Excuse me sir, this section is already reserved for our guest and his entourage," Skip voiced.

The unexpected visitor pulled on his cigar and blew the smoke in Dale's direction. Dale moved closer to the guest, but Skip quickly held his hand out, indicating no trouble.

"I ain't moving," he said as he pulled on his cigar.

"Sir, it's not really a choice, but we need you to clear this area," Skip said with a little more bass.

"Didn't you hear what I said? I said I ain't moving."

Dale cleared his throat just as Skip walked closer to his unfamiliar guest.

"Look man, I need you and your crew to leave this VIP section. Now, if you want a place to sit with your entourage, the owner can arrange that, but this area is already taken."

"How much is it then?" the customer asked while tossing crispy hundred dollar bills at Skip's face.

"What the fuck? Get your shit and move around or else I'll get your shit and move it for you," Dale said firmly.

Russ looked toward Skip and Dale's direction from the bar as the confrontational customer looked displeased and unhappy. He abruptly ended his conversation and walked toward the commotion.

"What's the problem?" Russ quizzed without looking at the guest.

"Man, we tryin' to tell buddy that this area is reserved, but he doesn't want to leave this area," Dale said agitatedly.

"It ain't about what *he* wants. Who the fuck is he?" Russ

asked as he stared at the guy pulling on his cigar.

"I don't know, but this cat ain't from 'round here."

Russ looked at him as he walked toward him.

"Hey man, what's the problem?" Russ spat.

"We ain't got no problems," he said while blowing smoke toward Russ face. "This is the best seat in this house, I can see everything."

"Yea, well this seat is reserved and roped off, but we have another spot where you and your guests can sit."

"Nah, this is good pimp," the visitor shot back.

"Pimp? Look man, I don't want no trouble and I sure as hell don't want Dade County coming up in here fucking up my shit 'cause I have a business to run. Like my boys told you earlier, these seats are already paid for so either you can remove yourself or they can."

The disgruntled customer placed his cigar in the ashtray, stood to his feet then peeled his glasses off and stared into Russ's eyes.

"Ric?" Russ said shockingly while taking a step back.

"Well, hello big brother."

Russ hadn't seen his brother's face or heard his voice since he left Vegas. Ric was bigger and his bearded face disguised his look, but his eyes were the same as he remembered when they were kids. Russ took a notion of his brother's demeanor and squared shoulders with him.

"Big brother?" Skip questioned.

"I see you still playing stupid," Ric barked.

"Skip and Dale, let me handle this," Russ said.

"You sure boss?" Skip said with fixated eyes.

"Yea, I'm sure," Russ replied without looking at him.

Skip and Dale backed away, but in ear shot range to give Russ some space. They alerted the other bouncers that a problem was spewing and they all placed themselves near the altercation as they watched Russ and his uninvited guest.

"So Ric, what brings you this way?" Russ spat.

"My fucking girl."

"Your girl?" Russ chuckled as he looked around staring at all of his naked girls in his club.

"We have some unfinished business that we need to take care of. When I found out she was out this way, I decided I would pay her a visit. Any time a bitch skips town and owes me money and I have to look for her, some shit is about to go down," Ric said as he rubbed his bearded chin.

"Well, it's a lot of cats coming in here telling me I got their girl, so join the club. What makes you different? 'Cause you're my brother? Look, like I said a minute ago these seats are reserved, so the rules still apply brother or not. When you see her after her shift is over, then you two can talk about it, but until then, I have a business to run."

"I don't give a fuck about your business, she's my business," he said as he walked towards Russ.

Several of the customers stared at the commotion just as the bouncers rushed toward the arguing men, which had taken a turn for the worst. Skyler hurriedly asked a young lady walking toward the dressing room if she could grab her and Dana bags in locker number seven. The young lady looked at her with a slight attitude until Skyler gladly handed her four nice crisp twenty-dollar bill enticing the woman who wasn't making much money. Skyler looked past the young lady toward Ric and Russ when their voices escalated over the music. She quickly looked at Dana with a piercing stare, but Dana ignored the stare and smiled back as she danced. Skyler eyed the front door, but Dana wasn't sure what she was trying to say with her eyes.

Skyler saw the men standing in each other's face yelling and shouting before Ric pushed Russ over and knocked down the table they were standing beside. The men tussled inside the roped section while the bouncers rushed in to separate them just as the young lady brought Skyler the bags. Skyler immediately ran toward the stage, grabbed Dana's arm, and pulled her off the stage while everyone looked at the altercation behind them. Just as they struggled to get through the crowd, Skyler and Dana ran into Clifton near the front door.

"Hey, where are you two going?" he said when they landed in his chest.

Skyler glanced back at the commotion when she heard shattering and breaking glasses.

"I need to talk to you Sky," he said with seriousness.

"We got to go, I can't talk right now," she said as she rushed past him.

The ladies pushed past Clifton and sprinted toward Dana's

car as if their life was on the line. Clifton wondered what the hell was going on with Skyler when his phone buzzed on his hip. He stepped forward until he heard a couple of gunshots ringing in the club, near the back. Seconds later, people stampeded from the entire club as they pushed, screamed, and knocked down whoever was in their way. Clifton hurriedly stepped out of the club before they reached him and spotted Dana's car. He quickly jumped in his car and sped off to follow them. He didn't know what was going on, but knew Skyler's name was attached to it. He jumped in his car to follow them just as the police arrived.

"What the hell was that about?" Dana finally said.

"We need to get our asses out of South Beach. Hand me a pair of jogging pants and a hoodie."

Dana searched through her duffle bag and pulled out their clothes and hurriedly dressed while they sped through the streets. Skyler looked in her rearview mirror and noticed a pair of flashing head lights. Dana's phone rang, but before Skyler could tell her not to answer Clifton's call, she answered.

"What's up Clif?"

Skyler mouthed to Dana that she wasn't taking his calls.

"What's up?"

"Don't tell him where we are going," Skyler whispered.

"What? Hold on," Dana said.

Dana handed Skyler the phone. She took a deep breath and only listened to what he had to say.

"Hello?.....What?.....I don't have anything to do with that......What?....No!" she said before quickly disconnecting the call.

Dana looked at her and asked her what was that all about when Skyler handed her the phone. They traveled north on interstate 95 for about two hours, losing Clifton in the wind. Skyler was now getting restless from the days event, but since Dana was fast asleep, she had to pull over and get a hotel room for the night. They both stumbled in the room before settling in the king size bed. The day's events unsettled Skyler. As soon as she settled in the bed, her phone buzzed again on the nightstand beside her as she drifted off to sleep.

Yellow tape and investigate...

The next morning Skyler arose to the Florida sun blazing through the hotel blinds. She stretched like a cat in a bed that didn't belong to her and slightly opened her eyes only to an empty bed. She glanced at the chair in front of the television set on the opposite side of the room, but it hadn't been touched since they occupied the room. She called Dana's name, but there was no response. Baffled and concerned, she walked toward the window and noticed Dana's car wasn't out in front. Quickly she scurried to her side of the bed, reached for her duffle bag hoping that her cash was still intact. She unzipped it and moved the money around. She zipped her duffle bag before dialing Dana's number, but it went straight to voicemail. She looked through the nightstand beside the bed to find a phone book to find out exactly where she was as she redialed her number.

Moments later, she jumped in the shower when Dana didn't call her back. She hurriedly slipped on a pair of jeans, a t-shirt, and a pair of flip flops just as her phone beeped. She picked it up hoping Dana was returning her calls, but it wasn't her. It was actually Clifton informing her that Russ and Ric were in a big drug bust last night. The witnesses mentioned drugs and its distribution inside the clubs, but quickly informed her that he covered for her and asked would she do the same for him. He didn't want to lose his business behind his cocaine habit and would compensate her if she stayed away. He told her to call him back at her earliest convenience so he could fill her in with the rest of the details, but as soon as she heard Dana's voice outside the door she quickly disconnected the call without hearing the rest of the message.

Skyler watched Dana walk through the door with the phone

glued to her face, laughing without a care in the world while telling someone she was on a vacation. Skyler stood up, stormed toward her then grabbed the phone from her ear and disconnected the call.

"What the hell Sky!"

"Where the hell have you been?"

"Well damn good morning to you too," Dana said.

"Where the hell were you?"

"I got us some breakfast at the huddle house up the street," she said as she handed her the bags. "You know, we do have to eat."

"Why didn't you wake me up? You could've let me know you were leaving," Skyler said in a much calmer voice.

"I tried, but you were knocked out. I showered, tried to wake you up again, but you were still knocked out. So, I left and grabbed us something to eat hoping you would be up and dressed by the time I came back," Dana said as she placed her keys and purse on the table near the door.

Skyler looked in the huddle house bag then smile coyly at Dana.

"Damn, you act like I was leaving you here?" she said when she walked past her.

"Were you?" Skyler said while grabbing their bags and putting them in the car.

"No. I just got us some breakfast so we can eat, that's all. Damn Sky."

"We need to keep it moving. We gotta go," Skyler said as she sat in the car.

"Is everything alright, Sky?"

"I don't have a good feeling Dana. Clifton said Russ and Ric were arrested and .....," Skyler said as she started the car and backed out.

"Your Ric?" Dana quizzed. "Ric is from Vegas? Didn't I tell you that Russ was from Vegas too?"

"Hell no!" Sky cranked the car and took off.

"Yes I did. I told you I walked in on him talking to some guy name Mark on the phone."

"Mark?" Skyler said with wide eyes.

"Yea, Russ was asking him a lot of questions," she stated.

"What's Russ's real name?"

"Russel Simmons."

"The fuck!" Skyler said as she hit the steering wheel.

"What is it Sky?"

"This is not good."

"What do you mean this is not good? What are you talking about?"

"I set myself up."

"How?"

"I mean, I did some things back home and Ric's name is written all over it. When I first linked up with him, everything was good or at least I thought it was. I was Ric's main girl until a new girl came into the picture and the way Russ treats you is the same way Ric treated me."

"They're both assholes."

"Yea, but Ric is much smarter than Russ and is a bigger asshole than his brother. He's such a manipulator and an extortionist."

"Russ is just as conniving as his brother," Dana said.

"I swear, Ric tried to clean me out but I had other plans."

"I'm glad you put me on. Russ was racking up while saying I was his girl."

"No problem, you just gotta know the game and you need to know how to play it."

Dana sat in silence as they continued on the highway.

"Why are we running, we didn't do anything wrong."

"You don't want a fresh start?"

"I do."

"So, tell me where you want to go," Skyler said.

"I'm down to go anywhere but I need to go back home and get my stash from my apartment floor board."

Skyler hesitated. She felt like it was too much of a risk to go back to South Beach . As Skyler reluctantly headed back to South Beach hours later, Clifton was at Night's Owl counting large amounts of cash so he could offer Skyler hush money. She knew too much about him that could lock him down for at least ten years, so the further away she was the better off he was. He glanced at his surveillance camera and noticed two detectives were headed toward his office. He put the money machine to the side and closed the safe then cleared his desk only leaving his order sheets out as if he was doing inventory. He stood to his feet and met them outside of his office once he knew they were approaching his office.

"Well, hello."

"Clifton Parks?" Detective Phelps questioned.

"Yes?" he said as he closed his locked office door.

"Can we talk to you for a second?"

"Sure, but I'm needed in the front for a second," he said as he stepped away from his office.

"This will only take a second."

"So will this," Clifton retorted.

He walked off leaving them near his office. When he stepped out of hind sight, they tried to open his door, but it was locked. They smirked at one another before walking toward the front. They looked around the restaurant and noticed Alana's pictures posted on the walls. They stared at the pictures on the wall near the tables near the back. Garcia walked toward her portrait and admired her beauty. The picture captured her standing near a wall outside in the rain without a smile. It was a black and white picture, but it zoomed in on her exotic look. Garcia looked at Clifton while he stood behind the bar pointing to his inventory. He handed a gentleman a sheet of paper and a young woman a booklet. He walked toward the detectives and grabbed a table.

"I do apologize for my delay."

"No problem my name is Detective Phelps and this is my partner Lieut..."

"We don't need an introduction Phelps. He knows who I am," Clifton said.

Lt. Garcia gnarled with a raised brow.

"Oh so you two know each other?" Phelps said with pause.

"I wouldn't say that, would you Parks?" Garcia said.

"Absolutely not sharp shooter," Clifton shot back sarcastically to Garcia.

"Okay then, Mr. Parks we have a few questions for you," Phelps said while looking around and behind him.

"Sure."

"First things first, I notice you have a lot of pictures of Alana Inacio hanging in here," Garcia said, glancing at the wall and refusing to take a seat. "Why is that?"

"Alana's the face of Night's Owl. We've been promoting her

modeling career for three years now."

"Face of Night's Owl?" Garcia said as he jotted in is pad. "Was she getting any proceeds from this?"

"I-I don't know what you mean."

"You know exactly what I mean. Are you paying her or does she get a free meal, you know that type of thing?" Garcia said sarcastically. "Is she getting compensated from your petty exposure?"

"Well yea," he said, leaning back in his chair, "she won five thousand dollars and ..."

"Five thousand dollars is a lot of money; wouldn't you agree Phelps?" Garcia asked sarcastically. "I mean, who's giving five thousand dollars away?"

"Well, I mean hey ..." Clifton said with a smile. "Well, I believe when you're fortunate to bless someone, you should pay it forward."

"Parks, cut the bullshit...," Garcia barked angrily.

"How the hell are you gonna ...," Clifton shot back.

"Alright, alright guys," Phelps referred. "It's obvious that we're not getting anywhere with this so how 'bout Garcia and I leave."

"How about that?" Clifton said as he stood to his feet.

"We need you to come to the station for questioning."

"Questioning? About what?"

"Alana Inacio," Garcia calmly replied.

Phelps handed Clifton his business card before they walked out of Night's Owl without saying a single word to him. Garcia just drove in silence and headed toward the precinct and as soon as he parked the car, he stormed out and pulled out his pack of Newport's.

Garcia paced back and forth in his office while the superfluous staff crowded Miami-Dade Police Department. He was not a fan of Clifton Parks and the more Garcia thought about Clifton exposing Alana around his establishment, his hatred festered. Instead of blowing a blood vessel, he swallowed a couple of pills before sifting through his notes on his desk.

Lt. Dezio Garcia Sr. had been on the force for almost thirty years but was silently on the verge of a mental breakdown. He worked night and day as an honest cop until his son was found decapitated and sodomized. Ever since then, he was a loose cannon ball when he worked on murder cases and everyone knew to stay clear of him except his new partner, Detective Raymond Phelps. His Captain insisted that he should take an early retirement due to his son's death, but Garcia convinced the doctors and his Captain that he was capable to complete and fulfill his duties on the force.

While Garcia busied himself in his office, Kris was patiently waiting for Alana Inacio's parents to walk through the morgue to identify her body. She gave the exact same speech to every parent or relative when they identified the deceased. As she patiently waited for them to walk through the door, she stared at Alana's jewelry which was in front of her in a plastic bag. She picked up the phone then dialed Hunter's number hoping he gathered prints from it.

"This is Hunter," he sang in the phone when he picked up on the second ring.

"Hey this is Kris, are you busy?"

"Not really. Just running a new set of fingerprint analysis, what's up?"

"Not much, just waiting on Inacio's family to walk through the door. They should've been here by now," she said, glancing at her watch.

"Yea, well Kris you and I both know it's never easy to see your loved ones in a morgue."

"Yea, I know," she said dryly.

"So, what's for lunch? Got anything in mind?" he said, quickly changing the subject.

"Not really, but Chipotle sound good."

"Wow, opting out of your daily salads? Is the autopsy report ready yet? You know Garcia will be down here like a bat out of hell looking for it."

"Please don't remind me, he already called asking for it," she said as she rubbed her temples.

"So, are you ready to make the speech?"

"I am never ready for the speech," she sighed. "Oh before I forget, did you dust or fume Alana's jewelry for prints at the murder scene?"

"No. I didn't even realize that she wore jewelry to be honest with you."

"Yea, they are in the plastic bag near her. I need you to get on that ASAP so you can check for any prints," she said with a raised eyebrow.

"Okay, how soon can you bring them up?"

"I'll send Anna," she said before disconnecting the call.

Kris informed Anna to take Inacio's jewelry in the plastic bag to Hunter's lab for fuming. She overemphasized to her to stay in the lab until the prints were fumed and the jewelry was placed back in the bag. While Anna signed out the jewelry, Garcia grabbed Alana's folder and headed toward Hunter's lab. He passed by Phelps office and noticed him leaning in his chair laughing on his phone as if he wasn't working on a case. Garcia made a mental note to address how critical the first forty-eight hours of homicide case are when he circled back. Garcia marched toward Hunter's lab and snatched the door open while Hunter ran a fingerprint analysis on his computer.

"Hunter talk to me, what do we have?" Garcia voiced.

"So far, nothing," Hunter said while staring at the monitor as it scanned thousands of fingerprints.

"What do you mean nothing?"

"I've been running this analysis for about thirty minutes now, but we don't have a match yet."

"Not a possibility?" Garcia said, standing beside him.

"Not a one."

"What about from the broken glass?"

"Just hers."

"Are you only searching locally?"

"Yes."

"Well, let's go outside of Dade County to see what we can come up with. At this point, we don't know who our suspect is or where our suspect is from."

"Sure no problem, I can run the IAFIS database."

"Thank you. Have you heard from Kris?"

"Yes, she just called. Anna is on her way up here so we can check Alana's jewelry for prints."

"Her jewelry? You guys didn't fume it for prints?"

"No. She said it must've been an oversight when she examined her body.

"That damn Kris, sometimes I swear," Garcia voiced just as Anna opened the door.

She walked in, greeted them and handed Hunter the clear

package.

Hunter removed the jewelry from the clear bag and fumed it. A small print appeared on the ring and necklace. He retrieved the print from it as best as he could, then place the jewelry back inside of the bag and handed it back to Anna. She thanked him then walked out of the room.

Garcia shook his head disappointedly. He disliked the way the case was panning. He took a deep breath, pulled out his cell phone and dialed Kris number. He left a message on her voicemail asking her to come to Hunter's lab with the autopsy report as soon as possible. He disconnected the call and stuffed the phone in his pocket.

"So Garcia, any luck on your end?" Hunter quizzed.

Garcia leaned against the counter then folded his arms across his chest. He looked toward his shoes then shook his head disappointedly.

"Tsk, not really," he said dryly, "I'm starting to get this feeling this prick is staring me dead in my eyes."

Hunter chuckled under his breath until he noticed Garcia's seriousness.

"What do you think?"

"I don't know what to think to be honest with you. I have worked on several cases similar to this one, but this one feels like it's getting away from me."

"Garcia, you know if anyone can solve this case, it's you."

"Yea," he said nonchalantly.

"You're the best we have out here in Dade County and I don't know what we're going to do when you officially retire."

Garcia glanced at Hunter then thought of his own son, Dezio Garcia Jr., who was murdered seven years ago. He leaned against the counter and wondered what kind of man his son would've been.

"Garcia, you okay?" Hunter asked.

"Y-yea, just thinking about..."

"Dj?" Hunter asked.

Garcia chuckled before looking away.

"You know Hunter, working on this case opens sore wound."

"Yea, I'm sure it does. It's not too much on you, is it?"

"No, no I'm good. Cases like these make me think of Dj's case. It still puzzles me that everyone is okay with a cold case on file."

"Have you requested to reopen the case?"

"I have, but Captain says I can't be the investigating officer."

"Why?"

"Family of the victim," Garcia said with raised brows.

"Have Phelps do it, and overshadow him," Hunter replied.

"I don't think he's the guy for the job. I have to wait it out and see, but I think that's a good idea. Food for thought, thank you Hunter."

"You know my dad would've jumped all over this."

"I know Hunter, that's why I do everything in my power to solve this cases. Your dad was a great guy."

"Well I tell you what, my father and Dj would be very proud of your accomplishment."

"Yea, I have my best memories with your father with my career," he said, "shoot, your father and I was the best Dade County ever had on the force."

"How's your new partner working out for you?"

"Ha, he's not. He's still wet behind the ears and to be honest with you, I'm not in the baby sitting business no more. I'm getting too old for that son."

"I understand," he chuckled, "when are you going to retire?"

"That's my plan, but it depends. I'll retire when this case is closed and the murderer is behind bars."

The men chatted and watched the print analysis speed through billions of prints until Kris walked up behind them.

"Hey Garcia you wanted me?" Kris greeted.

"So, when did you sneak in here?" Hunter said.

"Just a second ago."

"So back to business, any news?" Garcia asked.

"For the most part, I'm just waiting for the family to verify the body. You know, I was looking in Alana's file and noticed something disturbing."

"What's that?"

"She had internal and external bruises."

"Internal and external bruises?" Garcia said with a piercing stare.

"Yea, she had quite a few old and new ones."

"I didn't see any bruises on her when I checked her out."

"Me either, until I examined her thoroughly."

"Have you checked into her medical records?" Garcia quizzed

cautiously.

"I should be getting them tomorrow."

Kris walked toward the counter while shaking her head disgustedly. She'd seen different types of cases, but this one was malicious and heinous. She placed Alana's folder on the counter and opened it slowly. Garcia picked up one of Alana's pictures that Kris set aside and gazed at her paleness while his heart shattered inside. Kris pulled out the autopsy report and read it aloud while Garcia stared at her picture.

"The autopsy findings included a subdural hemorrhage in the cerebral cortex, presumably caused by blows to the head and two stab wounds, one in the thigh indicating that a double-edged blade had been twisted upward, downward and diagonally in the flesh and one in the genital area indicating that a blade had been inserted vertically."

Garcia covered his mouth then shook his head as he slowly placed Alana's picture back into her file folder.

"So let me get this straight. The blow to the head wasn't enough? The murderer stabbed her in the thigh *and* in her genitals?" Garcia asked.

"Yes, sick bastard," she mumbled.

"So, ahem," Garcia cleared his throat, "we have a murder victim. No murder weapon. No fingerprints and no witnesses," Garcia stated.

"It seems like our suspect is toying with you," Hunter said.

"Maybe. Maybe not. What we're dealing with is a psychotic suspect who obviously likes being in control," Garcia voiced.

"Garcia, control or not, your psychotic suspect has your full attention," Kris said.

"Yes, he does, but I tell you what, he's playing with fire."

"Seems like this guy is ruthless," Kris replied.

"Yea well, he better hope I never find his ass because I'm liable to cut off his fucking balls and stuff every inch of him in his damn mouth. Hell, he's already gotten on my bad side," he growled. "Hunter, make sure you get a match then call me on my cell as soon as you find out something, alright?" Garcia said while collecting his belongings.

"Will do."

"Oh and Kris, did you find out the results from the rape kit?" Garcia inquired.

"Again, our clever suspect made sure there were no sign of his DNA, but I did find some substance like KY jelly left behind."

Garcia gave Kris a mysterious look before he placed everything near Alana's folder.

"Kris, can I hold on to this file for a little while longer?"

"Sure."

Garcia walked out of Hunter's lab with Kris words replaying in his mind. He pulled out his phone to dial a number, but was distracted when he heard Phelps boisterous laughter in the hallway. He held onto Alana's folder, made a quick detour toward Phelps office. When he marched in his office, Phelps was still in the same position he saw him in earlier, leaning in his chair and laughing in his phone without a care in the world. Phelps quickly chopped up his conversation and nervously gathered the paperwork sitting on his desk when Garcia tossed the manila folder on his desk, closed his blinds then slammed his door.

"What the fuck are you doing?" Garcia said.

"I-I was ....."

"I don't give a damn about the excuse you're about to muster up, but I can tell you what you weren't doing! You're not doing what I fucking asked you to do and that was to pull up Clifton Parks rap sheet!" he exclaimed.

"I-I was....I just lost track of time."

"Yea, bumping your fucking gums! We can't waste any more time! Am I understood?"

"Yes sir."

"You're goofing off like this damn case is solved! You're just like all these other damn rookies who have no respect for the badge you wear!" he yelled.

Garcia covered his mouth then turned away from Phelps. He was outraged. He was on the verge of a meltdown, but knew he had to calm himself down before anyone noticed how emotional he'd been since he's been assigned to this case. Truth was Alana was his niece, his sisters' daughter, and the only thing on his mind was finding her murderer. Proper protocol was investigating officers couldn't work on a case if the victim was family, but he refused to let someone take her case and allow it to become a cold case like his son. He huffed and puffed as he paced inside of the rookie's office before Phelps cleared his throat.

"Ahem, I'm sorry 'bout that boss," Phelps said apologetically.

"Are you working on this case or not Phelps? Because there are too many other detectives outside of this office who want in on this damn case and I will not be shortchanged! I will get rid of you like a bad habit, am I understood?"

"Garcia, whoa... now hold on a minute."

"No you hold on a damn minute! My job as a Lieutenant is to make sure that cases like these are solved, am I understood?"

"Yes sir."

The once shuffled and busy police station was utterly silent. Garcia opened the blinds and stared at the staff as they tried to act as if they were busy.

"Don't let this happen again or I'll snatch this case right from under you. Am I understood?" he said with authority.

"Yes sir."

"So, since you were engulfed in your phone conversation, I would like to assume you were talking to someone who has some information for us regarding this case," he said with his hands on his hips.

Phelps hurriedly sifted through the scattered paper work on his desk as Garcia shook his head at his sloppiness.

"You know Garcia, um...I've called her cell phone carrier earlier so I can get a record of her calls and um....here's what they faxed me," he said as he handed him the documentation.

"Oh, you actually did some leg work?" he said sarcastically as he looked over her call history.

"And check out how many times that one number I circled called her around the time she was murdered."

"That doesn't mean anything," Garcia said as he studied her calls. "How far back did you go back into her call records?"

"I didn't go too far back, but I went far enough to see a pattern in her call history. I also got a number that belongs to an Anthony Carnes."

Garcia paused for a second without responding, not sure if he should explain to him why this case was so important to him.

"You know Phelps, I have a million and one things going on in my head these days so I'll cut you a little slack today."

"I'm sure having someone like myself as your partner is quite challenging when you really don't know my track record. I've been an investigating officer for five years and I plan to walk in your shoes one of these days."

"Is that right? Be careful what you ask for, these are some big shoes to fill," Garcia said with raised eyebrows.

"I know," Phelps laughed.

"So, let's get down to business, I think we need to start from the end then work our way back up to the beginning. Let's start with what's his name...?" he snapped his fingers until Sergeant Brown tapped on the door.

"What's up Brown?" Garcia greeted.

"Garcia. Phelps. There's a Jared Montgomery out here to see you."

"Jared Montgomery?" Garcia repeated while pointing at Phelps. "Put him in room two, we'll be out there in a minute."

Garcia watched Brown walk off until he disappeared before suggesting going back to Night's Owl after they speak to Montgomery. Phelps questioned Clifton Park's aloof demeanor when they spoke to him earlier as they walked toward the interrogation room.

"Montgomery, what brings you this way?" Garcia asked while shaking his hand.

"I wanted to swing by and bring you this."

He handed him several folders from Skyler Sutton's case he was working on. Garcia studied the pictures while Monte added more incriminating information about her and Clifton. Garcia quickly changed the subject and mentioned Anthony Carnes. Monte revealed some things he saw on his behalf and that was more for Garcia to work with. Garcia thanked him for sharing the information and asked if he could hold on to her file. Monte offered to help in any way possible to find Alana's murderer, but Garcia was slightly hesitant because he was still a suspect at this point. He told him to hang around and if they needed anything from him, they would give him a ring. They shook hands before parting ways.

"Phelps, let's pull up a home address for Parks and pay him a visit before he runs off and hides himself in his office."

"You took the words right out of my mouth, but let me get his priors printed out."

"Oh you don't have to print them out, I have them all memorized," Garcia said without a smile.

Phelps gave Garcia a pausing stare but Garcia gave him a reassuring smile before patting him on the shoulder as they walked down the hallway.

"Don't trouble yourself, it's a long story son. I'm going to call the judge to see if my search warrant I requested earlier this morning is ready for me to pick up," Garcia stated.

"We need to find out more about this Anthony Carnes as well."

While they were gathering information on Clifton, Mesa, the server at Night's Owl, greeted one of her regular guest. She sat her at her usual table, handed her a menu and complimented her with her usual glass of freshly squeezed raspberry lemonade while she looked over the menu. The settling ambience made the guest nod her head to the music while she lingered over the tasteful menu. She scanned the menu, but was interrupted when someone stood very close to her and cleared their throat. She quickly looked away from the menu and stared at him.

"What the hell are you doing here?" he said with clinched teeth. "I thought I told you to stay away."

"Clifton ...?" she said as he interrupted her.

"I told you I'd give you some money if you stayed away," he whispered.

"Yea, that," she chuckled. "And why are you giving me money again?" she said in a normal tone.

"I'm not playing around with you, Skyler," he whispered while leaning closer to her.

"Well, I want...."

"I'm willing to give you five thousand right now just so you can leave. I don't need anyone to see you."

"I'm hungry and haven't eaten a decent meal in....."

"Look, I-I ain't playing no fucking games with you, but you need to leave ...right now...," he growled.

"Here's your ice raspberry lemonade honey. Are you ready to place your order now?" Mesa interrupted.

"I'll take her order Mesa," Clifton said impatiently.

"It's okay. She just orders her usual and if that's the case then I can........."

"Mesa, don't you have a table to wipe?" he spat.

"Clifton?" a male server called out his name. "You got a phone call!"

"Take a message," Clifton shouted.

"It's really not a problem for me to take her order, I already know what she wants," Mesa said with a wink.

"Didn't you hear me? Go wipe some damn tables and I'll take care of her order," Clifton growled in frustration.

Mesa stared at him, slightly embarrassed by his actions. She looked at Clifton weakly before smiling to the customers who noticed the commotion. He tried his best to mask his frustration when he saw Lt. Garcia and Detective Phelps stop at the hostess station peeling off their shades.

"Damn it," he mumbled. "What the fuck are they doing here again?"

Clifton quickly called Mesa back to the table. She stormed toward him and demanded an apology when he asked her for a favor. He apologized when the officers walked toward the bar without looking their way. She took a deep breath, accepted his apology but was still agitated by his sporadic behavior as he walked toward his office hurriedly. While the detectives were busy showing off their badges and speaking to the servers, Clifton hurriedly buried incriminating evidence scattered on top of his desk. He rapidly paced around in his office for a place to hide the pound of cocaine until he remembered his uncle created a hiding place in his office for sticky situations.

He looked at the monitor to see where the detectives stood as he pushed the heavy desk away from the opening in the floor. He pulled the rug back, keeping his eyes on the monitor as he removed the floor piece. He quickly turned the knob to unlock his safe and noticed several envelopes stuffed with hundred dollar bills. He stuffed the cocaine in a box and placed it in the hole, near the envelopes without taking his eyes from the monitor. Quickly, he closed the safe and secret hideaway, threw the rug over it and slid the desk across it as quietly as possible just seconds before they knocked on his door.

"Parks, we know you're in there," Garcia voiced as he banged on the door.

He quickly stuffed his desk drawers with his dime sacks of cocaine and locked his desk before glancing over his office one last time.

"Clifton Parks," Garcia yelled again while banging on the door. Clifton hurriedly snorted the cocaine from his desk then snatched the door open. "What took you so damn long to open up Parks?" Garcia barked.

"Damn sharp shooter, can a man have some privacy?"

"Do I look like I give a damn about your privacy? I could've bust right through this damn door if I wanted to!"

"Not without a search warrant!" Clifton demanded.

"Got that," Garcia said as he tossed the warrant in his face.

Garcia walked past him and looked around his office searching for a clue, any clue while the search warrant laid on the floor beside Clifton's feet. Clifton watched them as they looked high and low for anything that looked suspicious. When it came to Garcia, he was a thorn in Clifton's ass. Garcia was the investigating officer who busted him for gambling and prostitution several years back, but the charges were mysteriously dropped and ever since then, Garcia has held a grudge toward him. Clifton leaned against the wall, stuffed his hands into his pockets and played with a couple of quarters he had in his pocket while they looked around his office.

"So Parks, I see you didn't kick your snorting habit to curve yet," Garcia said as he noticed the powdery residue on his desk.

Clifton scoffed under his breath.

"No reply?" Phelps asked.

Clifton looked at his shoes without responding to either one of them.

"Oh, so you're not going to respond, big shot?" Garcia stated.

"Sharp shooter, you're not here to talk to me, you're here with a search warrant. So just get whatever you're looking for so I can run my business."

"Hmph, so now you've grown a pair? Seems to me like you're hiding something," Garcia said when his cell phone rang.

Garcia pulled out his cell phone then answered it.

"Garcia. Yea?.....Really?.....A possible match?.... Le'me call you back."

"Let me get that surveillance disc the night you gave Alana a party?" Phelps requested.

"Sure, no problem."

Clifton walked toward his closet, unlocked and opened it wide enough so they both could see its entirety. He searched for the date, handed it to them then closed and locked it back.

"We'll return it when we're finished," Garcia said.

"I'm sure, but in the meantime, I need you to sign it out just in case they get altered."

"Altered?" Garcia scoffed.

"Yea, you never know these days," replying with a smirk. "Someone may have it in for me and ya know ...destroy it," he smiled slyly.

"You really are an asshole Parks. I thought you were the type of man to keep a backup copy," Garcia said as he looked over the disc carefully.

"I do, but if you fuck up my disc, it's on you Garcia," he said as he tossed his logbook in front of Garcia.

Garcia looked at it then signed it out and threw the pen down as if he made a statement.

"Anything else?" Clifton asked.

"Yes, the other night when we talked with you, you said Alana and her boyfriend left in a hurry, is that right?"

"Yes."

"Why?"

"Her ex-fiancé might've said a couple of words to her."

"Might've, huh?" he said as he pulled out his chewing gum.

"Yea, I can't recall."

"Really? Do we need to take you downtown so you can remember?"

"You came here to get what you wanted, you got it so don't you have someone else to fuck with?"

"I'm not in a rush, they can wait. What is her ex-fiancé's name?" Garcia retorted.

"Anthony Carnes."

"Anthony Carnes?" Garcia mused.

Garcia looked around the room one last time until Phelps phone rang. Phelps quietly exited Clifton's office, but Garcia stopped short from the door near Clifton. He looked at Clifton one last time before Clifton mumbled something under his breath.

"What the hell did you just say to me? Did you just threaten me?" Garcia said as he pushed him against the wall.

"You know damn well I haven't said shit to you. Let me go!"

"The next time I come in here and it takes you as long as it did to open this damn door, I swear I'll lock your ass up!"

"For what! On what grounds?"

"I'll think of something while I'm driving your ass to the precinct!"

"Yea right."

"I can lock your ass up right now for penny pushing dime bags of cocaine, but believe me, when I get your ass, it'll be something you'll sit with this time! Am I understood?"

Clifton looked away until Garcia threw his back against the wall.

"Am I understood?" Garcia said with clenched teeth as Phelps returned back to the office.

"Garcia?" Phelps called out when he tried to remove Garcia's hold from Clifton. "This is not the time for this. We can always come back for him. He's nothing."

"You're damn right he's nothing," Garcia said as he straightened out his jacket.

Clifton caught his breath then stepped away from him.

"You crazy as hell you ole' man," Clifton blurted.

Garcia snarled at him before storming out of his office.

"You alright?" Phelps asked Garcia when Clifton slammed his door.

Garcia shook his head when he leaned against the wall and covered his mouth. Phelps advised him to get it together before his actions were reported and Captain pulled him from the case. Phelps told him to go to the men's room and splashed some water across his face while he grabbed a couple of bottled waters. After returning from the men's room, Garcia took a deep breath just as his phone rang. He looked at his screen without paying attention to the patrons and accidentally bumped into a young lady.

"Oh I'm sorry," she pleaded.

When he looked up at her, he was a bit startled. "Ms. Sutton?" he asked.

"Yes?"

"Um, can I-I speak to you about a serious matter?"

He was immediately mesmerized by her beauty, but knew distractions could cost him handsomely.

"I'm sorry?" she questioned.

"My apology, my name is Lt. Garcia and I need to ask you a few questions," he said as he flashed his badge.

"Sure, would you like to sit at my table? I was just about to place my order."

He looked around, but thought against it.

"You know, actually I was thinking maybe you should stop my office."

"Your office? Am I under arrest or something?" she asked flirtingly.

He was slightly flattered by her charm, but didn't display it. Once she recognized his seriousness, she took a deep breath.

"So, back to my original question, am I under arrest or something?" she asked.

"Should you be?"

"I don't think so unless it's a crime to be fine," she chuckled while ironing out her wrinkles and rolling her neck playfully.

"I take my job very seriously."

"I can tell. You can take the stick out now," she shot back.

"Ms. Sutton, I'm not the mood for jokes."

"I was just playing around with you. You need to lighten up a little bit, you're too serious Mr. Officer," she said.

Her comment caught him by surprise, a pleasant surprise. A strong woman was always his weakness, but he knew she wasn't the woman he'd assumed. She was a woman of disguise, luring men to be her prey with her sparkling eyes and her quick witty attitude. He stopped in mid thought and focused on the matter at hand.

"Like I said, I would like to speak to you about a serious matter."

She looked around and noticed the patio near the back from everyone. She asked him if he wanted to talk to her outside and he surprisingly agreed. She heard a noise and quickly turned around only to see Clifton mouthing something to her near his office, but since he was acting crazier earlier, she dismissed it and walked alongside the officer. She walked toward the patio near the back that accented the welcoming view of the ocean. Clifton tried to send Mesa to the patio, but Phelps stood at the door with his arms folded and declined any services from Night's Owls employees.

"This bitch is trying me," Clifton gnarled.

Nothing is what it seems...

Garcia stared toward the ocean as his guilty conscience ate at him while Ms. Sutton excused herself to a very important phone call. As he watched the tidal waves dance in the ocean he thought about the promise he made to his sister about watching Alana, but the death of his son consumed him, leaving him devastated and brokenhearted. After his son's death, he minimized his phone calls from mostly everyone and he only called Alana once or twice a month with minimal visitations. He was depressed and popped pills like they were skittles just to get through a decent day of work. He'd mask his hurt by convincing the Captain he was capable of working, despite his son's death and although the Captain monitored him, Garcia knew his days of carrying a badge were numbered.

"Hello? Are you hard of hearing Mr. Officer?" she said with her hands on her hips, interrupting his thoughts.

"Wha-what?" he stammered. "What did you say?"

"Uh, you going to check out the view or talk to me because if not, I have other things to do."

He quickly looked at his watch, hoping he hadn't wasted too much of her time.

"I didn't hear you get off the phone, I apologize. I must've been engulfed with my own thoughts," he said as he quickly wiped his face with his handkerchief before stuffing it into his pants.

"I guess," she said nonchalantly, "so, Mr. Officer, you said you wanted to speak to me about a serious matter, I'm listening," she said agitatedly.

He quickly dismissed her sentiment and got right down to business.

"First thing first, my name is not Mr. Officer, it's Lt. Garcia."

"Excuse me, Lt. Garcia," she hissed.

"Secondly, how well do you know Alana Inacio?"

She rolled her eyes at him before she started to speak. "Fairly well, I mean, what the hell is this all about?"

"Could you answer the question, Ms. Sutton?"

"I know her well, but I do believe people will only reveal a part of them. So how well do we really know someone?"

"I was under the impression you two were close?"

"Impressions? They can be deceived," she said with a straight face.

"They can," he agreed.

"Are we done now?"

"No not exactly. Did she happen to mention to you that anyone gave her problems?"

"Look, Alana had her life and I had mine. We shared things but ..."

He looked at her with a puzzled look.

"Women," he mused to himself.

"What? Men give us problems when we don't entertain their boyish ways, so......"

"Hmph," he said with a raised brow.

"What *exactly* do you want with me?" she said while looking at her phone. "I have a meeting in less than an hour and it's on the other side of town."

"Okay, well let me get straight to the point. Where were you around seven o'clock Thursday night?"

"Hmm, I was here, near the bar," she said without hesitation.

"All night?"

"Yeah, but you need to know this because ..."

"Because Ms. Inacio was murdered Thursday night."

"She was what! Murdered?" she said horridly, covering her mouth.

He paused for a second when she stepped back, shaking her head in despair. It pained him to tell the story again, so this time he opted not to. Instead, he handed her his card and asked her to swing by his office in a day or two so she could answer a couple of questions. He left her standing near the banister grief stricken as he walked and stood beside Phelps.

"You okay Garcia?" Phelps asked without looking at him.

"Yea, just drained and ready to go."

Phelps glanced at his watch, then at Ms. Sutton before he looked at Garcia with a puzzled look.

"It's not even noon. You ready to call it quits for the day?"

"Yes."

"What about the girl?" Phelps asked when he turned to look at her.

"What about her? We don't have anything on her besides..."

"What about that stuff Montgomery showed us at the office? The case he's working on in Vegas and her pending charges."

"Alleged charges, and I'm still looking into that. But that's out of our jurisdiction."

"It seems valid to me."

"Nothing is what it seems Phelps. Nothing is what it seems," he repeated.

Phelps looked toward Ms. Sutton with a puzzled stare as she pulled out her phone. Garcia, in a single breath, told Phelps he was headed to the restroom then back to the station. Phelps quickly dashed toward Ms. Sutton as she talked on her phone.

"Excuse me, Ms. Sutton," he said in an authoritatively voice.

"Hold on for a second," she said as she covered the phone. "Yes, can I help you?"

"Yes, I would like to ask you one thing."

"Hey, you guys need to wrap up whatever you were discussing out here?" Clifton interrupted. "I have a reservation set out here and the party has arrived."

"As a matter of fact, Garcia gave you his card and here's mine. We will keep in touch..."

"Look, I don't need any more unwanted attention, so if you could take this somewhere else I would appreciate it," Clifton said nonchalantly. "Maybe you forgot, but this is my place of business. So, take your threesome and get the hell out of here," he said as he tilted his head in her direction.

Clifton watched them leave the patio area with sweaty palms and an accelerated heartbeat. He lied to Phelps just so he could distract them. He didn't have a party but he did open the patio so he could make his money. He walked off thinking about a plan, but his mind was too cloudy. Garcia was hot on his heels and he didn't need any more distractions from anyone else.

Garcia jumped into his Dodge Charger and sped toward the

precinct while Skyler tried to think of a plan. In the meantime, Micah and Monte met at a local Dunkin Doughnuts across town.

"Hey Micah, I'm glad you were able to see me on such a short notice," Monte said when they embraced.

"No problem. I needed a small break from everyone to be honest. This whole murder thing is devastating," she said, disguising her blood shot eyes with a pair of Louis Vuitton sunglasses.

"I know..., how's her family holding up?"

"Her mother is devastated and continues to blame Alana's father for her untimely death. It's just heartbreaking to see them go through something like this. I mean, they were just celebrating the news about her signing her modeling contract just days ago and now this?"

He covered his mouth then shook his head in disbelief while she painfully spoke. She looked away, discreetly wiping away her tears.

"So, now what?" he asked. "Have they discussed the funeral arrangements?"

"They haven't made any type of arrangements. I'm actually helping them out, so I'm arranging everything for them," she said in a somber tone.

He rubbed his chin then shook his head. He looked away then closed his eyes as he remembered her pretty face stained with blood.

"If you need some help, let me know," Monte said as he grabbed her hands.

"Okay."

"I'm serious. You got a lot on your plate and I know losing someone is never easy. So, don't feel like you have to do all of this on your own, okay?"

"Thank you, I really do appreciate it."

"No worries, does she have family here?"

"Surprisingly yes, her mother said her brother lives here, but I never heard her speak of him. Have you talked to the investigating officers?"

"Yes and no," he said with hesitation.

"Okay, so now what? Do they have a suspect?"

"I'm not so sure. I just know I'm waiting for them to clear my name."

"Clear your name?"

"Yes. Since I held her in my arms, they are saying that I tampered with her body."

"This is not good," Micah said while shaking her head. "Someone killed Alana and they are still walking around here, it could be anyone," she said softly.

"You're right but I hope they get the son of a bitch. My manners, would you like something to eat or drink?" he offered.

"I don't have much of an appetite these days, but I could use a tall Vanilla Latte?"

"That's it?"

"Yes."

He politely stood up then walked to the cashier and placed an order. He smiled at the flirty cashier but showed her no interest when he returned to their table. He placed latte carefully in front of her before sitting down across from her.

"You know Micah, I don't know, since Lana's been gone, I feel empty. I can still smell her on me. She's in my dreams, she's everywhere around me."

"I know you two were getting close," she said as she stirred her latte. "But you can't do this to yourself. She wouldn't want to see you like this."

"I know, but I just feel like this is all my fault."

"Your fault? Why are you blaming yourself for someone else's recklessness?"

"I should've stayed with her instead of leaving."

"Why did you leave?" she said as she sipped her latte.

"I ran down to get my luggage so we could leave at the same time and made a phone call."

"Alana invited you to spend the night?" she said with concern, finally removing her shades.

"Yea."

"Hold on for a second, she invited you over to spend the night? I knew she liked you but she never said anything else like that."

"I'm a gentleman, besides, we were just talking and we both revealed some things to one another."

"She opened up to you?"

"Yes, we talked about where we were in our lives and what we planned to do."

"You know I underestimated you," she said with a slight smile.

Micah smiled to herself when she thought about how happy Alana was whenever she talked about him. She looked at him as he slouched in his chair across from her and thought about Alana's school girl smile whenever she talked about him.

"What are you talking about?"

"I must admit, I did make her aware of the people she was surrounding herself intentions, including you. You came in and swept Lana off her feet. It was definitely nice to see her happy again. I'm glad it was you that fulfilled her last days, she needed a kismet spirit and it was apparent that's what you two shared."

"It felt like it," he said as he took a deep breath, "I wished we had more time."

"Don't we all wish that?" she said.

"She deserved to have everything she wanted," he said. "I would've made sure she had it."

"I believe that."

"Just so you know, I made a confession to Alana."

"A confession? About what?"

He placed his badge on the table then pushed it toward her latte.

"What's this? You're a cop? I thought you were the maintenance man," she whispered.

"Ssh, I was on an assignment posing as the maintenance man."

"Posing? What? Why?"

"I'm working on a very high profile case that I can't discuss right now."

"Oh my goodness, is it serious?"

"It's very serious, but I have to be very careful and cautious."

"So why are you telling me this? Have you told the investigating officers?"

"I did, but I feel like I owe you the truth."

"You really don't owe me anything, as long as you told Alana that's all that matters."

"I just felt like I needed to explain."

"Well, what did Lana say about all this? I mean, I'm sure she was upset."

"She was not happy at first, especially after her and Skyler got into it. That is one of the reasons why I went downstairs so I could show her my badge."

"Knowing Alana, I'm sure she wanted to see it. She needed conformation because if not it wouldn't have settled with her."

"Yea, I just wished I would've told her earlier. I didn't know what would come out of our friendship."

"He's a non-factor, but the best thing she could've done was walk away from him. He was too possessive and controlling for her, it wouldn't have worked out between them," Micah added.

"Yea, you right. She expressed her concern about how controlling he was to her. She mentioned his lack of supporting her dreams."

"And after all that, you mean to tell me you still didn't have any intentions?"

"No not at all, I was being a friend. She needed to talk so I listened. I made her laugh when he made her cry. I held her after he pushed her away and after spending time with her I honestly wanted to know more of her. I found myself wanting to learn more about her and the more we talked I knew then I had to tell her the truth."

"So why weren't you honest in the first place?"

"To be honest with you I never expected to meet someone like her. We had so many things in common and when my feelings surfaced, she was out of town doing her tours, but I respected her too much to tell on her over the phone. I wanted to tell her face to face."

Micah looked away, thinking back to the conversation she had with her when they were in the hotel about her circle of friends. Sadness quickly fell upon her as she crossed her arms and shook her head disappointedly.

"Listen Micah, for what it's worth, I really cared about her. I didn't want her to get on that plane thinking I would be here when she returned, but I couldn't leave without telling her the truth before I left."

"She and I just had this conversation about trusting people."

"I know, so did we."

"Okay, so now what?"

"Well, I wait here. I'm still a suspect in her case until I'm cleared, proper protocol."

"A suspect? Really? Then after that?"

"I'm outside of my jurisdiction, I have to go report back in," he said when her phone buzzed on the table.

She looked at Rafael's picture flash across her screen before answering it.

"Hello?....I'm okay. .....At the .....Yea, I'm sitting here talking to ....," she paused as she looked at Monte, "..Already...Can I see it? ......Okay, well call me when you're on your way.....Talk to you later...."

"Everything okay?" Monte asked when she disconnected her call.

"Yea. Rafael's doing the final touch up on her layout so the magazine can print it in a couple of hours."

"I can't wait to see it."

"Can I ask you something, off the record. Who do you think did this?" she whispered.

He leaned toward her without blinking.

"I don't have a clue. I've been asking the investigating officer if I can help out, but he just says until I'm cleared his hands are tied. He just told me to stay close."

"Close? To be frankly honest with you, I think Skyler did it."

"Whoa, are you serious?" he said in a light whisper when a couple of pedestrians walked past their table.

"I am."

"Why? I mean, they had a fall out but I don't think Skyler has it in her to ...."

"I don't trust her. I don't put anything past her. She's so full of lies and envy, there's no telling what she's capable of doing."

"Nah, I don't think she would do that besides she has too much on her plate as is, I don't think she would bring any more attention to herself."

"You never know what a person will do when their backs up against the wall."

"You might be right, but I don't know. I'm not convinced that Skyler would hurt Alana."

"You sure about that? If someone can hurt you with their words, to me there's no telling what else they can do."

He tried his best to mask his feelings toward Skyler as Micah continued to link Skyler as a suspect. He knew what type of woman Skyler was, but a murderer never crossed his mind.

"You're still not convinced? Did you see the look on her face when Alana mentioned her little cocaine habit?"

"I did, but that still doesn't point the fingers to her. It's quite obvious Skyler has some deep rooted issues, but a murderer? Nah. Just my honest opinion, not that it matters, Clifton bothers me. He's someone I think they should investigate."

"I have to be honest, I didn't. But where is he now? Where is Skyler? They sure haven't shown their faces round her since Alana's death."

"Sure haven't," he said with suspicion, when he looked around them.

"I wouldn't be surprised if they were plotting something," Micah spat.

Micah's shook her head disappointedly before her phone hummed on the table again. She quickly picked it up and looked at the unfamiliar number that flashed across her screen.

"Hello?"

"Hi Micah, this is Clifton. How are you doing?"

"How did you get my number Clifton?" she shot back.

"Raf gave it to me?"

"Rafael?"

"I hope you don't mind."

"I do mind actually."

"Is it true about Alana? She's dead?"

Micah paused for a second.

"Yes."

"Damn," he gasped. "Is there anything you or the family need? If and when you do, don't hesitate to call me."

"Thanks, but Monte already offered."

"Monte!" he said in with disdain.

"Yes."

"Well if you need an extra pair of hands, let me know. I'm 'bout to get out of here cause I'm tired of those investigating officers grilling me."

"Detectives grilling you?" she repeated, raising an eyebrow toward Monte.

"Yea, there's this cat named Garcia, who's a snake," he hissed.
"Garcia?"

"Yea, he's been coming here sniffing his nose 'round here like he owns me or something."

Clifton drew silent, not sure how to ask the next question.

"Did you hear that Monte is the number one suspect?"

"Is that right?" she said suspiciously.

"Yea, my contacts gave me an earful on how he's been in Garcia's face down at the precinct as his decoy. Monte doesn't even know them bastards are trying to set him up," he laughed. "Let them tell it, his story isn't credible."

"Is there any way I can call you back. I'm actually in a meeting."

"Sure. Sure. My bad, I didn't know. Yea, call me later."

She disconnected the call and shook her head disappointedly while Monte looked at her with a puzzled look.

"Everything ok?" he inquired.

"Yea, Clifton is such a liar, it's so pathetic," she said as Clifton's words replayed in her mind.

"I wouldn't put it past him," he said just as his phone rang. "Hello?.....Garcia?"

He mouthed that he would call her later, but he needed to take the call. She watched him jet off and for the first time she looked at his physique. He was very attractive and had nice dark features. A perfect gentleman with a badge. She sat at the table and allowed her thoughts to mingle as the breeze caressed her face while she wished Alana was sitting across from her sipping on a latte with her. She stood to her feet and grabbed her bag then tossed her cup into the trash can just before she noticed Skyler getting out of a car.

"Speaking of the devil," she mumbled to herself.

Micah slipped on her shades and walked back inside the shop so Skyler couldn't see her amongst the other patrons. She sat near the glass window quickly trying to redial Monte's number, but it went to voicemail. She played with her phone, trying to zoom in on her so she could video record her. Since she couldn't hear her, she tried to read her lips. She continued to adjust the camera until a car pulled up beside her. Immediately when she saw the person get out of the car, she zoomed in closer, peeled off her shades then stared at Skyler's guest with her mouth slightly opened.

"What the ....?" she mumbled.

Since her phone was fairly new, she had the hardest time trying to record the pair, but she managed. In a shock, she watched the pair talk as if nothing mattered for at least forty five minutes. Micah watched the pair embrace, exchange duffle bags before they drove off in two different directions. She redialed Monte's number, but it went to his voicemail again. Micah grabbed her bags, jumped into her car then headed toward the precinct. She was sure Monte was there talking with Garcia.

She sped through the streets, cutting corners hoping to dodge the red lights quick enough without getting a speeding ticket. She was still surprised at what she'd seen, but as she drove closer to the police department, she wondered if she should keep it to herself.

She sat at the traffic light wondering if she should mention anything to Monte at this point because he wasn't exactly cleared from Alana's case. The more she thought about it, the more she realized she couldn't trust anyone. She looked in her rearview mirror just as the turn light turned green and quickly made a u-turn.

Micah sat in her bedroom, on her bed, replaying the video on her phone. It didn't matter how many times she replayed it, seeing the pair together in public still shocked her. She sent the video to her email address then pulled out her laptop. A couple of messages came through her phone from Rafael, but she didn't respond. Once she signed on her to her laptop, she silenced her phone. At this point, she felt like she couldn't trust anyone and certainly didn't know who they kept in their circle when she wasn't around. As her mind pondered, she thought back when she and Alana visited an upscale restaurant for the very first time and met Clifton.

Immediately she and Alana liked the gesture but noticed he was like that with all the ladies. Micah knew he was a flirt, so she dismissed all of his advances. He never stopped, as she continued her thoughts, he slyly slid his number to her, but her disinterest made him introduce his friend, Rafael, to her. So telling Rafael wasn't an option either.

As she replayed the video over, she tried to read Skyler's lips but it wasn't clear enough. Just as the video started to play a knock sounded on her door.

"Who is it!" she called out.

"It's me babe," Rafael hollered. "Are you okay?"

She swiftly tossed everything in her laptop bag including her phone. She closed her bedroom door then rushed toward the front door. She looked around just to make sure she hid everything that could raise questions.

"Just a minute," she hollered.

She took a deep breath before opening the door.

"Hey Raf."

"Hey, you okay? I've tried calling you several times," he said before kissing her on her forehead and handing her a handful of flowers with a large sized envelope.

"These are nice Raf," she smiled. "What's this for?"

"I just wanted to put a smile on your face and the envelope is for you to open. I want your opinion about it, but since you haven't answered your phone I figured I would swing by," he said as he glanced around her living room.

"Oh I'm okay, really I am," she replied when she saw him glance around her living room suspiciously when he walked in.

"Well, you missed our lunch date too," he said, spinning around to face her.

"I totally forgot. I've been so busy with Alana's funeral arrangements it slipped my mind."

"Hmmm, I figured."

"I'm just trying to finalize a couple of things, ya know," she said, avoiding his eyes.

She placed the flowers on her coffee table then sat beside him when he sat on the couch.

"Before you open this, I wanted to tell you that I know you have a lot on your plate. But I've meaning to tell you a couple of things."

"Like what?" she asked nervously.

"First and foremost, I must be the luckiest man alive because I have the most incredible and amazing woman in my life," he said as he leaned toward her.

"Oh yea?" she smiled slyly.

"Yea and the second thing, I was thinking about us taking a trip."

"When?"

"Now."

"Now? I-I can't leave now, I mean, I'm helping Mrs. Inacio with the arrangements and whatnot."

"I know, but I was thinking how nice it would be if we just sailed the seas."

"And go where?"

"Where ever you want to go."

"Okay," she said dryly. "Can we discuss this after the funeral?"

"Sure, take your time," he said when she stared off.

"I just have a lot of things on my mind."

"Wanna talk about it?" he said as he pulled her closer to him.

"Not really," she said in a slight whisper.

"Alright, no pressure. I just want you to know that I've noticed you've been under a lot of stress and I thought maybe going away could do you some good. I just want you to take out some time for yourself before you have a nervous breakdown babe."

"I know. We will when this is all over," she said.

"I'm going to hold you to it," he said jokingly.

She looked away, refusing to say a word or look at him.

"I don't want to overcrowd you, but know that I'm here for you."

"I know," she said with a cracked voice. "Everything is different."

He pulled her closer to him and closed his eyes while she cried in his arms.

"I mean, this is just insane. When Monte called me Thursday night, I was a little baffled by what he said. At first, I thought it was a hoax or a sick joke until I opened my eyes and looked at the clock." Sniff. "I will never forget it. When I jumped in the car and headed toward Lana's, everything seemed like it was moving in slow motion. By the time I showed up at her place, it was chaotic. I mean," sniff, "you could smell death in the hallway before you even walked in her place." Sniff. "When I saw Monte, he was covered in her blood and that's when I lost it," she said as tears stained her face.

"What do you mean he found her? What was he doing there in the first place? I mean, I thought he said they were going out after they left Night's Owl?"

"After Alana and Skyler had words, she didn't feel like going anymore. Instead, she said they were going back to her place."

"How do you know this for sure? Wasn't Alana notorious for calling you when she invited someone to stay with her? Or if she intended to stay somewhere?"

"Yes but....."

"But what? What makes this time any different?" he quizzed.

"Raf, when we left Night's Owl, she told me their plans had changed, so I assume there was no need to call me," she said with slight agitation.

"Babe, I'm not trying to upset you. It just seems like Monte's name is written all over Alana's death," he replied with a serious look on his face.

"Monte didn't do it," she said matter of fact.

"How do you know?"

"Why would he? He cared about her."

"Or did he?"

"He showed me his..."

"He could've showed you anything to make you believe he's someone else or what he wants you to think he is."

"Rafael!" she said with disdain.

Micah stared at the wall hoping what he insinuated was a lie. She hesitantly looked at him while her own thoughts danced around in her head as he continued to talk.

"I hope, for your sake, that he didn't do it," he said with a final tone.

She leaned into his shoulder and tucked her legs underneath her without saying a word. He blew out a long sigh and kissed the top of her head.

She reached for the letter sized envelope, opened it then pulled out the contents and stared at it for a moment. It was his most beautiful work thus far. It was the cover of the rough draft of Alana standing in the ocean in front of the setting red-orange sun near black sand.

"Wow, this is absolutely beautiful," she mumbled. She stared at her picture in a daze as her tears welled back into her eyes. "She was beautiful."

"It came out amazing. She would be pleased. Babe, you sure you're not doing too much? I mean, you're helping the family arrange everything and ...."

"I'm just trying to stay busy. It seems like when everything is calm and quiet, her death hits me all over again."

"Just don't do too much. You're only one person."

"I know, but I don't mind helping out her family. Besides, she was the sister I've always wanted because I grew up in a house full of boys. You know we spent a lot of time together. We got our hair and nails done, went shopping together. Oh my goodness, even though she was my boss, she was a very good friend," she said as tears stained her face again.

"Baby, don't cry," he said as he wiped them as they fell down her cheek. "I know this is hard right now, but everything will be ok."

He grabbed her so she could lean into his chest. She pressed her body into his chest and thought about the days' events. She knew she had to tell someone, but the only name that came to mind was Monte. Telling him could damage the case since he was still a suspect, so she digressed from the thought. He kissed her softly on the lips before telling her he only stopped by to give her the picture. She walked him to the door and called his name softly.

"Raf?"

"Yes babe."

"Why did you give Clifton my number?"

"Did you mind?"

"I did actually. You know I don't like for other people to give out my number unless I'm asked."

"I'm sorry babe. He said he wanted to check on you and offer a helping hand. I didn't see anything wrong with that. He's really not a bad guy."

"Well, I choose the company I keep and he's one I stay away from."

"Don't think like that. You see what he's done for Lana?"

"I see what he's done for himself," she retorted.

"You sound like you dislike him."

"Let's say, I'd rather keep my distance from him."

"Okay, okay," he said. "I apologize for giving him your number without your consent. It'll never happen again."

She thanked him then closed the door after he walked away. She walked into her bedroom, picked up her purse then pulled out Lt. Garcia's business card she received when she arrived at Lana's place after Monte called her the night she was murdered. She immediately dialed his number. She left a message on his voicemail telling him that she was coming to the office first thing in the morning. She slipped inside of her covers, tossed the phone near her pillow then cried herself to sleep.

The next morning Micah arrived at the police station looking for someone who seemed remotely professional. A couple of officers stood around picking their noses, while the others gathered around looking at the internet. A man with a raspy voice approached her without smiling.

"Hello."

"Hi, my name is Micah Richardson and I'm here to see Lt. Garcia," she said as she walked into Miami-Dade County Police Station.

"Hold on for a second," the police officer stated as he picked up the phone.

Micah looked around the coffee stained spilled office as they smiled at her flirtatiously. She smiled weakly toward them then looked back at the pot belly officer who was helping her.

"Garcia, you have a Micah Richardson here to see you," he said into the phone.

The officer hung up the phone and leaned toward her with a smile until a rookie cop passed him with a stack of files close to his chest.

"Rookie, take this pretty little lady into one of the interrogating room near Garcia's office."

"I'm actually doing something for ..."

"I don't give a shit what you're doing. Do what I said now," he said authoritatively.

The rookie lazily smiled at Micah before he escorted her to an empty interrogating room. He told her Lt. Garcia should be out as soon as possible and offered her a cup of coffee, but she declined. She pulled out her laptop just as the doors opened.

"Ms. Richardson?"

"Yes sir?"

"Hi, I'm Lt. Garcia and this is my partner Detective Phelps again, how are you?" he said with an extended hand.
"I'm okay thank you."

Something was strikingly familiar about him, but she couldn't put a finger on it and it was beyond seeing him at Alana's murder scene.

"So, you called me yesterday saying you had something for me to see," he said, interrupting her thoughts.

"I did."

"Okay before we get started, could you tell me who you are to

Ms. Inacio?"

"I'm her...actually was her personal assistant," she said quietly.

"Oh okay, well what do you have for us," Phelps said as they pulled a chair beside her to look at her laptop.

The officers weren't sure what they were looking for and impatiently huffed just when Skyler appeared on the screen. They watched the screen as if it was a movie and Skyler was the debut actress, watching and listening for anything incriminating. As he watched the video, Garcia did a double take at the jaw dropping feature before looking at Phelps and Micah.

"I'll be damned, she has an identical twin sister."

Mirror image...

Tyler and Skyler Sutton shared the same facial characteristics, witty personality, weight, height, chestnut brown eyes and hair to match. They were mirror imaged twins and no one could tell them apart including their parents, which was the very reason why they weren't raised in the same household. They were separated when Skyler was sent to Brazil because of their demonic practical jokes they played on everyone. Tyler was raised by their father who was a genius in his own right. Determined to be her own person, Tyler refused to be an exotic dancer or pursue modeling like her younger sibling by one minute. She received a four-year scholarship from an Ivy League University which landed her a solid position as an Assistant Manager at a local bank outside of Vegas.

For four years, she learned the ins and outs of the financial chain before persuading her sister and her companions to invest their money with her. Tyler created a secret account for Skyler and hid the money in a place where Ric couldn't find it. Out of the blue, Tyler received a disturbing call from Skyler saying that she was in Miami and needed her right away. Tyler sensed desperation in her tone and quickly jumped on a plane to South Beach, following her sister. Exhausted and tired from the days' event, she checked into a hotel and quickly made herself a chilled Mimosa with fresh strawberries. As soon as she pressed her lips against the rim of her flute, her phone buzzed. She glanced at the time and quickly replied to the text, hoping to take care of some new unfinished business before her sister arrived. She sipped from her glass then laid across the bed and closed her eyes before she heard someone yelling and banging on the door.

"Open up Ty," a familiar voice yelled from the other side of the door.

Tyler recognized her sister's voice before opening the door and a smile grazed her face.

"Why are you so loud Sky?" Tyler asked Skyler when she rushed in. "What's the rush?"

"Gotta pee. Oh, don't close the door, my friend is getting the stuff out of the car," Skyler voiced from the bathroom.

"Friend?" Tyler mumbled to herself, while her brows met. "I thought we agreed, no friends."

Tyler closed the door slightly, moved the curtains to the side from the window so she could take a good look at her sisters' friend. She watched her carefully until she walked toward the door with a couple of bags in her hands. She held the door open until she walked in the hotel room without noticing anyone standing behind the door. She closed the door behind her and looked at her sisters' friend.

Dana turned around and smiled at the woman standing in front of her when she heard the toilet flush. She wasn't sure if Skyler's sister would be in the restroom long enough for her to sneak in a quick kiss, but as soon as she took one step forward the bathroom door swung open. In a state of shock, she quickly dropped the bags to the floor and took a step back when Skyler cleared her throat.

Dana jumped back, looked at one, then the other, in a daze as they conversed as if she wasn't in the room. She closed her eyes hoping to recognize the different tone in their voices, but she couldn't. Even their voices were the same.

"Damn Sky, you didn't tell me you were an identical twin," Dana blurted.

"We don't tell anyone," she said before looking back to her sister. "So what did he say Ty?"

"Skyler, we need to talk, *privately*," she said as she looked at her sister's friend.

Skyler looked at her sister then at Dana.

"What's the problem?" Skyler asked.

Tyler grabbed Skyler's arm then pulled her across the room.

"You know how I feel about bringing people when we meet," she whispered. "No one has ever seen us together and we promised that's how it was going to be from now on."

"Ty, chill out. She's good people."

"I don't give a damn about her being good people, you and I had an agreement," Tyler said with clenched teeth.

Tyler shook her head disappointedly just before her phone buzzed. She quickly responded to the message just as Skyler tried walked away.

"I don't feel comfortable talking business in front of your friend."

"So what are we going to talk about? I mean really Ty, I trust her."

"Well I don't," she whispered.

"I am in the room," Dana shot back.

They both looked at each other then paused before Skyler walked towards Dana.

Tyler watched her sister interact with her friend and took a long deep breath. She had a migraine headache, an interrupted business deal and now a new set of eyes watching her every move. She looked at her phone when it buzzed and responded quickly.

"How much money are we talking? You know the rules, we don't meet," she said to herself when she replied to the message.

There were certain things Tyler refused to share with her sister when it came to her business and vice versa. Tyler finished her mimosa before walking toward her sister and her friend.

"So you weren't even going to tell me?" Dana quizzed Skyler in a hushed tone.

"Dana please," Skyler shot back with widen eyes before her sister walked up to them.

Tyler looked past Skyler, concentrating on her friend oddly, until Skyler cleared her throat. She didn't feel comfortable talking about anything around her sister's friend, but she went with the flow.

"Ty, did you go there? What happened?"

Skyler was going to make Tyler tell her whether she liked it or not. Tyler rolled her eyes childishly.

"Ahem. Ty, hello? What happened?"

"He was rude and pissed," she said with a stare.

"Rude and pissed?"

"That sounds like him. Did you do what I told you to do?"

"Yes, I sat down and the server approached me. You should've seen the look on his face," Tyler chuckled then slapped her hands together. "He looked very uncomfortable. It was too hilarious, I just played along," she laughed.

"Isn't he sexy?" Skyler asked.

"He's too arrogant for me, but you already know he's not my type."

"What else did he say?"

"He really couldn't say much because his server was in the way, which pissed him off even more."

"Oh, must have been Mesa. Petite girl with a pretty face?"

"Yea."

"She's really good. She knows exactly what I like."

"I see. She gave me a glass of Vodka raspberry lemonade. What a delicate intrusion."

"You should've tried the Mango Martini, you would've liked that one too."

"Hell, before I could get a good look at the menu, Clifton started cursing me out."

"Clif....?" Skyler said until Dana interrupted her.

"Who? Clifton?"

"Hold up Sky, and who are you again?" Tyler asked Dana with a straight face.

"I'm Sky's.....," Dana said until Skyler cut her off.

"Friend," Skyler blurted out quickly. "And Dana, this is my sister Tyler."

"Friend?" Tyler scoffed, without taking her eyes off her. "So, how did you two meet again?" she asked Dana, ignoring Skyler's stares.

"Ty, you need to focus. What did he say?"

"We have plenty of time to talk about it Sky," Tyler shooed Skyler. "Anyway, I'm really curious who your friend is because this is a first," Tyler said sarcastically.

"Tyler!" Skyler exclaimed.

"No, I mean anyone that cuts off my conversation needs more than an introduction. She needs to speak so I'm letting her. Go 'head Dana, the floor is yours."

"Ty, why are you doing this?" Skyler said with clenched teeth.

"I have my reasons. I mean, I don't care for your men selection, but your interest in women has always been eye candy," Tyler said, undressing Dana with her eyes.

"Ty, stop playing?"

"You're so stiff, relax Sky."

"Ty, I know I asked you to switch for me, but don't drown me with all your foolishness."

Dana listened.

"Sis, you know we and it has its perks," Tyler said with a cynical laugh. "So like I said, I'm listening."

Dana relaxed a little when Skyler reluctantly explained to her sister how they met. Tyler listened intensely but her eyes saw more than two girls sleeping with each other. Something wasn't quite right, but instead of voicing it, she just observed and smiled at them. While the sisters conversed, Dana slipped away saying that she was tired and was in dire need for a long soothing bath. Tyler watched her disappear behind the bathroom door then stared at her sister.

"What?" Skyler quizzed.

"I told you that I didn't feel comfortable talking business around her. You see how she was all in our business? I wasn't even talking to her."

"Next time I will make sure I come by myself."

"I would appreciate it because if you're not solo, I'm not meeting you. I don't need people in my business."

"Ty, I have enough shit on my plate right now to be fussing with you."

"This is the very reason why you need to handle your business better."

Skyler looked toward the bathroom door then leaned closer to her sister.

"How can I when Ric brought his ass to Miami and he's still fucking with me?"

"See there, that's what I be talking about. I told you to leave his ass alone when you were at Scores. You should've listened to that crazy ass lady when she tried to tell you about him in the first place. But oh no, you can't tell Skyler shit," Tyler fussed.

Skyler grimaced while Tyler chastised her.

"So, what's new with Ric?"

"Who knows? Always muscling someone out of something. He's saying that I stole his money."

"Hell, you did."

"Shhh, no I didn't Ty."

"Why are you shushing me? He can't prove it, just keep telling your story. We can finesse your paperwork at the bank so it will look like you were saving your money long before him. He's just trying you."

"I hope you're right."

"I am. You should've never taken his money in the first place."

"That was my money! I worked my ass off for my money," Skyler said with clenched teeth, leaping to her feet.

"Hey, no need to raise your voice at me. You and I both know you gave it to him then stole it from him while his ass was asleep. Very smart Skyler," she said sarcastically.

"Whatever, I gave his ass plenty of money."

"Yea, like an ass. Just ignore him, all he's doing is messing with you."

"How can I? Now he's threatening me."

"Fuck Ric. One of these days you're going to listen to me. I keep telling you that these men you keep linking up with ain't hitting on shit. All they ever did was pimp you. Damn Sky, see pass the money and see it for what it's worth. I swear sometimes..."

"Nobody is pimping me."

"Hmph, that's what you think? I'll let you have that."

Skyler looked at her sister, but refused to say a word. Instead she just looked the other way disgusted by her comment.

"Look, I have a friend of mine that works at the bank here in Miami. I managed to pull a couple of strings so you can have access to your money here in Miami."

"All of it?"

"Of course not."

"Good, whatever is left back home, you can have it."

"I know. That money is in a savings account for Kyler."

Skyler quickly looked away.

"You really need to take care of yourself. This fast money is going to do you more harm than good in the end."

"This fast money is going to buy me a ticket out of here."

"And where are you going to hide this time? The D.R. or Paris? You need to stay put long enough and get some real business about yourself. As soon as I wrap up some unfinished business, I'm jumping on the first plane out of here. You all can have this."

Skyler tossed her sister her duffle bag hoping to shut her up.

"What's this?"

"Money."

Tyler unzipped it then quickly looked at her.

"Look at all these loose bills," she said in disappointment.

"It still spends the same."

"This is what you rather do in exchange for modeling?"

"There is no comparing to how much money I can get in one night instead of one set."

"Oh the bigger payout, the more intrigued you are."

"Yep."

"That's worth shattering your dreams?"

"I'm not getting into that," Skyler said, returning Tyler's piercing stare.

"Why not? You never want to talk about it."

"Because that's a closed chapter in my life."

"You know the stipulations Skyler."

"And so do you," Skyler spat.

Skyler walked off, thinking back when she lived in Brazil with Alana's family. Mr. Luis Inacio was the one who introduced her into modeling. A slight smile flashed across her face when she thought back when modeling brought her so much happiness until she remembered how it all ended. It was the eve of her fifteenth birthday and she'd won first place in the teen division with Alana placing second. The Brazilian community found Skyler's chestnut eyes and hair attractively odd, drawing in multiple first places. Skyler's beauty was nothing compared to Alana's, but Skyler's charisma captivated the crowd and won her the crown. She wasn't as shy as Alana and when Luis noticed, he began sneaking Skyler into older crowds where the prize paid more money. Once Luis convinced her to entertain the men, the payout became lucrative. Skyler's breast and curvaceous body lured Luis and his friend's attention. He would get her into more gigs in exchange for a rub or a touch, but it quickly turned into sex. Once she revealed to him that she was pregnant with his child, he shunned her. Quickly blackmailing and exposing her pregnancy which denied her any chance to model in Brazil and an immediate termination of her student exchange experience. Luis quickly shipped her back to Vegas with the money for an abortion with nowhere to go before she could tell anyone who the father was.

When Skyler returned to Vegas, she was heartless and scorned. She didn't want to carry the baby anymore and made adoption arrangements, but Tyler intercepted. Skyler told her that this would be their secret and the baby would become her niece. She promised to provide for her financially. When Skyler had the baby, she signed in the hospital as Tyler Sutton so no paperwork would be needed afterwards. Their father worked double shift when Tyler told him she was having a baby.

After Skyler tried to model with a growing belly but they agency denied her. When her mother refused to sign off the papers for her to expand her options outside of Nevada, she started exploring it on her own. She watched the child grow from a distance, resisting a connection with the child that mirrored her and Tyler.

When she reconnected with Alana, Skyler never mentioned her pregnancy but in Skyler's heart, she couldn't tell Alana that the child she was carrying was her half-sister, so she omitted it and swore to never repeat it.

"So that's it? You don't even care about her?" Tyler interrupted her thoughts.

"I never said I didn't care about her."

"You don't have to say it, you show it. You never ask about her. You never say her name and you never call her on her birthday which happens to be on the same day as Alana's."

"Tyler, I really don't want to talk about this right now."

"So, when are we going to talk about this Sky? You never want to talk about it."

"Ty please," she said, rolling her eyes.

"Okay then, fine. It's truly your lost. Kyler's amazing."

"And she has the perfect mother. I love you more because of it," Skyler said as tears welled in her eyes.

Tyler noticed her sadness and quickly dropped the subject. She walked up to her sister and hugged her. Without asking any more questions, she held her sister close to her while she imagined what it was like to have a child by her best friends' father. She stepped back and wiped her sisters' tears.

"I'm sorry. I didn't mean to get you so upset. That was wrong of me, I promise to never mention it again," Tyler said.

"It's okay. I know my mistakes."

"Yea, but it's not my place to remind you."

"Well, you're a better mother than I will ever be."

"I love her because she came from you."

Skyler smiled at her sister before noticing a business card on the table. She walked towards it and picked it up.

"Who is Lt. Garcia?"

"I saw him at Night's Owl. He's one of the investigators on Alana's case."

"Alana's case? What's going on with her?" she asked cautiously with pause.

"When was the last time you spoke to her?"

Skyler stopped in mid step as her heart rapidly paced in her chest.

"I don't know, it's been a couple of days," she guessed.

"Really?" Tyler said, not paying attention to her body language.

"Yea, but I need to call and check on her."

"I thought you and her talked quite often. Wasn't that the reason why you're here?"

"Alana's been doing her modeling thing so she's been out of town lately."

"Hmm, so I've heard," Tyler said. "I also heard she's dead."

"She's what?" Skyler said, spinning around.

"Dead."

Skyler's mind immediately spun into a frenzy. Alana's bloody face stained her memory, but the smell of Alana's blood sickened her. She looked around the room and met Dana's eyes when she walked out of the restroom.

"Are you okay?" Dana asked a pale Skyler.

"I need to....um....call...," Skyler said before passing out onto the floor.

When Skyler's body collapsed, Tyler and Dana hurriedly ran to her side while Lt. Garcia sat across from Russel Simmons. He twirled his ink pen while Russel tapped on the table and replayed the actions of the night.

"Ok Mr. Simmons, I heard you have a new girl by the name of Skyler Sutton that works there."

"Yea, Pretty Sky is what we call her."

"Pretty Sky?"

"Yea."

"Where is she from? Mind me asking?"

"From back home, Vegas."

"Vegas...," he repeated and jotted down.

"When was the last time you seen or spoke to her?"

"The other night, at the club, when the fight broke out."

"Do you know where she is at the moment?"

"No, but I'm sure Dana Ramirez knows where she is. Hell, it's more than likely that they are together."

"Dana Ramirez," Garcia jotted down.

"..and who's that?"

"My girl."

"Your girlfriend or your girl from the club?" Garcia said when a knock sounded on the door.

"I need your assistance," Phelps said.

"Mr. Simmons, can you finish your statement? I'll be right back."

Phelps filled Garcia in with Ric Simmons being uncooperative in the next room. Garcia marched in the room with a zero tolerance stance.

"So are you ready to talk now?" Garcia said as he closed the door behind him.

"Not until I have a lawyer."

"Well, you can get a lawyer Mr. Simmons, but we have already called Las Vegas Police Department. You will be extradited and will face the charges which are pending against you when you get there, but as of now you're being held here for questioning."

"Questioning? For what?" Ric growled, as he stood to his feet.

"Sit down," Garcia calmly said as three officers restrained Ric.

"The fuck? You told me if I cooperated with you, you would let me go!" Ric spat.

"Yea, that was before I received your thick ass file for facing charges of solicitation of prostitution, drug-smuggling, and whatnots. Should I go on?" he said, flipping through his file which was faxed over.

Ric sat down with rage as Garcia walked around the room, with his hands stuffed in his pockets, staring into the black window with his fellow officers watching him on the other side.

"So, Russ tells me that you two are brothers," Garcia said.

"Fuck Russ," Ric shot back.

"Oh, sibling rivalry?" Garcia said while staring at his reflection from the window.

"I ain't got shit to say to him."

"Yea, I get that," Garcia said nonchalantly.

"Fuck you!"

"Fuck me?" he said calmly, "throw his ass in holding cell four."

The officers escorted Ric to his feet then walked him to the holding cell while Garcia walked back to Russ's room, read over his statement then released him. He was very cooperative, thanked the officers and left the station.

Garcia looked at Phelps with frustration.

"Now, our issue right now is getting a lead on Inacio's case and that should be our *only* focus and not Parks' petty drug use. We need evidence that is concrete and that starts with those tapes. We have to watch those tapes, take notes and verify everyone's time checks. At this point, everyone is a suspect. The Simmons brothers, Parks, Ms. Sutton, her twin, Micah, Alana's fiancé and even Montgomery."

"Actually, they just cleared Montgomery," Garcia said.

"Good. That's minus one but look at what we have on our plate. We have seven people we need investigate and we don't have the time for any further distractions. Now, we need to sit down, watch Night's Owl and South Beach Estate tapes and screen check everyone so we can draw some type of conclusion or motive. I won't let your personal feelings entertain Parks right now. I swear to you, we'll get him, but right now, our focus is Alana and finding her murderer," Detective Phelps voiced.

Phelps sharpness slightly baffled Garcia, but he had a point. They had no clue and time was running out. His sister's plane had landed and wanted a full report of what he gathered when he sat down with her. He knew how painful it was to endure such tragedy from the loss of your own child. So for Garcia, delivering some news was better than none.

"Garcia?" Phelps repeated.

"Yea. Yea?" he stammered.

"You alright? Are you with me? Are we on the same page?"

"We are and you're right. I think I'm just so....," he tried to find the right words.

"Overwhelmed," Phelps suggested. "I know what happened to your son and I'm sure this hit close to home."

Garcia looked at him.

"You have no idea," Garcia said, as he pulled out a handkerchief.

"I know this is your last and final call of duty, but you're known for solving all of your cases and this one is no different. If it gets too much, just tell me what to do and I'll step in and do it. We're partners and that's what partners do."

Garcia smiled at Phelps and extended his hand.

"Partner?"

"Partner," Phelps repeated. "Now, do we need to bring Parks in for questioning?"

Garcia ran his trembling hand through his hair then took a deep breath.

"Yes," he said.

"Well let me get a warrant for his arrest and take it from there," Phelps said as he stood to his feet.

"Okay."

"I'll see you in a few," he said patting Garcia on the shoulders. "And remember, you don't have to carry this burden by yourself."

Garcia watched him walk off and thought to himself.

He reminds me of a younger me. He's gonna make a hell of a Lieutenant or even Captain one day.

Retracting my steps...

Lt. Garcia leaned his head into his folded hands which rested behind him with his eyes closed while the prescribed pills he'd taken thirty minutes ago digested into his system. So many different thoughts replayed in his mental archive, but things just weren't adding up when he jotted down what he knew about the case.

He picked up the phone, dialed the dispatch number then looked over his notepad.

"Lt. Garcia here. Can you pull up the recorded time for me when I was dispatched last week for the South Beach Estates homicide call?"

"Sure, give me one minute Lieutenant," she said, putting him on hold. He looked over his notes which indicated he spoke to Monte at ten thirty.

"Lt. Garcia?" the dispatcher called out when she returned to the phone, "the time recorded for you when you were dispatched at South Beach Estates is nine forty-five."

"Thank you."

"So, ten o'clock," he said aloud. "It took me about five to ten minutes to get to South Beach Estates...., but I was with Catalina....So, let's say I got there around ten after ten," he said, jotting the times on his notepad while his cell phone hummed.

He looked at it and smile to himself.

"Hello...," he sang in the phone.

"Hey babe, how are you?" Catalina said.

"I'm better now that your voice is on the other end of my phone."

"Are we still on for tonight babe?"

"Yes, what time do you want to meet?" Garcia said, glancing

170

at his watch.

"We can meet around ten o'clock, is that too late?"

"No, that's fine. I have a prior engagement at eight o'clock so that's perfect," he said, looking at his office phone.

"I've missed you."

"I've missed you too," he said to her.

"How's the case coming along?"

"The case is time sensitive."

"Hmmm....," she said as if something had distracted her.

"You okay?"

"Yea, let me call you back," she said.

"Okay," he said while disconnecting the call just as Phelps walked in the office.

"I got 'em," he waved the discs in the air. "You ready to watch them?"

"Sure am."

Garcia picked up his pad then stood to his feet. He trailed Phelps and quickly looked at his watch just to make sure he wasn't behind schedule.

"Okay man, I can sit here until seven o'clock. I have a date with Catalina tonight and nothing, I mean nothing or no one is messing up this date," Garcia said as he pulled off his jacket.

"I understand boss," Phelps chuckled to himself. "Let me hurry up and play this disc so we can see what we're working with," he said as they walked into the surveillance roomed office.

"Hey Sgt. Webster, my name is Det. Phelps and this is my partner..."

"The notorious Lt. Garcia," Webster said before shaking his hands.

Sgt. Webster was undoubtedly highly skilled and graduated top of the class, but there was one flaw. Sgt. Webster was a woman and most of the guys in the force didn't take her seriously. Her resume was quite impressive though. She inquired to the Captain about a possible detective job, but he always dismissed her inquiries. She also graduated from the University of Florida and majored in Criminal Justice, but that still didn't impress the Captain. She heard a lot about Lt. Garcia, but never met him and this was the first time she was in his presence.

"Hello, it's nice to finally meet you ...," Garcia said as he looked at her name badge, "Sgt. Webster."

"It's nice to meet you too."

"So, you're going to be the one to help us view these discs?"

"Yes sir."

"Good, let's get on the ball. We have a case to break."

"Great, Phelps did you pick up the disc?" she asked.

"I did, here they are," he said as he handed them to her.

"Please have a seat so I can tell you how this works as we view it. If you would like for me to stop, zoom in or out, just let me know.

Garcia pulled out a chair and sat beside Phelps and Sgt. Webster as they watched the Night's Owl surveillance disc on their fast paced Quad Security Systems Surveillance as the time read six o'clock on the bottom right hand corner of the screen. The surveillance was an excellent fast paced copy showing Skyler, Clifton and an unfamiliar woman setting the tables and placing ornaments in the center of each them. It showed Clifton storming off, and the ladies looked occupied until Skyler pulled something from her pocket. Garcia looked closely as the ladies snorted something from the plastic wrapped package. He quickly jotted on his notepad then looked back toward the screen. The ladies disappeared for forty-five minutes until Alana, Monte, Micah, and her male guest arrived.

"Pause that," Garcia blurted to Webster, "who is that walking with Micah?" Garcia asked, before looking at Phelps.

"I don't know, never seen him before," Phelps said, while taking a closer look at the screen.

Garcia jotted again, so he could reference it later.

"We need to get his name as well as the young lady with Skyler," Garcia said without taking his eyes from the screen. "They could possibly play a part in this investigation.

"Sure thing," Phelps jotted for himself.

"Okay, go 'head," Garcia said.

Webster proceeded and Night Owl's began to fill quickly. Clifton escorted Alana and Monte to their table, which was centered amongst the crowd. Phelps noticed Monte looking at his watch, but quickly remembered Garcia said he was cleared as a suspect from the case. Clifton busied himself and walked to the podium before the balloons filled the air.

"Go back," Garcia blurted.

Webster hit the back button, but wasn't sure what she'd

missed. Garcia voiced for her to stop it then replay it again. Phelps looked at the screen, but hadn't noticed anything out of the ordinary either.

"Stop," Garcia blurted again.

Webster did as instructed but she and Phelps weren't sure what they were looking at. Garcia's heart raced but instead of verbalizing what he saw, he simply studied the scenic view without uttering a word.

"Go 'head," Garcia said.

Webster continued to play the disc while Phelps asked her to give him an overview shot of the establishment and she did as follows. Garcia sat in a trance until Phelps called out his name again. Since he didn't budge, Phelps leaned toward Webster.

"Hit pause for me Webster," Phelps said to Webster in a whispery tone. "Garcia, are you okay?" he said, leaning up to him.

"Yea-yea, I'm alright, keep playing the disc," Garcia said in a nonchalant tone. "Don't worry about me, just focus on the screen so we can connect the dots."

Phelps noticed something odd about Garcia's tone, but refused to verbalize it while Webster was around. He was slightly taken aback by his comment and his mannerisms, but he didn't entertain it. Phelps figured the case was starting to get the best of him and left well alone. Instead, he leaned back into his chair and watched Skyler carry a beautiful bouquet of tulips to Alana's table. Webster, Garcia and Phelps watched Alana and Monte dance with smiles on their faces, but Garcia noticed a bigger picture other than them dancing. Immediately after they shared a dance and walked toward their table, a man walked in the background looking around suspiciously.

"Who is that guy that just came in?" Garcia voiced.

"I'm not sure," Phelps replied, looking at the man as if he'd seen him before.

Garcia jotted in his notepad of the man's description and kept his eyes on the mysterious guy as he walked toward a startled Clifton before publicly handing him a small package.

"So, is that Clifton's drug dealer?" Garcia voiced.

"Looks like it," Webster said.

"Yea, this cat is bold. I mean he does it all in the open," Phelps added.

"I tried to tell you, we can get him," Garcia said matter of factly.

"And we will," Phelps said reassuringly.

The officers watched Clifton look around before he walked his guest toward the exit door, but his guest took a detour. The guest walked away toward Alana. Garcia watched closely as Alana's table looked displeased by his presence when he arrived uninvited.

"Who the hell is that?" Garcia asked.

Garcia looked at Phelps with a puzzled stare before looking back toward the screen. The gentleman leaned toward Alana then she stood to her feet just as Monte grabbed her hand.

"Looks like Monte didn't want her to go," Phelps said.

"Looks like she didn't want to go either," Webster added.

She's just as stubborn as her mother, Garcia said to himself while looking at his niece.

Garcia continued to watch the film, but it was difficult for Garcia to read their body language. It appeared that the two of them were having a disagreement by the way she quickly snatched her hand away then looked away. Garcia immediately sat straight up in his seat, disliking what he witnessed, keeping his muffled comments to himself. The conversation between the two of them seemed heated, but the male guest mannerisms were easily compared to an abusive man.

"Did you see that?" Phelps called out.

"I did. We really need to find out what his name is and bring him in for questioning."

"We might have our suspect," Phelps voiced.

"Not so soon, we still have about two hours and forty minutes to play with."

"Two hours and forty minutes?" Phelps asked.

"Yes, that's the time I spoke to Monte while we were at Alana's," Garcia said, while looking at his notes.

Immediately, Garcia looked up and noticed the male guest storming off.

"Whoa, wait a minute. Back it up a couple seconds, why did he just storm off?"

Webster backed it up while they all watched the male guest talk to Alana near the bar. She tried to turn and walk away from him, but just as soon as she turned to leave she quickly turned and looked at him sharply. Seconds later, he grabbed her arm and like a raging bull until she snatched it away from him before he pointed his finger in her face then stormed off just as Skyler and Micah appeared by her side.

Garcia watched his niece on the monitor closely and realized to himself he hadn't participated in any of her modeling auditions nor supported her in her modeling career and that made his guilty conscience eat at him but he said nothing. Instead he dropped his head, shaking it slightly and notating something on his notepad in detail.

"Webster, stop it. Garcia, look at the screen," Phelps said, interrupting Garcia's thoughts as he jotted on his note pad.

Garcia looked up and noticed Micah cutting off Skyler's stride.

"What in the hell just happened?" Garcia voiced. "And you're sure we can't hear what they are saying Webster?" Garcia said, slightly agitated sitting on the edge of his chair.

"Um.....no, we can't," Webster said nervously.

Garcia studied the monitor, hoping to find something more incriminating that could've possibly led to her death. Since that was the obvious last public place anyone saw her alive, he felt like the clue was right in front of him. The time read seven thirty and things appeared chaotic, but he had to retract his steps. Skyler and Alana stood face to face while their hand gesture indicated they were arguing or having a heated discussion.

Quickly, Alana slapped Skyler just as Micah rushed in and pulled Alana away from her while Clifton pushed her back. Clifton turned to Skyler as if he was arguing with her as the other customers gathered their things when Alana, Monte and Micah left the restaurant. Micah's guest stayed behind and walked toward a heated Clifton. Garcia studied the screen carefully because Clifton handed him a small package, just moments after they stood and talked.

"Hit pause," Garcia voiced. "See that, this is the second time we caught him doing a transaction in his establishment on film."

"Ya know, I can print any picture you want from this monitor," Webster said.

"Can you?" Garcia said when he looked at Phelps.

"Yes, matter of fact, when we're done I'll do that so you can take the pictures with you."

"Thank you Webster."

"No problem Lieutenant."

Garcia stared at the gentleman on the screen as if he was taking a mental picture.

"You want to see the rest of the film?" Webster asked.

"What's the time on the screen?"

Webster resumed the footage and all of them looked at the displayed time which read seven forty-seven. Phelps noticed Skyler talking to the same young lady who helped her set the tables earlier. They were engulfed in a serious conversation until Clifton walked up to them with an attractive young lady by his side.

"You know what I was thinking...," Garcia said, turning around only to stare at the screen alongside Phelps.

Garcia was baffled when he saw Catalina hugged up with Clifton on the screen. He saw her earlier standing behind him near the podium, but thought that maybe she was there as a customer. Although it did puzzle him that she was in the background, he didn't know she knew Clifton. Countless nights, he remembered discussing many issues that concerned Parks and often wondered how he knew certain critical information. And now looking at the screen, everything made sense to him. He watched the monitor closely as she slowly kissed Clifton on his lips before they disappeared from the crowd with flirtatious smiles covering their faces.

Garcia covered his mouth, disgusted by what he witnessed then looked away. He saw Skyler sitting at the bar, like she said she was when they talked a few days ago, but his heart was now in his stomach and at this point, he'd seen what he needed to see.

"Webster, the display says eight o' clock, let's speed up. Alana and Monte left around seven forty-five so let's go to seven forty-five at South Beach Estates," Garcia said.

"Sure thing."

"Would anyone like anything to drink?" Phelps offered.

"No thanks," Garcia and Webster said in unison.

Garcia looked at his phone when it buzzed in his pocket. He looked at it, noticing Catalina's text message. It read, I miss you and can't wait to see you tonight."

Garcia closed his phone without responding to her message.

No words could express how he felt because at that very moment all he wanted to do was throw his fist into Parks mouth. He sat in front of the monitor until Phelps came back with a cup of coffee, stirring it, and checking his messages on his phone as well. Garcia checked the time on his phone before he put it in his jacket pocket, making sure he had enough time to go home and take a shower.

Phelps gave Webster the green light to put in the other disc then pulled his chair beside Garcia and shared his notes for a brief second.

"So what do you think? Do you think we've collected enough information so far?" Phelps asked.

"Not really. I think we have some evidence, but not enough concrete evidence at this point. I mean, there is so much more footage revolving around this case," Garcia said as he rubbed his temples.

Webster sped through the footage until seven forty-five displayed at the bottom corner of the screen. The monitor displayed a few tenants loitering and walking the hallway, but it wasn't overly crowded. Garcia looked at his watch then stared at his notes again while his mind pondered on Catalina and Parks. He scribbled something on his notepad just as Phelps called out his name.

"Garcia, do you have the time of death?" Phelps asked.

"I do," he said as he flipped through his notepad, "um, her autopsy report listed her time of death was between eight thirty and nine thirty," Garcia read.

Phelps watched the tenants come and go as they pleased without a care in the world. Some of them walked in with a crowd wearing one outfit, but left wearing another as if they were about to scout the town. They watched the footage until eight forty five when he saw Monte pull her close to his chest until the elevator took them to her floor. Garcia watched patiently as they reached her door and stepped inside.

"Now we wait."

A half hour later, they watched Monte leave and go towards the stairwell and disappear. Immediately, someone dressed exactly like Monte stepped off the elevator from the opposite side of the floor and walked inside of her place. The door closed behind him and in exactly thirty minutes, Skyler stepped off the elevator and stormed toward Alana's door. She pulled out her key but when twisted the knob, it opened. Skyler looked at the door awkwardly before stepping in.

"Whoa! Wait a minute, hold on, stop it. Stop it," Garcia blurted.

"What's wrong?"

"Now it's nine twenty. Go back, rewind it. I didn't see the first person leave yet, did you?"

"No," Phelps replied.

Webster reversed the footage.

"Stop!" Garcia said as he stood to his feet.

He walked toward the monitor and stared at the screen.

"What's wrong? What is it?" Phelps said as he stood beside him.

"How long does it take to go down one flight of stairs then come back up the elevator?" Garcia said with a stare.

"Maybe about five minutes, if that," Phelps replied.

"Whoa, wait a minute. Are you saying Monte came back another way?"

"Look at the screen."

"I am."

"It's obvious it's him, look at him. He knows where all the cameras are so there's no need to look up at them. He keeps his back toward the camera at all times because I'm sure he already checked them out."

"I don't th-..."

"Keep rolling Webster. Watch this," Garcia said while they watched the screen.

"Okay stop!" Garcia said. "How does he know that her door is unlocked?"

"It's probably instinct, he might've just ..," Phelps stammered.

"Instinct my ass. No one is going to walk up to your door and twist your knob without knocking unless you've been invited to just walk inside."

"Okay, but ...," Phelps said before Garcia cut him off.

"Something isn't right."

"Garcia, I think you're wrong about Monte," Phelps added.

"How so?"

"There is no way he could've been in two places at once. Didn't his boss clear his time?"

"Yea, but..."

"I'm just throwing things out there. We have the surveillance for the entire building, we can go on his floor to make sure he went inside of his place and never walked out, right Webster?"

"That's right. I have the footage, let me scroll and find it."

"But from the look of this video, it's quite convincing that it's a possibility that it could be him," Garcia added.

"I don't believe a man who wears a badge, would disrespect it."

"Just because he wears a badge doesn't mean he's a good guy. How many people in the force do we know take matters into their own hands and get away with it?" Garcia paced the area.

"Plenty, but he's not our guy."

"So what makes him different? We don't really know him. I mean we don't know his values, his respect or loyalty for the badge."

"No we don't, but we have to look at the facts."

Garcia walked in circles and shook his head. He looked at his notes, almost memorizing every line and then stood in front of a second monitor.

"Webster, what do you see?"

I need to retract my steps, Garcia mumbled to himself. *"Did I miss something?"*

"I'm not sure," Webster said.

Phelps stared at the man on the screen, noticing the man's entire outfit including his shoes. He had to look for his own set of clues. Garcia was a bag of emotions and he had to dig deep for his own set of clues, even if that meant overlooking things twice. Phelps memorized the man on the screen while Garcia stared at the other screen.

"Webster, roll this one too, I want to write down the time of events."

"Ok."

Phelps and Garcia watched two separate monitors and jotted down what they witnessed and the times of suspicions. Phelps stared at the second monitor as he watched the impersonator enter Alana's place. He noted the time Skyler arrived and the time she darted out toward the stairs. Within minutes, the murderer left behind Skyler but took the elevator. Thirty minutes later, Monte appeared from the stairwell with a small bag in his hand and opened her door. Phelps watched the monitor closely until the police arrived. Phelps told Webster to let the disc play as he rolled his chair toward Garcia staring at the third monitor. Garcia laughed under his breath, noticing the people at the bar.

"What's so funny boss?" Phelps said.

"You know, ever since Micah showed us that video of Skyler her twin sister, my mind has been running in circles."

"Why is that?"

"Because I'm starting to believe that no one knows she's a twin besides us and Micah."

"Why is that?"

"Because when I asked Skyler or least I thought I was asking Skyler about Alana, she seemed a little distant and uncertain about Ms. Inacio. I thought maybe it was just me, but after seeing this video made me rethink that whole conversation again especially when she said she was at the bar all night."

"Skyler said she, ...wait a minute, that couldn't have been Skyler because she left," Phelps said with a smirk.

"My point exactly."

"So, you mean to tell me that was her twin sister you were talking to at Night's Owl?" Phelps asked, with his hands on his hips.

"Yes it was."

"Whoa, so when did you know?" Phelps asked Garcia.

"I didn't. I was so engulfed with my own thoughts that I didn't pay any attention to it until just now."

"Damn, so do you think she's linked to this murder?"

"I won't say yes or no 'cause at this point, everyone is a suspect in my eyes."

"Well then, we should put an APB out on both of them," Phelps suggested.

"Whoa slow down. I don't think we should jump too soon and let the cat out the bag."

"Why not? They could've schemed up a treacherous plan by now."

"Oh I'm sure we're a little too late by now. At this point, we don't know anything about the twin we need to do a little digging. Never know what the Sutton's are up to."

"Well, how will we get that information?"

"Leave that up to me, I will fill you in with all the details as soon as I find out anything, but in the meantime we need to be careful we're not looking at the same woman since they are identical. Never know who's impersonating who, since they did it so well when I talked with her the last time."

"I know they are identical, but there must be something different about them," Phelps added.

"I'm sure it is because if not, we'll never know one from the other. In the meantime, we have to study these discs until we find it."

"Alright then."

"Oh before I forget, remember I said she said she was near the bar all that night?"

"Yes."

"Well, it turns out she was. Did you know they also wore the same dress?"

"What?" Phelps said in disbelief.

"Yes they did, matter of fact, Webster will you go back for me so I can show Phelps?"

"Okay."

Webster replayed the video as they watched her walk into Night's Owl at seven thirty while things were chaotic between her sister and Alana.

"Isn't she slick?" Phelps said, standing with his arms folded across his chest. "She was in the back all this time?"

"And no one paid any attention to her. Now get this, after the commotion ended look at Skyler. Watch what her and her female companion does," Garcia said, pointing to the monitor.

Phelps watched as they circled one another snorting cocaine.

"Wow, she has a habit."

"Indeed, but look how paranoid she becomes after she pulls out her cell phone. No worries, we have her phone records, so we can verify that."

"So is that the reason why she rushed over to her place?" Phelps concluded.

"I'm sure."

"Ok, so we know she left Night's Owl and by the way she stormed out, we know she saw something," Webster asked.

"Do you think she walked in while he was in the act?" Phelps questioned.

"Maybe. Maybe not. She could've walked in and helped, or startled the murderer. Until we talk to her and find out, we'll never what really happened."

"You think she saw murderer?"

"Whether she saw the murderer, the act or whatever, she didn't call it in which concerns me."

"I have a question. Who was the guy we saw Clifton talking to earlier?" Phelps asked. "We have names, we just need to match it to right face."

"Webster make sure you print those pictures out."

"On it right now."

"Now we can start trying to figure out these new faces."

"Okay, what about Micah's guest?" Phelps added.

"Oh I forgot about him, is from around here?"

"I'm not sure."

"I have seen his face somewhere, but I'm not sure where though," Garcia said with uncertainty.

Garcia looked at his watch and noticed his time was drawing near for him to meet his sister. His phone buzzed again in his pocket, but he simply ignored it.

"Okay gentleman and ma'am, I need to take care of some business so I will follow up with you later on this evening or first thing in the morning."

Phelps looked at the time, noticing three and a half hours had passed them.

"Garcia you want to pick this up in the morning?"

"That'll work."

"I will stay behind and grab the pictures from Webster."

"Scan them and send them to me regardless of the time."

"Will do."

Garcia thanked Webster again and nodded toward Phelps before he exited the door. He pulled out his phone and viewed Catalina's missed calls. He took a deep breath and redialed her number, hoping not to run a riot act on her.

"Hello?" she sang in the phone.

"Hello," he said dryly.

"Hey are we still on for later on this evening?"

"We are, unless you have something else planned," he said with a pause.

"No, I just want to spend time with you."

"Okay. Where do you want to go?"

"Surprise me."

"Sure. I will call you when I'm on my way," he said with a cynical smile forming in the corner of his mouth.

Tiptoeing on the other side ...

Dezio Garcia was nothing more than seven years older than his sister Aelah Inacio, Alana's mother, but compared to him she was a pit bull in a skirt. Ever since his sister's feet hit Miami's soil, he's been hesitant to see her. She traveled miles wanting answers to unsettling questions only he could answer, but with a guilty conscience and no concrete evidence, he hoped that all the long hours and late nights would pay off.

He paced back and forth inside his living room trying to rehearse the lines he'd practiced ever since he left the office. He quickly straightened out his shirt and took a deep breath when the doorbell rang. He hadn't seen his sister since his son's funeral, so when he opened the front door and saw her standing in front of him, his heart shuddered.

"Oh Dezio," she cried out, falling into his arms.

"Aelah," Garcia said compassionately as they embraced.

He closed the door behind her until it stopped abruptly.

"What the ....," Garcia said under his breath as he looked at the door.

"Be nice," she whispered. "It's Luis."

"Luis? You didn't say anything about him tagging along," he frowned.

"He's still my husband," she whispered, "and he *is* Alana's father."

Garcia looked past his sister at Luis. Luis closed the front door with the food in his hands with no help from Garcia. It was quite obvious that the two men didn't get along.

Luis Inacio never liked Garcia and the feeling was mutual. Garcia heard rumors about him years before he and his sister dated, but when he tried to warn Aelah about his ruthless behavior, she ignored her brother and eloped with Luis. Before Garcia realized the mistake she made, she was pregnant with their first child. Garcia knew Luis ran with a bad crowd, but trying to convince his sister was useless. He fed her lies and kept her pregnant with three boys until they had Alana.

"So, how are you holding up?" Garcia said to his sister.

"As best as I can," she said, trailing behind him. "I know this isn't easy for you either."

"It's not, but my concern is you. I will be okay, I can take it," he said with a deep breath.

"You've lost a lot of weight, are you sure you're okay?"

"Things are stressful these days," Garcia said with raised brows, "but I'm okay."

Garcia invited his sister into his sitting room as Luis trailed behind. He offered her something to drink, but she declined.

"I'll take a scotch," Luis blurted.

"Scotch?" Garcia huffed just as he felt his sister's eyes on his back.

Garcia looked at his sister, displaying a displeased facial expression. She nodded her head then found a seat just as Garcia walked up to his wet bar.

"Aelah, you need to try to eat," Luis said with concern.

"I'll try to nibble later, just put it on the table," she said.

Luis placed the food on the table then walked up to the bar beside Garcia.

"See you got the place looking good. Still small, but I guess big enough for you," Luis said sarcastically.

"Why the hell are you here? I don't have shit to say to you nor did I invite you into my house," Garcia said in a low growl.

"Well technically, we're family and this is a family issue," Luis growled back, hoping not to alert his wife.

"You know, Alana wouldn't be the topic of the discussion tonight if you weren't so damn money hungry."

"And if you were doing your fucking job, we wouldn't be here trying to get answers from you, now would we?"

"You can go to hell, " Garcia said with clenched teeth.

"I'll pass, but I would like a scotch on the rocks," Luis shot back.

"Get it your damn self," Garcia said before walking off.

He walked toward his sister as she patted the seat beside her while she nibbled on her food.

"I need to talk to you," she said.

"Sure," he said passively to his sister.

"So, Mr. M.I.A. Police Detective," Luis blurted, "have you found Alana's murderer?"

"Luis!" Aelah voiced, "you don't have to answer him Dezio."

"It's Lieutenant and as a matter of fact, my partner and I are working on some strong leads."

"You and your partner? What's the problem, you can't find Alana's murderer on your own?" Luis spat.

Garcia paused before speaking.

"You know considering the situation, I'm a little shocked by your behavior. I mean, Lana was murdered and all you have time to do is talk shit. What the hell is your problem?"

"I don't respect anyone carrying a badge."

"Luis!" Aelah said aloud, "I don't have time for your wikked ways. If you're going to sit in my brothers' house and disrespect him, get the hell out or do us a favor, shut the hell up."

Luis leaned into his chair and scoffed under his breath. He was already on Garcia's and Aelah's bad side. Instead of saying anything further, Luis just sipped from the glass and ate the food that sat directly across from him while listening to the two of them converse.

"So anyway Dezio, you said you and your partner have some strong leads?" Aelah quizzed.

"That's right," Garcia said, staring at Luis.

Garcia eyed Luis down before returning his attention back to his sister while she shook her head disappointedly at the two men.

"How could this have happened, Dezio?" she said in a soft cry. "*Ela nunca machuca qualquer um,*" she said in their native tongue.

Dezio looked away, trying to avoid seeing his sister cry. "No, she never hurt anyone," he said solemnly, "but I swear to you that I won't stop until I find out who did this to her."

"Good, that's the least you can do," Luis mumbled under his breath.

Garcia shot a vexed stare at him then stared at his sister.

"Luis, please. You're the real reason why we're sitting here having this discussion in the first place. When Lana said she was ready to come back home, you didn't listen to her. Instead, you dismissed her like always," Aelah shot. "You never cared about her."

"You robbed me of my child! You took my chance to...," Luis said before she cut him off.

"I robbed you of what! Being a father to our child!"

"Aelah please, I don't want to argue with you about this no more. You're not the only one who lost a..."

"Listen!" Garcia said aggravatingly, "there's a lot going on, no need to fuss. There's a lot of hurt and neither one of you are the blame."

Aelah looked at Luis. Luis looked away.

"When can we see her body?" she asked.

"We can go whenever you're ready.

"Have they started the autopsy report?"

"The medical examiner ran a toxicology report on her just to make sure she had a thorough autopsy."

"Why? She wasn't on drugs, was she?" Aelah said, placing her hand on her heart.

"It's just a precautionary procedure to see what was in her system."

Garcia grabbed his sisters' hand then pulled her close to him when she started to cry. He knew how heart breaking it was to bury your own child no matter what.

"What do you need me to do? You have everything you need for the burial services?" he asked wiping away his own tears.

"No, her personal assistant, Micah, has been very helpful with the arrangements."

"Why in the hell is a stranger helping with the funeral arrangements Aelah? For all we know, she could have something to do with Lana's death Aelah!" he said with rage. "We can't trust anyone!" he said as he stood to his feet.

"Don't you tell me what I should and shouldn't do! You're not helping me do anything, so don't tell me what I should or shouldn't' be doing," she said.

"That's a damn lie!" Luis yelled as he stood to his feet.

"Now hold on a damn minute!" Garcia faced him, standing in the middle of them. "If anyone is gonna do any yelling 'round here, it's gonna be me!"

Luis faced him, but Garcia didn't back away.

"This is between me and my wife," Luis shot back.

"Yea, well now it's between me and you. If I ever get wind that you put your hands on my sister, I'll kill you with my bare hands, damn a badge."

"Stop it Dezio!" Aelah screamed.

"Is that a fucking threat?" Luis said, taking a step forward.

"Luis! Stop it!" she yelled behind Dezio.

"No, it's a fucking promise!"

Luis growled but his bite was much too small in Miami. He threw up his hands and slowly backed away from Garcia. No one ever disrespected him like that and he would make sure Garcia remembered that. Aelah stormed past Dezio and pushed Luis in the chair.

"Get out!" she screamed.

Luis didn't move, instead he picked up his glass and tossed a portion of the drink in the back of his throat.

"Like I was saying, Micah was Lana's personal assistant. She's such a sweet girl."

"Aelah, whatever you do please don't tell her or anyone that I'm related to Alana. I don't want my Captain to snatch this case from me and give it to someone who's not experienced enough."

"Not a peep from me, but did you know that Skyler was living with Alana," she said, making Luis spill his drink.

Luis quickly jumped up and reached for the napkins. With Aelah and Dezio staring at him, he quickly blamed spilling his drink on himself on his clumsiness as they watched him wipe himself. Garcia's frustration was growing thin with his sister when it came to Luis.

"You need to get away from him, he's bad news."

"Dez, he's just..."

"Aelah, he's gonna get you killed. He's too reckless, but I told you that before."

"Whatever he does in the streets, he leaves it there."

"I'm not going to do this with you anymore. I've been telling you for years that one of these days he was gonna get you caught up with his web of lies."

Garcia looked toward the bathroom and shook his head when Luis walked away and listened to them carefully without making a big deal about anything else. Skyler's name made his skin crawl. Garcia listened to Aelah talk about her, but was shocked to know that she was an exchange student and an ex-model. He listened to his sister talk about the way she abruptly left Brazil to go back to the states.

While Aelah was sharing happy thoughts with her brother, Luis thought about Skyler and the recent pictures he received of the child he thought she aborted years ago. He never disclosed it to his wife, but ever since Skyler started sending pictures to him every other month, he knew he needed a plan. Garcia wrapped up their conversation and escorted them outside. He made a conscience decision to revisit Luis before they left. He waved to them as they pulled off and disappeared. He quickly glanced at his watch then walked back inside of his house. He put the food in the refrigerator and showered.

Eight forty-five arrived much sooner than Garcia had anticipated and yet he still wasn't sure how he was going to handle the situation with Catalina. It didn't matter how painful this was, a part of him was ready to get this over with. Truth was, he genuinely adored Catalina and had planned to spend the rest of his life with her. When he thought about it more clearly, she made everything in life clearer for him, but it devastated him to see the truth. To know the truth. The vision of her and Clifton kissing stained his memory and regardless how he felt about her, the trust was gone. He was a man of trust and anything less than that was undoubtedly meaningless. As the night grew before he reached her condo, he stopped by the store and picked up a beautiful bouquet of long stemmed white roses trimmed in red like he would've usually done when they hadn't seen each other for weeks.

This is it, no more Mr. Nice Guy after this, he said to himself.

When he spotted her in his rearview mirror, his loins grew heavy when he watched her hips sway. He was still a man and as a man, his lust was by sight regardless how he felt. She was flawless and the illuminated street lights complimented her skin complexion, but as she came closer, his heart caved in his chest when he thought about the reason for this date. His initial reason was to propose to her, but seeing her on the video changed everything. He didn't want his distance to alarm her so he quickly turned on his flirty ways, stepped out of the car as he walked toward her.

He immediately picked her up and spun her around, a gesture

he started years ago when he missed her. No need to change it up now, he knew this was the very last time he would spin her around. Once he stopped spinning her and she stared back at him, he looked at her differently. As much as he missed her, he knew she was playing him. He wasn't the type of man to mislead a woman nor did he want to be misled by one.

He stepped back and escorted her to the car, opening the door for her like a perfect gentleman. He knew their date was going to end quickly, so he tried his best to prolong it so her boy toy could spot her with him. His nemesis. After he closed her door, he walked around the car then hopped in. He carefully reached behind her seat pulling out her favorite bouquet of flowers.

"Oh Dezio, these are beautiful."

"Your favorites."

"Yes they are," she said, with a smile.

He smiled back at her, adjusted his mirror then sped off. He turned up his radio and played all of her favorite songs he made several weeks prior to the surveillance video. She listened and looked at him as if she was falling in love with him all over again.

"So, have you decided where we're going to eat?" she asked.

"I have," he said, taking a different route so she wouldn't catch on.

"Really, where?" she quizzed as she looked out of her window.

"I'm not saying."

"Oh, it's a surprise?"

"Sort of."

"I love the suspense. I must tell you Dezio, you really do take care of me."

He smiled, unsure if he should respond to that statement or not.

"Well you know it's not a surprise if you're looking. So, do me a favor...," he said.

"What's that?"

"Reach on the floor near your feet, pull out the blindfold out of that bag and put it on."

"Are we about to get kinky in a public place?"

"If that's what you want," he said, watching her put on the blindfold.

He stopped at the light and adjusted her mask. He didn't want her to see where he was taking her until they stepped inside of the restaurant. He sped off and headed toward Night Owl's while she sang along with no route in mind. As the music played he rethought out his plan. Everything had to be in order.

Once they arrived, he quickly glanced at her. Normally he wouldn't have handled a break up this like this, but since Clifton was in the starting lineup he wanted to make things interesting. He knew Clifton was a womanizer and knew he wouldn't be fazed to see her with another man, but since it was him, he wasn't sure how the night would turn out for her.

"Dezio?"

"Yes."

"Is everything alright? Why did we stop? Are we here?" she said, looking around with the mask still covering her eyes.

"Oh yes," he said, "I was just making sure I had everything."

He didn't' want to seem too anxious, so he performed his normal routine. As a perfect gentleman, he escorted her through the doors. Once they walked inside, he scanned the room, hoping to spot Clifton, but instead he saw a young lady walking toward them with a smile. He quickly stood behind Catalina and removed her mask as she blinked twice until her eyes met Mesa's eyes.

"I heard the food is good here," Dezio replied.

"Yea, but don't you think the restu..."

"Hi, smoking or none?" Mesa asked the pair, while looking at Catalina with a slight stare.

"It's her choice," Garcia said as she stood behind her.

"Can we sit on the patio?" Catalina suggested, looking toward the area and avoiding eye contact with Mesa.

"Oh I'm so sorry, that area is reserved for a party of twenty," Mesa apologized.

Garcia made sure that area was reserved, thanks to smart thinking and planning, he called it in earlier. He knew she would want to sit away from the crowd and the disgusted look on her face displayed it.

"Do you have any other tables away from the crowd?" Catalina inquired.

"We actually have one in the corner, near the back, how's that?" Mesa offered.

"That's fine, we'll take it," Catalina said uncomfortably.

Garcia chuckled to himself with a straight face as they walked toward the table, behind Mesa.

"My name is Mesa," she quickly introduced herself as their server when she sat them. "Here are your menus. Would you like to order something to drink?"

"Um..... sure. I'll take the peach ice tea," Garcia said first.

"And I would like a Mango Martini," Catalina said briskly.

"Okay, I will be back with your drinks," Mesa voiced.

"Okay, where is your restroom?" Garcia asked.

"Near the back," Mesa pointed.

"Okay, I'll be right back"

Catalina watched Garcia walk toward the restroom until he disappeared. She quickly pulled out her cell phone and dialed Clifton's number, but it went straight to his voicemail. She called several times back to back, but leaving three messages somehow filled his mailbox.

"Damn it!" Catalina cursed under her breath.

Mesa returned faster than Catalina expected and sat the drinks in front of her on the table.

"You got a lot of damn nerve coming here with another man," Mesa said discreetly. "You and I both know if Clifton saw you with him, he would shit bricks."

"Mesa, this was not my ...."

"You don't have to explain it to me. Just be glad his ass ran out of here like a bat out of hell about an hour ago."

Catalina looked away slightly uncomfortably.

"Look, between me and you, you're wasting your time with Clifton, but I'm sure you know that by now."

Catalina looked at a serious Mesa while Garcia walked toward the table.

"Could you do me one favor?" Catalina quickly asked, as she pulled out her compact mirror, so she can keep her eyes on Garcia as he walked toward her.

"Yes?"

"Whatever you do, please don't bring his name up."

Mesa shook her head with disgust before swiftly walking to her next table.

"So what do you think of this place?" Garcia said when he reached their table, looking around.

"What do I think?" she chuckled to herself. "It's nice, but why here?" she said as she looked around.

Before he could respond, Mesa walked up to their table, placed their drinks down and asked if they needed more time to look at the menu. Garcia stared at a very uncomfortable Catalina before she responded.

"Um, could you give us a few more minutes?" Catalina said.

"Sure," Mesa said.

"Um, before you go, what would you recommend?" Garcia interjected.

"Well, let's see. If you're in the mood for some good seafood, the Fried Lobster Tail is fried in our special batter and served with your choice of vegetables and an additional side."

"Does a salad come with that?" he added.

"It does. We have a house salad that is topped with steamed shrimp."

"Ooh, that sounds nice. I think I'll have that," he said before he turned his eyes to Catalina.

"Sweetheart, have you decided what you want to order?"

"No, I need a few more minutes," Catalina said, staring at the menu.

"Okay, take your time. Would you like a salad while you're looking over the menu Miss?" Mesa asked.

"Sure," she said.

Garcia watched Mesa walk away then glance around the room before he said anything to Catalina.

"Is there something wrong?"

"No."

"Really? You seem a little uncomfortable. You sure you're alright?" he asked.

She looked at him then scanned the area around them before leaning toward him.

"Why did you bring me here?"

"You said you wanted to go to dinner and you told me to pick the place."

"I understand that, but..."

"But what?" he said, leaning back into his chair. "You don't like my choice?"

"It's not that I don't like your choice, it's just that...."

"It's just what? The area is nice," he said leaning toward her.

"The food smells good too."

Just when she tried to respond, Mesa walked toward them and placed their salads in front of them.

"Thank you, it looks delicious," Catalina said.

"You are more than welcome. Whenever you're ready to order please let me know."

"I will, thank you," Catalina said with a smile.

"You're welcome," Mesa said before walking off.

Garcia watched Catalina fold the napkin in her lap and sampled her salad. She looked at ease, but just as Garcia looked past her, Clifton walked in the front entrance behind her.

"Why aren't you eating your salad Dezio?"

"I really don't have an appetite."

"Are you okay?"

"A couple of things are on my mind. For starters I'm an older guy. I'm about to retire and you know, I just might not, well you know.....," he stammered, hoping to stall the conversation a little until Clifton walked closer.

"You might not what?"

"You're almost twenty years younger than me, who am I kidding? I'm not a young man anymore."

"And that's why I'm in love with you because you're ......," she said before he interrupted her.

"You're in love with me?" he said doubtingly.

"I am. Since when have you ever questioned that?"

"I have my reasons."

"Care to share?"

"Is there anything you want to tell me?" he asked as Clifton walked toward them.

"No."

"Okay," he said when Clifton was a few steps away.

"I love you Dezio and I would never do anything to hurt you," she said loud enough for a passing Clifton to hear.

"Catalina?" Clifton quizzed calmly.

She looked at Clifton then toward Garcia. Immediately, her heart paced while she searched for a quick explanation. Garcia placed his fork down and wiped his mouth with his napkin then looked at her with a piercing stare.

"Hello Clifton," she said hesitantly.

"I see you got yourself a real sharp shooter?" he said

sarcastically.

"I can explain.....," she chuckled at Clifton.

Clifton looked at her then shook his head at her.

"No need to," Garcia said before she turned her attention back to him.

"Why the hell are you here? You couldn't think of another place to take your broad?" Clifton said.

"Figured this was her favorite place to eat since she's in here all the damn time," Garcia shot back as if she wasn't sitting across from him.

"Get the hell out of my restaurant and take her with you."

Garcia sat across from her and watched her stare at Clifton as he walked away. From the look on her face, she looked devastated by Clifton's nonchalant attitude.

"I can explain honey."

"No need. I've seen it with my own two eyes and you sit here and blatantly lie to me."

"No. it's not like that."

"It's not like that? And to think I was going to propose to you. You know Catalina, I thought you were different from all the other women I've met, but you're just the same."

"Dezio, it's not what you think."

Garcia pulled out the picture Phelps faxed him and placed it in front of her, next to her salad.

"Like I said no need to explain. The picture says it all, doesn't it?"

He reached into his pocket and pulled out a fifty-dollar bill. He placed it on the table underneath his plate and grabbed his keys just as she grabbed his hand.

"Babe, let me explain, me and Clifton have an arrangement. Please don't leave me."

He stood to his feet and pushed his chair up to the table. He covered his mouth and headed toward the front door while Catalina sat at the table. She heard someone walk up to her and looked up.

"Dezio?" she said as she looked up and saw it was Clifton.

"You told me he's not your type, old man Garcia. Guess you tried to play him. Tsk. Tsk. Tsk."

"You're not my type."

"Tonight I'm not? Oh I forgot, it's all about the money with you. You like who spends, I forgot."

"Damn you."

"Can I see you in my office please?"

Just a few steps later and a closed door, Clifton slapped her.

"Who the hell do you think you are? Bringing his ass in my fucking restaurant?"

"It wasn't my idea," she said as she grabbed the side of her face.

"Wasn't your idea? I bet it wasn't."

"How could you humiliate me like this Clifton?"

"Humiliate you? You are nothing, but an easy lay. I know you didn't think you were the only one?" he chuckled. "I keep telling you old man Garcia is going to give you worms. Besides, I have other shit on my plate than to worry about a bitch who can't hold up her end of the bargain."

"I did what I was supposed to do."

"Your job isn't done, so you better try to figure it out how to get back on his good side. I need to know when he is coming up here and what he has on me, am I understood?"

"Fuck you."

"No, go fuck your old man and get out of my face."

She looked at him then stormed out of his office. He laughed under his breath and shook his head when his phone rang.

"Hello?...Now is not a good time?"

"Because I said tonight is not a good damn time!" he yelled into the phone before disconnecting it

He dialed Skyler's number, but it was disconnected. He paced around his office for a few minutes before dialing Dana's number, but it was disconnected as well.

"Fucking bitches! I hate all you bitches!" he screamed into the phone before throwing it the wall across from him.

The downside of a let down...

A couple of hours later, Garcia found himself sitting in his closed dimly lit office with a banging migraine and bottle of scotch near his heart. The stained vision of Catalina kissing Clifton still jogged his memory, but the more he drank the more his anger festered. In addition, Luis made matters worse when he came by his house with his sister. When he finally took his last swig, he tossed the empty bottle in the trash can near his desk and leaned forward. He rubbed his temples and looked at the notepad sitting in front of him. He flipped the pages until he saw an unfamiliar manila folder sitting underneath the notepad.

He moved his notepad to the side and opened the folder that read to *Lieutenant from Sgt. Webster* which was full of enhanced photos from the surveillance discs. He picked the first one up with Skyler, Clifton, and an unknown woman. He sat it to the side, placing a post-it-note with a question mark on the unknown woman's face.

"Who are you?" he slurred to himself.

He looked at the pictures in sequential order as they had watched the disc and pulled a second set of pictures to the side which had Micah's unknown male guest.

"Who is Micah's friend? I swear I know this guy," Garcia mumbled under his breath.

He continued to scan through the pictures until he saw the man talking to his niece by the bar. He picked up the picture and stared at it, hoping that something could jog his memory.

He placed three pictures in front of him, but his blurred vision handicapped him. He stood from his desk and stumbled toward his bulletin board. He pinned the pictures of the three unidentified suspects in the center of the board while the other pictures surrounded them. After a few stumbles and a couple of pricks on his fingertips, from the pushpins, he finally sat in a chair near the bulletin board and fell asleep.

The next morning, his office phone rang loudly and his cell phone vibrated in his pockets which started him and caused him to fall on the floor.

"Damn it!"

He looked at his watch for the time as it read six fifteen.

"Who the hell is calling me this time in the morning?" he said aloud, as he struggled to stand to his feet.

He pulled out his cell phone and noticed twelve missed calls from Catalina when his office phone stopped ringing. He quickly shoved the phone back into his pants pocket as he scratched his shadowing beard. He walked toward his desk phone and dialed Phelps number with squinted eyes. He picked up the receiver when he heard his voice.

"Phelps?" he slurred.

He sat in his chair and explained to Phelps what happened the night before and how he managed to spend the night in his office with his bottle of scotch.

He disconnected the call and placed his cell phone in his desk drawer. He walked toward the wall locker in his office, pulled out his toiletries, a shirt, pair of pants and a towel. Before leaving, he stared at his bulletin board for about forty-five minutes hoping that the pictures would reveal some type of clue. After minutes of wrestling with the stench in his office and a banging headache, he finally opened the door, hoping to avoid everyone in the office as he headed toward the men's locker room so he could shower and shave before Phelps arrived.

After Garcia stepped out of the shower, Phelps walked in the locker room with a tall cup of black coffee and shook his head at his partner.

"You look awful."

"I feel awful."

"You okay?"

"Yea, just got a slight hangover."

Phelps laughed as they walked back to Garcia's clean office.

"Oh yea by the way, while you were in the shower, I asked housekeeping to swing by your office first. Man, I tell you...," Phelps informed.

"You didn't have to do that," Garcia said, patting him on his back.

"It's not a problem, but guess what's on this morning's front page," Phelps added as he handed him the local newspaper.

"I'll be damned."

"The reporters are all over this case, we need to do something quick. We need to make another statement or give a press conference to update the case. I thought Captain gave one the night of the murder?"

"He did, but we'll need to make another announcement to the speculators this morning," Garcia said, sipping on his coffee when they walked in his office.

"Okay, oh and I took a look at your bulletin board and it just came to me who that mysterious guy Alana was talking to near the bar."

"Oh yea, who is he?" Garcia quizzed.

"That's Anthony Carnes, he used to play in the NBA."

"Carnes?"

"It sure was."

"Bring him in. Matter of fact, bring everybody's ass in here that's on this damn board. It seems like everyone is talking about this damn case except for the people who were close to her. Maybe if we play everyone against each other, someone will unass some fucking information," Garcia said.

"I'm on it boss."

Garcia stood in front of his board wondering who the hell Micah's friend was. His face was so familiar to him, but he couldn't call where he had seen him before. He immediately placed his coffee on his desk then finally pulled out his cell phone from his desk to dial his sister's number, Catalina's name flashed across his screen. He quickly pressed ignore, sending her to voicemail then dialed his sister's number.

"Aelah?" he said when she picked up on the fourth ring. "Are you still asleep? ...I need you to do me a favor. ....Do you have Micah's number?.......Oh, yea?...Well, when she gets there will you send her to the station...,Yea, everything is okay, and I just need to ask her a few questions...No, she's not in trouble, just want to ask her somethings."

Garcia looked through the manila folder while his sister talked on the other end of the phone and came across Skyler's picture. He wasn't sure if he was looking at her or her twin sister, but shook his head at the thought. It was odd that they were that identical that you couldn't tell them apart, not a mole or a visual birthmark could separate the two. As he sifted through the folder, he came across another picture of Skyler. There was something slightly different about the new picture but it stood out like a needle in a haystack.

"Aelah? .... I need to go so I will talk to you later.......Don't worry much, as soon as I get a break in the case, I will keep you posted okay?....Love you too," he said as he disconnected the call while staring at the picture.

"Garcia?" Phelps called his name just as he placed the phone on his desk.

"Yea," he glanced up.

"Okay, I'm about to head to Park's place to rattle his cage bright and early before he tries to bury himself at Night's Owl."

Parks. Hearing that name made Garcia's flesh crawl and without cracking a smile, he looked at Phelps with a serious face.

"Good, and make sure his ass ride in the back of your car. He has priors and we don't want him thinking he has one up on us. He's liable to call anyone to cover his tracks."

"Will do."

"Oh, and as far as everyone else, let them come down to the office. No need to alarm anyone or ruffle anyone's feather until we have them in our custody."

"Remember, if they don't want to come to the station, don't make them. Just remind them if we have to get warrants for them, they won't like the outcome."

"Is that for everyone?" Phelps asked.

"Yes."

After Phelps left his office, Garcia dialed Monte's number on sped dial.

"Hey there, ...Can you meet me at the station? .....Good, see you in a few then."

He called the front desk and told the officer who spoke into the phone that he was expecting a visitor by the name of Montgomery. For fifteen minutes, Garcia sat in his office and gathered all of his notes from his bulletin board and rechecked his time line when his office phone rang.

"Lt. Garcia."

"Sir, Mr. Montgomery is here waiting for you."

"Good, send him to conference room B and tell him I will be there shortly."

"Yes sir."

Once Montgomery arrived at the precinct, he was escorted to the conference room while Garcia gathered three unknown pictures Webster printed out for him, hoping Monte could shed some light to him. He tucked it under his arm then closed his door behind him as he walked toward the conference room.

"Thank you for coming in on such short notice," Garcia said after he closed the door behind him.

"No problem, what's going on?" Monte asked.

Garcia laid the folder in front of Monte as he sat in front of him, hoping to read his facial expression.

"Could you look inside of the folder in front of you and tell me the names of the people that you know?"

"Sure," he said as he opened it carefully.

Monte noticed both Anthony and Rafael's pictures and called out their names. He studied the woman in the picture standing beside Skyler, but he couldn't recall her name.

"This is Anthony Carnes," he pointed out.

"So now I can put a face with the ex-fiancé," Garcia said as he stared at the picture.

"Yea, that's him," Monte said when he looked at Garcia.

"Do you know why is he the 'ex'?"

"She said he was too possessive. I told her that she needed to get a restraining order out on him after the incident at her place when she had a get together and at Night's Owl."

"Is that right?" he said, making a mental note to recall any orders placed on Carnes.

"She was convinced that he would never hurt her. I told her that she didn't know what a person would do during desperate measures, but she didn't seem too interested in taking it that far."

Stubborn just like Aelah, Garcia mused.

"Okay, so who is the guy with Micah?"

"That's Micah's guy friend, Rafael."

"Rafael?" he repeated. "Guy friend as in boyfriend?" he quizzed.

"Yea, I believe so."

"Hmph, thanks for clearing that up for me, I really do 'preciate it."

"No problem."

"I need you to do one more thing for me and that's it."

"What's that boss?"

"I need you to write a statement in your own words as what happened the night Ms. Inacio was murdered."

"Am I okay? I thought I was cleared?" Monte asked cautiously.

"You are."

"Am I now a suspect in this case?" Monte said as he sat up in his chair.

"No, no, no. You're a key witness and I just want to make sure you have your statement written out in your own words, you know proper protocol, and then we're done."

"You're not blowing smoke up my ass, are you Lieutenant?"

"No, not at all. Don't need anyone prying in this case. Just trying to cross all my T's and dot all my I's."

"Hmph," Monte said skeptically.

"Alright, let me be straight up with you, there's a slight problem and what I'm about to tell you doesn't leave this room," Garcia said as he stood up and looked out of the blinds, keeping his back toward him.

"Okay, shoot. I'm listening."

"...I think someone is trying to frame you."

"Frame me?" Monte said with more bass in his voice.

"Yes. We looked at the surveillance disc and it appears that you and someone else were dressed alike even down to the exact same styled shoe that night."

Monte covered his mouth then dropped his head.

"What?"

"Same suit, same color, same style ...even same shoes."

"I doubt that, my shoes were custom-made."

"They were?"

Garcia immediately spun around and stared at him with a raised brow.

"Well that's what the guy told me when I picked up my shoes near the shore."

"Hmmm, there's several little what not stores near the shore. Can you recognize the owner if you had to?"

"Of course. Spanish guy with a long salt and pepper ponytail with a goatee to match."

Garcia dropped his head then shook it before looking back at Monte. I should've known it was Santana. He has a small shop near the beachfront. He sells shoes, hats, belts......"

"Yea, yea, that's him."

"He's a crook. He's always nickeling and diming people with his only one of a kind custom-made products," Garcia revealed.

"Damn, are you serious?" Monte said while shaking his head.

"Yea, but do you still have the receipt?"

"I do."

"Good. Just keep it close by. We may need to make a visit to Santana. In the meantime, let's not discuss this with anyone. Never know who is waiting for new evidence."

"Sure thing," Monte replied suspiciously.

Garcia paced the conference room with a puzzled look on his face. He memorized Santana's thirteen-page rap sheet by hard, but tying him to this case was out the question. Garcia knew paying Santana a visit would ruffle his feathers and he would come clean about his recent customers.

"This is what I'm working with right now. You and Ms. Inacio were getting close and it was obvious she was interested in you as well. I'm sure there were several people interested in her so who knows, maybe someone was heartbroken. This could be a crime of passion, but at this point, we are looking at everyone and no one is excluded. I'm going to review the disc one last time to see what else I can find. Do you have any visual markings or tattoos?" Garcia said as he turned to face him.

"No, my tattoos are on my chest."

Garcia raised his eyebrows and walked toward the door while Monte trailed him before he left the station until he spotted Micah.

"Hi, I'm here to see...."

"Me?" he said playfully. "How you doing, Ms. Richardson?" Garcia asked politely as he walked up behind her.

"Ooh, please call me Micah. I'm making it, Ms. Aelah said you wanted me to swing by, is everything okay?"

"Yes, but I do need to talk with you for a moment?" he said.

"Sure."

He walked her to the conference room he just occupied with

Monte and handed her the same manila folder. He asked her the same questions, hoping she could shed more light on Rafael.

"Could you please tell me who this guy is?" he said as he pointed to Rafael's photo.

"Oh that's my boyfriend, Rafael Jai."

"How long have you two dated?"

"For about two years."

"So tell me about your boyfriend, how did you two meet?"

"It's kind of weird, it's like he just landed on my doorstep. He was referred to my agency, by who I'm not sure, so we tried him out. Our last photographer was relocating and we needed to replace him. We were skeptical at first, but when he showed us his work, we were captivated. The photos were absolutely stunning, so we signed him on to our modeling agency."

"So, he's a photographer?"

"Yes, his studio is three miles north of Night's Owl."

Garcia jotted down the information in his notepad.

"Okay, so he's that good?"

"Yes. Have you seen any of his work?"

"No, can't say that I have."

"You should see some of the shots he took of Alana, simply beautiful."

"Oh yea? I will make sure I look into it."

"Please do. He knows what to capture."

"So he has an eye for beauty?"

"He does," she said before she looked at her hands. "Lt. Garcia, should I be worried about something?"

"No. Just proper protocol," he said with a calming tone.

"Oh okay," she said as she relaxed a little.

"Let me ask you something and this stays between us."

"Sure," she said when she looked at him.

"Have you seen Skyler or her twin sister again?"

"Actually I haven't. The only time I saw them together was the day I recorded them."

"Hmph. That's weird. I thought that maybe you would've seen or heard from her by now."

"Well you know she wasn't *my* friend, she was Alana's."

"Yea. Who is the woman standing beside Ms. Sutton in the picture?"

"Um, I'm not sure what her name is because they never said

her name."

"Hmph, someone must know her name," he said aloud. *I just need her name so I can identify everyone in the picture,*" he said to himself as he rubbed his chin.

Micah looked at the pictures carefully before standing to her feet.

"I do thank you for coming in, but can I get you to write a statement on what happened the night that led to Ms. Inacio death so we can have it on file?"

"You're welcome and sure thing."

Garcia needed to know more about this Rafael Jai guy because something was unsettling about him. As he walked toward his office in deep thought, he spotted Sgt. Webster talking to a uniformed officer near the front desk. Garcia quickly darted toward her with a favor in mind.

"Sergeant?" Garcia said with an authoritative voice.

"Good Morning Lieutenant," they both said in unison.

"Sgt. Webster, can I talk to you for a second?"

"Yes sir," she said to Garcia. "I'll catch up with you later," Webster said to the uniformed officer.

Garcia pulled her to the side, away from the lurking officers who tried to surround them.

"Can you run a name for me? Rafael Jai?"

"Sure."

"I need you to find whatever you can on him. A fingerprint, mug shot anything on him ASAP."

"Okay, I'm on it. Let me see what I can dig up. Are you going to be in your office in the next few minutes?"

"If not, call my cell."

"Yes sir," Webster said before darting off.

Garcia stopped at his office to grab his notepad. He quickly glanced at his bulletin board once more before he left his office. Something was strikingly familiar about Rafael Jai's face, but as he stared at the picture, he couldn't connect the dots. It was if he'd seen him somewhere, maybe in passing or at a restaurant. Somewhere. He walked closer toward the board and stood in the same place for fifteen minutes until Sgt. Webster walked in his office and handed him several pictures of Mr. Jai. Garcia looked at the pictures in his hands, the one pinned to the board then at Webster.

"What's this?" he asked Webster.

"Rafael Jai. Apparently, there are several Mr. Jai in our database. Is there anyone in particular you're looking for?"

"Yes, him," Garcia said with his head, nodding it toward the board. "The men in these pictures look nothing like my Mr. Jai."

"You got an age for your Jai? If so, we can call the DMV and see what they have."

"Don't have an age, but his girlfriend is in one of the interrogating rooms and hopefully she won't be too alarmed if I ask her a few more questions about him."

"Is she starting to clam up?"

"You know actually, she's starting to get a little suspicious and I don't want that."

"Well, if you don't' mind, how about I ask her? She might not find it too offensive if it comes from me."

"Good idea. She's in the second interrogating room."

"Okay, I'll be right back. Is there any other information you need?"

"I can't think of anything."

"Okay."

Garcia handed Webster the manila folder before she walked toward the interrogating rooms. She knew this was a good chance to impress the Lieutenant. She looked over the folder Garcia handed her and made a quick study. Sgt. Webster closed the folder when she opened the door to the interrogating room Micah was occupying.

"Ms. Richardson?" she called out.

"Yes ma'am."

"Are you finished with your statement?"

"No, not yet," she asked with a puzzled look on her face.

"Okay, well let me know if you need more time."

"Okay. Is everything alright? Where's Lt. Garcia?" Micah asked as she looked past her.

"He was actually pulled into a meeting. He told me to come get your statement. My name is Sgt. Webster."

"Okay, nice to meet you. I was starting to think maybe I did something wrong."

"No everything is really okay."

"Oh okay. I was feeling a little nervous," Micah said with a smile.

"No need to get nervous," she said as she opened the file. "So how long you and your boyfriend been together. Is it serious?"

"Well, it's getting serious and almost two years...."

"You two make a beautiful couple."

"Why, thank you."

"He has a baby face he doesn't even look legal?"

"Oh my goodness, everyone tells him that when he cuts off his facial hair. That man is forty-six going on sixty."

Sgt. Webster laughed to herself, but slapped herself five for getting his age out of her.

"He looks exotic? Doesn't look like he's from around here."

"He's not, but I can't remember where he's from. He doesn't speak much about it, I do know he's an islander."

Webster continued to write. She knew she was in a good place to keep asking her more questions about Rafael without raising any red flags.

"Garcia told me that you're helping out Ms. Inacio's family so don't let me hold you. You have his card and here's mine just in case. Don't hesitate to call us."

"Will do, thank you," she said before she opened the door and walked off.

Webster smiled at herself just as Anthony walked into Night's Owl toward the bar on the other side of town.

"Hey beautiful, how ya doing?"

"Fine," Mesa smiled wide like a school girl.

"Is Clifton here?"

"Yes, he's in his office," she said as she wiped the bar.

"Alright, I'ma just shoot back there real quick."

"Is he expecting you?"

"Nah, so don't worry about calling him. I'll just surprise him," he said as he winked at her before walking away.

"Oh okay."

Mesa wiped her area while her female customers occupied her time at the bar. They all glanced at Anthony when he walked toward the back and shook their heads while they lusted over him.

"Ain't he fine," one of the female customers said.

"Yes he is," one of the patrons said.

Anthony knocked on Clifton's door until he finally snatched it opened.

"What?" he shouted.

"What's up stranger?" Anthony said, walking past Clifton. "What took you so damn long to open the door and why are you hollering?"

"I um......," Clifton stammered, "wha-what are you doing here?"

"I've been calling you about my money for almost a week and you still haven't gotten back to me, so I decided to pay you a visit. Ya know sometimes when you just show up uninvited you can see shit for yourself, wouldn't you agree?" Anthony said calmly.

"Ah, yea. Yea I agree."

"So," Anthony said as he sat on the corner of Clifton's desk, "where's my money?"

"I um...."

Anthony looked around the room disgustingly as Clifton walked toward his desk, shuffling his paperwork, and thinking of a believable answer.

"I can explain. See, I've been trying to ..."

"Avoid me," Anthony clarified.

"I haven't avoided you. You've been out of town."

"You have all of my contact info. You already know, this shit isn't my style. I'll leave that up to you, but from the looks of things, looks like you're losing control."

"Look Anthony, I've had a hell of a week and I needed something to, ya know, help filter some things out of my mind," he said nervously.

"Hmph, looks like you got a habit now."

"I don't have no damn habit, this shit ain't nothing. I'm just, ya know, clearing my mind from all this bullshit."

"Clearing your mind?" Anthony repeated as he looked at his iPhone when a message appeared. "So, I'm guessing the person you get your shit from apparently doesn't know you're dipping?"

Clifton looked away while Anthony stared at him watching his paranoid behavior.

"Man, are you alright?"

"Tsk. Hell nah," Clifton shot back. "I made a promise to Alana's father that I would look after her and he's already called demanding for us to meet."

Clifton watched Anthony put his head down.

"You know, you have the nerve to sit here and pretend that

you really gave a shit about her," Anthony said.

"I cared more about her than you ever will."

"Look, I will admit that I didn't handle shit right and my firecracker jealously streak got the best of me, but Lana and I understood each other," he said convincingly.

"Who are you trying to convince?" Clifton scoffed before he stood up and paced around in his office.

"I ain't trying to convince anyone. Boss man, I'm here to get my funds and I'm out. I don't need Dade county on my ass."

"That's too late, ole' Sharp Shooter been fucking harassing me."

Anthony shook his head then folded his arms across his chest.

"Yo, he got it in for you. I'm not here for all that shit. I need my damn money then I'm out."

Clifton walked toward his desk and pulled out five stacks from the top drawer and handed it to Anthony. Anthony counted the stacks of hundred dollar bills then smiled at Clifton before walking toward the door.

"Look man, you need to get your shit together and stop sniffing the shit you're 'spose to be selling. Get your mind right man," he said as he opened the door.

Just as Anthony opened the door, Detective Phelps and his accompanied uniformed officers were standing directly in front of him.

"Anthony Carnes? Clifton Parks?" Phelps voiced when he showed his badge.

Clifton and Anthony looked at the police officers with uncertainty.

"Yes?"

"I would like to ask you gentlemen to come with us to the station so we can talk to you about a homicide."

"A homicide?" they said in unison.

"Now, we can do this one or two ways. We can be civil and walk out of here like men or we can cuff you. It's your choice."

"Look man, I'm not sure what's going on, but I was just about to leave," Anthony said.

"Great, that means you can come to the station right?"

Anthony's nose flared.

"Mr. Carnes, this is not a debate," Phelps added.

"Hey, I'm more than willing to cooperate with you."

"Good. I'm taking it that since you were leaving you know where the station is, right?"

"I do."

"Good, see you there."

Phelps walked toward Clifton while the uniformed officers spoke to Anthony near the door.

"Mr. Parks, what about you?"

"What about me?" Clifton shot back.

"We need you to come to the station," Phelps replied.

"I'm so fucking tired of Dade County coming here to harass me," Clifton spat hysterically. "If it's not Sharp Shooter, it's you."

"Look, I have orders to come here and..."

"You have orders? From who? Sharp Shooter? Every time I look around ya'll keep fucking with me. I tell you what, I'm about to get me a fucking lawyer and sue ya'll asses."

"Go right ahead, it'll never hold up in court. We need you to come to the station Mr. Parks."

"I ain't going no damn where."

"Okay then, you're under arrest."

"For fucking what?"

"I'll think of something," Phelps said as he pulled out his handcuffs.

"Are you fucking serious!"

"You have the right to remain silent," Phelps said as he placed the cuffs around his wrists.

"Help!" Clifton yelled out.

"Anything you say can and will be used against you in a court of law..."

Immediately the uniformed officers left Anthony at the door and rushed toward Phelps to see what was going on when they saw Clifton kicking and yelling as Phelps read Parks his Miranda rights.

"Help me!" Clifton voiced at the officers as he tussled in Phelps arms.

"Settle down now, you're making a bigger deal than what it is," one of the uniformed officers said.

"I'm making a bigger deal than what it is? Every time I turn around, I'm the one in fucking handcuffs," Clifton spat.

"Settle down I said," the officer repeated when Phelps pushed

Clifton toward him.

"Shit, I could've rode with Anthony since he's going that way, but noo... ya'll want to embarrass me."

Phelps looked around Clifton's office while the officers escorted him to the car. Phelps walked toward his desk and noticed residue of cocaine lines near his phone. He shook his head before heading toward the door. He cut the light off then shut his door behind him. Mesa walked toward Phelps swiftly catching his attention.

"Excuse me? Is everything alright?"

"Everything is fine."

"What's going on?" she said with caution.

He ignored her and dialed Garcia's number and waited for him to pick up.

"Hey, just wanted to give you an update before I got there. You will not believe who we ran into... Carnes..., but I had to cuff your boy...disorderly conduct... headed there now."

While Phelps was en route to the precinct, Micah's phone rang. She looked at it and noticed Rafael's name on the screen.

"Hey Raf."

"Hey, where are you? I've been calling you for a couple hours, you alright?" he quizzed.

"Yes, it was in my purse, is everything okay?" she lied.

"Yea-yea," he said with a pause. "On my way to meet Clifton at Night's Owl for lunch," he replied.

She paused.

Why was he meeting Clifton for lunch? she thought.

"You there babe?"

"Yes. I am. I need to make some calls and need to call you back," she said hurriedly before they disconnected.

She sat in her car wondering why Rafael and Clifton were meeting for lunch. She never knew that they were lunch buddies and that bothered her. As she sat in her car, Rafael walked up to Mesa at the bar.

"Is Clifton here?" he asked politely.

"Actually, you just missed him."

"Really? We were supposed to meet for lunch."

Mesa looked around the bar before leaning towards him.

"I'm not sure what's going on, but Dade County just came and got him."

"Just now?"

"Like about five minutes ago," she whispered.

Rafael thanked her then jumped in his car and dialed only one number. Micah, but she didn't answer her phone.

While Micah got out of her car and walked toward Alana's condo, Luis paced back and forth in the hallway recalling a conversation he and a man by the name Feliz had previously.

"I got a job for you."

"Yea?"

"I need you to take care of some business for me."

"What kind of business are we talking about boss?"

"There's this girl by the name of Skyler Sutton. Find out what you can about her then we'll talk more."

"Okay boss. I'm on top of it."

Luis ran his fingers through his hair when the elevator chimed. He was so engulfed in his thoughts, he hadn't noticed Micah walking toward him.

"Hi, Mr. Inacio. How are you?" she said.

"Oh," he said in a startled voice, "....just trying to get some fresh air."

"You should walk on the beach, the air is nice outside."

"Okay thanks," he said as she walked past him.

He slowly turned around to make sure she was inside Alana's condo. He jumped on the elevator and headed outside. He dialed a number, but it went to voicemail.

As he rode down to the lobby, he continued his thoughts.

"I have some news about your girl," Feliz voiced.

"I'm listening."

"It seems like Ms. Sutton has been busy, she's in Miami."

"Why is she in Miami?"

"Looks like she's here with Alana."

"I need her gone permanently."

"Well, wire me some money and it'll get done."

"Since when do you tell me to wire you some money? I make the financial commitments when you have completed the task."

"Listen, I've been doing a number of jobs for you for years when it comes to her and I haven't seen no real money from this job, so now I want my money up front."

"Not until you get rid of Skyler, am I understood?"

"Not exactly. Until I see some paper, I ain't doing shit!"

"Feliz, you must've forgotten that you work for me. I make all the rules! I give the fucking orders, I don't take 'em! So, before you fix your mouth and demand some shit, you need to tread lightly!"

"You know you're a really funny dude. All these years I remained loyal to your ass and never once complained or asked for more money. I just gave you what you wanted. But things have changed. You hide behind an alias name, Kaiser to be exact, because you're a fucking coward. But I know you. I've been your right hand man for over twenty five years and I've never asked you for shit!"

"I'll get the money up for you because your loyalty means everything to me. Haven't I always taken care of you?"

"This is getting old. If you want me to do the job, pay me my damn money."

"Feliz, now you know there are plenty other cats that will do your job for you."

"Well, let them," Feliz said before disconnecting the phone.

Luis quickly made several calls to his key players for a new job. Feliz time has expired and he no longer needed the extra lip service when he put in an order. He just needed results and a payout was commissioned. He waited for a call to come through as he walked on the beach and watched the sun set waiting patiently for someone to call him to accept the job. No one called. He dreaded the next day, his daughter's funeral.

Laying her to rest...

Aelah Inacio dreaded this day, Alana's funeral. It didn't matter how many countless hours she stared at her daughter's beautifully draped pink casket, she still wasn't ready to say goodbye. She tossed and turned throughout the night with unsettling thoughts and a heavy heart. She trusted her brother with her daughter's life and still there were no answers, no promises, or suspects...just uncertain witnesses was the only closure she had to take to her daughter's grave in a few hours.

Aelah stepped on the balcony, looked into the darkened sky as the rain fell into the ocean and her tears stained her face. She cried constantly not believing that the day had arrived that she would have to bury her child. She looked into the heavens when the sky opened desperately asking God was this her punishment for selfishly recreating what he originally created. Her heart was broken. Shattered. Just like her daughters' dreams, and the longer she thought about it, the more she realized she wasn't ready to close the casket permanently.

As she watched the morning sky open with thunderous clouds and boisterous lightning, Luis stood beside her and comforted her as they looked out onto the ocean. He wrapped his arms around her while they both cried for two different reasons. Aelah cried because she promised Alana, no matter what, no one would ever learn the truth she hid from everyone. A secret which was so convenient to hide in the beginning was now becoming a heavier burden. Luis silently hoped that his personal affairs wouldn't haunt his family if Skyler wasn't contained. Aelah cried in his arms just as Micah knocked on Alana's bedroom door.

"Yes?" Luis called out, quickly wiping away his tears.

"I'm sorry, did I disturb you two?" she asked politely.

"Not at all," Aelah replied in between sniffs.

"The cars are here. They are ready for us to line up," Micah said solemnly.

"Thank you," she said, with a smile.

Micah noticed the hurt in their eyes and tried to form a smiled towards them before leaving them alone to bask their own moment. Aelah looked at Luis and grabbed his hand.

"Whatever you do, please don't cause a scene with Dez. I can't take that today," she asked as a tear fell from her eye.

He softly wiped her tear away and pulled her close to him.

"I promise not to make a scene with your brother. Today, is about Lana, nothing else matters sweetheart."

She took a deep breath before taking a good look at him.

"You've grayed more since we've been here," she said when she looked at his hair.

"Yea, I noticed that myself when I was putting on my tie," he said, trying to hide it.

She laughed a little, thinking about the days before mentioning his receding hair line. She grabbed her hat, purse and sunglasses then followed Luis toward the living room. Just as she walked into the living room, she saw her brother dressed in black standing in front of her.

"Oh Dezio," she said as she ran into his arms.

Micah noticed, but Luis quickly gathered Micah and his nephews so they could go to the car.

"We'll be downstairs, okay?" Luis said. "Take your time."

"Thank you," she said.

Dezio nodded at Luis just as he closed the door behind him.

"I know Aelah, I know this is hard," Garcia said, kissing the top of her head.

"Dez, please tell me something. I don't want to bury my baby with the thought that this case will go unsolved.

"I'm trying my hardest to piece this puzzle together. I swear if it takes my last breath, we will get an answer. Her murderer will not walk the streets of Dade County, even if I have to kill him myself."

Aelah looked at him and noticed something strange about him, he was teary-eyed but serious. For the first time since his son's death, she saw her best friend.

"Now, I just want you to know that I can't ride in the family car nor can I stand beside you at the funeral."

"I know. It will be too suspicious and if anyone notices anything they will pull the case right from under you and assign it to someone else."

"I just want you to know that I will be there. I'm going to try to position myself directly in front of you on the opposite side. Okay?"

"Okay."

"So whenever you look at me, know that I'm holding your hand from a distance, but I will be here afterwards. I promise."

"Okay Dez," she said dryly.

"Let's get you to the car. I love you."

"I love you too Dez."

"I promised mamã that I would look after this family after papai left."

"I know Dez."

He looked around Alana's place once more before they left and locked the door. He walked her to the car while some of the police officers conversed near the family car. Garcia insisted to the uniforms that he and Phelps should drive their car directly behind the family, for security reasons, and they agreed without questioning it.

Garcia walked up to Phelps blowing out long deep breaths. "You ready?"

"Question is, are you ready?"

"I don't have a choice."

Garcia slipped on his shades then looked around the cars before they got in. Garcia sat in the driver seat and pulled up behind the family car while Phelps looked at his phone. They followed the family car riding in a steady pace.

"Hey, you know I told Webster to keep a close eye on Parks."

"I heard."

"Can you believe that bastard was calling for help like somebody was beating him?"

"I can," Garcia replied.

Phelps looked at him with a cracked smile, but Garcia didn't return the gesture.

"You thought I was playing? As soon as I get back to the station, I got something for him," Garcia said.

"Whoa, wait a minute, we talked about this before. We're going to get him, don't worry about that. I've already started the process. We just need to make sure when we do, the charges will stick. But you know what, Carnes had a believable alibi, but things just didn't add up when I looked into it."

"What do you mean?" Garcia looked at him quickly.

"See here's the thing, I told Webster to look at the surveillance tape again and did you know that Parks left Night's Owl shortly after everyone left too?"

"He did?"

"And you know what's crazy, they arrived shortly right after another one, trying to blend back into the crowd."

"Now that's interesting."

"It looks like Mr. Parks might be a suspect after all," Phelps said.

"It's possible. Clifton could've raced over there to apologize for the unplanned showdown between her and Skyler, but things didn't go as he planned and knowing him, he could've spiraled out of control and it could've take a turn for the worse."

"Okay and to add insult to injury, but what if she asked him to leave and he didn't want to? It's overly obvious that he has some type of obsession with her. He seems like the type to not take rejection too well," Phelps added.

"Yea, well maybe he did it and tried to make it seem like Monte did it to cover this tracks," Garcia replied with running thoughts.

"Yea, I saw the way he kept eyeing Montgomery when he would get too close to her."

"Hmph."

"When I asked Mr. Carnes about his whereabouts, he said he was on a flight going to New York, but that was a lie."

"Was it?"

"Yes. Seems like our guy was a no show for his flight, he didn't check in."

Garcia rubbed his chin while they drove toward the church.

"Okay, so Carnes didn't get on that plane, but we don't have proof that Parks went to Ms. Inacio's," Garcia said.

"Maybe someone else inter intervened."

"But who? Why? What would make someone hurt her though? She wasn't a troubled girl and didn't hang around bad crowds ..," Garcia stopped abruptly in mid-sentence.

"You alright?" Phelps asked when he paused mid-sentence.

"Yea, yea.....I was about to say," hoping to come up with something believable in the next two seconds, "we need to keep digging?" Garcia said.

"I'm no fan of Parks, but I don't think he has the brains to do this," Phelps said when they arrived at the church.

They escorted the family inside the local crammed church. Garcia weakly escorted his sister to Alana's casket to view her body one last time before they closed it permanently. He looked at his niece lying in the casket, but a quick flash of his son's face stained his memory. He quickly closed his eyes then took a deep breath and silently wished he'd taken a couple of his pills. Aelah tugged on his arm slightly to shake him out of his trance. He cleared his throat then moved his lead weight legs toward her seat. He looked at Phelps then at the front door while several people shoved each other hoping to get in. He then called several uniformed officers to help him while the chaotic crowd was quickly turned away.

As everyone found their seats and they finally closed her casket, Tyler was in her room packing her things and booked a flight for the next day back to Vegas. She knew she couldn't help her sister anymore and it was obvious that she was addicted to fast money. She sat on her bed reviewing her bank account. She realized if something happened to her, no one could access Kyler's account so she immediately jotted a little note with the account numbers, user and password names and placed it where only Skyler could find it.

Tyler refused to tell her sister that she was involved in a money laundering scheme with several drug lords with hefty incentives for validating their money. It started when she blackmailed Luis and sent pictures of Kyler to his home address and threatened to expose his infidelity to his wife. Assuming it was Skyler, he quickly responded and asked her how much would it cost to keep the child hidden and she named her price. Since then, she hired a private investigator to tour Brazil to find out exactly what kind of work he did since the sum of money she requested was easily accessible for him.

Tyler designed a money laundering scheme to better handle large sums of money without her institution knowing. She never met any of her clients, it was always a bank account number, a cash deposit or a courier delivery, which allowed her to have an increase number of referred clienteles. Her latest customer wanted to meet with her a couple of days ago in New York, but she canceled at the last minute. Out of all her customers, the customer was beginning to work her nerves with their persistent meetings and frequent changes. She knew then, it was time to stop her operation and move around so she can lay low.

As soon as she closed her laptop, someone knocked on her door. She looked at the door with a puzzled look before looking at the time on her phone. She requested a driver, but it was still four hours away until her flight. Hopefully, Skyler got her message and was going to meet with her before she left town.

"What the hell?" Ty mumbled to herself when the banging continued on her door.

She quickly slipped her laptop in her bag then closed and placed her suitcase on the floor beside the bed. She crept toward the window and peeped out of the window to see who was knocking on her door, but her uninvited visitor stood in a blind spot. Tyler wasn't going to answer the door so she turned around to walk away from the door until her uninvited visitor hurriedly knocked again before revealing themselves.

"It's me, Dana. Please open Up Ty," she said in a low voice near the crack of the door.

Tyler rolled her eyes, contemplating if she should open the door or not before finally opening it. Dana's disheveled hair alarmed Tyler, so she quickly stepped back when Dana rushed past her hysterically, pacing back and forth in Tyler's room.

Dana looked at her hands nervously before looking at Tyler. Tyler knew that facial expression all too well, so before Dana said anything else she intervened.

"Why are you here?"

"I need to speak with you ..."

"See, this is a problem. The difference between me and my sister is that I'm a loner. I don't like people in my business and the favor is returned."

"Tyler, I'm really sorry that I came here uninvited, but I need to tell you this," she said in a ghostly whisper, "Skyler is hiding something and I think it's bad."

Tyler stared with a blank stare.

"I wanted to tell you because the two of you are identical and I didn't want you getting caught up in whatever she has done."

Tyler looked at a scared Dana then turned around.

"Where is Sky now?"

"I don't know. She just turned mad, throwing things at me, hitting me and cursing at me. She even went into my bag and stole my money."

"What! That's not like Sky."

Dana looked at her nails when Tyler shook her head. Tyler warned Skyler about bringing a third person to their meetings because they could tell someone that Skyler had two faces, an identical twin. Tyler new Dana could expose her, so she did what she usually did when Skyler got them in a whirl of trouble. She used her familiar looks to charm Dana.

"So, what am I supposed to do?" Tyler asked without taking her eyes from her.

"I need to clear my thoughts. You know, hanging around Sky has brought me a lot of trouble."

Tyler furiously grew suspicious about her sister's sporadic behavior, but voicing her thoughts was not an option. Dana studied Ty's every move so she quickly looked away and thought about the disturbed phone call she received from Skyler when she was in Vegas.

"You know, I'm not sure what's going on with Skyler these days, but like I said earlier, she and I are two very different people," she said with no expression.

"I don't want no type of trouble," Dana said.

"And neither do I. I have a daughter back home that needs me."

"I didn't know you had a daughter," Dana replied shockingly as she spun around.

Of course not, Skyler's not going to tell you that she gave up her daughter, Tyler mused to herself.

"I do and she's beautiful."

"You're a mom, what's her name?"

"Kyler."

"Tyler, Skyler and Kyler? Does she look like you two?"

"Spit image."

"Wow, triplets...in other words," Dana said in a jokingly way.

"So, you see my concern? I can't get tied up with Skyler's games and being here I can easily get caught up by mistaken identity. I need to go."

"Oh, you don't ever have to worry about me mentioning you to them."

"I would hope not. I do know people can be unpredictable and when they are pushed to the limit so there is no telling what can be revealed."

"Well, I won't say nothing."

"How much did she take from you in exchange for your silence?"

"I wouldn't feel right taking money from you. Besides, I said I wouldn't say nothing."

"Look, don't mention none of this to her, she will think we are against her and that's added fuel."

"I won't. She's been so antsy about everything lately especially leaving Miami."

"You need to go," Tyler stated.

"Listen, ever since she realized that her ex-boyfriend Ric and my ex, Russ are brothers she's been in a frenzy. Then when all hell broke loose at the club, she's been all paranoid."

Tyler rubbed her temples because she remembered that night perfectly. She remembered leaving her several messages on her voice mail that night. Tyler thought back to her sister's erratic behavior and grew extremely suspicious.

Tyler grabbed her bags.

"Drama finds drama," Tyler said while shaking her head. "Look, thanks for the heads up, but you gotta go right now. I'm not trying to get involved with my sisters' drama, that's her life and I have my own," Tyler said hurriedly.

Dana walked toward the door before Tyler called out her name.

"Hey Dana?"

"Yea," she said while spinning around.

"I have my reasons why I choose not to get involved with anymore of my sisters' affairs. I will tell you this, if you feel like she's involved in something, detach yourself quickly, because it will end badly."

Tyler reached inside of her duffel bag and pulled out fifty brand new one hundred dollar bills. Dana's eyes grew wider when she saw the duffel bag full of money.

"Here you go, remember to keep my name out of your mouth," Tyler said as she handed Dana the money.

Dana hurriedly stuffed the money inside of her purse then looked at her.

"Tyler?"

"Yes."

"Thank you."

Dana scurried out of Tyler's room and headed to her car. She quickly jumped in her car then sped off in the opposite direction while looking in her rearview mirror.

"Oh shit, I can't believe I just did that!" she screamed.

Her heart paced in her chest as she nervously ran the red light with no destination in mind. As soon as she picked up her phone to make a call, Skyler's name flashed on the screen.

"Yes?"

"Where are you?" Skyler growled quietly.

"Excuse me?" Dana shot back.

"Look, I said I was sorry for hitting you before you stormed out of here. I was frustrated and ..."

Dana didn't respond.

"Can we talk about it?" Skyler asked.

"There's nothing to talk about. You got mad over some dumb shit then hit me and took my money. Every time you get high, you spaz out and get all paranoid and shit."

"I know, I'm really sorry."

"I want my money back because it's mine," Dana replied, knowing she was hours from finally saying goodbye to her. "If so I'll be there shortly."

"Ok. Ok. I have it, see you soon."

I still can't believe my plan worked. I wasn't sure if Tyler was going to open the door or not. She easily chalked up the funds just so I can keep my mouth shut about her, no problem. I don't ever have to say shit about her or her twin sister. Now all I have to do is get my money from Skyler after I meet with the investigating officers who have been asking about me so they can clear my name then get the hell out of Miami and let Skyler deal with this shit, she said to herself.

While Dana was in route to the precinct, Sgt. Webster was at the police station wrapping up the information from the DMV on Rafael Jai. As soon as the fax came through, she read over the documents then quickly dialed Garcia's number while he was at the funeral.

222

"Hey boss, I hate to interrupt you, but I'll make this quick, your results are in with Mr. Rafael Jai......There are on your desk.....Are you going to swing by afterwards?......Good, I will see you then....Oh by the way, Captain said they are gathering Ric Simmons paperwork together so he can be extradited Monday. He also said he need you to sign off on some paperwork too......Okay, see you when you get in."

Garcia disconnected the call and replayed what he painfully witnessed. Watching his sister cry out for her daughter broke his heart and made him think of his own heartbreak.

"No! Not my baby!" Aelah screamed out in a desperate plea when they closed Alana's casket.

Losing a child was the most devastating experience a parent couldn't fathom, but losing them because someone took their life was even more excruciating. Garcia stuffed his hands in his pocket and held onto the cross as the ceremony continued while he thought of his son's death. No words, no amount of comfort or psychological help could endure the loss. He remembered the day when Aelah called him ecstatically when she found out she had a girl and all of the promises she vowed to give to her.

Now, instead of Aelah wearing a white dress on her wedding day where she could give her daughter away, she sat in a black dress, moments before she said her final goodbyes. Once the ceremony ended at the church, he escorted her to the family car.

"You will be ok Aelah," he whispered.

"This is just too much for me Dez, I just want to die. My heart is broken and my baby is gone," she said as the tears streamed down her face.

He hugged her and told her that her pain would never go away, no matter how many sleepless nights she would bear. He knew all too well how the missing heartbeat in his life felt.

When she looked at him, she quickly wiped his tear and told him that she loved him before she climbed in the car. He closed the door behind her, took a deep breath then walked to his car as they followed them to the burial site. When they arrived at the burial site, he sadly watched Luis escort her to her plot which was beside his son, Dezio Garcia Jr. He'd visited his grave just days prior to learning about his niece's death.

Garcia took a deep breath just before Phelps walked beside him.

Phelps looked toward the Inacio's family mourning the loss

of their loved one as they placed a single white rose on her casket. Garcia looked at his nephews sitting beside each other while his eldest held his mother's hand. Garcia immediately turned away as the mourners walked up toward Aelah and hugged her. Phelps looked on while observing her guests, hoping to see someone suspicious, but he didn't.

Garcia watched along hoping that no one noticed his emotional connection to the service. Aelah told him she was going to finally leave Luis but for now, he stood by her side. He looked mentally absent though during the service. Garcia kept his eyes on Luis and his mannerism, but something didn't sit right with him.

"Hey boss, you ready?"

"Yea...I am. I think I've seen enough for today. I need to go to the house later to check on the family," Garcia sighed solemnly.

Just as they walked off, Micah called out his name.

"Lt. Garcia?"

"Yes?" he said, spinning around to look at her.

"Ms. Aelah wanted me to thank you for coming out. She said it meant a lot for you to come out in her time of need," Micah said.

Garcia looked past Micah and stared at his sister. He nodded at her then placed his hand over his heart, a gesture they did when they were younger to imply that they empathized with each other. He watched Aelah placed both of her hands over her heart before looking back at Micah.

"Are you going back with them Micah?" he asked cautiously.

"Yes, just for a little while."

"Could you do me a favor?"

"Sure."

"Make sure you look after her."

"I will," Micah replied.

Garcia smiled at Micah then walked away. He quickly slipped on his shades seconds before Phelps turned toward him.

"You look a little pale, are you sure you're okay?"

"Yea. Yea. We need to get back to the station and find her murderer," Garcia said as they walked toward his car.

Honesty is the best key...

Garcia drove back to the precinct with several things on his mind. He knew as a seasoned detective he needed to take a step back and look at the whole picture and exhaust all investigative avenues to present the best case to the district attorney. The case was lingering but nothing added up. No one was talking. Everyone had an alibi. With countless hours of preparation and planning, they didn't feel any closer than they did weeks ago. He was so engulfed with the case, he hadn't really prepare himself for his approaching retirement date. He slightly formed a smile when he thought about sailing on the Atlantic waters and not having a care in the world. He made a mental note to go back to the marina to look at their boats again so he could make a final decision on which boat he wanted. Until recently, he wanted Catalina to share his sailing adventure with him, but she had other plans that didn't include him. He pressed his lips together as the thought of seeing her kissing Clifton stained his memory. Phelps noticed a quiet Garcia.

Phelps was starting to worry more about Garcia, but knew if he mentioned this to him he was only going to make up faulty and petty excuses. He noticed Garcia was antsy about the case or anyone who stood in the way while his mix matched clues frustrated him. He knew something was wrong with Garcia, but knew that Garcia would never reveal it to him.

"You look like you have a lot going on in that brain of yours, are you alright?"

"I'm alright. Why do you say that?"

"I mean, you're all over the place."

"Look. I'm on the verge of retirement and I learn that I'm on a case..., a case that happens to be closely associated to my heart. I want to retire with my perfect record of accomplishment, but honestly, it's not looking like it."

"What makes you think you won't? I mean, we are just minutes away from cracking this case?"

"Are we? Can you honestly look at the Inacio family and tell them that?"

"No, but I think..."

"You think what? Phelps, as much as I don't want to say this.....we don't have any concrete evidence on this case."

"Man, you have to admit we're working our asses off on this case trying to dig up more clues and...," Phelps said before Garcia cut him off.

"You think that's good enough?" Garcia quizzed. "Families want justice, they don't care about clues. Keep in mind, you are the final link in giving closure to these families. The arrest and prosecution gives most families some type of closure."

"I know. I know, just feels like we're just steps away from solving this case," Phelps said optimistically.

"And we might not be. There are things to look for. This is a career criminal, not someone who accidentally murdered her."

"We have interrogated everyone we listed, but they ain't giving up shit."

"Yea, well technically the Simmons Brothers aren't part of this investigation."

"Or are they? At this point, everyone is tied to someone in some way or another."

"Yea, now I believe that. The only people we haven't interrogated are Ms. Sutton, her friend or Rafael Jai."

"What about her twin?" Phelps added.

"Technically we have. Remember at Night's Owl?"

Phelps stared out of the passenger window without responding.

"I'm hoping Ms. Sutton friend will be here and give her statement."

"When we get back to the station, let's look at the surveillance tape one more time."

"Alright," Phelps replied.

While the men were in route to the station, Clifton Parks walked in the station with his lawyer and stood at the front desk. Sgt. Webster spotted him then walked up to him.

"How can I help you?"

"Yes, I'm here to see Sharp Shooter, I mean Garcia," Parks spat sarcastically.

"He's not here at the moment, but is there something that I can help you with?"

"No, but when do you expect him back?"

"Hmmm, what is this in regards to?"

Clifton looked at her before sticking out his chest.

"My attorney and I need to privately speak to him."

Sgt. Webster suggested for them to schedule a meeting with him. Clifton suggested to speak to the Captain with his attorney. Sgt. Webster was a little skeptical at first, but dialed her Captain's line and waited for him to pick up the phone.

"Yea....," Captain said as he snatched up the receiver.

"Sir, you have a," she said as she covered the receiver, "what's your name sir?"

"Clifton Parks."

"Clifton Parks is here to speak with you...since Garcia isn't here........okay?"

Captain Duvall snatched his front door open then walked toward the front desk. He was a short man, standing only five four, but no one ever mentioned his height. He walked towards Sgt. Webster then put his hands on his hips when he looked the gentlemen up and down.

"Clifton Parks?" he said as he took a good look at him.

"Yes."

"And who are you?"

"He's my attorney," Clifton chimed in.

Captain Duvall's patience was extremely thin and there were two things he didn't like, bullshit and drama. He looked over the attorney with hesitation until the attorney handed him a business card.

"Follow me," he said sharply as he turned away then walked toward his office.

Clifton and his attorney followed Captain Duvall in his office before he closed the door behind them.

Ten minutes later, Garcia and Phelps walked inside of the precinct side by side. Sgt. Webster swiftly walked toward them and pulled them to the side. She glanced back just to make sure no one was around as she told them Clifton Parks was in the

227

office with their Captain with his attorney.

"What? Right now?" they asked.

"He didn't give me any details at all, however he did ask for you first Lt. Garcia."

"So he opted to talk to Captain?" Garcia asked.

"You don't look worried," Phelps asked.

"I'm not. Parks just trying to get on Captains good side, but Captain has seen his rap sheets so that's the least of my concern," Garcia said.

Phelps watched Garcia walk into his office. He walked towards his partner's office and lightly tapped on the door.

"Come in," Garcia said, "are we missing something."

"I think we are close to finding a le...," Phelps said until Garcia's door flung open.

"Captain?" they both said in unison. "Is everything alright?"

Captain Duvall stood with his hands stuffed in his pants pocket and stared at Garcia for two minutes breathing like a raging bull. Phelps looked at Garcia then toward the Captain trying to figure out what the hell just happened.

"Would you like for me to step out?" Phelps asked.

"No need," he said before closing the door behind him.

"What's going on Captain?" Garcia quizzed hesitantly.

Captain walked toward Garcia's window, shut his blinds then leaned against the wall with his arms folded across his chest. He took a deep breath then began the inevitable.

"Garcia, I respect you and all that you have done for the force over the years. Your intimate details on finding resolutions has modified how the force will continue to grow," Captain stated.

"You already told me this before," Garcia replied with a pause. "What is this all about?"

"Why in the hell is Clifton Parks threatening to sue our precinct for harassment?"

"Get the hell out of here, he's just bluffing?" Garcia said as his eyes darted toward Phelps.

"He's already started the process. He brought his attorney here and the paperwork has been drawn."

"He can't do that, he's a suspect in our case," Phelps added.

"Yea, well he may be a suspect in your case, but that's not stopping his allegations. I don't need another lawsuit or any extra shit coming from anyone right now especially him."

"So, now what? What are we supposed to do? Just let him do whatever he wants?" Garcia asked.

Captain covered his mouth then shook his head.

"Parks attorney has thrown us a curve ball too."

"What's that?"

"He also came in here with accusations that your murder victim is your niece. Please tell me this is not true Garcia?" he said as he dropped his head, "tell me that you and Parks issues are just that, issues and these are just accusations."

Phelps stared at Garcia while their Captain spoke to them. Garcia refused to answer the question, but his heart wouldn't allow him to lie.

"I'm waiting on you to tell me that this is a lie," Captain said.

Garcia gradually looked toward Phelps then lastly at Duvall.

"I'm sorry Captain, ...but it is true," he mumbled under his breath.

Captain shook his head before pacing back and forth in Garcia's office. Phelps looked away without saying a word. That explained his emotional behavior and now it all made sense to Phelps.

"What! You of all people know protocol. You know damn well we're not supposed to be working on our relatives' cases!" he grilled.

"I understand that sir," Garcia said, "but..."

"There are not but! You are less than two weeks from your retirement and I'll be damned, of all people Clifton Parks is in here threatening us, we don't need this type of attention."

"Captain, I can explain," Garcia stated diligently. "I saw how these other detectives handle my son's case and I refused to sit back and watch them handle this case the exact same way. To this day, no one has an explanation and as a father I would like......closure," Garcia said unapologetically.

"But that wasn't your call Lieutenant?"

"You're right. It wasn't my call, but I made it and I don't regret it."

Duvall shook his head by Garcia's comment then looked away.

"Captain listen," Phelps added, "I've worked beside Lieutenant throughout this entire investigation and I'll admit, it's been tough, but by no means have we disrespected or harassed Clifton Parks. He's only saying that to cause distractions from this case."

Captain threw his hands in the air while he paced the room.

"That's not good enough Phelps. Parks is ready to make an announcement to the press and that leaves me and this precinct in a bind," Captain said as he walked toward Garcia's bulletin board. "Garcia you are a well-respected man and officer. I respect you even more because you swallowed your pride and gave your best shot trying to solve your niece's case. However, at this time you've placed me in a compromising situation and I only have a couple options for you."

"I'm listening," Garcia replied.

"I have to pull the case from you or you can hand the case to Phelps. Officially I can place you on administrative leave until you retire out. Just plan your retirement party and leave with high honors and teach Phelps what you know. Whatever you choose to do, stop by my office and let me know within an hour."

"Yes sir."

They both watched Duvall leave the office and close the door behind him. Phelps was stunned and wasn't sure what he should say. From the look of things, Garcia had enough on his plate.

"I apologize. I should've told you Phelps."

"It's okay. I'm sure you had your reasons." I'm sorry you had to go through the agony by yourself.

Garcia sat in his chair then looked at the ceiling.

"You know, all I ever tried to do was be the best investigator I knew how to be. I never thought in a million years that it would've ended like this. But I trust that you will do your best."

"What are you saying?"

"I'm saying, he's right. I'm giving you the case and for the remaining two weeks, I will shadow you and start moving my things out."

"Garcia, isn't there something we can do? Something we can say? I mean for crying out loud, Parks doesn't have that much pull, does he? I mean do you think I can solve this case by myself?"

Garcia sifted through his notes except for the DMV files Webster left on his desk earlier and placed them in a manila folder precisely. Phelps watched him carefully as he kept talking.

"So that's it?"

"Yes it is. I'm tired and I'm mourning."

While Phelps watched hopelessly, Garcia was slightly relieved that the truth was out. While he mentally rehearsed what he was going to say to Duvall, Clifton sat in Anthony attorney's car outside the precinct.

"Oh my god, did you see the Captain's face when I threatened him to sue the precinct for harassment? Oh my goodness," Clifton laughed hysterically as if it was a joke.

The attorney didn't respond.

Clifton said before he burst out into another boisterous laughter. "I mean, lil' man was pissed."

The attorney didn't smile nor make a single comment. Instead he shook his head disappointedly at Clifton while Clifton snickered and cynically laughed.

"You know, had I known that this was a joke to you I wouldn't have agreed to stand beside you while you humiliated yourself. I know what type of game you're playing and from this point on, I don't want to be involved. So for that, get out of my damn car."

Clifton abruptly stopped laughing and looked at the attorney with a puzzle stare.

"I told you I needed a favor, right? And I would pay you."

"Lose my number, keep your money and get the hell out," the attorney said angrily.

"Well fuck you then, you ungrateful bastard," Clifton said when he jumped out of the car.

He angrily slammed the attorney's door just as the attorney sped off. Clifton watched the car until it was out of site. Clifton quickly did a small victory dance, but stopped short when he looked at the phone nervously when the name appeared on his screen.

"Hello?...Um...., nothing ... ... A job?......What does it entail?...... Cash?......When do you need this done?......ASAP?.....Let me make some phone calls and call you right back," he said before disconnecting the call.

He immediately disconnected the call, jumped in his car as he headed towards Night's Owl. He pulled alongside a cab and saw the familiar face. He slowly trailed the cab until it came to a stop near an abandoned building. He parked several feet away behind an old dumpster and hurriedly jumped out of his car to follow her. He noticed she scanned the area carefully after she stepped out of the cab then looked toward the abandoned building. Clifton saw another dumpster closer to her and sneakily ran toward it while she talked to the cab driver before he drove away in the opposite direction. She quickly pulled out her cell then turned and walked away, keeping her back away from him while he crept up behind her without making a noise as he spoke in the phone.

"Hello?" Tyler said into the phone.

"So, what does it take for you to call me back?" he asked with his hands stuffed in his pockets interrupting her call.

"What!" she asked, spinning around nervously, "oh, it's you?"

"Yea, it's me."

"What do you want?" Tyler asked disgustingly, as she covered the phone. "And you followed me? You're a stalker."

"What do I want? You act like you don't know what I want," he said as he walked closer to her.

"I don't."

"What's your deal? Is this your retaliation of rejection? You already know what it was."

"What the hell do you want?" she realized then, he thought she was Skyler.

"Well, I asked you to call me the other night, but you didn't. I told you I would give you money if you stayed away, but I see you're still here and now you have the audacity to stand in front of me and ask *me* what do I want. It really doesn't matter what I want now, does it?" he asked sarcastically.

She looked past him, shaking her head disgustingly.

"Is that Clifton?" Skyler asked through the phone.

"Mmm hmmm," she replied.

"Call me when you're in this area," she said into the phone before disconnecting the call.

Clifton looked at her then looked toward her Louis Vuitton bag behind her.

"So, what brings you out here?" he quizzed as he looked around.

"Look, I have no dealings with you and you don't have any with me, so again I asked what do you want?" she said aggravatingly, storming past him.

He reached out to grab her arm, but she snatched it away

quickly. Within minutes, he rushed toward her and grabbed her neck.

"You don't know who you fucking with Sky," he growled.

"And neither do you," she said, when she kicked him in between his legs.

"Urghh," he screamed out as he held himself.

She ran past him and grabbed her duffel bag. She hurriedly unzipped it but before she reached inside of it to get her gun, he shoved her to the ground. Immediately, she lost her footing and hit her head on a sharp silver object. Clifton painfully walked toward her, but she didn't move from her fall. He called out her name, but she still didn't move. He walked towards her motionless body and lightly tapped her foot. He thought it was some kind of cat and mouse game until he noticed a speckle of blood underneath her nose.

"What the ...?" he cursed under his breath.

He looked around him hoping that no one saw him push her to the ground before pulling out his cell phone. He took several pictures of her then sent it to Luis. He heard a car approaching and took off running. He hid behind a dumpster refusing to look back until the coast was clear then jumped in his car and drove north so he wouldn't be seen.

"Oh shit," he said aloud. "I didn't mean to kill her."

As he drove away, Skyler reached the abandoned area where she was to meet Tyler. She called her sister's phone, but she did not answer. She felt like something was wrong and stepped out of a cab.

"Don't leave. I will be right back, okay?"

"Sure thing missy, but you're on my meter."

"Yea whatever man. I told you I would give you your money, after you take me to three places."

The cab driver threw his head back into his head rest when she walked away. He pulled out a pack of cigarettes and lit one while he waited and watched his meter run. Skyler pulled out her cell phone again, but this time when she called she heard a faint noise.

"Ty?" Skyler called out. "Damn, I know you're still pissed but geesh, don't you think this is a bit extreme," she said as she scanned the area. "In an abandoned area? Ty?" she called out again. "This is a bit much Ty."

When she walked further up she stopped in mid step in horror.

"What the fuck?" she said as she ran up to her sister.

"Tyler?" she cried out. "No!!!!!"

She remembered hearing Clifton's voice in the background and immediately rushed toward her sister's body.

"Fuck!" she cried out when she saw the blood that she'd lost.

She picked up her limp body and held her close to her broken heart. She knew if she called in her sister's murder, the police would automatically link Alana's murder back to her so she decided against it. She wasn't built for this. Too much was at stake and her tears streamed down her face as she cradled her sister back and forth in her arms, as she did Alana. She looked around to see if she could replay what could've happened to her.

First Lana and now this? she mused hurtfully. "I need you Ty, you are my person. I can't do this without you."

She wiped her tears away when she noticed her sisters' unzipped duffle bag beside her. Skyler looked at the bag then at her sister then gently placed her back on the ground. She grabbed her sister's purse, and duffel bag. She knew this was her only ticket escaping her life's drama. Ty was her ticket so she switched purses before kissing the top of her sister's head for the last time.

"I promise to raise Kyler the best way I can," she whispered to her sister.

She wiped away her tears and noticed the cell phone inches away from her. She stuffed it in her purse then walked back to the cab. She hurriedly closed the door and told the cab driver to drive while she looked out of the backseat window as he drove away. She then bent over and covered her face before silently crying to herself in the backseat.

Oh my goodness, Clifton killed my sister, she said to herself.

The cab driver asked her a few questions, but she didn't respond. Instead, she held onto her sister's belongings and thought about Kyler. She looked inside of her sister's purse and grabbed her wallet. She opened it and what she always feared most, stared back at her, a picture of her daughter. She looked at it then quickly turned it over before looking at it again. The more she stared at the picture, the more tears she shed. She hurriedly placed the picture back inside of the wallet and kept searching. She saw a set of keys, Ty's passport, driver's license, social security card and a piece of paper with different numbers scribbled on it in the duffle bag. She told herself that the woman she found was herself and she would now live as Tyler.

"I will now live as if I'm Tyler," she mused hurtfully.

She searched through Ty's phone and looked at the messages she hadn't cleared.

"I just transferred the funds to the account you provided ending in 1009.

She closed her sisters' phone and tilted her head back as she closed her eyes while her mind danced with so many thoughts. Her sister was doing something on the side, but what? She didn't know nor did she put any more thought to it.

"Cabbie, we need to make a detour. I need to stop by my room," she said as the cab driver made a u-turn in the middle of the street.

Back at the precinct, Garcia reluctantly walked toward Captain's Duvall office. He tapped on the opened door while Duvall searched the internet intensely.

"Come on in Garcia," he said. "Close the door behind you," he nodded his head.

"Thank you sir."

"Garcia, Garcia, Garcia," Duvall said before he covered both of his hands over his face. "I'm at a loss of words."

"I'm sure you are."

"So, have you given any thought to what I said earlier?"

"I have and I've given Phelps the case."

"He had the best teacher and I will assure you that this case, will get solved."

"Speaking of teaching someone, I do have a recommendation for his partner."

"Is that right?"

"Yes."

"Who?"

"Webster."

"Webster?" Captain asked with a piercing stare. "I don't think she's..."

"She's the perfect person. She's sharp, she's brilliant and you will have women looking up to this precinct because you made a Sgt. a detective."

"That's your suggestion?"

"My stipulation."

Captain looked through his blinds at the officers lurking around the office. He noticed Webster was busying herself with the files she held in her hands.

"Ok well you tell her the news. I'm sure she will appreciate the news coming from you."

"Thank you. Ya know Captain, I should've told you that she was my niece when it was confirmed that the murder victim was Alana Inacio."

"I can only imagine what type of emotions was brewing around when you heard her name. I'm sure you were horrified."

"That's an understatement," Garcia said.

"Well, take these final two weeks and transition out. I will call HR to see what you need to sign or sign anything at all."

"Ok," he said as his phone rang.

"Yea," Captain said into the phone. "He's in here....Okay Phelps."

Captain placed the phone back into its cradle and looked at Garcia.

"Is everything okay?" Garcia asked.

"I'm not sure. Phelps is on his way over here. He sounded rushed, so we will see."

Garcia rubbed his temples just as Phelps walked through the door.

"Hey, sorry to interrupt you Captain, but Garcia, can I see you for a second?"

"Sure, are we done Captain?" Garcia asked.

"Yea, we'll talk later. Go 'head."

"Okay."

Garcia trailed Phelps back into his office. Phelps closed Garcia's door and looked at him seriously.

"What?" Garcia questioned. "What is it? What's wrong?" he asked anxiously as Phelps just stared at him.

"...Skyler Sutton is dead."

"What! What do you mean she's dead?" he said while he scratched his head.

"It was just called in."

"Good Lord, if it's not one thing it's another with this damn case."

"That's why you can't abandon this case, boss."

Garcia looked at Phelps and knew this was the best time to tell him the news.

"Well I'm more than confident that you will be able to handle this case with Webster on your side."

"Webster?"

"Yes. I've already spoken to Captain and gave my recommendation for her to be your partner instead of those other guys he was thinking of."

"Sir, but she's not even...."

"Qualified? Man, she's better than anyone here including you."

"Me?"

"Just kidding," he joked. "I want her on this case with you I think she can really bring out the best of you."

"You really think so?" Phelps looked at him sincerely.

"I do. So make sure when you team up with her you lead her just as I led you. Gather all the information you can together and always be on the same accord. Whatever gut feelings you have, let her know and vice versa. Not sure if this is a break or not for the two of you, but this definitely raise concerns."

"I will."

"Good."

"Hey boss, you know things aren't going to be the same without you being here."

"Yea, I'm sure. Good thing is, I'm just a call away. Whenever you need me I'm there. When I get back from sailing for a while we can catch up."

"Sailing?"

"Yes, that's my retirement gift to myself."

"Must be nice. You got a boat?"

"I'm going in the morning to get one and I plan on taking it out for a spin."

"Ah man, I'm so jealous right now. Are you going to do any fishing?"

"Of course."

"Alright, well after you break it in, let me know. I just bought some fresh reels," he chuckled.

"I'ma hold you to it," Garcia replied.

Phelps took a deep breath.

"Well, I'm going to pack up my stuff then head out."

"You sure you don't want to stick around here to see the outcome of Ms. Sutton?"

"Nah," he said as he packed, "just keep me updated."

Phelps looked around Garcia's office then turned away.

"Phelps, when I'm done I will put everything you need for this case in a box and leave it on your desk."

"I was just dispatched," Phelps said just as Webster walked in. "You sure you don't want to stick around for a quick walk through?" Phelps asked Garcia again.

"Lt. Garcia, Captain said you wanted to talk to me?"

"I do, are you busy?"

"No."

"Good," he said as he looked toward Phelps, "let's take my final drive."

The last drive ...

Garcia, Phelps, and Webster arrived at the crowded crime scene that was filled with police cars, news reporters, two fire trucks, and an ambulance.

"I'll be damned," Garcia said as they walked closer to the taped crime scene.

Webster looked around the premises while she and Phelps trailed Garcia. She was overwhelmed by the news Garcia had relayed. She was finally going to transfer into investigations and Phelps was going to be her partner. A part of her knew that she couldn't measure up to Garcia, but he assured her that she was perfect for the position.

"Lieutenant," a uniformed officer called out when they walked toward him.

"Hey there...Williamson," he read on his name badge.

"I'm so glad to see you Lieutenant, let me fill you in on what's going on?"

"Actually, I'm not the lead investigator on this case, Phelps and Webster is taking this one," he said politely as he quickly introduced the duo.

The officer looked at Garcia with a shocked expression because everyone knew he was the only lead investigator of all the cases. Garcia quickly took note of his expression and immediately smoothed out a few wrinkles on the officer face.

"Williamson, they are just as good as me, besides you know my partner Phelps right?"

"Yes sir."

"Good. Make sure you treat him and his new partner, Webster, as if you were dealing with me. I assure you, you're in good hands.

Williamson formed a smile in the corner of his mouth.

Webster was a beauty and all the men lined up just to get to know her and he figured this would be the time to do just that.

"Oh, and no funny business either. She's tough," Garcia said as he patted his shoulder.

"Yes sir," the young officer looked past Garcia then glanced back at Webster.

Garcia stepped to the side and allowed them to lead the way. Garcia noticed several uniform officers talking to a homeless man near the scene. He instinctively turned to Phelps and Webster to give them a quick pep talk about what to look for and keep in mind with possible witness.

"Before we go over there, just want to run some things by you real quick. Not sure who he is or how much information he has, but you two need to check him out thoroughly. Make sure you introduce yourselves as the leading investigating officers to the surrounding officers. Webster, hopefully by next week, you can start wearing civilian clothes. I will make sure to put an order of business cards in for you when we head back to the office."

"Thank you."

"No problem, now go check him out and oh, before I forget Webster, here's a pad. Always carry one with you. You never know what you need to jot down and reference back to. You can have this one, it's fresh," he said as he handed his.

Webster nodded before she and Phelps walked toward the commotion as Garcia trailed them. He quickly noticed two separate tire tracks and voiced it aloud for them to look into it. He continued his stride until the homeless man walked toward them with Williamson leading him to Phelps and Webster trying to recall the series of events he saw.

While Webster was jotting down what the homeless man witnessed, Phelps and Garcia walked toward the other officers to learn more about the victim. Garcia observed the area and was pleased to know that Webster was holding up her end of the bargain. She had animalistic characteristics and that was going to be what helped her most in this male dominant industry. He was also pleased to know that her keen sharpness would be recognized by their Captain for what she's worth. He smiled to himself at the thought before they all resumed collecting information about the case. They walked toward the other officers until Kris walked beside them.

"You know Garcia, I hate meeting up like this. If you want to see me, all you have to do is come to my office," she said with a smirk.

"You're just full of jokes today," he chuckled. "Have you met Webster?"

"Not officially."

Kris nodded to Sgt. Webster then smiled.

"Finally a woman in investigations, welcome aboard," she said.

Webster smiled in return then followed Kris when she invited her to walk with her.

Garcia and Phelps stayed back to questioned the other officers who arrived before them. While they were jotting down their own notes, Webster knelt down beside Kris as she placed her markups near the body.

"I wonder what happened here," Webster said as she scanned the area. "Looks like foul play."

"Yea, it does," Kris agreed. She quickly looked at Webster with a puzzle stare.

"My background is Criminal Justice with an emphasis in Forensics."

"That explains it. We will work well together," Kris added with a smile.

Webster scanned the area.

"I was speaking to a gentleman who wouldn't give me his name earlier. He says he saw the entire thing."

"Is that right?" Kris quizzed.

"Yes, he had her license in his hand," she handed it to Kris.

"Skyler Sutton," Kris voiced. "Damn shame."

"Yea, looks like she could've been a model," Webster stated.

"You think this case is connected to that other model who was murdered?"

"Who knows, seems like we're going in circles."

Webster looked at the victim closely and realized she'd seen her face before. This case was indeed connected to the Inacio's case and she was one of the leading suspects on the surveillance disc. She jotted down some quick notes on her pad before Garcia and Phelps walked next to her.

"So talk to me Kris, what do we have?" Garcia voiced.

"Looks like our victim's name is Skyler Sutton all the way

from Vegas. Not sure what she was doing in an area like this."

"Look like she was looking for trouble," Phelps added.

"Well , trouble is what she got herself into," Kris added.

"Everyone out here is asking the same questions. Why would she come here of all places?" Garcia added.

"There is no visual evidence of physical or sexual assault and there's no matter under her nails. From the looks of things, she shows no signs of assault or strangulation, but there is blood coming from her head. Once I get back to the lab and clean her up I can give you more to go on," Kris voiced, unmoved.

"I wonder if the same bloody hands murdered both suspects," Garcia added.

"I wonder if the murderer came after her since it's possible that she saw him," Phelps added.

"I wouldn't argue with you on that one, but why would the murderer meet her all the way out here. Did she know him? Look at her things, her purse is open and there is no telling if the murderer staged this, took her money, credit cards or anything with value to it. Does she still have on jewelry?"

"Yes she does," Webster added.

Kris snapped several pictures in different angles so she could put them in her file.

"Well, gentlemen and ma'am, I'm about to wrap this up here and take her body back to the lab. If you have any more questions, come see me in a couple of hours. I can give you more to work with."

"Sure thing," they said in unison.

Webster combed the area while Garcia pointed out several things to Phelps.

"Webster, are you ready?"

"I am."

They walked past the standing officers and headed toward Garcia's car. Webster looked over her notes while Garcia finalized his duties to them. He told both of them to call if they needed some pointers every now and then. They agreed to call him on speed dial if they had any questions regarding the case they were working on. When they walked inside of the precinct, they noticed Duvall standing near Garcia's office talking to several officers until he spotted him. He walked toward Garcia to give him an update.

"She was a natural boss," Phelps interjected. "She's real sharp," he whispered when he walked past him.

Sharp? he mumbled to himself.

Duvall walked towards Garcia and shook his hand. Garcia then picked up his belongings and headed out for an early day. He tossed his box, with most of the things from his office in his trunk then spun around when a familiar voice called out his name. The sound of her voice jolted him which made him spin around quickly.

"Can we talk?"

He looked at her then looked away.

"For what? There is nothing to talk about."

"I know you don't want to talk about us, so I won't bother trying to discuss us."

"Thank you," he said in a disinterested tone.

"I do need to discuss something with you."

"Look Catalina, right now I'm not in the mood for anything," he voiced.

"It's about Clifton," she said in a tone close to a whisper.

He looked at her then shook his head in disbelief then turned away to walk off. She noticed the familiar look then tried a different approach.

"Clifton is trying to set you up Garcia. The lawyer he brought in was only to call your bluff," she blurted. "I swear to you."

He stopped in his tracks then looked around them to see who could've heard her.

"Get in."

He didn't know whether if he was making a wise decision or not, but he knew Catalina could help him get Clifton once and for all. He avoided her calls since the night he took her to Night's Owl. He pulled off from the precinct hoping not to regret his decision. He approached a red light and quickly looked at her.

"Start talking," he ordered.

"Look first of all, I want to apologize for everything. I can't explain everythi....."

"I don't care to hear an apology from you or your reasons. You said Clifton is trying to set me up and that's all I want to know," he said with a startling stare.

"Ok, where do I start?"

"From the beginning," he said when the light turned green.

"I met Clifton at the airport almost two years ago. He was......," she paused.

"He what?" Garcia asked when she stopped talking abruptly.

She paused for a second, wondering if telling him the truth was going to hurt him or help him. She toyed with her fingers.

He was slick with his words, always had a comeback line. He had a charismatic way about him that was alluring, but he also had a cocaine habit which was maintainable. After we introduced ourselves, he told me that he owned a beachfront restaurant, but I wasn't interested in him. One day he called me and asked me could I swing by. I was in the area, stopped by and he started talking.

"Talking about what?"

"At first just trying to court me until he got a phone call. He was arguing with someone by the name of Feliz. They stayed on the phone for more than thirty minutes arguing When I asked what was going on, he just said Feliz worked for some big time guy by the name of Kaiser."

"Feliz? Kaiser?" he repeated while she continued her story. "What the hell does that have to do with Clifton."

"Apparently, Clifton needed a financial favor and Feliz had someone to drop off a couple of stacks of cocaine."

"He was that comfortable to let you see that?"

"Yes, I was trying to get you what you wanted, but Clifton's sporadic behavior made me change how I dealt with him so I can get more information. So, I pretended to have an interest so I could go to his house. I soon learned they were running partners."

"Running partners, did she say where they were from?"

"Not that I can recall. I just remember him referencing it as 'back home'."

Garcia paused.

"Anyway from what he was telling me, Feliz was Kaiser's right hand man and was hired to complete tasks for him. But something has happened between the two of them and now Clifton thinks Feliz is trying to get him. Anyway, I don't know all the details, but something went wrong and Kaiser is furious. Now, after learning this I wasn't sure how this would matter so I ignored it until Clifton called and asked me to meet him and Feliz at his restaurant, but Feliz never showed up."

"Have you ever met Feliz?" Garcia asked.

"No."

"Do you know if they ever met up?"

"No, and you know what's pathetic, Clifton doesn't even know what Feliz looks like?"

"You have got to be kidding me, that's just like Clifton. He's so reckless."

"You mean to tell me Feliz could be standing in front of Clifton and he wouldn't even recognize him?"

"That's what he told me."

Garcia listened intensely just as he pulled up to an empty parking lot. Nothing Catalina was saying made any sense to him, but he made sure to make a mental note on this issue.

"Out of the blue, Clifton received a strange call from Feliz saying he thinks Kaiser was playing him like a rag doll and he was going to give him a dose of his own medicine."

"A dose of his own medicine? Wait, you do know that what you're saying makes no sense. It's almost useless, but I'll tell Phelps and Andersen look into it."

"Garcia, I'm not sure if it mattered or not, that's why I stayed silent on it. Besides, Clifton was so high he didn't even know he had the call on speaker when Feliz called."

"Look, I think I've heard all that I can tolerate when it comes to him. I've never been his fan especially since I busted him with gambling, prostitution, and drug trafficking a few years back. I learned a lot about Mr. Parks. He's originally from Chicago, but he stayed with his dad's best friend who he called his uncle when he was seven. His uncle passed and left his entire estate to Clifton."

"You were the one who busted him for gambling, prostitution and drug trafficking?"

"Yes I did and ever since then, I've been his least favorite person."

She paused for a second before continuing.

"Small world," she added. "Have you ever heard of a guy by the name of Anthony Carnes or Barnes?"

"Carnes. What about him?"

"Well his lawyer came in town and I overheard them plotting up a scheme to scare off a couple of people for a nice amount. I just wanted to tell you that you are on that list."

"They already came by."

"Damn," she covered her mouth, "Is everything ok?"

"Everything is a mess. They have threatened to press charges against the precinct."

"Don't worry about it, it's just a fluke. Besides he's just a sports attorney. He probably just flashed his business card and left the talking for Clifton."

Garcia hit the steering wheel with his fist. He was boiling mad, but no matter how mad he was, Clifton called his bluff and it worked. Even if the sports attorney was a flute, Clifton blasted him in front of his boss which made him lose his position on the case.

Catalina closed her eyes when she heard him hit the steering wheel with his fist. It pained her to know that she aided in all of this, but tiptoeing with his nemesis sealed the deal. It cost her more than her happiness, she lost a lifetime of secured happiness. Had she known that he was 'Sharp Shooter,' she would've handled everything differently. The more she pondered about the situation, the clearer things became. It all made sense now, but she knew words wouldn't heal the hurt she caused him.

"I am so sorry I betrayed you. I never meant to hurt you nor did I ever want you to find out this way. I should've told you."

He stared at the steering wheel while she confessed. The lingering thoughts of a younger man enticing her made him avoid her confession at all cost. She waited for him to say something, but he did not. The suspense was killing her.

"Say something. Your silence is killing me. I know my dishonesty led to all of this," she said nervously.

Garcia didn't move a muscle.

"Hello? Are you going to say something?" she said while staring at him.

"I want to hate you," he said solemnly as he turned to look at her. "You're not only a liar, you're also reckless."

As soon as his words left his lips, she quickly turned her head as her tears immediately streamed down her cheeks leaving nothing else to say.

"Would you like for me to take you home?"

"Yes," she said in a low tone.

Her tone was familiar. A tone that usually weakened him

before and after all the hurt she caused him, it still weakened him now. He took a deep breath before quickly glancing over at her while he caught a tear stream on her face before she wiped it away.

"Lina, why did you lie to me? Why didn't you tell me the truth? Was he worth it?" he asked.

"At first, I didn't think it mattered because you said from the beginning that you didn't want to have a serious relationship, and no he was not worth it."

He paused, regretting to have made such a statement.

"I know I said I didn't want to have a serious relationship in the beginning, but things changed for me. They didn't change for you?"

"I never wanted to have a casual thing with you. I also didn't want to pressure you into something that you clearly stated you didn't want from the beginning. I understood the seriousness of your job so I tried to give you the space you needed."

She paused for a second when she heard his phone ring.

"I'm not going to answer it."

That was a first. He always answered his phone regardless what they were doing. She raised an eyebrow then continued to speak.

"I started to busy myself when you started canceling our trips and dinners. I always came last to your job. Clifton put me first."

He swallowed hard because he knew her reason. It was the same reason his first wife left him. There was so much to say. He had so many questions to ask, but knew the timing wasn't right. He drove in silence until he pulled up alongside her condo.

"I really do hope you find it in your heart to forgive me," she said before she stepped out from his car.

Within seconds of responding, she hurriedly closed the door and walked away. He knew his words would linger with her until he reached out to her, but too much hurt settled within him and he refused to give in. When he drove away from Catalina's, Clifton was busy stirring around in his office. He scanned his entire office as he replayed the conversation he had with Skyler before he shoved her to the ground. His mind raced thinking of a believable alibi, but who was going to believe his side of the story?

He knew Dade County was watching him with a fine tooth

comb. He had only one option, leave South Beach, get his money and head to the Dominican Republic for a little while to lay low. He paced through his office once more before looking through his desk drawers. He glanced at the monitor making sure no one was coming towards his office. He hurriedly grabbed his bag and stuffed every piece of content that was in the safe. He zipped the stuffed bag then closed the safe. He took his final glance of the room, grabbed his coat, cut off his light and headed toward Mesa.

"Mesa, I need to talk with you for a minute," Clifton swiftly said as he glanced around his restaurant.

"What's up? Everything okay?" she quizzed when she noticed his Louis Vuitton bag beside his feet.

She wiped her hands on her hand towel before walking toward him suspiciously.

"Yea, yea," he stammered, "we need to talk privately. Do you mind if we walk out on the patio?"

"No, not at all."

Mesa quickly told the second server that she was stepping away for a few minutes to talk with Clifton. Clifton hurriedly walked on the patio then quickly stuffed his hands in his pockets so Mesa wouldn't see him tremble.

"Hey, what's up? What's going on with you Clifton?" Mesa asked cautiously.

He looked around while scratching his shadowing beard.

"I need you to trust me right now," he whispered.

Mesa looked at him.

"Are you alright?"

"Yes. No. Yes. Look," he shook his head, "I rather not tell you what's going on 'cause I'm sure those detectives will be snooping around here in a couple of hours, so here's a crash course. You have the other key to Night's Owl still, right?"

"Yes, and?"

"Okay, you remembered I told you I was gonna make you my silent partner one of these days because you've been so loyal to me?"

"Clifton, you've been telling me that for several years now, so why should I believe you now?"

"I know, I know Mesa," he said rapidly, "anyway, I've signed everything over to you and I'm officially making you my silent partner. It's been legally drawn up for five years now."

"Five years? When were you going to tell me?"

"After I was busted, I added you then just in case if I was going to do some real time. I didn't want them taking my shit from me. I'd rather give it to you 'cause I know you will do right by it, besides you're like family to me."

"Don't I have a voice in this matter?"

"Legally you do, but if you don't want it, I will have to make arrangements for someone else to be my silent...," he said before she interrupted him.

"No- no-no, no, I'm not saying I don't want it, but I would've liked to have *known* about the changes. So, since I've been a silent partner for five years, when will I see my back pay?" she asked.

"I have fifteen thousand dollars on me right now, cash. Is that okay for now?" he whispered.

"Fifteen thousand dollars on you right now, are you insane?" Mesa voiced.

"I can't really get into that right now, but will you handle the restaurant for a while?"

"I don't know how to run this, I mean, you pay people and order ....."

"You know how to run this place, you did it for months while I was locked up and our sales were great. Just keep doing that. If you need to hire someone, then hire someone."

"Clifton, I think..."

"Mesa I have everything in the second drawer for you to follow just in case it slipped your memory. I know this is a lot to take in and I know this is last minute, but if you can do this one thing for me, I swear I will make it worth your while."

Mesa looked at him as he repeatedly wiped his nose. She knew all about his bad habits and his bad business handlings. She was the one who saw his swollen black eyes when his gambling habits went awry with all of his bad tactics, but still never judged his ways or his recklessness.

"Look, I have to leave right now, but I will call you as soon as I figure some things out. I don't want to tell you anything right now because I don't want you to carry that burden when they try to sweep things in here."

"They?" she quizzed.

"Dade County and they will be coming, I assure you. But you

have nothing to worry about. They can't come in and search without a warrant and they damn sure can't close these doors."

"But I have so many questions....."

"I know, and I will answer them soon."

He reached into his shoulder bag and pulled out three envelopes stuffed with cash and hurriedly handed it to her. She glanced at them but quickly placed them inside of her apron while her heart paced inside of her chest.

"Whatever you do, don't place it in the bank all at once. You never know whose watching. I have to go in here and tell the staff something so just follow my lead and I promise to keep in touch as soon as I figure something out," he said before spinning around, preparing to make a speech before his final exit.

He quickly asked the staff to gather quickly so he could make a quick announcement.

"Hey yo, listen up real quick. I need everyone's undivided attention. I have good and bad news. Real quick, the good news is that I'm looking to open another Night's Owl in another location, but the bad news is that it's in another state."

Everyone clapped their hands and cheered out for a celebration.

"Whoa, not too soon, I don't have anything concrete right now but in the meantime, Mesa will be in charge. Everything goes through her until I return. I will be in touch. Not sure how long I will be gone, but I plan to franchise Night's Owl. Hopefully, when I come back I can bring a contract and some blueprints of the new establishment," he lied. "Okay, playtime is over, everyone get back to work."

He watched his crew scatter amongst themselves as they celebrated with each other. He didn't want to scare them off and this was his only escape.

"Are you sure you have to do this? I mean, is there any way we can fix this without you leaving?" Mesa quizzed before reaching for his hand.

"This is the only way," he said as he squeezed her hand in his before he released it.

He raised one of his eyebrows, pressed his lips together, displaying his dimple, then turned and walk away. Mesa stood there in a daze when he walked out of Night's Owl. A part of her wanted to run behind him but she knew something was terribly wrong and his reason had everything to do with those detectives.

Clifton hurried himself to his car, tossing everything in the trunk without looking up or around him. He jumped into his car and dialed only one number, Luis. His call was forwarded to his voicemail which infuriated him. He stopped at the red light and stared at his phone. No sooner when the light turned green, Luis name flashed across the screen.

"Luis?"

"Clifton, we need to meet. Meet me at the dock in fifteen minutes."

"Gotcha," Clifton said before he disconnected the call.

He spun the car around and headed to the dock about a mile up. He knew this meeting was sure to be his final meeting in South Beach. He rushed through the streets while the local police officers cruised the area scouting for petty criminals. He rehearsed to himself what he was going to say when Luis stood in front of him until he looked at the taxi that pulled up beside him at the red light.

"What the fu...?" he said shockingly to himself.

He quickly looked away then glanced back to the car one more time just to make he saw correctly. The woman in the car beside him was applying lip gloss in her compact mirror and from the looks of it, she looked just fine. He watched the taxi speed off without moving a muscle while the cars blew their horns behind him.

"It can't be. It's impossible. I saw her, I was with her, she's... Skyler's dead," he mumbled to himself.

He drove in distress while Skyler headed toward her sisters hotel. Skyler looked through her phone, hoping that Dana would return her phone call, but she hadn't. Instead, she laid her head on the backseat while the vision of her sister's blood stained her memory. It finally settled in that her sister was dead and just like Alana, she left her twin sister alone with the hopes of escaping her own demise. After the cabbie took her to her sisters' hotel, she gave Tyler's entire luggage to the cab driver. Before the cabbie closed the trunk, she noticed a plane ticket itinerary sticking out of the side of the duffel bag. She grabbed it and headed to the backseat.

"Damn it," she said to herself, "Las Vegas, here I come."

She instructed the cabbie to head to the airport. She was right on time, she was leaving South Beach and all of its horrid memories behind. Her plane was leaving in a couple of hours and everything was looking in her favor. Her only regret was pretending that she didn't know her sister's fate. She looked out of the window and wondered where Dana was, but Dana made sure to stay her distance from Skyler.

While Skyler was headed to Miami's International Airport, Monte's phone buzzed in his hand as he sat in the cab.

"Garcia? Everything alright?" he said into the phone. "What's going on?....Yea, my Captain has ordered me back to Vegas unless I have Skyler in my custody......What!... She's dead? ......Have you verified this? Have you seen her body?...I guess.... my job is done here then.......Can you fax the office the news in a report. I will. You too," he said before ending his call.

Monte looked through his pictures in his phone. He smiled at the sight of Alana while the sun kissed her. Sadness drew upon him as he stared at her picture as he rode to the airport. His memories in South Beach would be treasured.

When fate walks directly to you...

A couple of hours passed, Monte found his seat on the plane. He wasn't quite ready to say good bye to South Beach just yet. He wondered if Alana was alive, would she be occupying the seat beside him. He paused for a second when the thought about their last conversation. He placed his phone in his shirt pocket, close to his heart. He slipped on his shades then closed his eyes, but quickly opened his eyes when he heard a familiar voice.

Skyler walked past him talking to the flight attendant. He quickly pulled out his cell phone and dialed Garcia's number, but it went to his voicemail.

I thought he said he saw her body.

Monte peeled his glasses from his face and took a quick picture of her on his phone. He quickly forwarded the picture to Garcia before they announced for all electronic devices to be turned off. He watched her every move without taking his eyes away from her.

Meanwhile, Garcia sat at home looking inside of the manila folder Webster placed on his desk about Rafael Jai. He stared at his laptop and pulled up several missing persons website the office often frequented. He would often work from home and since he still had access to the dashboard. He quickly typed in Rafael Jai's name in the database search hoping to learn something new. Immediately, Rafael Jai's picture came up, along with his date of birth, hometown, occupation and how long he's been missing.

"I'll be damn," he said aloud.

He stuffed everything back into the manila folder headed toward his car. The first place he wanted to go was Night's Owl so he could pistol whip Clifton, but quickly decided against it when he drove past Night's Owl and headed toward the Marina. He'd plan to meet a buyer several days later to pick out a boat, but he felt like getting a sneak peek on the inventory. He needed to clear his mind and to make sense of what he saw on the internet. When he arrived at the Marina, he opened the manila folder once again and looked at the contents. He knew he had everything in front of him, but he felt like a small piece was missing, the name. He grabbed the folder then walked alongside the dock noticing several guys were cleaning their boats, but from the looks of it, none of them captured his attention.

"Excuse me sir, is there anything I can help you with?" a gentleman asked.

"Umm, yes. I have a scheduled appointment in a couple of days but since I was in the area, I just dropped by to check out your inventory."

"Well today is certainly a good day to check them out. We have a couple potential sellers out on their boats. Go out there and talk to them. Since the weather is clear, you might want to ask them to take the boat for a spin. Then, maybe you guys can work out a deal."

"I think I will do that," Garcia said.

Garcia walked toward the dock and introduced himself as a potential buyer. He inquired about the boats and the asking price while Clifton stood near the dock looking for Luis.

"I'm here," Luis said.

"Good, let's get this over with."

"Thank you for sending me the confirmation pictures of Ms. Sutton. Since you delivered me what I asked for, here's your money," he said as he handed him a leathered briefcase.

Clifton opened the briefcase just enough to see the enclosed taped money. He separated the bills in one stack just to make sure Luis wasn't setting him up. He could never play it too loosely. He slowly displayed a smile then closed it rapidly when Luis assured him it was all there.

"Okay, well our business is done, right?" Clifton asked a serious faced Luis while extending his hand.

"Not exactly," Luis said without acknowledging the handshake. He moved closer to Clifton. "I was hoping you could do me one last favor."

Clifton looked toward the ocean and contemplated about Luis statement.

"I don't mind doing favors for you, but I need to handle some very personal business first before I can conduct any other business."

"Personal business? I can pay you whatever you need to compensate your time," Luis commanded, "because Clifton, this matter is extremely personal to me."

Clifton looked at his watch and shifted in his stance. Luis noticed his hesitance and immediately pulled out a sealed yellow envelope.

"Whenever you get a moment, take a look at this and get back to me. I know this is last minute and I understand you have to take care of your needs before you can take care of anyone else's, so give me a call within four hours to let me know if you can take care of this matter or not."

Clifton looked at the sealed envelope. He looked around just to make sure no one was watching him. Once he turned to look at Luis, he was out of sight. Clifton became ultra-paranoid and quickly walked to his car. He pulled out his cell phone and dialed Mesa's number. As soon as she answered the phone, he instructed her to meet him in the back of the restaurant quickly. Her tone seemed a bit skeptical, but he wasn't taking no as an answer. He disconnected the call, jumped in his car, and placed the envelope Luis had given him moments ago on top of his briefcase in the passenger seat.

Clifton drove toward Night's Owl rethinking Luis's proposal. On one hand, he wanted to make some extra insurance money, but on the other, it wasn't worth it. He knew he had a head start in front of Dade County and the sooner he left South Beach, the better. He arrived near the back of Night's Owl, sending Mesa a text letting her know he was there. While he waited, he glanced at the large envelope and wondered what was enclosed. He kept looking in his rearview mirror to make sure no one was following him. As soon as he picked it up and opened the envelope, the contents fell faced down out of his lap with a post-it note attached to the back.

"Feliz Santos," he read.

Before he could flip the 8 x 10 picture around, he heard a tap on his window. Tap. Tap. Tap. He quickly jumped in his seat and stuffed the contents back inside of the envelope and rolled down the window.

"I didn't hear you come up?" he said.

"I know," Mesa said, leaning in his car. "As scary as you are, you need to look up at all times, you never know who's behind you."

"Whatever, look, I need to give you this," he said as he gave her the leathered briefcase, "lock this in the secret place in the office."

"Oh, you mean, *my* office right?"

"Yea, your office."

"What's in it?" she asked.

"It's yours. Make sure you invest it, but don't call me afterwards on this phone. I will call you with a new number."

"Damn, seems like you're about to ....."

"Like I said, the less you know, the better off you'll be. Anyway, I'll be in touch."

"Take care of yourself."

Within minutes, he sped off knowing he'll never return to South Beach. He drove toward a cell phone shop to get another cell phone. He grabbed the envelope and picked out a phone when he went into the store.

While he waited for them to process his transaction, he pulled out the picture and read the name Feliz Santos post it note on the back of the picture again. He looked around him just to make sure no one was hovering over him.

"What the ....?" he said when he snatched the post it note from the back of it and turned it over and stared at the picture again.

"Sir? Your phone," the woman said at the counter holding his phone.

"Thank you," he said as he quickly handed her the money and a little extra when she gave him another number with a different area code.

While Clifton hurried back to his car, he noticed a missed call from Micah. He tried to call her back from his new cell, but she didn't answer.

Micah kept denying the call from an unknown number and was happily engaged in her phone call with Rafael.

"So you're still going to sell it and buy us a bigger one?"

"Yes," he said with a smile. "I'm getting rid of all the old stuff and getting everything new for you. You have showed me I can be a better man and I intend on showing you the world."

"You don't have to do that Raf," Micah said.

"I do. I must change my old habits."

Micah finally felt like things between her and Rafael were finally getting better. Ever since Alana's death, she finally felt like she was getting back into her routine. Things between her and Rafael were better than before and finally she felt like he was the one. She finally agreed to sail with him without a destination mapped out. She was finally going to live on the edge, something Alana always told her she should do at least once.

"You there?" Rafael asked.

"I am," she said.

"I have something to tell you," she said with a smile.

"Oh yea?"

"Yes."

She smiled to herself just before she parted her lips to reveal her news, but a beep on her line interrupted her thoughts. She quickly looked at the screen and saw the unknown number flash across the screen several times.

"How can I help you?" Rafael said to someone else.

"Raf, are you listening? I really want to tell you something."

"Babe, someone is here to look at the boat, so as soon as I finish up here, how about I come get you and we go out to eat so you can tell me the good news."

"Okay," she said disappointedly.

"So, how can I help you?" Rafael said to the gentleman who walked up to him.

"Uh yea, I wanted to check out your yacht. The guy from the office said you guys were looking to sell and your boat caught my eye," Garcia said.

"I sure am. Come on."

"She's a beauty," Garcia complimented.

"Thank you."

Garcia looked at the man with pause.

"So what do you think?" the seller asked.

"I'm sorry, what did you say?" Garcia asked.

"I said, what do you think? You want to come up and look

around? You're more than welcome to take a look," the seller suggested.

Garcia agreed to check the boat. Just as he stepped on the boat, an eerie feeling quickly rushed over him, signaling a very bad vibe. He tried to mask his discomfort as he looked around the yacht, but his instincts wouldn't let him ignore the feeling. The seller continued to wash and polish the chrome trimmings, paying the inquisitive buyer no mind.

"So you're looking to buy?" the seller quizzed.

"I am. I'm looking to buy in a couple days, but it depends on the price," Garcia said trying to entertain his small talk, while forcefully jogging his memory.

As a detective, he always followed his instincts, but he couldn't remember having a conversation with him. His face looked familiar. The seller grabbed his hand towel and picked up his cell phone.

"Um I need to make a phone call so you're more than welcome to look around," the seller advised.

"Um....excuse me...um...," Garcia said, realizing he didn't get his name while he was dialing a number.

The seller quickly covered the phone and stated his name just as Micah answered the phone.

"Santos," the seller said.

"Hey baby," Micah said in the phone. "Are you hungry?"

"Raf, I'm looking for a place to have lunch, but I'm not really hungry. Where do you want to eat?"

"It doesn't matter babe. I have a potential buyer on the boat. I just wanted to let you know, ok?"

"Okay well don't let me mess up your money."

As he chuckled on the phone, Garcia walked around on the yacht and admired the Burgundy and Mahogany custom furniture. The floor base of the yacht had hardwood finishing. The top level had four burgundy small wrap around chairs with nice coffee tables centered in front the chairs. The second level had two bedrooms, one near the front of the boat and the second one with a master bathroom. Garcia noticed everything was customized and the color scheme complimented both levels of the yacht. When Garcia went back upstairs, he saw the owner of the marina next to the boat.

"So you like what you see?" he hollered at Garcia.

"I do, she's a real beauty," Garcia shouted back.

Micah overheard Garcia's voice. She immediately thought back on how adamant the officers were about questioning Rafael. Her heart started to pace in her chest while she debated whether or not to tell him what happened months prior.

"Babe you there?" Raf said in the phone.

"Raf...?" she called into the phone. "Raf?"

"Babe..., you there?"

The call dropped and there was no signal. He stuffed the phone back into his pocket when the service slipped to no service just as the buyer walked up to him.

"Do you mind if we take her out on the water?"

"Not at all, I was just about to ask you if you wanted to take a spin."

Santos started the engine then pulled up the anchor. The engine hummed like a kitten purring. Garcia smiled at the sound and closed his eyes while Florida's sun kissed his face. They pulled out the dock as the cool breeze filled their nostrils as he listened to the sea gulls crying as they flew across them. With his eyes closed, different faces flashed in his mind as the sound of the water splashed against the yacht.

He paced himself and thought about all of the countless investigations he diligently solved except his son's and niece. The many faces of different suspects flashed through his mind like a spinning wheel and not a single suspect was doing time for their murders. Almost in an instant, the wheel came to a stop. He looked at his mental portrait from different angles. He opened his eyes slowly and stared at his niece murderer steering the boat he was on. An eerie feeling came over him as his body quickly tensed up. He saw this man only on videos, but everyone else saw him in person, as Rafael Jai.

Before he left the house, he searched on the internet for Rafael Jai, but he couldn't figure it out. The real Rafael Jai was reported missing six years ago, but since his body wasn't found his case was unsolved and now cold. His family accepted it and never investigated it any further.

"So what do you think?" Santos said.

Garcia played it cool and pretended to be interested in his boat while he looked around to see if anyone else was on the waters.

"I think I want to know the speed of this sucker," Garcia said with a motive in mind.

Santos smiled at him and showed off the yacht's speed. Garcia walked closer to him, pretending to be intrigued by the boat. Instead he wanted Santos to go toward international waters. Santos pulled out a cigarette and his paperwork on the boat and gave it to Garcia. He wanted to get rid of the boat today and he was going to make Garcia an offer he couldn't refuse.

"All of the maintenance is up to date."

"I see, Garcia said as he looked at the paperwork.

"Hey, I didn't catch your name ..."

"It's Dez," Garcia said, realizing he didn't want to reveal no further information to him.

"Okay, well those are all of the records, but if you need more, I can get them to you."

Garcia looked at every signed document and noticed a Feliz Santos as the owner. He instantly thought about what Catalina said about him.

Feliz Santos? Garcia said to himself.

Garcia's scrambled thoughts were everywhere when Santos continued to entice him to purchase the boat.

"I can give it to you for a steal. I just want to get rid of it."

"So, what's the rush?"

"Just ready to start a new life with my lady."

"It's always good to start over," Garcia stated.

"It is," he replied causally.

"So, you're the only owner?"

"Yep."

"You traveled a lot in it?"

"I have for business, never pleasure."

"Business?" Garcia quizzed while shaking his head.

Garcia listened closely.

"Yea, I used to take tourists on the water until I started renting out the yacht. I tell you, it's a lucrative business."

Santos shut the engine off so Garcia could feel her sail. Garcia had to strategically plan out his next few moves because there was no way he was going to let Santos take him back to the dock. Without a badge, he didn't feel obligated to do the right thing anymore. Garcia was finally going to take matters in his own hands. He leaned over the rail and stared at the deep blue ocean and pondered a way to get the truth out of him once and for all.

While Garcia was looking for the right signal, Clifton tried his attempt at calling Micah again.

"Hello?"

"I need to talk to you," he said hurriedly.

"Who's number is this?"

"It doesn't matter. I won't take much of your time, but you need to get away from Rafael."

"What!" Micah chuckled. "You just won't stop, will you?"

"I'm serious."

"Yea right Clifton."

"Listen to me, I can't go into details, but I'm leaving town. Shit has gotten out of control and something bad is about to happen and I don't want you in the middle of it."

"Middle of what?" Micah said with no concern.

"Look, Rafael is using an alias name. His real name is Feliz Santos and someone put a hit out on him."

"Wha-what? This is crazy. He's a photographer, you're insane."

"Micah, I get it. I'm a jerk and an asshole, but I put this on everything I have. Your life is in danger if you stay with or around this man. I have to go. This will be the last time you hear from me."

"Whoa. Clifton wait, what do you mean? Where are you going? My life is in danger?"

"Yes. Now I need you to do one favor for me."

Micah was now confused, scared, and baffled from Clifton's accusation.

"You need to get in touch with Garcia and tell him exactly what I said. He will protect you. I have to go. Leave before it's too late."

"I think I overheard Garcia's voice at the Marina with Raf-...."

"You need to leave before you end up dead...."

Micah heard the dial tone in her ear and she was lost in her own thoughts. She picked up the phone to dial Rafael's number, but it went to his automated voicemail. She walked in her bedroom and searched through his things to see if she could find anything on Rafael. She searched through his drawer, but all she saw was a few of his clothes. She looked in the medicine cabinet for any prescribed medicines for him, but saw nothing. She checked his mail, but everything came to him as R. Jai.

She paced in her living room and dismissed Clifton's accusations about Rafael. She thought about his words over and over again before grabbing her purse and keys. She held onto her cell phone and headed toward the Marina.

She calmly convinced herself that Clifton had it all wrong and was going to ask Rafael herself. When she pulled up thirty minutes later, she noticed several cars in the parking lot and Rafael's motorcycle. She smiled to herself when she saw it but the smile disappeared when she didn't see the yacht.

"Ma'am, can I help you?" the owner said to her.

"Um yes, I'm looking for someone by the name of Rafael Jai. He docks his yacht here."

"Rafael Jai? Um, name doesn't ring a bell to me," he said when he scratched his head.

"R. Jai?" Micah said instead.

The owner shook his head.

"I know everyone here ma'am. Are you sure you're at the right Marina?"

"Yes, he's motorcycle is parked out front."

"He said he was going to take a buyer out on the water."

"Ma'am, we have several people on the water taking potential buyers on out."

Micah paused for a second. It seemed like she was on a merry go round, spinning in circles where she stood. She was getting nauseous. She didn't want to say the other name Clifton gave her, but she had no other choice.

"What about ... Santos?" she said skeptically.

"Oh yea, now he's on the waters. He's trying to sell that yacht today."

Mortified by what the owner said, Micah took a step backwards and covered her mouth. She pulled out her cell phone and dialed Garcia's number, but his phone went to voicemail too.

"Dammit!" she said.

"Is everything alright?" the owner said.

She backed up, spun around, and ran toward her car. She sped off without saying anything else. She went back to her house, stuffed her clothes in a luggage bag, grabbed her laptop and the pictures of Alana Rafael took of her. She swiftly looked around and left everything the same way she left it. She closed the door and headed to the police station hoping to find Garcia's partner.

Back on the waters, Garcia knew they would be headed back soon so he quickly switched the conversation.

"How long have you been in Florida?" Garcia asked.

"Been here for about six years now."

"Oh yea, what do you do?"

"A little this and that, what about you?" Santos said, inhaling on a cigarette.

"Ah, I'm retired."

"Retired? Must be nice," Santos said.

"It is."

"So what do you think?" Santos asked before he turned around stretching his arms apart as he welcome the breeze and faced the ocean.

Garcia quickly stood to his feet and stared at the man in front of him. All the feelings he had inside was fuming and he did the only thing he could think of.

"I think this is nice, but I'm a little confused about you selling this beauty."

"I don't want to sell the boat to just anyone. I want to sell it to....," he said when turned around.

Garcia stood in front of him with a loaded glock 9 mm pointing at his face.

"Hey...now," he said as he raised his hands in the air, "I don't know what type of games you're playing, but Dez I-I don't have any money."

"I don't want your money," Garcia said calmly.

"Look, man, we don't have to do this. Just tell me what do you want?" Santos asked frantically, as he was caught off guard.

"I want the truth!" Garcia shouted.

"Wha-what are you talking about? I am telling you the truth. This *is* my boat and I don't want to sell it to just anyone..."

"See, you're smooth. You walk around here and make people think you are this person but in reality you're not."

"What!"

"See," Garcia said as he waved the gun towards him, "I know

your secret."

"My secret?"

"And what puzzles me is why?" Garcia said while he pointed the gun at him. "Of all people, why her?"

"Who is her?" Santos wasn't sure what Dez was talking about now and didn't want to give away anything.

"Ay, so you really don't know who I'm talking about? So you're that heartless?"

"I'm sorry, I'm not following you," Santos said skeptically.

"Wrong answer," he said as he shot the gun missing him only by inches.

The next shot will hit you.

"Look, whatever you want you can have it. I don't want no trouble."

"Trouble? You are trouble!"

"Look, what the fuck is this about?" Santos said as he looked behind Garcia at the covered seat where his gun was stored.

"You know what, you almost got away, but I had a hunch that I couldn't let go. At first, I knew you looked familiar to me, but I couldn't put my finger on it. I just let you kept talking while I figured out where I saw you before then it hit me. I saw your face with a young lady. Micah."

"Whatever you do, please don't hurt Micah. I plan on marrying her."

"Marrying her? I'm sure she doesn't even know that type of man you really are."

Santos knew at that moment, the man standing in front of him knew more than he revealed. He wondered if Kaiser sent him to kill him. He chuckled under his breath and put his hands down.

"Okay, now I know what this is about. Kaiser sent you here, right?"

"Kaiser?" Garcia quizzed.

"I know he sent you to kill me. That's how he works. If you don't kill me, he will get someone to kill the both of us. It's always a lose-lose situation with Kaiser. I'm done. I refuse to fight back. I want out anyway. I'm tired of this shit. I'm tired of his rules, his ways and his deceit. I'm the only person who knows the real him and maybe that's why he sent you here. That's a good one, to act like you want to buy a yacht."

Garcia wasn't sure if he should reveal who he was, but there was obviously something else going on. He played the role just to see how far it will get him since he was talking.

"Well, you know how Kaiser is," Garcia added.

Santos carefully scanned the area and tried to get Dez to walk around, but he stood still without a flinch.

"So how much is he paying you to kill me?" Santos asked.

"Don't worry about that."

"Oh let me guess, ten stacks? Did I get it right?"

Garcia didn't respond.

"Well, I hope you got some of it before he sent you down here because I'm sure he's on his way back to Brazil."

"Brazil?"

Garcia immediately became interested, but masked his curiosity.

"Brazil? He didn't say anything about Brazil to me."

"He won't. He was only here to ....well that's not important. He's going back home to run the streets all over again."

Brazil?

"Yea well, fuck Kaiser. Fuck his family."

Santos ran up on Garcia and before he knew it, he pulled the trigger. The gun blasted off and hit him in the side. Santos stepped back, covering his wound with his bloody hands. He fell to his knees and laughed. Enough was enough and Garcia was tired of playing this game with him, but before he could ask him anything, Santos mumbled something.

"What did you just say?" Garcia questioned his mumble.

"I regret nothing..."

Garcia stepped back, feeling slightly nauseous from his statement.

"She never did anything to you! You took an innocent girl life...and for what? What does she have to do with any of this?"

"I'll tell you for what?" Santos said in excruciating pain. "Kaiser wanted me to hit a lick, chick by the name of Skyler...," he said in between breaths."

"Skyler? Why?"

"She had a baby by him..., yea, it was an accident, but he shipped her ass back to the states. Back to Vegas," he said slowly.

"Skyler?" Garcia mused. "Has a baby by him?"

Garcia was growing frustrated from Santos slow confession. He was talking in circles and nothing made sense. He held onto his gun while Santos crawled around and sat against the bench.

"Yea, Kaiser was my running partner, but we started beefing when he wouldn't pay me for the jobs I completed."

"He paid you?"

"Yea...," Santos said weakly. "He pays for everything. He paid for me to get my photography license, paid me to relocate, snatched up the photographer Rafael Jai then paid me to impersonate him."

Santos laughed.

"He wanted me to get Alana behind the lens. You know, he wanted her to become a real model. The real Rafael was shy, never wanted the exposure, but his work was impeccable. I mirrored his work, reinvented his name and made a name for him. Not my type of field, but Kaiser paid me nicely so hey.., I took the job."

"So, was Alana worth it?" Garcia said.

"Honestly, I had no attachment to it. As long as I received my payments, I did my job. That was until he made it personal."

"Personal?"

"Kaiser was pissed when he found out that Skyler was staying with her."

"So, was it the case of mistaken identity?" Garcia said in a hopeful tone.

Santos grimaced as his breath became shorter and weaker. He shrugged his shoulders.

"Keep talking, if not I'm going to put three holes in you like a bowling ball," Garcia said with authority.

Blood was coming out Santos mouth and Garcia knew he lost too much blood, but he needed to know more information. He needed to know who was Kaiser. Kaiser was the mastermind behind everything.

"It wasn't Kaiser's call," Santos said, "but when he refused to give me what I worked for, I decided to put my own touch on his job. Revenge is a bitch."

"Who is Kaiser?" Garcia demanded.

Santos didn't respond, he just closed his eyes as tight as possible and shook his head. He looked at Garcia and with one final breath, he managed to say it in a whisper.

Garcia knelt down beside him and shook him furiously. "What? Who the hell is Kaiser?"

"Kaiser is... Luis In-aci...o..," Santos said with his final breath.

Garcia stared at him. Did he just hear him correctly? He shook him hoping to get him to say more. He said nothing. Not a single breath was left in his body. The man who killed his niece was dead. Garcia looked at the sky and screamed as loud as he could. The pain shot through him and his rage grew in a matter of seconds with blood stained eyes. He stood to his feet and looked at the man slumped over in his own blood. He aimed his gun toward Santos head and shot two bullets in his head with no remorse. He removed his clip and placed it on the seat behind him. He walked to the back and stepped down closer to the water so he could rinse his hands. He looked around him and saw several beach towels. He quickly stood up, grabbed the towels, and headed toward Santos.

He picked him up, slinging one arm across his shoulder and propped him up against the rail. He reached in his pockets, grabbed his phone, wallet, and his keys before tossing him overboard watching him fall into the waters. He tossed his gun and the clip in the water behind him.

"Now you're shark food asshole," Garcia said.

He watched his body sink towards the bottom. He knew the blood from his body would catch the attention of the killer sharks. He turned away and looked for another weapon on the boat. He searched thoroughly under the cover seats until he found Santos gun and shot himself in the shoulder so it could look like they were in a tussle. He turned the yacht around and headed toward the dock while he sat with only one thing on his vengeful mind. *Luis*

www.ingramcontent.com/pod-product-compliance
Lightning Source LLC
Chambersburg PA
CBHW070659280626
47159CB00022B/991